Dear Readers,

Many of you have beer
books: *Sing Softly to M*
reprinting them in this one volume called *Loveseekers*. It's an appropriate title because, as different as these two stories are from each other, they both emphasize the desire for love that overcomes what seem to be unfortunate beginnings. After many years in my own long, happy marriage, I am a believer in the power of love to conquer all.

Sing Softly to Me takes place in Wyoming during the bitter winter months, where Tom Clary struggles to maintain his ranch and care for his ailing sister-in-law. He makes a hazardous drive to Minnesota to bring her sister, a nurse, to come and help out. It doesn't look like it will be a jolly winter because Tom and the sister have met before—and they don't like each other . . .

Gentle Torment begins at an even rockier point in a relationship. Lindy Williamson has left the South for Alaska, leaving behind her life with Jake, her ex-husband, to start a new life as a single woman. When Jake comes North to try to win her back, the fireworks erupt.

These two stories are set in territories where the winter is harsh and the people are independent and rugged, my kinds of places and my kind of people. I hope you find yourself identifying with them and caring about them too. Write to me via my Web site or care of my publisher; I'd like to learn your reactions.

Sincerely,

Dorothy Garlock

www.dorothygarlock.com

Also by Dorothy Garlock

After the Parade
Almost Eden
Annie Lash
Dreamkeepers
Dream River
The Edge of Town
Forever Victoria
A Gentle Giving
Glorious Dawn
High on a Hill
Homeplace
Hope's Highway
Larkspur
The Listening Sky
Lonesome River
Love and Cherish
Midnight Blue
More than Memory
Mother Road
Nightrose
On Tall Pine Lake
A Place Called Rainwater
Restless Wind
Ribbon in the Sky
River of Tomorrow
River Rising
The Searching Hearts
Sins of Summer
Song of the Road
Sweetwater
Tenderness
This Loving Land
Train from Marietta
Wayward Wind
Wild Sweet Wilderness
Wind of Promise
Wishmakers
With Heart
With Hope
With Song
Yesteryear

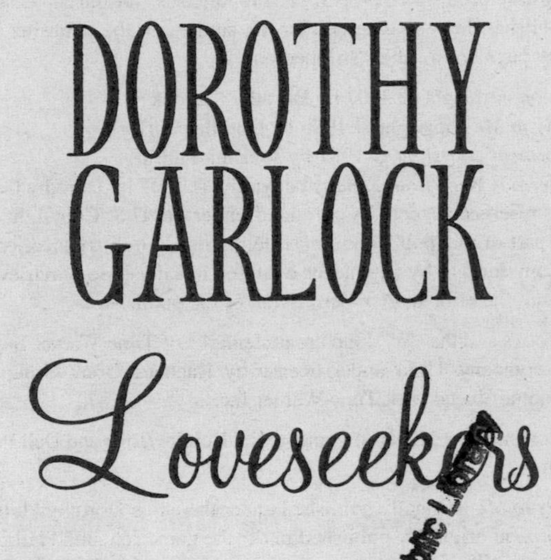

WARNER BOOKS

NEW YORK BOSTON

This edition published by arrangement with Berkley/Jove and Dell Publishing Co., Inc.

Sing Softly to Me originally published under the name Dorothy Phillips.
Gentle Torment originally published under the name Johanna Phillips.

Cover design by Diane Luger
Cover photograph by Herman Estevez

Warner Books
Hachette Book Group USA
237 Park Avenue
New York, NY 10169
Visit our Web site at www.HachetteBookGroupUSA.com

Printed in the United States of America

First Mass Market Paperback Printing: May 2007

10 9 8 7 6 5 4 3 2 1

Table of Contents

Loveseekers

Book One

Sing Softly to Me

For my lifelong friend
Marie Hook

CHAPTER ONE

"*Burr* . . . I must have holes in my head to live here!"

The muttered words came from lips stiff with cold. Snow covered the trees, bushes, and sidewalks, reflecting the feelings of the young woman who hurried toward the large, brick building that loomed ahead of her. A feeling of coldness permeated her, spreading its numbness to her fingers and toes.

"Oops!" Her foot hit an icy spot. She regained her balance and pulled her striped stocking cap farther down over her ears. "I'll be latc *again,*" she moaned. Five A.M.! she thought. What an ungodly hour!

The cars that passed beneath the streetlights were eerie, shrouded in fog, as were the forms that hurried toward the building, their breath suspended in the cold northern air.

Passing through the entrance of St. John's Hospital, Beth nodded to several acquaintances who were coming off duty and heading home to warmth and companionship. Their exclamations at the raw bitterness of the winter weather were soon lost to her. She walked briskly down the highly polished corridor to the nurses' lounge, where she shed her coat and hung it in her locker. She adjusted the starched white cap on her thick, dark hair and ran down the hall to the elevator.

The sixth-floor bell sounded as the elevator slid to a silent halt. The doors opened to a busy scene of nurses, doctors, orderlies, and other medical personnel.

"Oh, damn!" Beth murmured nervously as she hurried to the nurses' station. Her eyes were intent on the stiff back of her supervisor, who stood checking a chart with a young nurse. She was late again!

"Did he find you?" A clear voice came from beyond the still backs and bent heads.

Beth turned to find her friend Jill smiling at her. "Find who?" she asked.

"You. A man was just here looking for you. I told him you came on duty about ten minutes ago and probably went up to check on young Joshua in room six thirty-five. He went in that direction. You've obviously missed him." Jill came from behind the desk. "You'd remember him if—" She broke off suddenly, flipped open the metal chartboard in her hand, and began to explain the doctor's instructions for a new patient.

"And what is your excuse this morning, nurse?" An authoritative voice came from behind.

Before Beth could conjure up an answer, the Dragon, as the supervisor was called by the staff, was paged over the intercom. Both nurses sighed with relief when the elevator doors closed behind her.

"It only postpones my chewing out." Beth sighed.

"Yeah. She won't forget. But I want to tell you about this guy who's looking for you. He's tall . . . rugged, and all man! He looks just like the cowboy in the cigarette ads, I swear he does. I can just see him riding the range, roping a cow, doggin' a steer, or whatever they do. Oh, glory! There he is!"

Beth felt her cheeks grow warm. Her eyes encountered lively gray-green eyes. She could feel him appraising her from the top of her nurse's cap to the tips of her white shoes. He continued his inspection while his long strides covered the diminishing space between them. His large, muscular frame was covered by a shearling coat, unbuttoned, and a rich, bottle-green sweater. A brown Stetson was pulled low over his wide forehead and rested above straight dark brows—dark as the thick, bushy mustache that accented his strong, frowning mouth. His intense gaze held hers, making her aware of his sheer, powerful masculinity in a way that sent a shiver of panic through her.

"I've looked all over this damn hospital for you, Beth." His voice was deep, husky, and held more than a hint of annoyance.

Beth's blue eyes remained fixed on him. "I just came on duty."

"I need coffee. Where's the cafeteria?" He moved to take her arm, but she stepped back.

"Follow the sign, you can't miss it," she said carefully, staring up at his stern face. "I'm on duty. I can't leave the floor."

"When do you get a break?"

"About nine. But I don't always take one."

"And you won't this morning."

"No."

"I'm neither rapist nor mugger, Elizabeth."

"What do you want, Thomas? Why are you here? Has

something happened to Sarah? Has she had an . . . accident?" Her head began to spin. That's why he's here! My sister had an accident!

"No, she hasn't. I'm sorry if I scared you. I've been driving all night and I'm tired and hungry. I need to talk to you." His voice grew louder with his impatience.

"That's a relief, but lower your voice." Beth glanced at Jill, who stood gaping at him with a dreamy look on her face. Beth had to admit he was something to gape at, but Jill, who stood frozen in admiration, was making a fool of herself.

Beth's gaze came back to Thomas Clary. He hadn't changed one bit during the last three years. He was still as confident, still as arrogant, still as overpowering, as he had been when he came to attend the wedding of her sister and his brother. She had been nineteen then, and helpless with adoration. Now she was twenty-two, and far more capable of assessing a man.

"How've you been, Beth?"

"Fine." She didn't look at him. What the hell did he care? He'd gone away without a word. He'd kissed her, squired her around her hometown for a week—had made her fall in love with him. She'd waited, thinking he'd call. It had taken a year for her to get over him. Now here he was . . . in living color!

His eyes assessed her critically, moving over her short, shiny brown hair, to the big blue eyes with their dark lashes. His eyes narrowed as he gazed at her mouth, and her lips trembled at the image that came swiftly to mind—Thomas taking possession of her mouth, kissing her as she had never been kissed, making the kisses she shared later with other men seem almost . . . boring. His gaze traveled to the firm breasts rounding out the white uniform, and he smiled a secret smile while she burned with resentment. Slowly, coolly, he let his eyes roam over her from the narrow waist, down over slim hips and long legs to the tips of her white shoes, and back to her eyes, now sparking with indignation.

"You're thinner, and . . . more beautiful."

She did her best to return his gaze coolly. What she really wanted was to tell him to get the hell out and never come back. Instead, she said, "You'll have to excuse me. I've got my rounds to make."

His brows came together in a scowl of displeasure, and a pleased flutter punctuated her already rapid heartbeat.

"Just a minute." His massive body shifted to block her path. "I've driven nine hundred miles in the last two days and I'm dead tired. I'll go take a nap and be at your place at six o'clock. You be there." He turned abruptly on his heel and walked away.

"Wow! You've been holding out on me," Jill accused, after he was gone.

Beth was in a perplexed state of shock. Thomas Clary, here. Three years ago she would have given anything to see him come striding down the corridor toward her. But now she wanted no attachments. He'd broken her heart once. It had been like the end of the world for her, as if she had walked off a cliff or into an airplane propeller. She had almost failed to pass her exams because of him. She had wanted to scream, tear her hair out, or lie down and die. She had done none of those things. She did the only thing possible for her to do—put him out of her mind and wrapped herself in her work.

Now she wished desperately that he hadn't come. He

had said Sarah was all right. So what does he want with me? she wondered, her thoughts swirling in confusion. She tried without success to force the image of his dark face and green eyes from her mind.

Jill was still babbling about the "cowboy," and Beth was lost in thought when the Dragon reappeared, causing both women to flee to their respective duties.

The busy activities of the day helped Beth keep the evening confrontation with Thomas from her mind. Three babies were born during her shift, one premature. The infant needed the expert care that Beth was qualified to give, so her day was spent in the busy routine of helping to save, then monitor the tiny bundle of life which the parents had so eagerly awaited.

When the shifts changed, Beth stayed on to discuss the needs of the fragile premie with the oncoming nurse. By the time she headed home, she was drained and longed for a good soak in a hot tub.

The weather had worsened during the day. Blowing snow was whirling through the streets, stalling traffic, and Beth was thankful her small apartment was only a few blocks away. She hurried along, even jaywalking in her haste to get to her apartment. Home, she thought. It's not much, but it's mine. One large cozy room with a tiny kitchen, a small bedroom, and a minute bath was the place she called home.

Beth reached the large old Victorian house, and in her haste to get in out of the cold she almost collided with her neighbor Mrs. Maxwell on the porch.

"I'm sorry. I didn't see you," she exclaimed, steadying the elderly lady.

"I'm all right, dear. I just stepped out to check the

weather and get the paper." The tiny woman smiled up at Beth.

"Be careful. The porch is slippery. You don't want a broken leg."

"I should say not. It would cut down on my dancing."

"You're incredible!" Beth smiled.

"You're only as old as you think you are, my dear. And while you're still young, you'd better get you a man before all the good ones are taken."

"Trying to get rid of me, huh?"

"You'd have a lot more fun," Mrs. Maxwell confided with a giggle.

Beth laughed and stomped the snow from her shoes. Inside she climbed the curved staircase to the second floor and unlocked her door. Two apartments shared the floor and hers was the smaller one, but it had a small fireplace in the living room, and she loved the high ceilings and long windows. She had often reflected on what an elegant home it must have been in the early years, before it was converted into apartments.

Keeping her thoughts carefully away from the coming meeting with Thomas, she put the teakettle on to boil, turned on the stereo and listened to the classical strains of a concerto. She made a cup of tea and carried it with her to the bathroom.

Ten minutes later she was relaxing in a steamy, hot bath. Just what I need to loosen the kinks in my back and neck, she mused, and sank deeper in the clawfooted tub, until the water reached her chin. With her eyes closed, she allowed her mind to dwell on the early morning meeting that had shaken her to the core.

Thomas had come all the way from Wyoming to see

her. What could he possibly want to talk to her about? It was urgent, she realized, otherwise he wouldn't have come directly to the hospital after driving all night. It had to be something to do with Sarah.

Beth and her sister had not been close while growing up. That was due partly to the thirteen-year difference in their ages and partly to the fact that they were half sisters. Sarah was ten years old when her mother died. It had been a horrendous blow to the sensitive young girl. Her father had tried to bridge the gap, but Sarah's adolescence and hurt all contrived to push him further from her. She returned to her boarding school after the funeral, a grieving, unhappy little girl. Two years later her father remarried and Beth was the result of that marriage. Sarah's stepmother tried with love and understanding to break through the tough barrier that surrounded the young girl, and eventually she succeeded. By the time Sarah was ready to go out on her own, she and her stepmother had developed a warm, loving relationship.

After Sarah was graduated from college, she took a teaching job at an American military base in Europe, then transferred to other bases around the world. She met Steven Clary, an American service man, and when he was discharged they came to Minnesota to be married. At that time Beth was nineteen, in her second year of nurse's training, and ripe to fall desperately in love with the man who came out from Wyoming to be his brother's best man.

A year later both her parents died in a freak accident caused by a faulty furnace. Beth sent a telegram to Sarah, who came immediately. They made funeral arrangements, grieved together, and took comfort in knowing that they were sisters and had each other.

Beth was jarred from her thoughts by a loud knocking on her door. Mrs. Maxwell, she muttered silently. You're a darling, but sometimes a pest. She got out of the tub, wrapped a huge towel around her, and went to the door, fully expecting to have a bowl of chicken soup or something equally nourishing thrust into her hands.

"Interesting." Tom's gray-green eyes traveled from her startled face down to her wet, bare shoulders, then down to her breasts, barely concealed by the clinging towel. "May I come in?" he asked, then walked into the room, leaving her holding the door.

"It's only five o'clock! I didn't expect you so soon," Beth protested.

"No? I'd have sworn you did." Amusement played over his face as his eyes toured her figure. Beth's cheeks flamed.

"Make yourself at home," she invited sarcastically as he removed his coat. With as much dignity as possible, she stalked across the room.

"I'll be glad to help—"

She slammed the door on his words, and fumed. Damn him for coming early! She quickly toweled herself dry and pulled a pair of snug jeans up over her long slim legs. She was annoyed with herself for not thinking that he might show up before the appointed time. After slipping on a light blue turtleneck and a bulky navy sweater, she ran a brush through her hair. She was glad for once that it curled on its own. Looking at her reflection in the mirror, she applied a touch of lipstick.

The young woman who looked back at her had short,

dark hair cut in a wedge that showed the tips of her ears then tapered to the nape of her neck. She had deep blue eyes set far apart and fringed with dark lashes; a small, straight nose that even in the middle of winter was covered with freckles; high cheekbones, her best feature, she thought; and a soft, luscious mouth that she thought was too wide. I'm as common looking as an old shoe, she thought as she looked at herself. Oh, what I'd give for a little more sophistication.

Tom was sprawled on the couch. His eyes swept over her and he grinned. "I prefer the towel."

Beth, usually ready with a comeback, could think of nothing to say. She felt a telltale warmth invade her cheeks again. Damn him!

"What do you want to talk about?" she asked crossly.

"I'll tell you over dinner." He got to his feet, slung on his coat, then plucked hers from the rack beside the door.

She folded her arms across her breasts and waited, her eyes looking unflinchingly into his. "Is this your way of inviting me to dinner?"

"Should I have sent an engraved invitation?" He grinned cockily.

"Did it ever occur to you that I may already have a dinner date?" Her chin lifted and there was rebellion in every line of her body. He gazed at her defiant face with such intensity that she almost cringed. He knows! she thought. He knows that I was desperately in love with him!

"No. Now stop hedging and c'mon. You know you're going, I know you're going, so let's go."

"You haven't changed a bit," she flared. "You're still as conceited as ever." Her voice lashed him with bitter, unguarded words.

"Yeah?" His smile said he was proud of it. "You've changed. You didn't use to be so shrewish. I remembered you as being a real sweet little girl."

There was amusement in his voice. She wanted to retort that she was no longer the young, gullible, *little girl* she'd been three years ago. It had taken her a long time to erase his image from her subconscious. Night after night she had dreamed of him, despising herself for her inability to control her mind. But she had conquered her obsession for him, and now here he was, bulldozing his way back into her life. She wanted to put up further resistance, but what was the use? Clinging tightly to her dignity, she slipped her arms into the sleeves of the down coat he was holding for her.

"Button up. It's freezing out there."

Beth pulled the hood of her parka up over her head and put on her mittens. Then, holding fast to her resentment, she stalked ahead of him out the door.

It was dark outside now, and the temperature had dropped. An icy gust of air met them at the door. Tom took her arm and propelled her toward a four-wheel-drive vehicle parked across the street. Once inside he quickly started the engine and turned on the heat.

"It'll take a minute to warm up. God! It's cold here," he grumbled.

Beth huddled far down inside her coat, wishing fervently that she had one as warm as his. She was shivering, almost uncontrollably, from nerves and the cold. It was impossible to keep her teeth from chattering.

"You sound like a typewriter." He laughed and gave her a sideways glance.

"It's not funny, dammit!"

"You'll be warm in a minute."

This is crazy, she thought. Why did I come out with him? What in the world does he want to talk about? He could have said what he had to say in my nice warm apartment. They drove in silence, while Beth's mind churned with curiosity.

"I understand the Depot is a good place to eat." His statement broke the silence and hung in the cold air between them.

"I wouldn't know. I never eat there." The Depot was the classiest restaurant in town. That kind of dining wasn't covered in her budget. She was sure of one thing—she wasn't dressed for a place like that. Her mind was still working feverishly as they parked in front of the old building that housed the finest eating establishment Rochester, Minnesota, had to offer.

"I'm not sure about this." Her blue eyes sought his.

"Why?"

"I'm not dressed for this place."

The firm lips twitched under the dark mustache. "Don't worry. You look fine. You just might be the best-looking woman here if you took that frown off your face."

He laughed at the look of exasperation that followed the frown, and got out of the car. With great reluctance she opened the door and stepped out onto the snow-packed drive. The wind buffeted her as she walked beside the tall man who held her arm in a powerful grip. They passed through the double doors of the restaurant and into the warmth of the elegant interior.

They were met by a hostess dressed in a long velvet skirt and silk blouse. She glanced briefly at Beth as Tom helped her out of her parka, then dismissed her and gave her attention to him. Beth felt terribly conspicuous in her jeans and sweater, but managed to appear nonchalant as she followed the hostess, very conscious of Tom close behind her. They were ushered to a quiet table, partially secluded from the view of the other diners.

One glance at the menu told Beth she was definitely out of her league. There were no prices on the menu! Fighting not to let herself be intimidated by this place or this man, she armed herself with her pride. She glanced at the menu, and gave Tom her preferences with cold formality.

Once their order was taken by the waiter, who seemed to materialize as if by magic, Tom settled back in his chair, indifferent to his surroundings. His eyes settled on Beth. She looked everywhere but at him, causing a slight smile to twitch at his lips.

"You're going to have to look at me sometime, you know."

"Thomas—"

"Sarah, my mother, and you are the only people who have ever called me Thomas."

His softly spoken words caught her by surprise, causing her to look straight into his eyes. Once captured, she couldn't look away. He continued to study her, his eyes traveling over her flushed cheeks, flashing blue eyes, and the tip of her tongue, which darted out to moisten her suddenly dry lips.

Beth despised herself for blushing. It was a curse that at her age color could flood her face at the most inopportune times. She forced herself to return the stare in exactly the same way he was eyeing her. He was a handsome man—rugged and very masculine. He's a man's man, she thought. A man another man could depend on. He's a woman's man too.

Deciding that the best defense was a good offense, she attacked. "Okay. You've played your little game long enough. You've got me dangling in suspense so out with it."

"I want you to come back to Wyoming with me."

It took several seconds for Beth to grasp what he'd said. "Go . . . with you to Wyoming? You can't be serious."

"Oh, but I am." He wasn't smiling.

"But . . . but—"

He raised his hand to silence her as the waiter approached with their dinner. He watched the expressions flitting across her face, and it occurred to him that, although she wasn't what would be considered a beautiful woman, she certainly was the most *alive* woman he'd met in a long while. Where was the naive child he'd known three years ago? After the wedding he'd kicked himself all the way back to Wyoming for staying a week instead of the three days he'd planned. They had danced, swam, gone to the races, laughed at each other's bad jokes. To him, it had been a pleasant interlude. He'd not realized until the very last day that Sarah's little sister might have a crush on him.

"First we're going to eat our dinner," he said when they were alone again. "Mainly because I'm starved, and also because you'll be more rational with a full stomach."

"You've lost a few bricks!" The words were dumb, juvenile, and she was instantly ashamed of them. But dammit, his presence was disturbing. She thought that at the age of twenty-two she had a reasonable amount of poise and confidence. She had worked for a year in the emergency room at the hospital and had seen the ugly side of life—atrocities she'd not even imagined. She'd been proud of the way she handled herself, but her self-confidence was nothing compared to what *he* carried around.

The meal was delicious—cooked to perfection and served beautifully. Beth ate, but hardly tasted what she was eating. Her mind and her stomach were not at all compatible. Go to Wyoming? What for? Sarah was all right—he'd said so. She waited for him to finish eating, furious that he could eat such a large meal as if nothing momentous had happened. He finally finished and the after-dinner wine was poured. She could contain her curiosity no longer.

"Will you please say what you've come to say," she demanded.

"As I told you before, I want to take you back home with me."

"I'm not deaf! You said that thirty minutes ago. Why?"

The large masculine hand lifted the fragile wineglass, swirling its contents before lifting it to smiling lips. "Because I want you to."

A flash of anger engulfed her. He's playing with me and enjoying every minute of it! She ground her teeth in mute rage, grabbed her bag and got to her feet.

Tom reached out and grasped her wrist. "I'm sorry, Beth. Sit down. Somehow, I can't resist teasing you. You rise to the bait so beautifully."

She resumed her seat but remained poised for flight. He took his hand from her arm, but the warmth of his touch remained, sending danger signals up to her flustered brain, telling her that if she made one move, his hand would snake out again faster than a whiplash.

"Sarah has multiple sclerosis."

"Oh! Oh, my God! Why didn't you tell me at—"

"Don't worry. They think the disease has been arrested."

"Arrested? Arrested?" she blurted angrily. "For how long?"

He ignored her outburst and spoke calmly. "Sarah's been staying with me ever since she found out about the illness. Up until now she's been able to manage on her own, with the help of my housekeeper. But she needs someone with knowledge of the disease. She needs her sister, the nurse."

"Why didn't she tell me?"

"She didn't want to upset your life."

"But she's my sister!" She looked away from him, her face pale.

"Yes."

Beth's medically-trained mind clicked into gear. "How long has she known?"

"A year."

"A year? Then it must have been discovered right after Steven was killed."

"It was. She didn't let me get in touch with you then, because you were about to take your Minnesota board, and she thought it was more important for you to get your nursing license than to come to Wyoming to be with her."

Beth groaned, remembering. Sarah had called her shortly after Steven's accident to tell her when the funeral would be. Beth hadn't especially liked her sister's husband, but she'd wanted to go out to be with Sarah. But Sarah had refused, saying she was fine, there were lots of friends who were helping out. And she'd insisted it was more important for Beth to get her nursing license. She'd said very little about Steven's accident—she seemed reluctant to talk about it, and Beth had never pressed her for details—and never mentioned her illness.

"Why didn't you bring her here to the Mayo Clinic?" Beth demanded, needing to lash out at someone, wanting an excuse to be angry.

"I tried, but she wouldn't come. She's had the best medical care available. What she needs now is companionship, someone close to her."

"She's had you. Or are you too busy to give her your time?" She knew she was being unreasonable. She could tell by the look in his eyes that he thought so too. But his eyes also told her that he understood the hurt that was making her irrational.

"She doesn't know I've come for you. I'm sure she wouldn't want to interfere with your life."

"It'll take me a while to make arrangements to leave."

"I'm starting back the day after tomorrow. That's enough time."

"I can't leave that soon. I'll have to give notice at the hospital. I can't just pull out and leave on a moment's notice. I'll come out in a few weeks."

The waiter came with the bill. Tom paid him, and the waiter acknowledged the generous tip.

The cold air, when they left the restaurant, revived Beth's senses somewhat. She was still in a numbed state over the news of Sarah's illness. The drive back to her apartment seemed to take only seconds, and they didn't speak until he parked the Blazer in front of the old Victorian house. Leaving the motor running, he switched off the lights and turned to her. Despite her inner turmoil, she was terribly conscious of him. To her extreme discomfort, he sat studying her. The light from the streetlight shone on his face, and when she looked at him, his eyes held hers relentlessly.

"This afternoon I took the liberty of speaking to your supervisor. She agreed to give you a leave of absence due to the family emergency. . . ." He paused while she drew an angry breath. "Starting tomorrow."

"You had no right to do that! I can take care of my own business, thank you! I'm not a child."

He gave a low whistle. "No, siree. You certainly are not a child, *now*."

She could see the flash of white teeth, and knew he was laughing at her. Her Irish temper flashed out of control.

"You're arrogant and hateful and . . . belong in the loony bin!" Too furious to go on, she opened the door to escape his hateful presence.

His low laugh only increased her anger. "You're just a bundle of cheer. I can see that we'll have a great time on the way home."

"Forget the *we* stuff, mister! When you leave, it will be without me!" She slammed the door with all her might, and ran up the walk to the safety of her home.

CHAPTER TWO

THERE WAS A great deal on Beth's mind as she got ready to leave for her sister's home. Sarah's condition was always in her thoughts—how could she not worry about her, especially when she hadn't seen her in such a long time? Beth wished she'd been there to help her sister with all she'd been going through—Steven's death and her illness.

There were also her apartment, friends, and most important, her job being left behind. Her call to her supervisor had confirmed that she'd been given a leave of absence.

"It's perfectly understandable," the Dragonlady had said, as if butter wouldn't melt in her mouth. "Mr. Clary told me of the difficulty in finding a live-in nurse and insisted that I call your sister's doctor. The doctor spoke highly of Mr. Clary and said he was one of Cody's leading citizens. Mr. Clary explained why it was so necessary for you to leave at once."

He explained, Beth thought with irritation. I'll just bet he did, and oozed charm while he was doing it.

Resentment and frustration over Tom's high-handed method of ending her employment increased until her anger overflowed when he knocked on her apartment door two mornings later. She considered, for several wild moments, refusing to open it. She could easily ship her things and catch a plane for Wyoming.

"Eliz-a-beth! Do you want me to kick up a hell of a racket out here?" he shouted after the tenth rap on the door.

She flung open the door. He stalked in and picked up her suitcases without comment, seeming oblivious to her anger.

They left Rochester in the eerie morning darkness, headed south, then west on the interstate. Beth sank down in her seat and buried her face in the fur collar of her parka. Exhaustion overcame her, and with an odd sense of detachment, she promptly fell asleep. She woke once, conscious of the motion of the truck, then it lulled her back into an uneasy sleep, her head resting uncomfortably against the door.

Sometime later the sudden stillness of the truck awakened her. The only sound she heard was the soft purring of the motor.

"Wake up, sleeping beauty. We're making a pit stop."

"Where are we?"

"We're on Interstate 90. I need to stretch my legs and use the facilities."

Beth sat up, stretching her cramped body, trying to ease the kinks in her back. A wide yawn escaped her, but she quickly covered her mouth with the back of her hand.

"You've got the classiest snore I ever heard."

"I don't snore!" she snapped. She knew he was teasing

her, but she welcomed the excuse to vent her anger at him.

He smiled, clearly amused. "C'mon. The nippy air'll perk you up."

She didn't want to leave the warmth of the truck, but reluctantly followed him up the path to the brick building operated by the Minnesota Highway Department.

Later, through a dull headache, she watched Tom come out of the building and down the walk toward her. Even in her anger she had to admit that he was something to look at. The shearling coat and Stetson added to his charisma. Jill's comparison of him to the man in the cigarette ads was accurate. Tom Selleck, move over, here comes Tom Clary! she thought.

"Feel better now?" he asked as he threw his coat into the backseat before getting behind the wheel.

She sucked in her breath and nodded, intensely aware of his broad shoulders as he reached behind the seat for the thermos of coffee.

"Going to pout all the way to Wyoming?"

"Maybe."

Suddenly he reached out and brushed her hair back behind her ear, making her start and turn toward him. At that moment he captured her chin with his fingers.

"Look, Beth. I know you don't want to ride back with me. But you're here. Make the best of it." His long fingers moved to the ridge of her jaw, gently stroking, persuading.

She did her best to return his gaze coolly. She wanted to jerk her head away, but she didn't, couldn't.

"I resent your meddling in my personal affairs the way you did," she murmured.

"It got the job done, didn't it? That old battle-ax would've fought every step of the way to keep you."

Beth turned her head to the window. "Every time I speak to Sarah, she assures me she's fine," she said with a worried frown.

"She always says that," he told her. He turned away and started the motor. "But she needs you now."

Interstate 90 was a long straight ribbon of highway running east and west. The flat Minnesota farmland, now frozen and covered with a thick blanket of snow, soon gave way to the equally flat fields of South Dakota. The landscape was broken occasionally by a farmhouse nestled in a grove of trees, their leafless branches stark and cold. Herds of cattle huddled together in their pens.

At noon they stopped briefly to fill the gas tank, pick up lunch to go, and refill the thermos.

"Can't we stop long enough to eat?" Beth asked irritably after several near spills with a steaming cup of coffee.

"I want to go as far as possible today. The station attendant said a snowstorm was brewing over the mountains."

"So what? The highway department keeps the roads plowed."

He smiled, and his mustache twitched. "You're in for a surprise, Florence Nightingale. A Wyoming blizzard is the granddaddy of all blizzards."

"It can't be too different from a Minnesota blizzard," she said stubbornly. "The roads are seldom closed in Minnesota."

"You can't compare Wyoming to Minnesota. Every thing in Wyoming is bigger and better. Even the blizzards." His eyes glittered devilishly. His amusement deepened as she tossed him a glare.

"That's a crock!" she told him with a laugh.

"Uh-huh," he said, and kept smiling.

Soon the scenery, as it flew past the windows, started to change ever so slightly, becoming less flat, more hilly, but still with few trees, except around the farms. The towns along the highway were small, few, and far between. Beth knew it would be dangerous to be stranded out here at this time of the year. A person in a stalled car could easily freeze to death.

The truck ate up the miles. The sky changed, turning gray as clouds gathered ahead of them. When it grew darker in the afternoon, Tom switched on the CB radio and the chatter of voices invaded the silence.

"Breaker, breaker—one-nine. Does anyone out there have a copy on this lonesome ol' boy truckin' east? Anyone got their ears on?"

After several seconds another voice answered. "Ten-four, good buddy. I gotcha. You've got the Woodpecker, here. Go ahead."

"Howdy, Woodpecker. Ya got the Red Baron back atcha. Where'ya headed?"

"All the way to thc Big Apple. I've been'a slippin' and slidin' since I left that Shaky Town. Go ahead."

Hoarse laughter crackled over the speaker. "Ten-four."

"This ol' eighteen-wheeler's kept me on my toes, a keepin' her between the ditches. I been all over this concrete ribbon. Rain, sleet, ice, then snow. They've throwed everythin' at me but pretty girls and sunshine. Go ahead."

"I just started my run. I'll take the front door and give a shout if I see those ol' smokies."

"Ten-four, Red Baron. Put the pedal to the metal and we'll be in the Apple in no time a'tall."

"What'cha hauling . . ." The voice faded as they passed out of radio range.

"What's Shaky Town?" Beth asked.

Tom's eyes left the road long enough to meet hers. "That's Los Angeles."

"Oh. What else did he say? I was lost after breaker, breaker."

"Pour me a cup of coffee and I'll tell you."

She passed the hot cup to him after he had negotiated a bend in the highway and passed a slower car. Her fingers touched his and the contact sent warning signals through her. Watch it, she thought. Don't let yourself think of him as anything but Sarah's brother-in-law. Don't forget the heartache of three years ago.

"Almost everyone who uses a CB radio has a radio name, or handle as they call it. A few use the call letters issued to them by the FCC." He shifted in the seat, settling into a more comfortable position.

"Do you have one?"

"Uh-huh."

"Well . . . what is it?" she asked, when he didn't volunteer the information.

"Goat Roper."

"Goat Roper?"

"Yeah. You've got to admit, it's different." Smile lines crinkled the corners of his eyes and he gave her a quirky grin.

Words almost failed her. "If . . . you say so," she said, much too reasonably, and attempted to swallow the laughter that bubbled up.

They lapsed into silence and Tom concentrated on his driving. The loose snow, stirred by brisk winds, made for poor visibility at times. It was easy to be bored with the scenery. It seemed to go on and on without anything to break the monotony.

He must be tired, Beth thought. She had offered to drive earlier, but he refused, saying he knew the highway. Then with a quick glance at her and a twist to his lips, he'd added, "Besides, I don't know what kind of driver you are."

"You thought I was a pretty good driver three years ago," she'd snapped, and then mentally kicked herself for bringing up those days, so long ago, when they'd had such a wonderful time together.

They had stopped only one time since noon, and Beth's stomach was growling with hunger. Tom was tense—she could see it in the way he gripped the steering wheel. It was becoming more and more difficult to see the edge of the pavement.

RAPID CITY. She was barely able to read the sign as they whizzed past.

"We'll stop there," Tom said. "Do you think you can last another twenty miles?"

"I don't know. My stomach is slowly chewing its way to my backbone, and my fanny doesn't feel so good, either." Every bone in her body ached. She wanted something to eat, a hot relaxing bath, and a warm bed, in that order.

"I know the feeling," he replied with a deep chuckle. "I want a gigantic rare steak. We'll get a room, some dinner, and hit the hay."

Tom wheeled the Blazer into the drive of a Holiday

Inn just off the interstate. Leaving the motor running, he went into the office. Beth watched him through the window as he signed the register.

"We're set for the night," he said when he slid into the truck.

"Thank goodness."

Due to the late hour and the weather, few people were in the dining room when they arrived for dinner. The service was quick and the food good. They ate in silence.

"We're leaving at six in the morning," Tom said when he left her outside her door.

He knocked on her door at five, dressed, packed, and ready to go.

"What time is it, for chrissake?" she asked sleepily.

"Shake a leg. There's a storm warning out." He came into the room carrying his overnight case, his coat slung over his arm. His eyes missed nothing in their quest. They roamed down from the top of her dark tousled hair and sleepy eyes, lingered on her breasts outlined by her blue robe, and moved to her small bare foot. Resentment burned through her, and she stalked to the bathroom.

"I never knew a man who was so consistently early!" she flung at him before slamming the door.

He was standing beside the door, holding her coat, when she came back into the room. She slipped into it, and he turned her gently around to face him. His hands rested on her shoulders, his warm gaze focused on her face.

"Got your long johns on?"

She wanted to say something clever, but could think of nothing, so she nodded mutely.

"Good. The temperature is dropping and it's starting to snow again. We'll be headed right into it. I know you don't want to be stuck out in the boonies, with me." His voice held a smile.

"You're right about that." Her chin was level with his chest. She was too close to him, and drew back. "As long as you're in such a hurry, let's go."

It was snowing hard. Tom unlocked the passenger door, then moved around to the back and loaded their suitcases. The motor started the instant he turned the switch, and while they sat letting the engine warm up, he brought out the thermos.

"This'll thaw you out." He grinned as if he had just pulled a rabbit out of a hat.

"I hope so. Oh, Lordy, it's cold!" She cupped the mug in her mittened hands. The steam from the cup warmed her face, the coffee her insides. "Mmm . . . I needed that." She smiled at him. "Did the tooth fairy leave it?"

"Uh-huh. She left these too." He passed her a cinnamon roll wrapped in waxed paper, then laughed as she attacked it, smearing frosting on her cheeks in the process. He lifted a finger and wiped at her cheek, then stuck the finger in his mouth. "Mmm . . . pretty, and you taste good too." His eyes flicked over her face, studying every contour. Beth felt her body grow tense under his gaze. She almost lost herself in his luminous green eyes, and forgot to eat. A finger on her nose jerked her back to reality. "Your nose is cold. Want a doughnut? They're not as good as the chocolate-covered ones we got that day we went to see the statue of Paul Bunyan and his Blue Ox, but they'll do."

She shook her head in numbed silence. He remembered. Even as he handed her his coffee mug to hold while he drove the Blazer back up the ramp to the interstate, her mind refused to let go of the remark. He'd remembered the trip to Bemidji, and the picnic beside the lake, and the doughnuts they'd bought at a small stand. . . . Every minute of that day had been firmly etched in her memory. She began to shiver, but not from the cold.

The highway was slippery—ice, topped by snow. The sky was full of snowflakes, their density making it difficult to see, although the truck's headlights forged a path into the darkness. Tom expertly maneuvered the truck along the highway, which was starting to dip and sway with the hills. He switched on the CB radio and listened to the truckers discuss the road conditions.

"I'm thinkin' about puttin' ice skates on the eighteen-wheeler," one voice said.

"Ten-four. I'm havin' a problem keepin' the rubber side down."

"Well, you're in for it. I just came from Sheridan and it's bad. Real bad."

"Breaker, breaker," Tom interrupted.

"Go ahead, breaker."

Tom pressed the button on the microphone. "You got the Goat Roper. Can you give me a road report?"

"Which way ya headed?"

"Headed west."

The speaker echoed with nonhumorous laughter. "Lordy, Goat Roper. I've come from there and I've had me a time keepin' this toboggan between the ditches. It's a snowin' and a blowin' clean past the mountains. Go ahead."

"Are they trying to keep the interstate open?"

"They're tryin', but don't know if they can keep it up. I came on at Sheridan. Where're you headed?"

"Cody."

"Keep your eyes peeled, Goat Roper. There's four-wheelers and eighteens sprawled all over the road."

"Ten-four. By the way, what's the handle?"

"You got the Bluebird out of Albert Lea, Minnesota, flyin' back at-cha. That other mean ol' boy is the Beagle out of Red Wing."

"Thanks for the comeback and the info. We'll be heading west with caution. Have a safe trip. Catch you on the rebound. Goat Roper is clear."

"That's a big ten-four, Goat Roper. Have a safe one. You still with me, Beagle?"

"Still got the back door. Just keep on a truckin'."

Tom switched off the radio and gave Beth a quick, concerned glance. "There's a truck stop ahead. We'll stop there for a road check before we go on. Those big trucks can plow through some pretty good drifts."

Beth didn't answer. There was nothing she could say to improve the situation. It was snowing harder now. The wind whipped the white fluff across the road in blinding sheets, causing Tom to slow the truck until they were barely moving. Even with the heater on, it was cold in the Blazer, and Beth huddled down inside her coat, trying to keep her teeth from chattering.

"Reach behind you and get the blanket off the rear seat," Tom instructed.

Beth didn't hesitate. She turned to crouch on the console between them and reached for the blanket. Suddenly the truck slid on an icy spot, making Tom jerk the wheel to the right. She was thrown against his shoulder, clutching at the shearling coat to stop her fall. Her hand grabbed at his chest, slipped, and finally came to rest against his warm neck. She could feel his muscles clench as he worked the steering wheel to stop their slide toward the ditch. The truck bumped to a stop against the snow piled on the shoulder of the highway. He turned his head. Their faces were so close that she could feel his warm breath on her mouth. Silence. Suddenly Beth felt frightened. Frightened that this man would bring her pain, break her heart . . . again.

"You okay?"

She nodded, her thoughts a jungle of confusion. His hand came up to cover hers, warming it, before moving on to brush her cheek lightly. She recovered and moved away, reaching for the elusive blanket. Back in her seat, she covered herself, wrapping the blanket tightly around her legs. Tom reached over and tucked it around her shoulders.

"It's maybe five or six miles to the truck stop. We'll make it."

He got out and cleaned the windshield wipers. Then, moving slowly, he steered the truck back onto the snow-covered highway. They had not met or passed another vehicle for a long time. It was as if a curtain had been drawn around them, leaving them isolated from the outside world. The truck edged along, the only sounds being the wind and the rhythmic swish of the wipers.

Beth glanced at the man beside her. He was peering intently ahead, trying to see through the driving snow, moving cautiously, in case a car ahead had stalled or slid to the side. His hands gripped the wheel, his strong fingers curled around it. She remembered the feel of his hands on her bare arms, her back, and his fingers curled around her breast when he kissed her. She rushed into speech in an effort to control her runaway thoughts.

"Is it much farther?"

"I don't think so. Although it's hard to see any landmarks." His voice was weary.

Miraculously, the sign indicating the exit to the truck stop was visible. Tom edged the truck onto the shoulder, slowly guiding it off the highway, careful of the ice. They drove down the ramp, slid through the stop sign, but managed to turn onto the highway and drive the remaining hundred yards or so to the truck stop. The parking lot was full. The snow whipped and swirled around, making drifts connecting one vehicle to another. Tom eased in beside one of the huge semi-trucks, its engine still running, creating an eerie cloud of vapor.

It was then that Beth realized she had been holding her breath, and she released it with a long sigh.

Tom echoed her sigh and said, "I wasn't so sure we'd make it."

She looked at him with a smile in her eyes. "I never doubted it for a minute."

"That's because you weren't driving."

"I'm glad I wasn't." She was still smiling.

"So am I." He wiped his fingers across his mustache, then stretched his arms as wide as he could in the confines of the truck. "It's going to be crowded in there, but it'll be warm."

Beth was immensely grateful for the arm across her

shoulders that helped propel her to the large restaurant connected to the station. She gripped Tom, her arm around his waist as they struggled to keep their balance on the icy surface of the drive.

The heat hit them as they stepped into the crowded room. Holding onto her mittened hand, Tom threaded his way between tables to a booth near the window. The other half of the booth was occupied by a bearded man in a red wool cap. He moved his coat so they could sit down.

"Been here long?" Tom asked.

"Since this morning." The man answered Tom, but looked at Beth.

She removed her hat and mittens and struggled to get out of her coat. Tom pulled the sleeves from her arms. He stood and shrugged out of his own coat, then made his way through the crowd to the counter.

Beth glanced at the man opposite her, then looked away quickly when she saw him eyeing her speculatively from her head to her breasts, then down to her hand, bare of rings.

"That your man?" he asked softly.

She was saved the necessity of replying by Tom's return.

"The scuttlebutt is that the storm'll blow itself out tonight." He handed Beth a cup of steaming hot chocolate. "I thought you might be getting tired of coffee."

"Thanks. I am." She moved over to make room for him to sit beside her.

"You folks live around here?" The man spoke with a New England accent.

"West of here," Tom said. "You?"

"Boston." He spoke with his eyes on Beth. "Your wife's not used to this weather, is she?"

"I—" A nudge from Tom's knee stopped Beth's denial.

"What makes you ask?" Tom's eyes were sharp and narrow, searching the man's face. He watched the eyes go directly to Beth's left hand.

"No reason. I—"

A commotion at the door caused the man to break off whatever he was going to say. A man had come in supporting a woman. Her head rested against him and blood was running down her face.

"My wife's been hurt!" There was panic in the man's voice.

Beth was on her feet. "Let me out, Thomas." Years of conditioning in the emergency room of the hospital put her into immediate action. She reached the couple quickly. "I'm a nurse. Sit down and let's see about stopping the blood. Thomas, I've got an emergency kit in the truck. Will you get it, please."

CHAPTER THREE

WITH BETH ON one side and her husband on the other, the stunned woman was led through the crowd to the booth. The bearded man got up and Beth pressed her down onto the seat. Bright red blood ran profusely down the woman's face. She was frightened and clutched her husband's hand.

"Is there anything I can do?" The hesitant question came from a young waitress, whose face matched the whiteness of her uniform.

"Bring clean cloths and a pan of water, please. It always looks worse than it is," Beth said to the injured woman as the waitress hurried away.

"I'm all . . . blood!"

"Head wounds bleed a lot. Does your head ache?" Beth examined the long ugly gash on the right side of her forehead.

"No."

"That's good. How about your vision? Are you having trouble focusing?"

"I don't think so."

Beth glanced up. Tom was shouldering his way through the crowd. He placed the first-aid kit on the table. "How're you doin'?"

"Okay. I can tape it until she gets to a doctor for some stitches."

"We were barely moving when we hit an icy patch and skidded out of control and headed for the ditch," the husband explained. "She hit her head on the dash when we jerked to a stop. Luckily we were close to the truck stop."

Beth felt in complete control of the situation, relaxed and confident. Her competent hands performed their ministrations, cleaning and soothing at the same time. "Will you get antiseptic and sterile pads from the case, Thomas?"

He placed the articles on the table. "Anything else I can do?"

"Hold your fingers here." She placed his fingers on each side of the wound. "Press the edges together so I can tape them."

His body was curved against hers, his arms encircling her as he reached around to assist her. She was terribly conscious of his warmth and strength as they shared their task.

"Thank you," she murmured when he took his hands away.

"You're most welcome." He smiled into her eyes.

Beth covered the tape with a sterile pad and carefully bound the woman's head with a cloth bandage to hold it in place.

"That'll have to do for now. As soon as you can, see a doctor. You'll need some stitches."

"Thank you, ma'am. We really appreciate it," the anxious husband told her.

"I'm glad I could help." Beth sat down and Tom sat down beside her.

"You'd better get your order in," the waitress said. "From the looks of this crowd, I doubt if the food holds out."

"Thanks for the tip." Tom's smile seemed to fluster the girl. Her eyes sparkled and clung to his. Beth thought she looked like a hungry kid staring in the window of a candy store. They placed their order and the young waitress reluctantly moved away.

The hamburgers and french fries were delicious. Tom ate his and placed another order. While he waited, he helped Beth finish off the fries on her plate. When she laughingly protested, his hand came from the back of the booth and gently tweaked a strand of her hair.

"I'll pay you back," he whispered in her ear.

They smiled into each others eyes and new life began to pump through Beth's tired body. She just barely resisted the temptation to press the length of her thigh closer to the long, muscular one that lay lightly against hers. Usually she could think of something flip to say, but all that came to her mind was how beautiful his eyes were, and she couldn't say that.

The waitress removed the dishes and carefully wiped the table. Beth was sure the extra service was due more to the teasing smiles and light banter that passed between her and Thomas than to the large tip he'd slipped under his plate after he paid the bill.

The other couple left the booth in search of a telephone. Tom moved his hand to the back of Beth's neck and gently massaged her sore muscles with his fingers.

"Tired?"

"Mmm . . . yes." She knew she should casually lean away from him, but her muscles loved what he was doing. His strong fingers worked magic, playing sensually along her neck, up into her hair, down over the tight cords of her neck. "That feels good," she murmured contentedly.

"You can do the same for me sometime."

He's far too handsome, Beth thought, watching him in the dim light of the restaurant. Her eyes returned again and again to the smooth skin, hard cheekbones, and firm lips beneath the russet brown mustache. Suddenly she felt an inchoate fear of this man, a fear of the completeness she felt when she was with him, a fear that he would become, once again, too important to her. She didn't like the way she was beginning to feel about him. She'd put that schoolgirl crush out of her mind, it was all behind her. His dark lashes lifted and his green eyes locked with hers. His face was so close she could feel his breath, soft and warm on her wet lips.

"Will you?"

"Will I what?"

"Rub my back, little screwball." He chuckled, and the lines in his face shifted. "I think I've almost put you to sleep."

"If you don't stop, I'll fall face-first on the table."

"I can't let that happen." He pulled her against him, holding her with his arm around her shoulders. Her stomach tightened with nervous apprehension when his hand forced her head to his shoulder. "This is kind of nice, isn't it?"

"I don't know what you're talking about," she said tightly.

"Silly, foolish, independent little cuss," he whispered with soft amusement in his voice. "Relax and lean on someone for a change. It won't set women's lib back a hundred years if I hold you."

Beth wanted to speak, but her voice seemed to have dried up. Inside her a wild, strange voice shouted a warning. *Be careful!* She was consumed with a variety of emotions—mainly fright, because what she was feeling was so strangely familiar, and regret, because she wasn't sophisticated enough to handle her feelings.

The other couple came back to the booth and settled down to rest, much the same as Tom and Beth were doing. The restaurant began to quiet down. Lights were turned down and people dozed. A few of the travelers played cards or talked, their voices subdued.

She felt Tom's breath on her ear before she heard his soft whisper. "Comfortable?"

"I'm fine. You?" she whispered back, lifting her head to meet his eyes.

"You don't hear me complaining, do you?"

Her eyes dropped to his mouth. The firm lips under the dark mustache twitched into a grin as he saw her eyes move over his face. The hand that held her moved to cup her upper arm and rub it gently. She could feel his heart beating under the palm of her hand. Their eyes met and Beth felt a strange drowsiness. The warmth of his body against her was making her feel so relaxed that almost against her will, she lowered her head to his chest.

His fingers came up to turn her face toward him, then stayed to caress her cheek gently before moving on to her ear.

"You like being a nurse, don't you?"

"Yes, I do."

"You're good at it. You handled things well, little Florence Nightingale."

"I only did what I've been trained to do." His hand on her ear was chasing coherent thought from her mind. In the semidarkness his features were unclear, except for the firm lips stretched over white teeth as he smiled. "I've been trained to handle emergencies, Thomas. I've helped to put many a mangled body back together. You do what you have to do."

"Cool-hand Luke, huh?" There was a definite note of respect in his voice.

For an indeterminate time she was aware of nothing except the scent of a masculine body: a combination of wool, leather, and soap. This was Thomas. Thomas was here, holding her. She turned her face to soft flannel that pushed against her nose as gentle breathing lifted his chest. She felt each beat of his heart against her cheek. I wonder what kind of patient he'd be? she mused. There's one thing for sure—he'd only have to ring once. The nurses would fall all over each other to take care of him.

"What are you thinking about? What caused the chuckle?"

"I was visualizing you as a patient."

"I'm a good patient."

"I bet! Men, as a rule, are terrible patients. When were you in the hospital?"

He shifted farther down in the seat, taking her with him, holding her firmly, while his other hand moved to pull his fur-lined coat over both of them.

"It was while I was playing football at Oklahoma State. I had knee surgery. Everyone, especially the nurses, made my stay . . . most pleasant."

"I bet they did!"

"There was one who—"

"You don't have to explain. Every hospital has one or two who serve beyond the bounds of duty."

The mustache brushed across her forehead. "Are you one of those?"

She didn't look up. She didn't dare. "A good nurse is firm, efficient, and impersonal."

"Firm, efficient, and impersonal," he echoed. "Sounds dull."

"That would depend."

"On what?"

"On what kind of a patient you are."

"I might try to pull you into bed with me," he said softly, his breath warm and moist on her forehead.

"I know all the correct moves. It would never happen."

"So it's been tried, huh?"

"Several times."

He pulled the coat closer around them, his large shoulder shielding them from the others in the room. Beth's mind was in a spin. Why am I allowing this? Why don't I move away? His fingers caressed her cheek before moving around to trace the outline of her lips. Unconsciously she held her breath as his fingers continued their exploration, stopping to caress her earlobe, then losing themselves in her rich dark hair. He held her head firmly against his shoulder while his mouth dropped to follow the path his fingers had taken. He gently brushed her cheek, his breath coming softly to her parted lips. She felt his lips trace a path, and then he was pressing them against hers. Her hand moved to stroke his cheek, his neck, then fastened tightly to his collar. His kiss was exquisitely gentle, demanding only what she was willing to give in return. It seemed to Beth that the world stood still while she was held close to the broad chest by the brawny arms of this man who had thundered back into her life and turned it upside down again. He deepened the kiss before he raised his head and looked at her.

"No—" she said breathlessly, but the word was muffled by his mouth as it returned to her own.

"Shh . . ." His mouth wandered over her face. "Let me kiss you. We deserve it after what we've been through today."

"No—"

"You're all grown up. . . ."

She didn't know what to make of his words. She hated herself for letting him hold her, kiss her. She meant nothing to him. Nothing.

He stroked her hair, then whispered. "It was a nice ending for our third day together. Go to sleep. It'll be morning soon."

Sleep was the furthest thing from her mind, but as he continued to smooth her hair, she closed her eyes. Her hand gripped his shirt, then relaxed as she fell asleep. Several times she felt him move, seeking a different position to ease his cramped muscles. Each time he cradled her closer against him. She burrowed into the nest made by his arms, giving herself up to the warmth and comfort he provided.

"Wake up." The words were accented by a gentle shake, interrupting Beth's beautiful dream of floating in a warm scented bath.

"Mmm . . ."

"Rise and shine. The bugle blew an hour ago."

Beth's blue eyes, heavy with sleep, opened to a room that was still dim. She saw two buttons, then a chest, topped by a firm chin. One of her arms was wrapped tightly around his waist. She lay partly on top of him, their tangled legs hanging off the end of the seat. Consciousness returned like a slap in the face. She struggled to sit up, pushing herself away from him.

"What time is it?"

"Almost six o'clock. Do you hear anything?"

She cocked her head to one side and listened. "The wind has stopped blowing! When?"

"Several hours ago. The snowplows have gone through."

The intimacy of the night vanished with the early morning light. Beth felt her cheeks redden with his inspection, and quickly excused herself to go to the restroom. She splashed water on her face, brushed her hair, added a touch of makeup, and wished she had her toothbrush.

Get a tight hold on yourself, Beth, old girl, she said silently to her reflection in the mirror. Thomas is not only good to look at, he's tough and wild as a hawk. He thrives on the unconventional and unexpected. He kissed you because he deserved it, like he said. And he thought nothing of holding you in his arms. He held you before and it meant nothing. Haven't you learned a thing?

Feeling ridiculously self-conscious, she went back to the booth and slipped in beside Tom, carefully stashing her purse on the seat between them.

"I ordered your breakfast. Here it is." He smiled at the waitress, an older one this time, but she was no less affected by his charm.

Beth looked with dismay at the stack of toast, the two fried eggs, and several fried sausages.

"I never eat this much!"

"Force yourself. No telling when we'll stop."

With the first bite she realized how hungry she was, and quickly cleaned her plate. She sipped the hot coffee and watched people prepare to leave. The weary travelers were eager to move on. Truck drivers were calmly discussing such things as jackknives and frozen gas lines, while women were bundling up their children for the walk to their cars. The howling wind had stopped, but it was still bitter cold. Beth heard a soft purring noise and wondered what it was. Finally, after several minutes, she asked Tom. "What's that sound?"

"Diesel engines."

"I never noticed it before."

"You didn't notice it yesterday because of the wind, but they were running even then."

"They ran all night?"

"Sure. They may not start again if they're turned off." He fingered his chin, covered with a brown stubble, and Beth forced her eyes to move away from him. "Also, if they're hauling a special cargo that must be kept at a specific temperature, the engine has to run to maintain the heater or refrigerator on the trailer." He smiled at her. "Make sense?"

"I guess so. I never thought about it."

"Most people don't." He motioned for the waitress to refill their cups.

Just then, the woman with the bandaged head and her husband came to the booth. "We're going," she said, "but we couldn't leave without saying thank you again."

The man shook hands with Tom. "Let me add my thanks too."

"Be sure to see a doctor," Beth urged.

"I will. Bye."

"We'd better get a move on too. Do whatever you have to do while I pay the bill." Tom moved toward the cash register that sat at the end of the counter, pulling on his coat as he went.

Beth went to the restroom again, and when she returned, the restaurant was even more crowded and Tom was nowhere in sight. Thinking he had gone to start the car, she went through the crowd toward the door. Then a voice stopped her.

"Where ya goin', pretty thing? You been here all night?"

Beth looked into the bloodshot eyes of a young man who couldn't have been much more than a teenager. He had a stubble of a beard on his face and a silly grin due, she was sure by the smell of him, to too much liquor. She gave him an icy glance and tried to move by him. The maneuver brought her close to the wall, and before she realized it, she was pinned there by his arm, blocking her way to the door.

"Are ya tryin' to give me the brush-off?" His sour breath assaulted her.

"I'm not trying to give you anything, junior. Bug off!" She tried to dart under his arm, but he moved it downward and stepped closer, so that his body shielded her from the view of the others in the restaurant.

"You ain't goin' to be friendly?" He looked over at two men lounging against the wall. "She ain't gonna be friendly," he announced with mock disbelief, and one of the men laughed.

"Okay, buster. You've had your fun. Get out of my way." Beth spoke in the quiet professional tone she used when talking to an unruly child in the hospital.

"Let 'er go, Harley. She don't wanna play," one of the other men urged.

"Well, I do!" The boy's voice turned ugly, and he moved closer, until his body was against Beth's. She still wasn't frightened. Out of the corner of her eye she could see people passing by and could hear the hum of voices in the restaurant. She brought her arms up between them and pushed.

"You cocky little . . . creep! Get away from me or I'll scream so loud I'll burst your eardrums!"

He stood his ground, as if daring her to open her mouth. When she took a deep breath, his hand flashed out, but before he could touch her he was flung back with such force that he stumbled into a group of truckers on their way to the door.

Tom reached the boy before he could regain his balance, and shoved him against the wall, bouncing his head on the hard surface.

"If you want to play with someone, punk, I'll play." Tom waited, his eyes like bits of hard green glass.

The boy looked up in fright at the angry man towering over him. Finally he scooped up his hat, and with his two friends pulling him along, he hurried out the door.

Beth was astonished at the violence of Tom's attack. She had been confident she could handle the situation. With her back braced against the wall, she could have brought her knee up sharply and rendered the boy helpless, without causing a scene. Her face burned with embarrassment as her eyes swept the sea of staring faces.

Tom reached for her arm and ushered her out the door without saying a word.

CHAPTER FOUR

THE COLD WRAPPED Beth in its icy blast as she slipped and slid her way to the parking lot. She had to concentrate on keeping her balance on the frozen surface as well as keeping up with Tom's long strides. He unlocked her door, then moved around to the driver's side.

Beth's temper began to simmer at a low boil. "There was absolutely no need for you to use such a heavy hand against that boy."

Silence.

Tom inched the truck forward until he could see if the road was clear, then eased it out onto the highway. The plows had pushed the snow into high mounds on each side of the parking lot entrance, making it difficult to see oncoming traffic. Several trucks were already rolling down the ramp to the interstate and Tom pulled in behind them.

"You didn't have to push him into the wall," Beth persisted stubbornly. "You might have caused a concussion."

He gave her a cold glance and then turned his attention back to the highway.

"Thomas!"

"Hush up!"

Had she heard him correctly? she wondered.

He looked at her, read her expression, and repeated the words slowly for emphasis. "Hush up!" His voice was low, toneless, and she heard the anger beneath the surface.

"Why did you—" she began.

"Force is the only language a punk like that understands." The smoldering glance he gave her would have melted an icicle.

"I could have handled him."

"How? By saying 'Oh, please don't!' " He mimicked her voice.

"No. By using a few of the things I learned in a self-defense course."

"You obstinate little mule!"

Beth gave him a withering look. "No more obstinate than you, Mr. Clary."

"I'm sure you've taken care of obnoxious pests before, *Miss* Marshall, but this time there were three of them, and they could have hustled you out the door before you had time to bat your eyes."

"I could have handled it," she said stubbornly, though grudgingly admitted to herself that he was right.

"You think so?" His mouth twitched, but he managed to suppress his smile. "Forget it."

His dismissal of the subject made Beth all the more determined to not let the issue slide by.

"There are ways of dealing with an unpleasant situation without resorting to violence," she said primly.

He shook his head slowly. "You *are* mule-headed!"

Beth refused to take up the challenge of that statement, and turned to stare out the window. She gazed with unseeing eyes at the snow-covered landscape. But this was only a ploy to mask the turbulent emotions churning within her.

Three years ago he had been fun, and charming, and had worn his magic as casually as he did his shearling coat. Now she realized there was a depth to him she had not seen before. A relationship with him would not be an easy one. She sighed deeply. Where was the gentle man who held her in his arms last night?

The altitude was higher as they drove on. Snow covered everything, rounding out sharp angles, giving the trees and boulders a softer appearance. Evergreen branches hung heavy with the accumulated snow. Dark clouds ahead of them cluttered the gray sky.

"The only thing that could make this weather any more disagreeable would be for the wind to pick up," Tom said drily. "The snow would block the highway in a matter of minutes if it began to drift."

Beth thought over his words for a few minutes. "What about your cattle? How do you feed them in this weather?"

"Most of them are brought in to feeding stations. But for the ones out on open range, we fly the bales of hay out in a small plane and dump them. It's quite a ride." He flexed his shoulders in an attempt to ease his tense muscles.

"What about the horses?"

"They're brought to the homestead in the fall. The mares that are in foal are stabled. The yearlings are quartered in another area of the ranch."

"It's like frontier days."

"Not quite."

"Wouldn't Buffalo Bill be astounded to see hay being dropped from a machine in the sky? Basically, life on the range hasn't changed all that much, according to cowboy movies. Cowboys still need horses to round up cattle and . . . do all that other stuff." She finished with a wave of her hand.

"Tell you what. When we do all that 'other stuff,' you can come along." His eyes were laughing now, his face relaxed. This was the charming side of his personality. With an effort Beth looked away from his starkly masculine profile.

"Have you always lived in Cody?" She needed something sane and sensible to say, something to distract her thoughts.

"Except for my years at college and my stint in the Marines. Both Steven and I grew up like wild Indians." His voice was laced with melancholy. "I was two years younger and four inches taller than Steven. He used to say that I got the legs and he got the brains. We both loved horses, and from the time we could walk, we each had one." He slowed the Blazer and carefully guided it over an icy patch of highway. "We played all the usual pranks on each other while we were growing up. He was my brother, but also my friend."

"You were lucky. It doesn't always work out like that."

"After Steven finished college, he joined the Navy. He wanted to see the world. It seemed like every six months he was transferred to a different part of it. He loved traveling, seeing new things, meeting new people. After my three years in the Marines, I was ready to come back to the ranch. Dad died shortly after that. Mom was shattered, but she's tough. She picked up her life, and now travels—sometimes alone, or with a group. It's worked into a sort of new career for her. She guides tours all over the world. I guess that's where Steven got his wanderlust."

There was a long silence while Beth absorbed this brief bit of family history. She had always felt a little guilty because she hadn't liked Steven. She didn't really know why, unless it was because he was almost *too* perfect. He was handsome, polished, and polite to the extreme. Sarah had been reluctant to mention Steven since telling her of his death, and Beth wondered if her sister were still grieving. Finally she asked Tom about Steven's accident, because she had never heard the details. Tom seemed uncomfortable, but after much hesitation, he began to speak.

"Steven was driving into Cody when he was killed. A rock slide had partially blocked the highway, and he swerved to avoid it and collided with a truck. It was tough on all of us. Sarah hadn't been feeling well, and about that time tests revealed that she had multiple sclerosis, but she hadn't told anyone. It was a double blow."

Beth was silent. Lord, she thought, first our parents, then Steven, and now this dreadful disease. How had Sarah managed to keep her sanity?

"I still don't understand why she didn't call me. No job is more important to me than my sister. Of course I'd have come to help out. Sarah would have done the same for me."

"I doubt it was just the job that made her decide not to tell you at the time. I remember her saying it had been tough on you to uproot yourself from the family home after your parents died. You had studied hard to get your licence and it wasn't fair to upset you."

"I talk to her a couple times a month and she's never said a word about not feeling well. She tells me she's happy and that she's loved helping you out around the house since Steven died."

"Her condition has stabilized. There's no emergency, as I told you. She doesn't know that I went to Rochester to get you. That's a decision I made on my own. In the first place, I thought that if you were the person Sarah says you are, you'd want to know and want to be with her. In the second place, Sarah needs her family. I think it will make all the difference in her attitude."

"She's had you." She remembered saying that once before. She didn't know why she said it again. Perhaps it had something to do with the deep, quivering breath he had taken when he finished speaking.

"Yes. She's had me." It wasn't a positive admission, and Beth's brows drew together in puzzled thought. "She has good days and bad days. But mainly she needs companionship. She loves her home and it would kill her to have to move to a nursing home to get the care she needs. What better way for her to be able to stay at home than to have her sister, the nurse, with her." He glanced at Beth, then abruptly changed the subject. "It's twenty-five miles to Cody and the ranch is seven miles beyond. We can stop at Cody and stretch our legs."

"It's my fanny that needs the relief. It'll never be the same again."

"Wait until you've spent a day in the saddle," he said with a teasing grin.

The day dragged on. Beth felt as if she had been in the

Blazer forever. But it wasn't until her stomach growled and she glanced at her watch that she realized how late in the afternoon it was. The roads were icy, so progress was slow, despite the fact that the traffic had thinned with the coming of evening.

Beth yawned and stretched. "I'm tired, but not as tired as you are, I'm sure." The rhythmic movement of the truck had made her drowsy. She smiled at him when he glanced at her.

"Hot food, a shower and shave, is what I need."

"Funny you should mention that. I was thinking the same thing."

"I didn't know you shaved!"

"Fun-ny!" she countered with an impish grin.

Cody appeared at the end of the long curved highway and stretched out toward the gentle slopes of the mountains. They followed a yellow school bus into town, then turned off the highway. They parked in front of a cafe whose sign boasted the best steak in the Northwest.

"What a trip!" Tom said as he shut off the motor. "My shoulders feel like they've been in a straitjacket."

Beth watched him. Being tired did nothing to diminish his virility. When he looked at her, his eyes were like the green foam on a turbulent sea. His nose was proud, the shadowed cheeks faintly grooved with fatigue. He was a handsome, powerful man. He caught her look, smiled at her, and reached for his coat.

"Let's get out and stretch our legs."

"Every muscle and bone in my body is protesting," she groaned as she slid from the seat to stand on shaky legs.

"Tom? I thought I recognized that bucket of bolts." The voice came from behind, and a stocky man in a leather coat and stocking cap came toward them from across the parking lot.

"Hi, Pat. How ya doin'?"

"Fine, Tom, fine. Here today, gone tomorrow. You know how the cable business is—go where the business is or go without." His friendly blue eyes matched the wide smile on his face. He looked at Beth and waited, plainly wanting an introduction.

Tom's hand rested on her arm. "Beth, meet Patrick O'Day, a wild Irishman."

"Pleased to meet'cha, me darlin'." He snatched the cap off his head and bowed over her hand. "Don't let this rogue scare ya. I'm Irish, yes . . . but wild, never!"

Beth smiled. It was impossible not to. The man's dark brown hair hung down over his ears, and his cheeks were pink from the cold. But it was his eyes that drew her attention: they were pale blue, and crinkled with smile lines at the corners. He wasn't as massive as Tom, nor as handsome, but he was attractive. He released her hand reluctantly, but held her with his eyes.

"We're going in for a quick bite, Pat," Tom said. "See you around."

"Mind if I join you?" His smiling eyes were on Beth. He didn't see the frown that crossed Tom's face, but Beth did, and she wondered about it.

Pat and Tom were greeted by friends as they followed the waitress to a corner table. The cafe was small and reflected the western atmosphere with checkered tablecloths and a rough plank floor. It had been hours since breakfast, and Beth was hungry. The waitress, dressed in jeans, a plaid shirt and a cowboy hat, took their order.

"Are you a rancher, Mr. O'Day?" Beth asked over the din of western music blaring from the jukebox.

"Pat. Call me Pat." He laughed as he said it. "My company does aerial and underground work, mainly for the telephone company and cable television. It's too cold to work here at this time of year, so I'm heading for warm country."

"When are you leaving?" Tom asked pointedly.

"I'm not sure. It depends." He smiled at Beth with open admiration.

She blushed. "Your work sounds interesting."

"It is. I'll tell you about it over dinner some evening, if the ol' hoss, here, don't have his claim staked."

"Beth's here to take care of her sister, Sarah," Tom informed him flatly.

"Sarah? I wouldn't have guessed you were sisters."

"We're half sisters, actually. I'm terribly anxious to see her."

"She's had a raw deal." He frowned, then a slow smile spread over his face. "I'm sure you'll have some free time. I'll show you the sights."

"That would be nice of you," Beth said, avoiding Tom's gaze.

"I'll give you a call."

The waitress brought large hamburgers in baskets. The delicious odor wafted up. Beth inhaled deeply and laughed. "Mmm . . . good! I'm starved."

"Didn't the ol' hoss feed you?" The Irishman's eyes were warm on her face.

"Not since breakfast."

"I'd a looked after you better'n that," he said with a caress in his voice.

"Don't blame me, blame the weather. We've had a hell of a trip." From his tone Beth knew that Tom was in no mood for light banter.

"We caught the edge of it," Pat said. "I saw Herb in town yesterday. He said they'd been hauling hay, gettin' ready for the blizzard."

"Herb's a good man. I knew he'd handle things, but I'm glad to be heading home."

"You're damn lucky to have him. I know several ranchers who'd give their right arm to get him away from you."

Tom ate quickly and rose to leave as soon as Beth finished. "Ready?" he asked.

She picked up her purse and glanced at the other man. "It was nice meeting you, Pat."

"My pleasure." He smiled at her as if she were the only woman in the world. "I'll call you," he said softly.

"I'll see you before you leave," Tom told him as he helped Beth into her coat.

"I'm sure you will." He winked openly at Beth.

It was dusk. The sun had moved behind the mountains, casting long shadows over the valley.

"Why the come-on to Pat?" Tom demanded as he eased the truck back onto the highway.

Beth looked at him with disbelief. "What?"

"You heard me. You couldn't have sent the message more clearly if you'd written a letter."

"I didn't give him the come-on. I tried to be nice to him because he's your friend. That's all!" She couldn't believe her ears. He was angry! What was going on? "I was just being—"

"Yeah, I know. You were just being . . . friendly."

He was silent after that. The lights of Cody were left behind as they turned onto a snow-covered gravel road. Tom maneuvered the Blazer expertly, but Beth clutched the door handle as they swung curves and plowed through snowdrifts.

Tall, stately pine trees lined the winding road; beyond them were large, open spaces.

"We're almost there." Tom slowed the truck and turned to look at her. "You can let go of the handle now."

"Are you sure?"

"Uh-huh." She heard a chuckle after the grunt.

"This is beautiful country, even covered with snow."

"I love it. I wouldn't live anywhere but here."

"I can understand why." She gazed out the window and caught sight of something in the trees. "I think I saw a deer!"

"Could be. They're thick as fleas. Federal land adjoins mine and they're plentiful."

"They're so beautiful. How could anyone shoot them?"

"If they're not thinned out every so often, they starve. The land can only support so many."

"I know, but those soft brown eyes—"

"You'd have made a lousy pioneer."

"That was different," she argued. "It was kill or go hungry. I could shoot one if my family needed food."

"Have you ever fired a gun?"

"No."

"I'll give you a lesson, in case we ever run out of meat."

"I'm not sure I want a lesson, thank you," she retorted, and hugged herself with her arms.

"You should learn the fundamentals. There may be a time when your life will depend on it."

"All right. But I'm not going to shoot anything."

"God, I hope not. The only thing you'll shoot at is a target."

The road bent to the left, and Tom turned sharply to the right and onto a wide drive. They had been driving parallel to a split-rail fence for a few miles and this drive was the first break. A tall post flanked the drive, and suspended over it was a large wooden sign: GRIZZLY BEAR RANCH.

"I didn't know your ranch had a name."

"My great-grandfather named it."

Evergreen trees lined the lane as it wound back toward the mountain. As the trees began to thin, Beth glimpsed the ranch house. Even from a distance it looked huge. As they drew closer, she saw it was made of logs. It was nestled there as if it were part of the trees and mountains that surrounded it. It was two-storied with a wide covered porch. A gigantic stone chimney rose into the sky at one end of the house and was emitting a trail of smoke. A thick layer of snow covered the roof. Shrubs and bushes were scattered around the yard, but they were almost buried under the snow. There were buildings to the back of the house and to the side. It was a large complex.

The door rose as they approached the garage, and Tom drove the Blazer inside. After switching off the motor and turning on the inside light, he turned and looked at Beth for a long moment. Finally, he spoke.

"You may be surprised when you see Sarah, Beth, but don't let it show. She's not to be upset." He spoke quietly, but his tone conveyed a firm message.

A streak of fear raced through her heart. What did he mean? Oh, Lord! "I'm a professional, Thomas. Even if Sarah *is* my sister, I won't allow my anxiety to show."

"I understand that, but—"

"You don't understand anything about me," she blurted. "How could you? I knew you . . . briefly, a long time ago. And less than a week ago you came bulldozing your way back into my life. You don't know me at all."

"Has it been less than a week?" he asked in a low, husky tone, and swung open the car door.

CHAPTER FIVE

BETH'S MIND WAS whirling with conflicting thoughts. She tried to slow her steps, hoping to regain her composure before facing the sister she hadn't seen since so much tragedy had come into her life. Tom's hand was firm on her shoulder as he ushered her toward the house.

"C'mon," he urged impatiently. "I phoned my ranch foreman and he's told Sarah that you're coming."

They went up a couple of steps and into a side entry. Thick rugs were laid out on the tiled floor to soak up the snow carried in on overshoes. After slipping off their boots, they silently removed their coats, and Tom hung them on pegs hanging along the wall.

Beth followed him through a door to the kitchen. A dim light was on over the range, and a big dog stood in the middle of the room, wagging its tail. Tom switched on the ceiling light.

"Hello, girl." The dog came eagerly to him and he fondled her ears. "Where is everyone?"

The house was so quiet, it was eerie. Beth glanced around the large kitchen. It was equipped with contemporary cabinets and appliances, but set against one wall was an antique sink, complete with a red iron hand pump and filled with plants. In the middle of the room was a round oak table and high-backed chairs. The far end of the room was used for casual living, with a massive fireplace, chairs upholstered in red and white check which matched the wallpaper, and a long, low couch. The room had a warm lived-in feeling.

"What a marvelous kitchen," Beth said, her eyes roaming around the room.

"Efficient too. I had it done to Sarah's specifications. She almost drove the builder nuts."

Tom gave the dog a final pat on the head and straightened up. He was the only familiar thing in the quiet, unfamiliar room, and when he reached out his hand, Beth's went out to meet it. A quote from her father came to mind: "You can trust a man whose eyes smile when he does and who is kind to animals."

The ring of the telephone broke the stillness. Still clutching her hand, Tom reached the wall phone.

"Yeah, Herb."

Beth wondered how he knew who it was, then saw the numbered lights on the phone and realized the ranch had an intercom system. From the look on Tom's face, she knew the news he was getting wasn't good.

"Wasn't that kind of sudden? Why did they decide that right now, and how in the hell did you get her to the hospital?" he asked in a deadly calm voice. Then, after listening and nodding: "Yes, she's anxious to see Sarah." The green eyes shifted to Beth. "Was Sarah frightened when you got stuck? No? Jean was right to stay with her. How long will she be there? A week or longer. Damn!

We'll go see her in the morning. You may have to open up the lane again if the wind comes up. Yeah, Herb. Thanks for watching for me. I was beginning to wonder what happened when no one but Shiloh came to meet me. Things will work out fine now that Beth's here. She'll be able to give Sarah the shots and save her that long, hard trip to town. Yeah . . . bye."

He put down the phone gently and turned to Beth with a worried look. "They took Sarah to the hospital yesterday. Something about a pain in her back. They want to change the medication, try something new."

Oh, Lord! Beth thought wildly. Why didn't he come for me sooner? A flush touched her cheeks as her eyes sought out his face. The message in her features was loud and clear. He knows that I'm not as calm and collected as I pretend to be, she thought, and wondered if he realized he was still gripping her hand.

"How about making coffee?" he suggested gently. "I'll bring in our suitcases."

"The small one has my overnight things. No need to bring in the others. Tomorrow I'll find a room near the hospital."

Tom's expression was enigmatic. He reached behind her and opened a cabinet door.

"The coffee's in here. Do you like waffles? There should be some in the freezer. Pop a few in the toaster. That hamburger we had in town was just an appetizer."

Trying to disguise the nervousness building up within her from the feel of his hand on hers, and the blatant caress of his thumb against her wrist, she blurted angrily, "I think I can handle that."

Tom lounged against the counter, his arms folded,

Beth's hand trapped against his chest. She tried to pull it away, but he refused to let go. A slow smile warmed his face. A dark shadow of beard and tired, half-closed eyes were the only indication of the long rough drive he had just finished.

"I bet there isn't much you can't handle when you set your mind to it," he murmured.

"May I have my hand back, or do you plan to keep it permanently?" Her throat was tight and she snapped out the words. She had to get away from him so she could get some control over her mind.

His eyes assessed her critically, moving over the dark, tumbled hair to the blue eyes glinting at him. When his eyes settled on her mouth, her lips trembled at the image that came swiftly to mind: his hungry, probing kiss taking possession of her as she willingly allowed him that possession. His gaze traveled to the firm breasts rounding out the sweater she wore, and he smiled before he lowered his head and planted a quick kiss on her lips. The familiar soft brush of his mustache sent a weakening thrill through her.

"Stop it!" She jerked back angrily.

"Okay," he said good-naturedly. His long body straightened and he stretched his arms in a gesture of tiredness, bringing her up against him. He folded his arms behind her, pinning her arm behind her back.

She tried to move away. Her heart was pounding like a scared rabbit's and she was sure he could feel it beating through her thick sweater.

"Are you out of your mind?" she demanded breathlessly.

"I think so. I'm so damned tired I just might be off my

rocker. Aren't you going to offer me a little comfort and try to soothe my frayed nerves?"

"Only if you think a swift kick or a karate chop will help."

He laughed, but she wondered for the hundredth time why she had come here with him. How was she going to be able to avoid him in the days ahead?

Abruptly he released her and moved toward the door. "Make that four waffles and the coffee strong," he told her, knowing full well how he was irritating her.

Beth stared at the closed door and wished desperately that her heart would slow down so she could think clearly. She didn't want to feel anything for him, nothing at all. He was trouble with a capital *T*. Now her worry over Sarah was making her too vulnerable to cope with him, and she resented it. That accounted for her heart's nervous flutter, she reasoned angrily.

She brushed a hand across her forehead and picked up the coffeemaker from the spotless counter.

The dog, Shiloh, stood waiting beside the door for Tom, completely ignoring Beth's presence. Beth was delving into the freezer for the waffles when Tom returned from outdoors. She didn't look at him until she saw her two large cases out of the corner of her eye.

"Thomas!" She followed him to the stairway. "Thomas! I'll only need the little one for tonight."

He walked up the wide carpeted stairway without looking back, and her anger flared. He was the most impossible, domineering person she had ever met. "You'll just have to bring them down again in the morning," she called as he disappeared down a hallway at the top of the stairs.

The big dog followed closely behind Tom. Beth turned back to the kitchen feeling sick and exhausted. She just wasn't prepared for the agony of having to fight him at every turn. "You've got yourself into a sweet stew this time," she muttered. "You haven't had your head screwed on right since you met him."

Tom came downstairs and crossed to the outer door again. Beth turned her back and refused to look at him. She heard him murmur to the dog, "Watch out for the bear-cat in the kitchen, Shiloh, or she'll bite you."

Beth tightened her face muscles to keep from smiling. She needed to stay angry. It was her only defense against his masculine charm.

Tom made three trips from the garage to the rooms upstairs, and by that time the coffee had brewed and the waffles were ready. She put them on a plate and set it on the end of the counter.

"Aren't you going to eat?"

"I'm not hungry," she snapped.

"Have coffee with me."

"I seldom drink it at night. It keeps me awake."

"You need something. Sit down and I'll make you a cup of chocolate."

"Chocolate has caffeine too. Besides, your waffles will get cold."

"I'll heat them in the microwave. You're just being stubborn again. Sit down."

Beth gave a resigned shake of her head and settled on a padded bar stool at the counter. Minutes later he set a steaming cup before her, with a plump marshmallow floating in the warm foam. It smelled delicious. And the warm hand that lingered on her back when he set down the cup sent ripples of pure pleasure through her.

No words passed between them while he ate his waffles and she sipped her chocolate. When he had cleaned the plate and poured himself a second cup of coffee, he reached over and clasped her hand.

"Go on up and take a good hot bath. I'll clean up down here. One of Sarah's rules—whoever makes a mess in the kitchen cleans it up before they leave it."

"Do you always obey Sarah's rules?" The words sounded caustic, and she wished them back immediately. She felt even worse when he ignored them.

"Your room is the second door to the right."

The bedside lamp was on when she reached the room. She looked around and her eyes lighted with appreciation at the queen-sized bed covered with an intricate tapestry spread. Matching long drapes framed the small-paned windows. The furniture was white French provincial; the lamp shades and a deep, soft chair were covered with a dusty rose fabric.

Beth loved the furnishings. She stood quietly for a long moment and let herself enjoy the unexpected beauty of the spacious room. With a soft, tired sigh, she picked up her cosmetic case and went into the adjoining bath. She filled the tub, poured in a generous amount of fragrant oil, and sank into the warm bath.

Thoughts of Tom tormented her as she lay back and let the warm water ease the tension from her tired body. The memory of the kisses they shared last night had refused to dim during the day. She could close her eyes and feel the soft touch of his lips and the gentle brush of his mustache against her face. Damn! She had been kissed before, even by him. It was the damn mustache then, and it was the damn mustache now! Why had she let him hold her and kiss her? She knew she was playing a dangerous game. My God! Hadn't she learned anything from that disastrous encounter so long ago? He had taken it for granted that his attentions would be welcome. With his good looks, she doubted if he was ever refused. For the first time she wondered if he had a steady woman friend, or a lover. A man of his good looks and virility was bound to seek physical release. His commanding presence and the magnetism of his personality would arouse most women with hardly any effort at seduction on his part.

She tried to turn her thoughts away, but they persistently returned to Tom. She wondered if her surrender to his physical presence satisfied a deep need in her for security through male dominance and possession. Her one affair, while trying to blot Tom from her mind, had left her with the feeling that sex was a frustrating experience, and she had come to terms with the belief that perhaps she was a woman with a low sex drive. Now she was not so sure.

Beth lay in the tub and looked at the ceiling. She could no longer deny that Thomas Clary had only to look at her to set her heart pounding. She had to turn off her feelings for him or he would make her into a docile, mindless robot willing to do and be whatever he wanted her to be. Damn him! Her body had matured along with her mind during the three years since she had believed herself so desperately in love with him, and the intensity of her response to him was proof that her burgeoning needs had been denied too long.

She dried herself with a thick towel, dusted herself generously with powder, and applied a light lotion to her face. Dressed in her pajamas and robe, she padded barefoot into the bedroom and turned back the bedcovers.

A soft knock came on the door seconds before it opened. Beth turned in astonishment as Tom casually walked into the room as if they had been living together for years.

"I heard the water pipes gurgle and knew you'd let the water out of the tub" was his only explanation.

"Oh?"

"I've built up the fire in the fireplace. C'mon down and see the rest of the house."

"Thank you, but I really want to get to bed."

"So do I, but I'll wait until we're better acquainted."

"If you're trying to shock me, it won't work. I'm not a trembling child, nor am I frightened because we're alone in the house." She looked at him in the mirror of the dressing table, and saw that he was grinning.

"Thank God for that!" he murmured. "C'mon." He took her hand and pulled her toward the door.

"Stop, Thomas. I don't have any shoes on."

"I noticed. You don't need them. I'll bed you down on the couch and you can tuck them under you."

"You'll . . . what?"

"Poor choice of words. You can sit on the couch and keep your legs tightly together. I promise not to attack you, although . . . I'd certainly like to." His eyes twinkled as her mouth tightened and her nose lifted in defiance. They were at the head of the stairs, and he was two steps below her. She tugged on her hand and he turned. Their eyes were even. "C'mon, or I'll kiss you right here."

"I wish you'd stop playing your adolescent games," she said crossly. "I'm a grown-up, professional woman and would appreciate being treated like one."

"You don't look like a professional woman. You look like a scrubbed little kid." His eyes held so much mirth that she had to whip up her resentment to keep from smiling.

"*You* don't look as if *you* were lifted from *Esquire*."

"You noticed? Three minutes in the shower, two minutes to shave, two minutes to jump into my clothes. Seven minutes . . . all for you." A smile tugged at his lips, as if he were completely unaware of her belligerence.

He's flirting with me, she thought, and lifted her hand to brush the thick swath of dark hair from her forehead. His own dark hair was wet and tousled, and the terry shirt he had pulled over his head clung to his damp shoulders. He had on soft, faded jeans and . . . white socks! She wanted to laugh. She hadn't seen a man in white socks in years. His strong male ego needed a setback, she thought, so she did laugh.

"White socks?"

"Sure. I always wear them in my boots." He was totally unperturbed by her amusement. He raised dark brows. "As a nurse, I thought you'd approve. C'mon, your feet will be getting cold."

Beth allowed him to lead her down the stairs and back to the living area in the kitchen.

"I thought you wanted me to see the rest of the house."

"You can see it in the morning." He led her to the couch and pressed her down.

What's the matter with me? she fumed. He's either leading or pushing me into whatever niche he wants me in, and I follow like a lamb being led to slaughter. She felt a strong desire to jump up and go sit in the high-backed chair opposite the couch. At that instant his eyes met hers.

"Sarah has to have a high, solid chair. It's impossible for her to get up out of low ones without help."

Beth sank back down on the couch. Damn him! He can read my mind. She sucked in her breath and looked around as if concentrating on the room, but she was intensely aware of him moving to the stereo.

"Do you get good television reception out here?" She had to say something; the silence was making her feel ill at ease.

"Are you a TV fan?"

"Not really."

"Sarah is. She loves it. We had the cable run out here so she could watch a movie any hour of the day or night."

"I've never had the time to become addicted to TV."

"Want to see if there's a good X-rated movie on?"

She knew he was trying to shock her again, and she refused to take the bait. She shrugged indifferently, sorry that the gesture was lost on him. He had turned his back and was fiddling with the controls on the stereo. When the music reached her ears, she jerked her head around in surprise. She didn't know what she had expected, but it certainly wasn't Beethoven's "Moonlight Sonata."

Her eyes sought his and her lips parted in one of the warmest smiles she had given him.

"Do you like that?"

"I love it," she said softly.

"Somehow, I thought you would." He sat down on the couch, leaned his head back, and stretched his long legs out in front of him. "Now, this is my idea of a pleasant evening—a crackling fire, a quiet house, soothing music, and"—he rolled his head and faced her—"a pretty woman all ready for bed."

Color flooded her face. His eyes glinted devilishly, his lips twitched in an effort not to laugh. He *was* flirting with her, but it wasn't going to work! She'd had male patients who had tried to jar her out of her calm reserve, but she had never had to try as hard as she was now to keep her composure.

His hand snaked out and grabbed hers. "I'll stop teasing you. You're too tired tonight, and it's no fun unless you fight back. Come over here beside me and stretch your feet out to the fire. I'm enjoying this even if you're not."

"No—"

"Yes." His arms pulled her over against him. "Now, isn't this better? Relax. You're stiff as a poker." He reached down and straightened her legs, then lifted her bare feet and rested them on one of his jean-clad legs. His arm encircled her and he pressed her head down onto his shoulder. "Ah . . . you smell good and feel better." He buried his nose in her hair. "Just like ol' married folks, sittin' in front of the fire when the chores are done and the kids in bed."

"Thomas—"

"Mmm . . . ? If you've got anything to say, you'd better say it now, because I'm going to have to kiss you in a minute."

"Now look! You work too fast for me. I've only known you—"

"Three years and five days and four nights. I didn't sleep a wink one of those nights. I didn't want to miss out on a minute of the time your tight little body was pressed to mine. Did I tell you that your little bottom is a nice handful?"

"Stop it, Thomas!"

He let out a bellow of laughter. "God, I love it when you get your back up!"

"Enjoy yourself while you can. I'm going into town tomorrow. I'll stay at the hotel. I'll spend my days with Sarah as her private nurse. If she's not coming back for a week or two, there's no need for me to stay here."

"There's every need for you to stay right where you are."

Beth sat back and closed her eyes. I won't argue the point with him now, she thought. She tried to relax, but everything about him—his physical attraction, his personality—made that impossible. She wondered if he could feel her insides trembling. She tried to ignore the warm hand that slid up the loose sleeve of her robe to stroke her arm with long slow movements. His head moved, his breath fanned her mouth, and her eyes flew open.

Amusement, curiosity, and surprise all mingled in his eyes as he looked at her. "You're trying awfully hard to stay ramrod stiff and not enjoy this. Loosen up. I haven't raped a woman in over a week now!" His tone was teasing.

She put her hand on his chest to push him away, but it was like pushing against a mountain. Her lips tightened and she kept them that way even as he covered them with his. Oh, God, she prayed, help me to hold out against him.

"Eliz-a-beth." His lips left her for an instant, and his tone was cajoling. "Beth." His voice was a mere whisper against her mouth. "Your lips are as tight as a miser's purse. Let me in."

"No. Thom-as—"

"Yes . . ." His fingers were pushing her hair behind her ears as his mouth silenced her protest. "Mmm . . ." The sound came from his throat, and his arms locked her to him.

Beth had not imagined such an assault on her senses. She wanted to surrender to the excitement of his touch, her mouth responding to the insistent persuasion of his. The kiss deepened. His hunger seemed insatiable and his caress became savage, his skilled sensuality blotting out everything but his power over her senses.

"Beth . . . Beth, your mouth is so . . . sweet," he whispered, his lips moving to her eyes. "You were sweet before . . . but now . . ." The soft feel of his mustache on her face drove her into a frenzy of need, and she lifted her fingertips to his cheek and pulled his mouth back to hers. He responded instantly to the urgency of her desire. His tongue gently stroked her inner lips, the moist, velvet texture sending spasms of delight down her spine. She drove away any thoughts that might shadow the bliss of the moment.

He lightened the pressure of his mouth so that their lips were touching gently. "Soft, sweet, delicious. I had forgotten your mouth tasted like this." His voice was no louder than a sigh.

Her arm slid around his neck. She was drowning in sensuality. A sweet, unbearable erotic pleasure-pain had started in the pit of her stomach and spread to her womb with throbbing arousal. She gently worked her fingertips between his mouth and her cheek and stroked the soft hair above his lip.

"Do you like it, sweet?" The words were breathed between nibbles on her fingers.

"I love it."

She angled her head so that their noses were side by side and rubbed her face against his mouth. She heard a soft sound come from his throat and felt the trembling in his body as he buried his face against her neck. His hand had burrowed inside the robe and under the top of her pajamas. Softly, gently, he first cupped, then stroked her breast, fitting it into his palm, his thumb resting on the swollen nipple. When he pressed her down onto the couch with gentle insistence, Beth's desire raged war with her instinct that this was a dangerous game she was playing.

"Thomas . . . we shouldn't—"

"I know we shouldn't. It's too soon for you. I'm trying hard not to grab you and take you upstairs to my bed. I want to love you all night long . . . I wanted to last night—" His lips covered hers very lightly, his tongue caressing the edge of her mouth. "I want to love you very gently, until you ache for more."

CHAPTER SIX

BETH KNEW SHE should stop this headlong flight into sensuous pleasure, but the weight of Tom's body pinned hers to the couch and played havoc with her desire to escape. Her fingers caressed his thick hair. His mouth nuzzled her throat, then moved slowly lower to explore the breast his hand had exposed. Emotions, long dormant, surged uncontrollably through her when she felt his tongue caress her nipple. She stifled the desire to cry out when his lips, then teeth, nipped lightly at it.

"Please, Thomas . . . we must stop!"

Suddenly a cold, wet nose thrust against her face. She moved her head to the side to evade the dog's tongue. Tom raised his head and was immediately accosted by the insistent animal, who whined, then barked for attention.

"Dammit, Shiloh, what is it?" he said thickly. The dog continued to bark, her tail swishing rapidly from side to side. Then she jumped up and down and ran toward the back foyer.

"I think she needs to go outside," Beth suggested.

Outside was the magic word: it sent the big red dog

into a frenzy of barking. She raced to the door and back again to thrust her nose into Tom's face.

"All right, Shiloh, but your timing is lousy!"

Tom's fingers lingered on Beth's exposed breast, then gently pulled her robe together and buttoned it. He eased himself up to lean over her, and his fingers played with the curve of her jaw.

"Saved by the dog," he teased. "And she isn't even a Saint Bernard."

Strong currents of embarrassment kept Beth from looking at him. He'd wanted to make love to her, and . . . *bang*, just like that, she'd been a pushover! Oh, Lord! I've never been so stupid in all my life, she thought wildly.

"C'mon, dog. I may just feed you to the bears," Tom said to the dog on his way to the door.

Beth heard the outside door open and scrambled to her feet, hurrying up the stairs to the sanctuary of her room. She closed the door and leaned against it. Tom was a man familiar with seduction. Even with her lack of experience, she knew that only too well. Fighting back the feeling that she had made an utter fool of herself, she sat down on the edge of the bed. The lamp cast a warm glow in the room. She flipped it off and slid beneath the bedcovers. When a door closed downstairs, a quick surge of blood sent her heart galloping. She heard the dog come bounding up the steps, followed by the even tread of the man who had turned her emotions into such a riot of confusion that her seriously ill sister was taking second place in her thoughts. She held her breath as his footsteps neared her door.

"Good night," he called. "If the road conditions permit, we'll go into town in the morning to see Sarah. Okay?"

"Okay," she replied. She exhaled the long breath she had been holding. I've lost control, she thought, moaned softly, and turned on her stomach, clutching the pillow. His very presence is more than I can handle right now. Her face burned with embarrassment as she thought of how she had welcomed the intimate touch of his hands. It hadn't taken much at all, and she was panting in his arms. "Ohh . . ." She burrowed her head deeper into the pillow, trying to erase the image of his face from her mind's eye. Finally she turned and stared into the darkness until she slid into a fitful sleep that held dreams of green eyes and sensual lips beneath a soft curve of mustache.

Beth opened her eyes to a gray room. The sun was concealed behind rolling clouds., and the wind, whipping around the corners of the house, caught and held the tall pines in its icy grip, tipping them back and forth with its force. Loose snow fell against the windows and piled in the corners, making a Christmas-card scene. She didn't want to leave the warm bed, but forced herself to throw back the covers and stumble to the bathroom on legs stiff from the long ride in the truck. She splashed cold water on her face and scanned her reflection in the mirror. She didn't look any different, she thought. But then, how was an idiot supposed to look? She did feel better about the situation this morning, so she told the face looking back at her: you've been a pushover. Just chalk it up to being overtired and let it go at that.

She dressed in navy wool slacks and a white turtleneck

topped with a Norwegian ski sweater, her Christmas gift to herself last year, and went downstairs. The kitchen was empty, but the radio was on and a voice was giving the weather report. She poured a cup of coffee and sat on a bar stool to listen. The detailed weather report didn't sound good. More snow was in the forecast along with high winds: Oh, that's just great! she thought. More snow, more wind. Just what we need.

The door opened and Shiloh raced in. Her paws were covered with snow. She stopped in the middle of the room to shake, then bounded over to Beth, nuzzling her arm and almost upsetting the coffee cup in her hand.

"Hold it, girl," she said, laughing, and eased the cup of sloshing liquid to the counter. She reached for the dog's ears and rubbed gently. Tom was leaning against the doorjamb. She knew he was there, but she refused to look any higher than his stockinged feet while she petted the dog. Out of the corner of her eye she saw the feet approach the counter, and then they were planted firmly as he sat down on a bar stool.

"How about scratching my ears?"

She glanced up. A smile lifted his mustache, and she lowered her eyes to the dog.

"If I did anything to your ears it would be box them." She hadn't meant the retort to be humorous, but he laughed, and after a while, so did she.

Tom reached over and took a sip of her coffee. He was warmly dressed for the outdoors. Snow dusted his shoulders and she could smell the cold air that permeated his clothing.

"Well, what's the verdict? Can we make it to town?" Beth was instantly proud of her calm voice.

"Sure. If we get stuck, Herb will come with the tractor."

"Okay. Give me a few minutes to get my things together."

"There's no need. I'm thinking that as long as you're here, the doctor will let Sarah come home. This is where she wants to be."

Beth stood and moved to the door leading to the stairs. "But what if he won't allow her to come home?" The question hung in the air.

"Then we'll consider what's the next best thing to do."

A thoughtful frown covered her face as she went up the stairs. What did he have in mind? With determination in her every move, she packed her overnight case, and without giving herself time to wonder what Tom would say when she appeared with case in hand, went back downstairs.

She could hear a motor running out on the driveway and Shiloh's frenzied barking. She put on her snowboots, heavy coat, and pulled a wool stocking cap down over her ears. The blast of cold air almost took her breath when she opened the outside door. Her eyes watered and she turned her back to the wind as she hurried to the Blazer parked in the drive. A cloud of vapor from the exhaust rose and was scattered by the force of the wind.

Before she could open the door, something hit her on the back. She half turned, and—*bang*, a snowball whizzed by, missed her, and flattened against the side of the truck. Sheltered by the Blazer, she turned and looked back to see Tom and Shiloh romping in the snow. He was wearing an orange insulated jacket and a blue stocking cap. As she watched, he scooped up another handful of snow and formed it into a ball. She opened the door at the same time he launched the missile. The snowball went through the open door, hit the window on the driver's side of the car and smashed, filling the seat with snow.

Beth jumped in and slammed the door, giggling, and fervently hoping the heater would melt the snow and leave a wet puddle in his seat.

"Coward! Come out and fight!" he yelled.

Beth put her thumbs in her ears, wiggled her fingers, and stuck out her tongue. Seconds later a snowball smashed against the window. Thinking he had to be part Eskimo to stand the frigid cold, she watched him play with the dog. Then, with the dog nipping at his heels, he walked across the drive to talk to a man on a huge green tractor with a snowplow attached to the front.

By the time he opened the door to the Blazer, the snow in the seat had melted, but Beth had forgotten about it until he took a towel from beneath the seat and wiped it dry.

Tom's green eyes twinkled at her. Cold had reddened his cheeks and a fine film of snow lay on his head and shoulders. He radiated health and vitality.

"Brat! Why didn't you wipe off my seat?" he grumbled.

"Why should I? You threw the snowball."

His grin was wicked. "Brave, aren't you? Just you wait, my girl. You've got one coming." He removed his gloves and picked up the microphone to the CB. "Breaker, breaker, Geronimo. Got a copy on the Goat Roper?"

"I gotcha, go ahead." The voice that barreled in on the speaker was so loud that Beth flinched.

Tom turned down the volume. "Ten-four. Keep your ears on, we may need you to come pull us out of a drift.

The Goat Roper and the Little Mule are headed for Cody." He signed off and hung up the mike. He was grinning devilishly. "Fits, doesn't it? And to think, I just now thought of it."

"Brilliant. You must be very proud." Beth was trying to maintain her cool reserve and was failing miserably. Her lips were pressed tightly to keep from smiling, but her bright blue eyes flashed him an amused look.

The east-west road was clogged with drifting snow. The tractor had cut a path, but it was apparent that the swath would be filled in again soon. The blowing snow made for poor visibility, and Tom sat hunched over the wheel, concentrating on his driving. Beth didn't speak until they reached the highway and turned south.

"Who is Geronimo?"

"Herb, my foreman." Tom sat back and relaxed. Traveling with the wind at their back made for easier going.

"Does he live at the ranch?"

"We have two tenant houses. Actually we have three, but one isn't in use now. Herb lives in one and my head stockman and his wife, Jean, live in the other. Jean has been helping out at the house and went into town with Sarah. Herb was divorced about five or six years ago. His wife longed for the bright lights and went back to Denver. That wasn't their only problem, I guess, but it was the major one. Herb misses his daughter and makes several trips a year to see her. She spends some time here with him in the summer."

"Does the daughter share the mother's fondness for the bright lights?"

"Lord, no! Susan's a long-legged twelve-year-old in love with her horse. She's a real sweet kid," he said, cautiously swinging the truck around a stalled car. "If her mother wasn't such a bitch, she'd let her stay here with Herb, but then she'd lose the generous child-support payment."

"You sound bitter."

"I am. You'd be, too, if you could see how happy that kid is while she's here and how she looks like a little whipped pup when she has to leave."

"You like kids?" Beth stared at him suspiciously. There were many facets to this unpredictable man's character, and this was a new one.

"Sure, don't you?" He gave her a searching look, then his voice deepened to what sounded like a growl. "Don't tell me that you're one of those career women who don't like kids."

"I didn't say that. Of course I like children. I plan to have some . . . someday. That is if—"

"Some?" he cut in.

"More than one," she snapped.

"Why are we quarreling? I want that too." He smiled, and there was a mischievous glint in his eyes.

She started to contradict him, then, remembering how he enjoyed raising her hackles, she forced an indifferent shrug. His small chuckle told her he had read her mind, and she decided she'd rather die under torture than give him the satisfaction of knowing how he affected her.

Speechless now, she leaned back in the seat and tried to ignore him. From the corner of her eye she caught his sideways glance at her, but she stubbornly looked straight ahead.

"Are you warm enough?" he asked abruptly, turning

the louvers on the hot-air vents. A waft of warm air flowed over her.

"Sure. I'm fine," she said stiffly.

"How come you've not married? Were you waiting to snag a rich doctor?"

This time she let herself look at him, her eyes following the clear-cut line of his set profile.

"Why do you ask?" She fumed for a moment, waiting for him to reply, and when he said nothing, she rushed into speech. "I haven't married because I haven't found the right man. Not that it's any business of yours. When I marry, if I ever do, it will be forever. My kids will not be shuffled back and forth between divorced parents."

"My sentiments exactly."

"Furthermore, here's a small bit of news for you to file away for future conversations when you feel inclined to pry: I don't indulge in casual relationships."

"You sound pretty bitter," he said. His eyes clung to her face for as long as it was safe before looking back at the road. "What happened? Did you have an unhappy love affair? Did someone jilt you?"

"No!" she said quickly, cutting him off. He mustn't know that it was her old feelings for him she was thinking of. "I don't want to talk about this anymore. Forget it, will you?"

"Sure," he said with a shrug. "That's the hospital ahead."

The sidewalks were ice-covered, and the wind biting cold. Beth walked beside Tom into the brick and glass building, his hand firmly grasping her elbow. He stopped at the information desk to ask for Sarah's room number, spoke to several people, then ushered her to the elevator. This was familiar territory to Beth. Hospitals always smell the same, she mused. Her nurse's training shoved her mind into its professional channel and her anxiety about seeing Sarah was overshadowed by her desire to speak to the attending doctor and get a detailed report on her sister's condition.

The door of the room was ajar when they reached it. Tom stepped back so she could enter the room alone. She steeled herself to expect the worse, and pushed open the door.

Sarah, in a maroon robe, was sitting in a chair beside the window, a paperback novel in her hand. Her blond hair was swept up and pinned loosely at the top of her head, exposing her long slender neck. She looked beautiful and fragile.

"Elizabeth! Oh, darling, I'm so glad to see you!" She held out her arms and Beth went to her with tears clouding her vision. She leaned over and kissed her sister, then grasped her hands and stood back to look at her. Sarah was thinner; it was evident in the lines at the sides of her mouth, in the skin on her neck, and in her slender wrists.

"You silly, crazy woman!" Beth exclaimed. "I'm so angry at you I . . . could beat you! Why in the world didn't you tell me about this?"

Tears now flooded Sarah's eyes. "I didn't want to worry you. I've never really been a part of your life, not that it was anyone's fault. At first I was angry at Thomas when Herb told me he'd gone to Rochester to get you;

then, selfish woman that I am, I was glad, and have been counting the hours until you got here."

"You should have known that I'd want to come and be with you." She returned her sister's teary smile. "I'm sure I can get a job right here in this hospital, and I can see you often."

"Oh, Beth, I'm so glad you're here. I wanted you to come, but I didn't want to interfere." Tears rolled from her violet eyes. "Now that our parents are gone, there's only the two of us left."

Beth released Sarah's hands and took off her coat. "Yes, and how foolish we've been to live so many miles apart. There was really nothing to keep me in Rochester except my job."

"Where's Thomas? That man is stubborn as a mule. He has a one-track mind, and for months it's been on getting you out here."

Beth smiled. "I'd say he was more mule-headed than stubborn."

"I heard that." Tom's big frame filled the doorway. "Are you two ganging up on me?"

"Eavesdropping?" Beth said brightly.

"Sure." He dropped a kiss on Sarah's forehead. "Why not? How ya doin', sweetheart?" His gaze was honed in on Sarah's face and his voice was full of loving concern.

"I'm all right," Sarah said firmly. "Now, why did you bring my little sister out in this blizzard? Don't you know there's a travelers' warning out, and this town is full to overflowing with busloads of people they've taken off the highways?" She shook her head, but gazed at him affectionately. "Sometimes you and Herb don't have a lick of sense. You both need a keeper."

Tom's eyes went from Sarah to Beth. "You two are more alike than I thought. You're both bossy."

"I'm not!" The denial came out sharply, and Beth wondered again why this man's teasing could prick at her and make her so angry so quickly.

"Now, I can't have the two people I love the most quarreling," Sarah said. "You'll have to learn to ignore him, Beth. He loves to tease, especially if he thinks he's getting under your skin."

"That's easy for you to say," Beth said, eyeing Tom, who leaned nonchalantly against the wall, watching her so intently that butterflies began to flutter in her stomach. "Sometimes he's as hard to ignore as that blizzard out there."

"Speaking of the blizzard, I don't think you two should stay in town very long. The last report was that they're pulling the snowplows off the highway." Sarah's worried eyes flicked from one to the other. "As much as I'd enjoy a long visit with you, darling, I'll feel more comfortable when I know you're safely at home."

"I'm staying here." Beth didn't have the courage to look at Tom. "I'll get a room nearby. You'll have your own private nurse. How about that?"

"Oh, dear. I'm afraid that isn't possible." Sarah looked at Tom for confirmation. "I doubt if there's a vacant room to be had in town. You don't know how it is here at a time like this. The town will be filled to the brim. Motorists, skiers, hunters . . . all will be stranded here until the storm is over. You'd best go back with Thomas. He'll take care of you."

"I brought my overnight case and a uniform." Did she hear Tom swear under his breath? she wondered, and turned slightly, so that his face was out of her line of vision. "I want to speak with your doctor, Sarah. There's a chance I can stay right here in the nurses' quarters temporarily. Or—"

"Stubborn!" The word sounded grating, issued through clenched teeth.

Beth ignored him. "How about the room Jean is using? She came into town with you yesterday, didn't she? No doubt she'll want to go back home with . . . him." She tilted her head toward Tom, but didn't look at him.

Sarah's eyes bounced from one to the other. "Jean's staying with her mother. She'll be disappointed to have her visit cut short, but I suppose—"

"Beth's going back with me," Tom said firmly.

"Some women may like an arrogant, forceful man, but I'm not one of them," she snapped. "I make my own decisions. I want to see Sarah's doctor, I want to know if there's a position available here for me, and I want to assure him—"

"Beth . . . ," Sarah said quietly.

Beth turned and saw the distressed look on her sister's pale face. "I'm sorry, Sarah. I just want to be with you."

"Sarah will need you when she comes home, which will be as soon as the storm lets up," Tom informed her. "Dr. Morrison told me so this morning. He'll give you complete instructions at that time."

Beth turned on him. "You talked to her doctor this morning? Why didn't you tell me?" With an effort she kept her voice under control.

"If you remember, we didn't have much time to talk.

You slept in and didn't even have time for breakfast. Is that why you're so cranky?"

"We were together all the way to town!" Beth reminded him furiously.

"We were talking about other things."

When he grinned at her, she let loose with a swear word. It slipped out before she could hold it back.

"Ladies don't swear." He was laughing, and it fanned her anger.

"Ohh . . ." She thought of several things she wanted to say, but Sarah was shifting uncomfortably in her chair.

Tom leaned against the wall, his hands in his pockets, his dark hair ruffled from the wool cap he'd been wearing earlier. His eyes glinted when he looked at her, but softened when he watched the worried expressions flit across Sarah's face. He moved away from the wall and squatted down on his heels beside her chair.

"Herb and I will come and get you just as soon as we think we can make it in the station wagon. Herb said he had quite a time getting you here and said a flat no when I suggested bringing you home today. You won't mind staying a few more days if you know Beth's waiting at home, will you?"

Beth listened with shocked surprise at the wonderfully patient way he spoke to her sister.

"Don't you think I could go home in the truck, Thomas?" Sarah's hands had come up to his shoulders, and her long slender fingers smoothed the hair at the back of his neck.

"And force Jean to cut short her visit?" he chided gently.

"Oh, that's right. But, darling, I'll worry until I know you and Beth are home. Will you call me?"

"Sure. I called this morning, didn't I?"

Beth felt like she was eavesdropping on an intimate conversation. Tom treated her sister as if she were the most precious thing in the world—treated her more like a lover than a sister-in-law.

"Yes, and you got here before I had time to worry." Sarah raised soft, loving eyes to Beth. "This is the most dependable man in the world, and I love him dearly." She reached for her hand. "I want you two to be friends, like you were when he came to the wedding."

Beth was silent.

"For once she's speechless, Sarah. I'll have to remember that line and use it when I want to shut her up."

"Darling, stop teasing her." Sarah looked at him with such a radiant expression that Beth knew her sister did indeed love him, but with what kind of love? "Life doesn't stand still around this one long enough for it to be dull, Beth," Sarah said while Beth shifted from foot to foot, uncomfortable with her thoughts.

Tom rose. "We'd better get going. Herb will be waiting for us at the turnoff. That east-west road will be drifted shut for sure."

Sarah held tightly to Beth's hand. "I'm the luckiest woman in the world," she said softly, her eyes misty with tears. "I've two of the most wonderful men in the world taking care of me, and now you, darling. I'll be home soon. Oh, Thomas, won't we have a wonderful Christmas with Beth with us?"

"You bet, Queeny. We'll have the best ever. I'll put in an order for a truckload of mistletoe." His laughing green eyes flashed a look at Beth's face, and she prayed the heat she felt wasn't reflected there.

"Queeny?" she said sarcastically, wanting him to know she thought the nickname ridiculous.

"Thomas and Herb call me that. They tell me that I'm queen of the hive." Sarah's small laugh was nervous, and she gazed fondly at Tom. "If you'll help me out of this chair, love, I'll walk down the hall with you." With his hand beneath her arms, he lifted her to her feet. "The most aggravating thing about MS is getting up out of a low chair," Sarah confided when she was standing. "Thomas fixed my chairs at home so I can get up easily."

Sarah walked confidently, with no sign of the staggering gait characteristic of the disease. Beth's experienced eye noticed this, and she felt a degree of relief that the illness had not yet progressed to that stage. Sarah was taller than Beth and very slender. Where Beth was considered attractive, Sarah was considered arrestingly beautiful, with her fine-boned face, and skin like porcelain. She walked between Beth and Tom as they went down the corridor to the elevator.

"What do you think of the house? Thomas let me remodel and decorate a couple of years ago. I love it. Of course, I liked the cottage too," she added hastily, then explained. "Steven and I lived in one of the cottages. After he was gone, Thomas insisted that I move up to the house."

"It's beautiful," Beth murmured. She felt trapped, and her heart started thudding unpleasantly.

"Call when you get home," Sarah said anxiously.

"Worrywart!" Thomas accused, and kissed her cheek.

The elevator door opened, and Beth gave her sister a quick kiss. Tom held the door so she could enter, then it closed, blotting out the sight of Sarah's gently smiling face.

CHAPTER SEVEN

SNOW WAS FALLING thick and fast. Whipped by a brisk wind, it swirled around the truck like a thick fog.

"I'll have to leave the window open a crack until the defroster can take over," Tom said. His words were the first spoken since they got in the truck.

Beth stole a glance at him and told herself that she was ten times a fool for being here with him—for going back to the ranch where they would be alone in the house for no telling how long. It was intimidating—he knew exactly what he wanted and how to go about getting it. He was the most controlled person she'd ever met. Even when he had thrown the boy against the wall at the truck stop, his fury had been controlled. He was extremely capable, and according to Sarah, dependable. It was disgusting, she decided irritably, for one man to have so many admirable qualities.

Knowing he was fully occupied maneuvering the Blazer through the dense, blowing snow, she watched his hands on the wheel. Beth felt a shivery thrill remembering those hands moving over her bare flesh, gliding, caressing; strong hands that could crush or be exquisitely gentle. Damn! Damn! She'd better get that thought out of her head. Is he in love with Sarah? Is she in love with him? The unwelcome thought stumbled on the heels of the first one. Sarah was only a few years older than Tom, and it was logical that he could fall in love with his brother's widow.

The truck stopped, but Beth, lost in thought, was unaware of it.

"Don't be afraid. We'll make it okay." His hand left the wheel and lightly squeezed her mittened ones.

"I'm not afraid," she said absently, and something inside her trembled. "I was only thinking."

Tom guided the truck around a stalled car. "What about?"

"Nothing . . . everything . . ."

"Everything?" he echoed. "Sarah will be just as she is for a long time. They don't expect her to get any worse, but no better, either. As you know, MS is unpredictable and affects people differently. Sarah is one of the lucky ones."

"Yes, I know." She stared at him helplessly, cold to the heart. Better to let him think she was worrying about Sarah than to let him know her mind was on *him*.

They were moving slowly, the Blazer plowing through the drifts building across the deserted highway. When Tom blindly reached for the mike attached to the CB radio, Beth picked it up and placed it in his hand. He turned quickly when their fingers touched and gazed at her. His eyes held hers for a timeless second before he looked away.

"Breaker, breaker, Geronimo. Have you got your

ears on?" He waited and repeated the call. There was no answer. He handed the microphone back to Beth. "We're not close enough for Herb to pick us up." He looked at his watch. "I told him we'd be back about noon. It's after that now. It's slower going than I thought it would be."

The motor strained when they went through a drift, and the wind buffeted the truck. It was a scary white world, and Beth was extremely glad that Tom was there with her.

"Talk to me Beth." The sound of her name coming from his lips made her heart lurch. She was trying to think of something to say when, to her utter amazement, he began to sing in a low, controlled voice. "I'll take you home again, Kathleen. Across the ocean wild and wide. To where your heart has ever been, since first you were my blushing bride. . . ."

His voice washed over her as if his hands were caressing her skin. Reverberations echoed up and down her spine. A longing to snuggle close to him and have the words he was singing hold a real meaning slowly enveloped her. She tried to shake off the sensation and looked straight ahead, conscious that he turned to look at her often as he sang.

When he finished, she clapped her mittened hands in silent applause. "Bravo! You sing beautifully." She knew her face was flushed and her voice weak. She tried to disguise it with a small cough.

"I've got all sorts of hidden talents." He laughed, and the small wrinkles appeared at the corners of his eyes. "I can make biscuits, sew up a rip in my jeans, use the plunger when the plumbing clogs, and I can . . . can tomatoes."

"Bully for you! You'll make someone a lovely wife someday! Hey—look out!"

Tom saw the small foreign car stalled on the highway at the same time Beth did, and put on the brakes. Although they were moving slowly, he couldn't stop the truck. They slid into the car and pushed it into a snowbank beside the road.

Beth gave a small cry as she was flung forward, only to be held back by the steely strength of Tom's arm as it shot out to hold her.

"Sonofabitch!" The word exploded from him. "Why in hell didn't they push that thing off the highway?"

As he spoke, the doors of the small car opened simultaneously, making it look like a small bug with big ears. Two men got out. They wore sweaters and insulated vests, but their heads and hands were bare. Tom cursed again as they hurried to the truck. He rolled down the window and the cold wind blew snow into his face.

"Man, are we glad to see you. We damn near froze to death." The man who spoke was young. He peered into the truck. "Will you give us a ride into Cody?"

"No," Tom said flatly. "I'm not going back. But I can't leave you out here, either. Get in. I'll take you to my place."

"We'll pay, man. We want to get to Cody." A second face appeared beside the first. Both faces were red with cold, both needed a shave, and both had shifty eyes that swept over Beth, then scanned the back of the Blazer.

"I'm not going back, take it or leave it. You can come

to my place or stay here and freeze to death. The choice is yours, but make it quick."

"You're not giving us much choice, mister. We'll go with you. We'll get our things from the car."

Tom rolled up the window.

"I don't like them," Beth said quickly.

"I don't either." Tom reached across to open the glove compartment. He took out a small pistol and slipped it into his pocket.

"Do you think—" she began, eyeing the gun with apprehension.

"I don't know what to think. It's best to be sure." He swore again when he saw the men coming back. Each carried a cloth duffel bag, and one had a rifle. Tom rolled down the window on Beth's side. "Hold it! You don't get into my truck with an uncased gun."

"Holy jumpin' hell, man! We don't have a case, and it'll be snatched if we leave it in the car."

"All right. Hand it in, butt first." Tom drew the gun into the car, checked to see if it was loaded—it was. He ejected the shells, then with the butt on the floor of the truck he leaned the barrel toward Beth. "Hold onto it," he instructed, then to the men, "Okay, get in." He leaned forward to release the back of Beth's seat. The men squeezed behind her and into the back of the Blazer.

She could feel their eyes boring into the back of her head. She turned sideways in the seat so that she was facing Tom. At least she could shout a warning if they made a move toward him. And she would do something, although she wasn't sure what it would be. After glancing at them, she decided they were in no condition to do much to anyone. Both men were shaking from the cold and rubbing their hands together and blowing on them. Their faces were not far from frostbite.

Tom was driving in the middle of the highway now. Occasionally Beth could see the white line where the wind had cleared the snow. They passed another stalled vehicle. One of the men remarked that they had passed it before they had stalled and that it was empty.

"Breaker, breaker, Geronimo—" Tom had called almost continually for the last few miles.

"Ten-four. I got ya." The voice that came back was faint and crackly.

"We'll be there in a few minutes."

"Ten-four. I'll be watchin'."

Tom handed the mike to Beth. "Call him again in a little bit, honey. From now on I've got to watch for the turnoff."

Honey! He had said it naturally, as if it were an endearment he used all the time. She strived to close her heart against the thrill, and took the mike from his warm fingers.

"That's neat!" the younger of the two men said. "You ain't takin' no chances, are ya, mister?"

"A man's a fool to risk more than he has to in this country," Tom said drily.

"I'm Mike Cotter. This here's Jerry Lewis." His laugh was more like a sly snicker. "He's not the movie star, but he's kind of funny sometimes." He snickered again.

A quick glance told Beth that Jerry Lewis didn't think it funny at all. He had a scowl on his face.

"This your wife?"

Tom didn't answer, and the man lapsed into silence. When Tom spoke it was to her.

"Give Herb a call, honey."

There it was again! She glanced at him this time. He wasn't teasing her. His brows were drawn together in serious concentration. As she watched, she saw him glance into the rearview mirror. He's keeping an eye on those two, she thought. He doesn't trust them any more than I do. She pressed the button and spoke into the mike.

"Breaker, breaker, Geronimo—"

"Ya got me—" the voice boomed.

"There he is. Dammit, I went past him." Tom braked to a halt, backed the truck, and cautiously turned onto the graveled road.

"Okay, let's go." Herb's voice boomed.

The big, green machine moved through the snowbanks, the V-shaped blades making a path. Tom stayed a reasonable distance behind because several times Herb had to back up and make a second run at a drift before he could make a path for the truck.

"Who's in the bunkhouse, Herb?"

"Frosty and John. Gus and Smitty stayed at the line shack."

"I've got two more for the bunkhouse. We'll drop them off there before we go to the house."

"Got-cha."

Tom pulled up behind the tractor when it stopped. The snow was blowing so hard that Beth could just barely see the outline of the buildings. Tom put on his stocking cap and gloves.

"Here's where you get out, fellows." He nodded to Beth to open her door, then unhooked her seat and waited for the men to squeeze out from behind her. The younger man reached for the rifle.

"Leave the gun," Tom said curtly. "You can take it when you leave."

"God, man! You're sure as hell one suspicious cuss." This came from the man called Jerry.

"You're damn right, mack. And I'm alive to prove it. You can wait out the storm here, but understand one thing—you play by my rules. Now grab your gear and follow me."

In seconds the three were out of sight. Alone, Beth slumped in the seat. A trembly sigh escaped her lips. She hadn't realized she was so tense. A new awareness of Tom dominated her thoughts. He was definitely a man of contrasts. She thought of him—tender, affectionate, his eyes warm with loving concern for her sister. That was the kind of man she had dreamed of loving. Then, there was the hard, unfeeling, cold-eyed man who'd grabbed the cowboy in the restaurant and sent him spinning into the wall. She shivered at the thought. Violence was repugnant to her and had become increasingly so during the time she had spent in the emergency ward at the hospital. She had seen the results of violent behavior—battered women and children, gunshot cases, fights—Could she love a man capable of such actions?

Love? Oh, for crying out loud! She had gotten over her love, if you could call a girlish crush love, for this man a long while ago. She was attracted to him, and yes, she wanted him physically. There was no disgrace in *that.* She was a healthy, adult woman. Not that she would jump into bed with him just to satisfy her sexual desires, she told herself firmly. Her dream had been to meet someone, become friends first and then lovers, building a solid foundation for their future together. Then, *bang!* He had come back into her life, and she wasn't sure she was strong enough to resist him.

The day went quickly. After Tom called the hospital and they both spoke to Sarah, assuring her that they had arrived home safely, Beth made sandwiches from the leftovers in the refrigerator and heated a can of soup.

"Herb'll be in to eat with us tonight." Tom was stepping into an insulated snowsuit. "Do you think you can rustle up enough grub for two hungry men?"

"Sure. You're not the only one with hidden talents. What time? And what about the other men? Who cooks for them?"

"Jean cooks when she's here. But they won't go hungry. There's a kitchen and supplies in the bunkhouse. They can manage." He pulled on a ski mask and raised the lower part of it so that it fit his head like a stocking cap. Shiloh was waiting expectantly. "Not this time, girl. We'll be going on the snowmobiles, and there's no room for you. Stay here and keep Beth company." He turned to face her. "I'll call you from the barn if we'll be later than six."

She nodded. "Don't forget your gloves." She picked them up off the counter and handed them to him.

His fingers caught and held hers. "I like having you in the house, Beth," he told her quietly. "I like knowing that you'll be here when I come back."

She didn't know what to say. She felt a strange slackness in the pit of her stomach. Her eyes were drawn to his, and she was moved by the tenderness she saw there.

"It's . . . dangerous going out in a blizzard. I hope you know what you're doing," she said calmly, proud of the steadiness of her voice.

"I do. That's why Herb and I are going together. We'll take two machines and follow the fence line. We'll be okay." He was still holding onto her fingers, and now he pulled her closer.

"Hey, I've got dishes to do," she protested weakly.

"This won't take ten seconds."

His fingers slid up under her hair at the nape of her neck. He bent his head, without any appearance of haste, and his lips tingled over hers. Her eyes closed slowly. Then, horrified by her lack of resistance, she opened them.

"Do you want chicken or steak for dinner?" she murmured.

"Surprise me. I think you'll find everything you need in the freezer and the pantry."

"Okay." Beth wondered why she felt so faint. The swimming sensation in her head couldn't be caused by his touch alone. The hand behind her head was holding her firmly, and she couldn't move if she wanted to. Liar, her common sense whispered; he's not holding your feet!

"I want to kiss you again." His voice was a rough, seductive whisper.

Shock held her silent for a moment, then she swallowed. "Well, get on with it. I've got dishes to do," she said at last, trying to smile scornfully.

His fingers moved around to her chin and he held it with his thumb and forefinger. He kissed her again, more deeply, his lips clinging, seeming not to want to leave. The kiss was soft and agonizingly sweet and tender.

"You taste like a peanut butter and jelly sandwich," he whispered. Their eyes locked in a silent duel. She was determined to not look away or he would know how his kiss had shaken her.

"Strange, considering I just ate a peanut butter and jelly sandwich." She spoke as lightly as she could and was pleased there was no tremor in her voice.

"Amazing." He gave her a lazy, amused smile.

She wished he would go. She wanted to be alone, to give her mind time to recover its balance. He reached behind him and opened the door. Only then did she step away from him. I've got to keep it light, she warned herself. Let him think casual kisses are the norm with me.

"Amazing," he said again.

It took every ounce of her will to tilt her head saucily and quip in a slightly breathless voice, "Maybe I'll be invited to appear on 'That's Incredible.' "

"Not without me, you won't." He stepped backward through the door, and just before he closed it, he said, "Think about it."

She did. Minutes passed while her mind grappled with answers to the questions flooding it. What did he mean, amazing? What were her feelings . . . his feelings? Was it purely physical gratification he wanted . . . she wanted? Dammit! Why was her stupid heart beating so violently? Cripes! I need a bath and two aspirin.

Later, Beth decided she liked being alone in the house. A hot bath and aspirin calmed her nerves and brought out the practical side of her nature. She resisted putting on the blue velour lounging suit that flattered her slim figure and made her complexion look so peachy, and dressed instead in worn jeans and an off-white turtleneck sweater.

While in the tub she had decided to make Swiss steak and mashed potatoes for dinner. The only question was how much to cook. Would it take more than one potato to fill a hungry man'? I'll cook two each, she decided. Whoever heard a man complain about too much food?

The foreman was a surprise. Beth had visualized Herb as being older, perhaps middle-aged. He was a man in his middle or late thirties, a large man with brooding dark eyes, black hair, and sharply etched features that proclaimed an Indian heritage. Tom introduced them. Beth smiled and nodded. Herb acknowledged the introduction solemnly.

"It smells good in here. I hope you've cooked enough." Tom caught her eyes and grinned.

"That I can't guarantee, but there must be food here to feed half of Custer's army."

Halfway through the meal the phone rang. Tom's long arm reached for it.

"Hi, Sarah. How'er ya doin', hon?" His smile was beautiful; there was no other way for Beth to describe it. "We're doin' all right. Now you stop worryin', hear? Yes, Herb's here too. And yes, I'll see that he doesn't take any chances in the blizzard. But, hon, he's a big boy now!"

Herb had stopped eating and was watching Tom. His dark brows were drawn together expectantly.

"Yeah," Tom was saying into the phone. "I hope she's a better nurse than she is a cook! Okay, okay—I won't tease her." He shoved the phone in Beth's hand.

"Don't mind him, Elizabeth," Sarah said. "He takes some getting use to."

"He doesn't bother me in the least. I've discovered he's got an inflated ego and that he's all *blow* and no *go!*" She could barely hear Sarah's words over Tom's whoop of laughter.

"It sounds like you're having fun. I wish I were there with you," Sarah said wistfully.

"I wish you were too. Before you come home I'll need to consult with your doctor."

"I've already told him about my sister, the nurse. He's anxious to meet you," Sarah said. "My nurse is here frowning at me. Do you suppose I could speak to Herb for a moment? I'll call you again in the morning."

"Sure. Have a good night. Here's Herb." Beth held out the phone and the big man got to his feet.

He turned his back to the table while he spoke to Sarah. "The weather isn't as bad as the news makes out, Sarah. Tom and I went down to the line shack and every-thin's fine. No, I'll stay in the room over the garage tonight." He listened patiently, his shoulders hunched, his dark head bent. "I'm goin' to have to start callin' you worrywart." His chuckle was low and affectionate.

Beth looked up to see Tom's eyes on her. Were both of these men in love with her sister or was it an unromantic love they felt for her because she was beautiful and frag-ile and inspired their protective instincts?

"Now, Sarah, turn that mind of yours off and have a good rest. We'll bring you home just as soon as the roads clear. Okay? Yes, me too. Bye now." Herb hung up the phone and sat down. "She's always afraid we'll get lost in the blizzard," he said with a worried frown.

"It happened to one of our neighbors a couple of years ago," Tom explained. "He got lost between the house and the barn and froze to death. Ever since that happened, Sarah's been panicky during a storm."

"There's a very real danger. It happens a couple of times a year in Minnesota." Beth refilled their coffee cups.

"That's right. You're from the cold country too." She thought Herb's voice was soft for such a large man.

"I'm no stranger to blizzards. I hope you two like peach cobbler. That's what you're having for dessert."

"Sit down, honey. I'll get it." Tom lifted the plates from the table and took them to the sink.

Herb took away the empty serving dishes. I can't believe this, Beth thought, and sank back into her chair. They grow a different breed of man out here in the West. She felt a momentary flash of envy when she thought of their gentle concern for Sarah, then instantly regretted her jealousy. Her sister deserved every good thing she could get out of life.

Swiftly and efficiently the men cleared the table and served the dessert. Afterward, Tom filled the dishwasher while Beth stored the leftovers in the refrigerator.

"Is there anything you can't do?" she asked when Tom whipped off the tablecloth and set in its place a wooden bowl filled with huge pinecones.

"A few things, I guess. But I'll try anything once, and some things several times before I give up on them." His laugh was low and sensuous, and a brief shiver ran along her nerves. "Go on, sit down and watch the news. I'll finish up in here."

Beth sat at one end of the sofa with her feet tucked under her. Tom came and sat at the other end. She saw him watching her quietly. Something in his eyes seemed to draw her into their mysterious depths before she managed to look away.

An hour passed. Lost in her own thoughts Beth had no awareness of time. The pictures flickered across the screen, the actor's voice soft in the quiet room. She glanced at Herb. He sat in Sarah's chair, his head resting against the back, his eyes closed, his long legs stretched out in front of him. Tom was equally relaxed, although he seemed to be watching the screen with half-closed eyes.

Beth felt totally at peace before the crackling fire. She was trying to stifle a yawn when Herb rose to his feet and stretched.

"I think I'll turn in before I fall asleep in the chair. Thanks for the supper."

Beth unfolded her legs and stretched them out in front of her to allow the blood to circulate. As soon as Herb left the room, she stood. Before she could say anything or move away, Tom grabbed her hand and tugged. She flopped back down on the sofa and was immediately cocooned in his arms.

"Tom—"

"Ssh!" He pulled her head to his shoulder.

"Don't—"

"That word isn't in my vocabulary, and I don't want it in yours, either." His dark face was adamant, his lean jaw set and firm.

Through blurry eyes she saw his lips nearing hers, and felt powerless to turn away.

CHAPTER EIGHT

BETH WAS IN the most tormented quandary of her life. She didn't understand the part of her that snuggled in Tom's arms and eagerly lifted her lips for his kiss. What had happened to her all of a sudden to wash away her resolve? She didn't want to get involved with him again. But his mouth was incredibly sweet as it closed over hers, gently forcing her lips apart. His arms, unlike his lips, were unyielding and determined around her. Feeling desire curl in her stomach, and the exquisite ache that throbbed in the core of her femininity, she fought desperately to keep her senses. *This must stop!* She tried to turn her face away from his, but he caught her lower lip gently between his teeth and refused to allow her mouth to leave his. When she ceased to resist, he moved his lips over hers, stroking, touching, playing lightly; and then, in what seemed like a pleasurable eternity, he deepened the kiss. Her fingers, seeking the warmth of his skin, moved to his throat and the pulse that beat so rapidly there.

When the kiss ended, she stared at him with glazed eyes. Desire misted her vision and she failed to see the tenderness in his eyes. She tried to hide her aroused emotions with pretended anger.

"May I go now?" she demanded.

"Are you sure you want to?"

She looked at him for a long while. Obviously she was losing her mind, and what little she had left he could read like a book. Never had it been like this. What she had felt for him three years ago was puppy love compared to this. She longed with all her heart to lift her hands to his face, hold his cheeks in her palms, let her thumbs trace the contours of his lips and her fingertips feel the softness of his hair.

"I'm not going to sleep with you." The words tumbled from her trembling lips. Her breath quickened and her insides were a turmoil of sensations. As she spoke, his arms fell away from her.

"Is that what you think?" he asked with a queer, unfamiliar huskiness to his voice. "You think I'm angling for a quick lay?"

"Well?"

"If it happens between us, it happens, Elizabeth. We're adults, and neither of us is so naive that we don't realize we're physically attracted to one another." He slipped his hand down her arm and interlaced his fingers with hers.

"It's too soon! I don't—I'm not—" The feeling that she was strangling began to grow in her.

"I'll never hurt you, darlin'."

She wanted to speak, wanted to ask him to give her time to get used to the wild, wanton desire that swept over her when she was with him. He was almost a stranger, yet so dearly familiar. She knew he fulfilled everything she wanted in a man. She had instinctively known it three years ago.

"I'm not a man who takes, darlin' Elizabeth." He made no attempt to conceal the yearning in his eyes or the vulnerable expression on his face. "My woman will share with me all the joy of our coming together."

Swimming in a pool of confusion and desire, Beth felt the silence that followed his words wrap around her. *His woman!* Tom studied her quietly and then released her hand. It wasn't at all what she wanted him to do.

"Thomas?"

"Not until you're sure it's what you want, Beth."

Her stomach twisted in a knot. Why couldn't she lean forward and wrap her arms around him? That would be answer enough for him. But she couldn't do it. She couldn't make the first move. Slowly and carefully she got to her feet. She was beginning to realize with increasing force that she wanted more than anything in the world to have his hands run over the most intimate and sensitive parts of her body, to have him look at her with love in the depths of his compelling green eyes. Reason waged war with the hunger that gnawed at her. She wasn't ready for a casual affair with him. There had to be commitment first. It was as simple as that.

"Good night." Her eyes were haunted and dark with despair.

"Good night, Beth." For an instant the mesmeric eyes held her in a thick embrace, then she walked unsteadily from the room.

Beth woke from a sound sleep and peered into the darkness, trying to read the digital clock on the table beside the bed.

Blackness.

She rolled over and stuck her hand out, groped blindly for the edge of the table and found it. The room was icy cold. She shivered and felt along the table until her fingers found the lamp switch. The click failed to produce the light she expected. The electric power was off. While trying to decide if she should stay in the warm bed or wake Tom, she heard a door close downstairs. Not stopping to think about it, she threw back the covers and reached for her flannel robe. The cold penetrated the robe—her body was chilled and her teeth began to chatter. She felt her way along the wall to the door.

The hall was equally as dark. She stood for a moment, then saw a faint beam of light downstairs. Had someone broken into the house? *The men from the stalled car!* The thought flashed through her mind with the force of lightning.

"Thomas!" Her voice was almost a squeak. "Thomas!" This time her call was loud and carried with it a hint of panic.

The beam from the flashlight traveled up the stairs.

"I'm down here, Beth. The electricity is off. Stay where you are and I'll come up." Tom talked while he moved up the steps. "This happens every once in a while. Usually our rural electrical system is reliable, but that's a pretty strong wind out there tonight. Were you frightened?" He kept the beam of light focused on the floor even when he reached her.

"Maybe a little. What do you do about heat?"

"I've built up the fire in the fireplace. It'll have to do until we get the power back to run the furnace. We've got a generator that will keep the heat tapes on the water pipes going, and the water pump running. *Whoof!*" He made a blowing sound. "You can see your breath in here already. Do you want to go back to bed or come down to the fire?"

"I'll . . . come down."

Beth began to shiver, and it was only partially due to the cold. A quick glance told her Tom was wearing pajama bottoms, and an unbuttoned flannel shirt was all that covered his torso. His hand, wrapped firmly around her side, was meant to guide her down the darkened stairway, but it had the effect of a potent stimulant and her breath started to come in jerky little gasps. She took several deep breaths in an attempt to calm herself.

A fire was blazing in the fireplace, and she moved away from him and went to kneel in front of the blaze and hold her hands out to its warmth.

"It doesn't take long for the house to cool off." She forced herself to speak. When there was no answer, she turned and saw the beam of the flashlight at the end of the room. Then she heard a door close, and Tom came back to her with an armful of blankets. He turned off the flashlight and draped one of the blankets around her shoulders.

"Thank you. That feels good."

"This only happens during a severe storm. I don't remember it happening at all last year." He sat down on the floor beside her and rested his back against a big square ottoman. The firelight flickered over his tousled hair, his face, and down over the mat of hair that covered his chest. He seemed immune to the cold.

Desire, that elusive, unfamiliar feeling she had felt last night and again earlier this evening, spread over her. His eyes held hers in a sensuous embrace, and without being conscious of it, she swayed toward him. His arms opened, then closed around her. She was safely ensconced against his firm, warm chest. She felt the sigh that went through him before she heard it.

"This feels good," he said, echoing the words she spoke earlier, but with a different meaning. His arms exerted just enough pressure to lift her so he could settle his long legs, knees slightly bent, on each side of her. The blanket had fallen from between them, and now he spread it out to cover them. Beth was conscious of the masculine part of him pressed tightly to her hipbone. "When I grow too old to dream I'll have this to remember. . . ." He sang softly in her ear.

"You sing very well."

"Thank you. Now be still and relax. I'll get you warm."

Relax? How could she relax when the primal push she felt inside her was sending her reeling into a world of sensation? Enthralled by his nearness and the effect of his masculinity, she wasn't sure of anything but the force of the sexual awareness that throbbed between them. He lifted a hand to brush her hair away from her face, tucking the silky strands behind her ear. He stroked her cheek before his fingers moved to her throat. Beth was entranced, having lost all touch with rational thinking. She tipped her head, her eyes seeking then losing themselves in his. Her fingers spread and her palm rubbed in a circular motion against the rough hair on his chest. He seemed to be as mesmerized by her as she was by him. It was as if the world had fallen away, leaving only the two of them.

Tom searched the depths of her gaze as she explored

his. And then, slowly, he lowered his head until his lips were a fraction of an inch from hers. The sweet scent of his breath, the tangy smell of his skin, and the firm warm flesh beneath her hand were like a powerful drug that started a craving for fulfillment deep in the center of her being.

A small sigh forced itself from between her lips, and her hand slid up to his throat, then to the back of his neck. Her defenses were down. The core of passion that had long lain dormant flared into life, and driven by desire, strong and pure, she fastened her lips to his.

Tom welcomed her kiss with a response so strong that he trembled. The arm that held her to him was rock hard, and the strong fingers behind her head held it so he could deepen the kiss. Beth quivered at the heady invasion of his mouth and ran the tip of her tongue along the sharp edge of his teeth in welcome.

Somewhere along the way she realized that the pressure of her hand at the back of his neck was no longer needed, and she let it slide, palm down, over the curve of his shoulder and down to the taut flesh beneath his shirt. His skin was warm and hard. Her fingers savored the firmness and discovered little areas that quivered beneath her touch.

"Darlin'." He spoke thickly, his breath coming in uneven gasps that matched hers.

It took Beth a minute to recover from the trance of arousal. Slowly she opened her eyes. His face was so near she could feel the movement of his eyelashes against her cheek. His hand began slowly to smooth the robe from her shoulders.

"Let me feel your breasts against me, sweetheart. . . ."

The tenderness of his tone caused a wild, sweet singing in her heart. His mouth moved over hers, soft and then hard. She felt the tremor that shook him when the softness of her breasts touched the hair-roughened skin of his chest. She closed her eyes again as he pressed her hips against the rock-hard part of his body that had sprung to life during their kiss.

"Sex has got to mean something for me," she gasped. "I just can't do it for desire alone!" Her body was a total contradiction to her words. Her arms circled his waist and she moved intimately against his arousal with a tormented sigh. "Oh, Thomas—"

"Don't think about it, darlin'. We may be desperately in love—I don't know. I only know that I've never felt like this before, and I think I'll die if I can't feel every inch of you against me. I want to feel you surrounding me, wanting me. Pretend that you love me, darlin'. Just for a few hours pretend you love me more than anything, that I'm the center of your world and you're the center of mine."

The emotional plea echoed in the far depths of her heart, bringing a mistiness to her eyes and a tightness to her throat. Her arms tightened protectively around him and her innermost thoughts leaped to her lips.

"I don't have to pretend. More than anything I want to make love with you. I love you. I've always loved you. You fill my heart, my thoughts, make my world a joyous place. I'm here, I'm yours—"

"Oh, love . . . oh, my sweet love . . ." His answer was a groan that came from deep inside him.

Beth knew without doubt that she would remember the look in his eyes until the day she died. The expression she saw there was more than gratitude for the gift of sex. It was as if he had waited all his life for something precious, and at last it had been given to him.

Her hands yearned to touch his face, and they did. Her palms pressed his beard-roughened cheeks. When she leaned back, the blanket fell away. The chill was momentary. His hands, work-hardened, moved to cup the gentle fullness of her breasts in a reverent and tender way.

"I love you." A soft whisper came from the lips touching hers. They were three very familiar words, but now she believed them, because she wanted to believe them and because she was beyond thinking or feeling anything except rising passion and building need.

Without further words or thought, in lazy, loving movements, they lay down on the rug beside the fire and he slid the clothing from her body and his. He covered her with his male body and pulled the blanket up over his bare back. Resting on his elbows, his chest barely touching her breasts, he smiled down at her.

"You're beautiful." His voice was low, soft, dreamy. He seemed to be savoring each minute, each second.

"So are you." Her hands drifted over his back in exploration of the curving muscles, sought the indention of his spine, and followed it to taut hips that she pulled against her thigh.

"I want to love you slowly . . . if I can. I want to remember every sensation, every look, every whisper. Tell me what you told me before. I want to see your eyes when you say it." His eyes were aglow with love and desire.

"I love you. You mean everything to me." Oh, dear God! she thought. I mean every word of it. I really do, and he thinks it's pretend! She grasped the smooth hard flesh of his hips and held him to her.

"Beautiful, beautiful Elizabeth. A beautiful name for a beautiful woman." His mouth opened against hers and his urgent tongue sought and found the sweetness of hers. Beth's heart stopped, then sprinted into a mad gallop. "I love you," he whispered against her cheek. "I love you," he whispered against her mouth.

Oh, yes, I believe you! her thoughts spoke silently to him. *For tonight, I believe you.* The long, lean, muscular body moved over hers. There was no awkwardness, no hesitation. Her arms lifted to slide around his shoulders, and his hands burrowed beneath to lift her up to mold the soft contours of her body to his. It was all so natural. There was no waiting. They became one both emotionally and physically. She felt his weight pressing down on her, and she opened to meet him. With one long, slow drive he filled her emptiness. They were complete and they sensed it at the same time.

"Darlin' . . . how we fit, darlin', how we fit! Oh, woman, you were made for me, and I'll never let you go." The green eyes burned with exultation.

She closed lovingly around him, feeling not only her sensations, but his. She arched toward him instinctively, but he was the master, moving slowly and deliberately, prolonging every single bit of the wondrous heaven as if it had to last a lifetime. Beth didn't need his hands to guide her; she knew what he wanted her to do, just as he knew what she needed.

Together they journeyed to the top of the precipice and beyond, soaring into space in a brilliant blaze of rapture.

Together they drifted slowly back through a glowing haze of passion.

Neither of them moved for a long moment, giving their hearts and lungs time to regain their natural rhythms. Beth could feel the tiny aftershocks of climax in the heated sheath that enclosed him. His taut muscles loosened, his head sank onto the floor, and his lips touched the spot beneath her ear. They lay still, sharing the sweet aftermath of fulfillment, bodies still joined, drugged by sensuous pleasure.

"Am I too heavy for you?" A soft whisper.

"No."

"I'm glad. I don't want to leave you." He flicked the line of her jaw teasingly with the tip of his tongue.

"I'm not fragile. I like you there." She circled his shoulders with her arms and turned her face to his. Their lips met in a long, tender kiss while she shifted her legs slightly to cradle his hips more comfortably between her thighs.

Tom lifted his upper body and supported it by both elbows. There was a seeking look in his eyes. "Beth?" Her name was a murmured, husky whisper. "Elizabeth . . . sweet . . . ?"

She knew what he wanted to know. "Unbelievable. How can I describe it?" she whispered. "Beautiful . . . a whole new world. Oh, Thomas—I never knew it could be like that." Her words came softly in marvelous discovery. She caught her breath as his face was transformed with love and laughter. If she didn't know better, she would have thought the glistening she saw in the brilliant green eyes was caused by tears.

His lips moved to hers. Gently and tenderly he held

them captive in a long, lingering, trembling kiss. Tendrils of delight wound all through her body and a delicious tickling began to build deep in the part of her that surrounded him. When he would have moved his lips away, she followed with her own, and his sigh was a mingling of pleasure and need.

Tearing his lips free, he murmured, "Darlin', darlin'," and shifted his position to roll on his side, taking her with him. He reached for the back of her knee and pulled her thigh up over his hip, holding her there.

Beth's heart was beating fast, like a trapped bird under her breast. The delicious tickle increased, and she pressed her breasts into the soft hair on his chest. They began to move together with the smoothness of velvet. His hands were everywhere: on her back, her breasts, pressing against her hips. Her breath came in short gasps as they moved together, fitted and welded, while the light from the flickering fire poured over them.

Then came the moment when they stopped moving and simply clung, winging through space into a new and glorious heaven. It was as if skyrockets were bursting inside her, cruising through her veins, tingling in her scalp and down to her toes. She gripped him, wanting it to go on forever, partaking of his love in a whirl of wonder. *This was love!* This was the strongest emotion in the world. It held everything together. It was what poets wrote about. She had not understood it before. It was bliss, to have his body linked to her body, his heart beating against her heart!

Beth lay curled in his arms, and even as they rested, their lips sought and their hands soothed. It was so peaceful, this blessed togetherness. She was sated, filled with the wonder of her newfound sensuality. Tom nuzzled her neck, holding her close. She could sense that he didn't want to leave her, and it made her love him all the more.

"I've got to put more wood on the fire."

"I know."

"I don't want to move." His hand glided down her back, exerting just enough pressure to mold the full length of her naked body more tightly to his.

"You can come back." Her lips were parted against the warm smooth skin of his neck. She sucked on it gently and caressed it with the tip of her tongue.

"It's almost daylight. Herb will be coming in soon."

"Oh!" Mortified, Beth pulled away from him and reached for her gown.

Tom laughed softly. "Don't worry, honey. He'll have to come through the garage, and I threw the inside bolts. I don't exactly trust the two we picked up today."

The fire was only burning embers now, and in the dim light Beth saw the gleam of Tom's naked body as he stood to slide into his pajama bottom and shirt. Would her life ever be the same after this night? She had not realized the bliss, the oneness that could be felt with another human being. It was as if she had become an extension of him, would forever be an extension of him. Her eyes devoured him as he bent to place the logs on the grate. What were his intentions now that they had shared the most intimate act that can be shared between two people?

Beth wrapped her robe tightly around her and sat on the couch. Tom poked at the fire until the logs caught, blazed, and crackled, then turned his back to it and looked at her. She couldn't see the expression on his face, and a quick spear of fear pierced her. What was he thinking? Did he think this was the norm for her? Did he think that as a nurse she was accustomed to seeing naked male bodies and often indulged in casual sex? Say something, her mind screamed. When he didn't say anything, her mind urged her to explain, to tell him that she'd only been with one other man and that had been in an attempt to purge him from her thoughts. But she didn't say anything and her great, blue eyes locked on his face.

"What are you thinking?" he asked, and came to sit down beside her. He pulled the blanket up over her and tucked it behind her shoulders. Beneath it his fingers caught hers and crushed them in a tight grip. When she didn't answer, he asked, "Have you ever been in love?"

It was uncanny how he could sense her thoughts.

"I thought I was at one time."

"Did you feel with him what you felt with me?"

"No." It was the faintest of whispers. He was talking about her sexual experience, she was referring to her feeling for him three years ago.

He put his arm around her and pulled her close. "I'm glad," he said softly, proudly. Her head rested against his shoulder, and he leaned his cheek against her forehead. "Was he the only one?" She nodded, and he said again, "I'm glad."

It was very quiet, very peaceful. Beth stared into the fire and moved her palm across his chest to burrow into the space beneath his arm.

"No regrets?" His whisper accompanied light kisses and the brush of his mustache against her brow.

"What's this? Twenty questions?"

"No," he said after a long pause. "I just want to know all about you."

"I'm sorry." She turned her face into his neck. "I'm so confused."

"*Confused* confused? Or happy confused?"

"Both, I guess." She tilted her head to see his face. "We took a gigantic step in our relationship and—"

"Are you sorry?" The words were muffled against her lips.

"It was a beautiful sharing experience. I just don't want you to think—" She halted in mid-sentence, not wanting to phrase her fear.

"You don't want me to think you're easy. Is that it?" Not waiting for an answer, he pressed his lips softly to hers. When he lifted his head, the corners of his mouth were raised in a half smile. "Honey, you're far from easy. That first night in Rochester I wanted to beg you to let me stay with you, but I knew you'd throw me out on my ear."

"You didn't even like me."

"Mmm . . . I played it cool, didn't I?" His eyes twinkled mischievously. "I thought you were an adorable kid when I came to be best man at the wedding, but when I came back and saw the woman you had grown to, I was determined you were going to come home with me. If you'd dragged your feet, I was going to get sick so you'd have to take care of me."

"Sick? That reminds me—I noticed that you're terribly warm. You may have a fever." She moved her fingers to the base of his throat and pressed the pulse beating there. Her own pulse raced so fast that she couldn't count his.

"Having you in my arms is enough to make my temperature rise." His fingers searched beneath the robe for her breast.

"Are you feeling all right?" Beth ran her hand over his

heated flesh. Now that she thought of it, his skin had been warm when she came downstairs; hers had been a mass of cold goose pimples.

"Of course I feel all right, little Florence Nightingale. But if it will keep you fussing over me, I'll be happy to get sick." A hard rap on the kitchen door startled them. "There's Herb. Give me a kiss, love. " Their lips met in tender, nipping, bittersweet kisses. The hard-knuckled rap sounded again, and Tom raised his head. "Thank you, darlin'." He got to his feet, bent to tuck the blanket snugly around her, and reached for the flashlight.

CHAPTER NINE

THE WIND STOPPED blowing when the sun came up. Beth pulled back the draperies that covered the large picture window and looked out over a winter wonderland. White snow, piled by the wind, lay in picturesque drifts several feet deep. Icicles, clear and sparkling in the sunlight, hung from the eaves of the house. Happiness danced in Beth's heart like a snowflake in the wind. I've got years of love saved up for you, Thomas, darling, she thought.

The man who was constantly in her thoughts had gone out to the utility buildings to check on the generator. As soon as he left the house, Beth had dashed upstairs to brush her teeth, have a quick wash, and dress in layers of warm clothing. Now she busied herself bringing all the houseplants into the kitchen so they would have the benefit of heat from the fireplace.

Then Sarah called.

"Is everything all rigbt out there?"

"The electricity went off last night," Beth told her. "Thomas called the power company and they told him they had crews out looking for downed lines. In the meantime we have a fire in the fireplace and the generator is keeping the pipes from freezing." Beth couldn't suppress a giggle. "Thomas set a pan of water on the grate to boil. When he put the coffee in it, it boiled up and almost put out the fire."

"You sound happier this morning."

Oh, I am! My whole world has changed since last night, she thought. Aloud she said, "I guess I'm getting over the shock of the long trip."

"They're saying on the news that this is the most severe winter we've had in several years. All the major highways are closed and several deaths have been reported among stranded motorists. It'll take several days to dig out and get things back to normal." Her voice ended on a wistful note.

"Herb said this morning that just as soon as they have the essential chores done he'll start opening up the road to the highway. As it turned out, it's a good thing you didn't come home with us yesterday. The only warm place in the house is the kitchen. The rest of the rooms are cold as ice."

"My plants—"

"All safe. I brought them into the kitchen."

"Oh, Elizabeth, I'm so glad you'll be there when I come home!"

"So am I."

"Tell Thomas and Herb that I know how busy they are at a time like this, and that there's no mad rush for them to come and get me. I'm just fine here, although I miss being home. And Beth . . . Thomas is really a sweet and gentle man."

For a long time after she hung up the phone Beth

thought about what Sarah had said. *Thomas is really a gentle man.* What a strange thing to say. With a deep breath and a long sigh, she remembered how gentle, how considerate, how loving he had been.

It was almost noon when she heard the soft hum of the refrigerator and saw the light come on over the electric range. The power had been restored. Now, to make a really good cup of coffee and heat some canned soup. She'd have a hot meal ready when Herb and Thomas came back to the house.

It didn't take long for the house to warm up once the furnace fan was set in motion. Beth turned on the radio to hear the weather report. It was fifteen degrees below zero. It couldn't be *that* cold, she thought. It looks so beautiful out there in the white stillness.

When Beth heard a noise in the entry between the garage and the kitchen, she hurried to the door and flung it open. The smile of welcome on her face was quickly replaced by a puzzled frown when she saw Jerry Lewis, one of the men she and Thomas had picked up on the highway, standing before her. He stood silently grinning at her, with his hands in his pockets. She recognized the expression on his face immediately. *He was stoned!*

"Hi."

"What do you want?"

"Do I have to want somethin'?"

"Why are you here?" Beth kept her tone even.

"It's cold . . . out here," he said stupidly. His eyes were opened wide, the pupils mere pinpoints.

"I know it is. You'd better go back to the bunkhouse, where it's warm."

"Ain't no women out there."

Moving as naturally and as calmly as possible, Beth stepped out into the entry and picked up a coat that had fallen from the rack. When she turned back she found that he had moved around her and was going into the kitchen. She darted around in front of him.

"Hold it! I didn't invite you into the house."

"I know it." He spread his feet wide apart to steady himself.

"Please leave."

"Whaaat?"

"Leave. L-E-A-V-E. Go on back to the bunkhouse."

"I wanta stay here." He reached for her, and she stepped away.

"Your friend will be looking for you." Her voice had risen in pitch, and she reminded herself to stay calm.

"He ain't no friend. He's a bastard."

"Is that right? I really would appreciate it if you would leave, so I can get on with my work." Her heart began to beat in double time and her legs felt weak, but she knew she had to appear completely confident.

"I ain't goin' to bother. I'm just goin' to look at you."

"That's very flattering, but Mr. Clary will be angry if he comes and catches you here. He was kind enough to offer you shelter. The least you can do is respect his hospitality." Beth knew immediately that she shouldn't have used such strong words. His face tightened and his expression turned ugly.

"I don't care 'bout him! I could blow him away . . . just like that!" He snapped his fingers.

"I'm sure you could, but what would that prove?" Beth took a deep breath. She was beginning to feel frightened, and she searched her mind for every bit of information she'd learned on how to handle a situation such as this.

"It'd prove that I don't have to take nothin' from nobody," he replied belligerently.

"I see. Do you live in Cody?"

"Hell, no. I live in L.A."

"You're a long way from home. I'm sure you're not used to this cold weather."

"I ain't wantin' to talk 'bout no weather. I come to see a woman." He reached for her again, and Beth deftly sidestepped.

The outside door opened and Shiloh came bounding in, then slid to a halt when she saw the stranger in the kitchen. Behind her, Tom's tall form filled the doorway. Something in his expression brought back to Beth's mind the strange statement Sarah had made earlier. *Thomas really is a gentle man.* He looked anything but gentle now. The intensity of his expression, laced with the dark scowl and beetled brows, was intimidating enough without the added leverage of the vicious oath that burst from his lips.

"What the hell are you doing in here?"

The man looked at him blankly, his head wobbling when he turned it. "What's it to ya, cowboy?" He grinned, seeming enormously pleased with himself.

Tom reached him in two steps. A heavy hand on his shoulder sent him spinning toward the door. "Did he touch you?" he bellowed at Beth as he moved.

Beth was shocked by the savagery of his tone. "No! He's stoned, Thomas. He's out of it. Don't you understand?"

"You're damn right I do. The low-life bastard! I've got

no patience for dopers." He gave the man a vicious push. "Get the hell out of here!"

"Stop it! He's in no condition to go out there. He'll never find his way to the bunkhouse."

"Tough! That's his problem." With his hand clamped to the man's shoulder, Tom propelled him through the garage and shoved him out the door.

Beth grabbed her coat from the hook and followed. Jerry was picking himself up out of a snowbank where Tom had shoved him. He was still grinning when he got to his feet.

"Hey, what's goin' on?" Mike Cotter was running through the snowdrifts toward them.

"Get your stuff together. I'm taking you back to your car," Tom ordered, glaring at the man, his jaw muscles pulsing as he fought to contain his anger.

Beth waded through snow that reached halfway to her knees and put her hand on his arm. "How, Thomas? How can you take them? You'll never get through."

"Herb and I'll take them on the snowmobiles." He swore viciously. "The bastards have been shootin' drugs in the bunkhouse." He looked down at her as if just realizing she was there. "You don't have your boots on," he said impatiently, and swung her up into his arms. He carried her to the doorway. "Get back in there and dry your feet. I'll be back as soon as I get rid of them."

"Thomas . . ."

He didn't answer. He was the same as after he'd roughed up the cowboy in the restaurant. He seemed to retreat into himself. With apprehension gnawing at her, she watched him follow the two men across the snow-covered yard. Half an hour later she stood at the window and watched the two snowmobiles leave the ranch, headed toward the highway.

Twice she had seen Tom lash out with what she considered unnecessary force. All her life she had despised violence of any kind, and her sister was aware of that fact. Twice Sarah had made the remark that Thomas was a *gentle* man. Why would she say that? Was Thomas unable to control his temper? Was that why Sarah was trying to assure her that Thomas *didn't* have a violent nature? She didn't want me to build up a dislike for him before I got to know him, Beth decided.

The afternoon passed slowly. After cooking a roast, banked with potatoes, carrots, and onions, Beth kept a vigil at the window and looked out into the early evening darkness, hoping to see lights coming up the lane. Doubts assailed her. It was still in the back of her mind that there was more between Sarah and Thomas than friendship. Was Sarah in love with him? How could she possibly not be in love with him? By six o'clock Beth's nerves were stretched almost to the breaking point.

When she finally saw the two beams of light approaching the house, she heaved a tremendous sigh of relief and tried to ignore the thudding in her chest. It was a strange but pleasant stirring within her, and she had a fleeting impression of how pioneer women had felt when their men returned from a dangerous mission.

She was taking the roast from the oven when she heard the familiar voice scolding the dog and telling her she would have to stay in the foyer until she was dry enough to come into the house.

"Hi." Thomas came through to the kitchen and leaned on the counter. Herb followed and closed the door.

"Are you hungry?" It seemed to Beth a sensible bit of chitchat while she was taking the roasting pan to the counter. Then she saw Thomas's drawn, tired, utterly weary face. The muscles in his jaw knotted as he clenched his teeth.

"I'd like some of that hot coffee, honey. I'm cold clear through to my bones." He pushed himself away from the counter, went to the fireplace, and stood with his arms folded on the mantel.

Beth darted a glance at Herb and saw that he was watching Tom with concern on his dark face. Her mind skittered in panic, and she went to join Tom where he stood with his head resting on his arms. Now she saw his broad shoulders shivering, and knew the reason for his clenched teeth. He was trying to keep them from chattering. She lay her hand on his arm.

"Are you sick, Thomas?"

"No, honey. Just tired and cold. It's been a hell of a day."

"Let me take your temperature. You have a fever. I'd like to know how high it is."

"Not now, sweetheart." The lines on each side of his mouth deepened. "I want to sit down for a while." The green eyes passed over her quickly. He sank down into a chair and leaned his head back wearily.

Beth took the Indian blanket from the back of the couch and draped it over him, tucking the ends behind him and down into the sides of the chair. She brushed the hair back from his face, then rested her hand lightly on his forehead. It felt hot and dry. She should have known this morning that he wasn't well! She continued to castigate herself while she put the teakettle on to boil. She'd make a toddy if there was any whiskey in the house. Herb had gone down the hall to the bathroom. When he returned, Beth was waiting for him with the question.

"Is there any whiskey in the house?"

The big man moved easily. He reached into the cabinet above the refrigerator and brought out a bottle.

"A slug of this will warm him up quicker than anything."

"I was going to make a toddy, but perhaps you're right." She poured a small amount in a glass and took it to Tom. His eyes were closed. He looked so quiet and weary sitting there. Tenderness welled through her as she brushed a lock of hair back from his forehead. His eyes opened at the touch of her hand.

"Drink this and it'll warm you."

"I don't think I can, honey." He turned his face away from the smell. "My stomach isn't behaving very well."

Beth set the glass on the table. "Why don't you go up, take a hot bath, and go to bed? It could be that you've got a case of the good old-fashioned flu."

Tom's hand came out from under the blanket and searched for hers. She met it with a firm clasp. His eyes were bright with fever, and he squinted against the light from the lamp.

"My head feels like a thousand hammers are pounding on it," he said regretfully. "Tonight, of all nights, when I wanted to be with you, I feel like I've been hit by a semi."

"You didn't feel good this morning," she accused gently. "Why didn't you say something?"

"There was too much to do. I took a couple of aspirin and thought that would take care of it."

"Aspirin is not a cure-all. Come on, let's get you into bed."

Tom grinned in spite of his pain. "Just the words I've been wanting to hear."

Before she spoke, Beth glanced quickly to see if Herb had heard the remark. He was putting the food on the table.

"Are you sure you can't eat something?"

"Don't turn all nursey on me, love. I'm sorry I'm going to have to take myself away from you, but I feel like hell." He lurched to his feet and on unsteady legs made it to the stairs. Holding onto the railing, he climbed them and disappeared in the hallway above.

Beth stood looking after him, then moved to follow. Herb's voice stopped her.

"Give him a little time. No man wants his woman to see him throw up."

It was a while before the import of his words reached Beth's worried mind. When she turned to look at Herb, he was smiling gently.

"I'm not his—Did he say that?" Anger and embarrassment vied for dominance.

"No. But I saw the change in him this morning. It could only have been because of you."

Beth felt the warmth come up her neck to her face. "I suppose you think that—"

"I don't think anything. Everyone needs someone. Tom more than most."

Beth looked at him steadily. His dark eyes seemed challenging and vaguely envious. "How about you?"

"Me too." He waited a moment and said, "I'll go up

and see if he's in bed. He has to be pretty sick before he'll give up."

"He may have Asian flu. He has the symptoms. If he isn't better by morning, I'll call and talk to his doctor. It may be that someone will have to bring out some medication."

"No problem. I can always get to town on the tractor, or someone can fly it out and drop it."

"That's a relief to know."

While Herb was upstairs, Beth put the roast back in the oven to keep warm. She was sure Herb would be hungry even if she and Tom were not. What a strange and gentle man the foreman was, with his quiet, dark face and soft voice. He was a man she could have fallen in love with if she hadn't met Thomas first.

Beth waited for what she considered a reasonable time before she went upstairs. She went to her room first and took stock of the medication in her first-aid kit. There wasn't anything there that could combat the infection causing Tom's fever. She had aspirin, of course, and a very mild form of penicillin tablet. Tom needed fluids, and probably the only thing he could keep in his stomach would be carbonated beverages. Thank goodness there were plenty of those on hand.

The door to Tom's room was ajar. Beth cautiously pushed it open and went inside. There were no lamps on, but in the light coming through the open door of the bathroom, she saw Tom on the bed and his discarded clothes on the floor beside it. Herb came out of the bathroom with a glass of water in his hand.

"He doesn't have anything left in his stomach, that's for sure."

"It'll be good if he can sleep." Beth stooped to pick up the clothes.

Herb set the glass on the table beside the bed. "He'll be all right while we eat supper. Sarah will be calling soon."

"She said she'd call around seven. It's almost that now."

"I won't tell her that Tom's sick. It'll just worry her. Time enough for that tomorrow."

Beth folded Tom's sweater and lay it on the bureau. "I'll let him sleep a couple of hours, and then I'll wake him and take his temperature."

Beth and Herb talked to Sarah when she called, and Herb smoothed over Tom's absence by saying he was upstairs at the moment. By the time the conversation was over, Beth was almost sure the foreman was in love with her sister. It was in the tone of his voice, his gentle encouraging words, and the softening of his harsh features when he talked to her. Now it remained to be seen if Sarah returned his affection or if it was Tom she had given her heart to.

"Did you have any more trouble with the men when you took them to their car?" Beth inquired casually.

"Not much. We ran into a highway patrol officer and turned them over to him. It wasn't only pot they were using. They had some hard stuff too."

"Thomas has quite an explosive temper," she ventured shyly, and stole a glance at him.

He shrugged. "At least *he* tries to control it, which is more than I can say—" He broke off in mid-sentence and raised his coffee cup to his lips. Beth waited for him to say more, but when he spoke again, it was to tell her that this year they had driven the cattle into feeding pens and it was lucky they had because some of them would have died during the storm.

While Beth put the dinner things away, Herb went back up to check on Tom. "He's still sleeping," he told her when he returned. "I'm going to turn in. If you need me, punch number two on the dial. The phone will ring in the rooms above the garage."

"Thank you, I will. Good night, Herb."

Beth made sure the doors were locked and the lights off before she went up to her room to put on her granny gown, robe, and slippers. With the first-aid kit under her arm she went down the hall to Tom's room. The bedside lamp was on, and he watched her come into the room.

"How do you feel?"

"I'm freezing. Do you suppose you could find some extra covers?"

"There's a down comforter in my closet. Do you know where I can find the heating pad?"

"Sarah may have one in her room." He closed his eyes again.

Beth found the heating pad, plugged it in, and slipped it into the bed beneath his feet. She covered him with the extra comforter, moved a chair beside the bed and sat down.

"I'd take your temperature if I weren't afraid those chattering teeth would break it," she joked.

"I'll be okay in a little while. You could get in here with me and keep me warm. Jane Russell did it in an old movie I saw on TV."

She laughed softly. "I don't think you're quite as sick as you make out."

"I want to hold you. I want you to hold me." There was longing in his voice and his eyes pleaded with her.

Without hesitation she stood up and slipped out of her robe. His arm raised the covers and she had a glimpse of his naked chest before she lay down beside him and drew his head to her shoulder. With her free hand she tucked the covers firmly around him, then wrapped his chilled body with her arms and cradled him close. He snuggled his face into the curve of her neck with a sigh.

"You feel so good."

"Shh . . . go to sleep." Her lips moved over his forehead in soft, soothing kisses.

Gradually he relaxed and stopped shivering. Beth's warm hand stroked the muscular thigh that lay across hers, trying to bring warmth to his chilled legs. She wasn't sure if what she was feeling for him was love for a man or the kind of love she would feel for a child. It was probably a mixture of both. All she knew was that she wanted to give to him whatever he needed.

Long after he was warm and sleeping, Beth lay with her thoughts going in several directions. Three years ago she had been sure that she loved this man, but with absence the love faded. Could it return with such terrific force that it was capable of consuming a person? They had satisfied each other's needs last night under the guise of pretended love. It had been his idea to use the word. Was she a substitute for her sister? The thought was so painful that her eyes flew open to stare at the ceiling. Tom stirred restlessly, and she raised her head so she could see his face. A new wave of feeling swept over her, one of tenderness. And she wondered if this man, of all men, was capable of making her life complete. Being too weary to try to answer the questions that plagued her, she gave herself up to the luxury of holding him, and finally she dozed.

The sound of Tom's voice woke her. She was so relaxed that at first she only thought she'd heard his slurred words. His body was hot and he had one bare arm out from under the covers. She covered him and tried to move a little away from him, but his arms closed around her and clamped her tightly to him.

"Damn you!" he muttered, and turned his face into her shoulder, rocking his head back and forth as if in torment. "Oh, Sarah! Goddammit! It's always been this way."

Beth was instantly alert. Her first thought was to wake him, because she didn't want to hear what he was saying, but then he began to talk again.

"Don't cry, Sarah. I'll take care of you." He groaned and flung out his arm. "You're pretty and sweet . . . don't worry. No one will ever know. It isn't wrong, Sarah . . . It isn't wrong to feel this way. . . ." His voice died away to incoherent murmurs and then silence.

A coldness settled around Beth's heart as if someone had plunged it into a freezer. Somewhere in her mind she had known all along that there was something more than a brother/sister relationship between Tom and her sister.

So many things fell into place now. Thomas moving Sarah up to his house, his concern for her, the urgency to bring her back from Minnesota to take care of her. His willingness to allow Sarah to decorate his house was a sure sign that he didn't intend to marry anyone else. Why was he keeping his feelings a secret? It had to be that he didn't want to hurt Herb, knowing that he, too, was in love with Sarah. No, that couldn't be. Men were seldom that considerate of other men's feelings where a woman was concerned. Maybe Sarah didn't return his love, and he had brought her here to make Sarah jealous—Beth's thoughts whirled in a riot of scornful accusations against both Thomas and her sister.

What are you going to do now, you fool? How could you have been so stupid? Tears slid slowly from the corners of her eyes and rolled down into her cheeks and into her hair. When Tom had recited the poetic words *I love you*, he had told her they were pretend, so how could she blame him now? How could he have known her words had come from her heart?

Easing her legs from their entrapment between his, she inched herself away from his long, hard body. Sleeping soundly, he didn't stir when she moved his limp arm aside and slipped out of the bed. She stood beside it for a long moment and looked down on his relaxed features. *You're a bastard*, she mouthed. A handsome, charming, cheating bastard, or you'd never have made love to me when you're in love with my sister.

The misery in her body grew, encompassing her heart and expanding into her soul. She hurried to her room before the volcano of tears erupted within her. At least some of her questions were answered.

CHAPTER TEN

BETH USED THE hours before dawn to condition herself for the new day. She counseled herself sternly. It wasn't as if she hadn't faced disappointment before. She had no one but herself to blame for not heeding the squirming little worm of doubt that had tried to wiggle into her reasoning. Almost light-headed with the conflict in her brain, she bathed, dressed, and went downstairs. The heaven had lasted for only a few hours; surely the hell couldn't last forever.

Appropriately enough, the sun hid behind a bank of gray clouds. Gloom permeated the house and was suitable company for Beth's sagging spirits. Herb was in the kitchen. He poured her a cup of coffee while telling her he had looked in on Tom and found him still sleeping.

"I'll plow snow if nothing else comes up to claim my attention," he told her.

The rest of Beth's fading courage went out the door with Herb. She dreaded the moment she would face Thomas.

It happened sooner than she had expected. She looked up from the stove where she was cooking an egg, and there he was, leaning against the door frame. His hair was rumpled from sleep and there was the shadow of a night's growth of beard on his lean cheeks. He had slipped into a pair of faded jeans and a gray sweatshirt. Beth felt a fierce rush of resentment that he could stand there so calmly when her stomach felt as if a couple of cats were inside, clawing to get out.

"How do you feel this morning?" A calm voice and slight smile masked the wrenching ache that tore at her heart.

"Like I've been run over with a steamroller, and weak as a cat."

"I have a remedy for that. Sit down, I'll fix you some toast and eggs." She bent to take the egg poacher from under the counter, and when she straightened he was beside her. "Running around with bare feet is no way to get over the flu," she said coolly, and busily filled the pan with water.

Tom moved behind her and placed his hands on either side of her and braced himself against the counter. "When I went to sleep last night you were in bed with me. Why did you leave?" He pushed the hair away from her ear with his chin, and put his lips there. She shivered once, then bunched her shoulder to escape his touch.

"I'm busy, Thomas."

He pressed against her hips, imprisoning her against the cabinet while his tongue caressed her earlobe. Beth felt the unmistakable pressure of his masculine sex against her buttocks and tried to turn from it, but his hands had found their way up under her sweater and his palms flattened her breasts. Using more strength than was necessary, she dropped the pan in the sink and pushed him away from her.

"Stop it!"

Undaunted, he grinned at her lazily. “Are you a grouch this morning, sweetheart?”

“Yes, I am. I didn’t get much sleep last night.” Beth seized the excuse for her behavior.

“You didn’t get much sleep the night before, either.” A smile tugged at the corner of his mouth.

Sudden, hot anger rose in Beth. Cool it, she cautioned herself. If you lash out at him he’ll know that what happened between you was more important to you than it was to him. Important? What a mundane word to describe it!

“You *are* feeling better this morning.” She retrieved the pan from the sink and refilled it with water. I can’t stand this, she groaned silently. Then, Yes, you can! Buck up, girl. Salvage your pride.

“I feel better. I must have had the twenty-four-hour misery that makes the rounds once in a while. I’ll take it easy today.”

Beth walked around him to get to the stove. “Herb said to tell you he’ll start plowing out the drive.”

“Did he say anything about going in to get Sarah?”

“No,” she said flatly. “How many eggs?”

“Two. Did Sarah call last night?”

“Yes. Herb talked to her. Toast?”

“Two, to start.”

Beth was proud of the way she was handling herself. She had managed, with a great deal of effort, to remain calm during one of the most difficult situations she’d ever had to face. She refused to let her tears have their freedom and even contrived a small, cool smile when she set his breakfast before him.

“You said you didn’t sleep well?” His voice had become taut, and when his hand shot out to close around her wrist, she felt the tension in his fingers and it added to her own.

"Only so-so," she muttered, and lifted her shoulders in a careless gesture.

Tom's facial muscles tightened. "Are you feeling okay?"

"Sure," she said lightly, and moved to pick up her own plate. He was forced to release her arm.

"Then why in hell are you acting like a cow with her tit caught in the fence?"

Beth managed an indignant huff. "Just because you have the twenty-four-hour misery, that's no excuse for being vulgar."

"Vulgar!" The sound that came from him was like a snort. Anger flickered in the eyes that raked her face before they became unfathomable.

"More toast?" she asked evenly.

His brows lifted and then fell. "No, thank you." His tone had turned decidedly cold.

Somehow, the morning passed. Beth was upstairs when Sarah called, so she was spared the pain of having to pretend that she was all bubbly with good feelings. She could hear Tom's voice, but couldn't and didn't want to hear what he was saying. Just for a moment she allowed herself to cry silently. Biting her lip, her eyes filled with tears before she hurried to the bathroom to dash them away with a spray of cold water. Oh, God! Am I going to be able to carry this off? she wondered.

When she went down to the kitchen to prepare lunch, Tom lay sprawled in the chair. He looked up when she came into the room. He still hadn't shaved and his face wore the look of a man with a lot on his mind.

"You're awfully quiet today," he observed.

"Am I?" Beth tried to smile and hoped her attempt at brightness would succeed. She went to the refrigerator and took out the cold roast in an effort to avoid a discussion. She was aware that Tom had come up behind her, and she moved before he could touch her.

"What's the matter with you? You act like a pup with its tail in a crack."

"First I'm a cow with my tit caught in the fence and now a pup with my tail in a crack. Flattering."

"I don't need any of your smart-ass answers," he snapped.

"I'm all right. See, I'm smiling." She spread her lips, showing all her teeth. "Will Herb be in for lunch?"

"I doubt it. Damn!" He struck the counter with the flat of his hand. Beth jerked her head around at the sound. She watched his features harden in a surge of anger.

"How do you feel about hot beef sandwiches for lunch?" Her voice was hoarse with the strain of attempting a normal tone. She leaned over the sink and ran water over her hands. As she reached for a towel, she heard the sound of a snowmobile close to the house. By the time she'd hung the towel back on the rack, the doorbell was ringing. Tom stalked to the door and flung it open with such force that the dog backed away and didn't dart into the kitchen as she usually did.

Beth greeted Pat O'Day with an overbright smile.

"Howdy, darlin'!" he said with a wink. "I see you haven't forgotten me."

"Of course not. Did you come out from town on your snowmobile?"

"Sure did. I came across country, as the crow flies. It's

the only way to go." He stood grinning at her, his bright eyes openly admiring.

"You're in time for lunch." Beth glanced at a grim-faced Tom. "That is, if you can eat last night's leftovers."

"You betcha. I'm not fussy. I'll eat anything that don't bite me first." He glanced around at Tom. "Herb tells me you're under the weather, ol' hoss."

"Nothing to speak of," Tom said drily. "How's Herb doing? Has he got to the end of the lane?"

"Yeah. He's out to the gravel road. The county man is coming up from the other end. They should have the road open anytime now." Pat turned his attention back to Beth. "What can I do? I can't stand to see a pretty woman workin' all by herself."

Beth smiled at him. It was almost impossible not to. "I'll be glad for your help. Cooking isn't my long suit." She avoided looking at Thomas. "But you must wash your hands first. Cook's rule number one."

"May I interrupt long enough to excuse myself?" Tom stood, adamantly fingering the stubble on his chin.

"Go ahead, ol' man. Don't let me keep you from anythin'," Pat said cheerfully. "You don't have to entertain me. Just watchin' this pretty thing is all the entertainment I need."

Tom gave a derisive snort. Beth met his eyes briefly, but long enough to see the disapproval reflected there. Then with characteristic arrogance he stalked from the room, leaving her seething with impotent rage.

During lunch Beth had the uncanny sensation of sitting on the edge of a volcano about to erupt. Tom had come to the table with a freshly shaved face and wearing an open-necked knit pullover shirt. Beth refused to acknowledge that the flutter in her heart was caused by the familiar scent of his aftershave when he passed behind her chair. She was immensely relieved that it wasn't necessary for her to hold up an end of the conversation. The men discussed the storm, cattle feeding, and the underground cable business, leaving her free to concentrate on getting the fork from her plate to her mouth and the food down her throat without choking on it.

Surely it will become easier, she told herself. This is the first day. Tomorrow will be better, the day after that better still. That was the way it had worked before, so why not this time? I've only got to get through this day, she reasoned. Tomorrow Sarah will be home.

Beth was thankful for Pat's company. After she loaded the dishwasher she found him bent over a huge jigsaw puzzle laid out on a card table in the living room. She wasn't a puzzle fan and hadn't tried to put any of the pieces in place, realizing it was Sarah's project because of the raised chair beside the table.

"Sit down and give me a hand," Pat urged. "I'm a puzzle freak from way back. Can't resist 'em."

A couple of hours passed almost pleasantly. Finally Pat's interest in the difficult puzzle began to wane. "Would you like a ride on my machine before I head back to town?" When he stood beside Beth, their eyes were on a level. His eyes were blue and merry, hers blue and desperately trying not to mirror the misery she was feeling.

"I'd love to go. How cold is it?"

"Not as cold as yesterday. Only nine below, but no wind to speak of."

"Super. Give me a few minutes to get on my long johns."

"I'll be glad to help," Pat called after her as she started up the stairs.

Beth turned to smile at him and saw that Tom had come in from the family room and was watching her from the doorway. The light retort died on her lips and she continued on, hurrying to get out from under the critical, angry blaze of his intense green eyes. She couldn't help shivering at the thought that very soon she would have to account for her actions.

Pat started the snowmobile and Beth slipped into the seat behind him. The snow was light and the churning lugs of the machine left a soft, white cloud behind them. Beth's spirits rose as they headed for open country. The breeze rushing against her face and the snow whipping around her cleared her head and soothed her taut nerves.

Pat was a pleasant companion who laughed easily. His wolfish, flirtatious ways were a come-on that was not meant to be taken seriously. Beth was comfortable with him.

At the top of a hill he stopped the machine and grinned over his shoulder at her. "Your cheeks look like two red apples."

"Crab or Delicious?"

"De-licious. Definitely Delicious."

"You've got a line a mile long, Patrick O'Day."

"Nicest thing anyone's said to me all day." He got off the machine so she could turn around. "Look at that view. Pretty, isn't it?"

Beth followed his gaze. Spread before them was a panorama of ranch buildings surrounded by tightly branched pine trees. Her eyes dwelled on Tom's house for a long moment and then on the three smaller houses behind and to the left of it. She wondered which one of them Sarah and Steven had lived in. Farther to the west she could see the feeding pens and the utility buildings, but her eyes kept coming back to the long brown house with smoke curling from its chimney.

"It looks like a scene on a Christmas card," she remarked.

"Yeah, it does," Pat said seriously, and then laughed as if he disliked having to say something serious. "I'd better get you back. I don't think ol' Thomas was too pleased that you came out with me. He looked like he was about to blow a fuse."

"He's had the flu. I don't think he feels well today." Beth smiled carefully. "A nurse gets used to grouchy patients and pays them no mind."

It seemed to take less time to get back to the house than it did to reach the hill. Almost before Beth was aware of it, Pat eased the machine up to the garage door and turned off the motor.

"Thanks. I enjoyed that."

"My pleasure. We'll do it again." A drift of snow hanging on the eave of the roof let go just at that moment and cascaded down on Pat, showering him with the white stuff. He looked at Beth accusingly.

"I didn't do it," she said. "It wasn't my fault." She began to back away. He stalked her and she turned to run. "I didn't do it!" she shrieked between peals of laughter. When she saw that he was going to catch her, she grabbed up a handful of snow and threw it at him. The snowball connected just as he reached for her and they went tumbling into the snow.

"I'll teach you to laugh at me!" Pat sat astride her and calmly washed her face with a handful of snow.

When he let her go, he ran to the snowmobile and Beth sat up, sputtering. "I'll get you for that, you . . . jerk!" she yelled.

He laughed uproariously, put the machine in gear, and roared away.

Beth sat in the snow for a moment before she rolled to her knees and stood. She glanced at the house and saw Tom standing in the window. Immediately tension returned, winding around her until she thought her taut nerves would snap. Not wanting to face him just now, she walked around to the back of the house, toward the bunkhouse, tack house, machine sheds, and barns. She passed them and walked on toward the three small houses, each set in its own landscaped yard. The houses were small compared to the big house. They looked to be two-bedroom cottages.

As she walked along, a glimmer of an idea struck her. Tom had said that there was no one living in one of the houses. She wondered if he would allow her to live there. Sarah didn't need a live-in nurse, and by living out here she would be able to avoid Tom and still be available to care for her sister. How could Tom refuse the request?

Feeling better now that there was in sight, at least, one solution to her dilemma, she trudged head down back to the house.

Only Shiloh met her at the door. One quick look told her she might be able to make it to her bedroom without running into Tom. Without haste, in case he came out of one of the rooms and was watching her, she went up to the room that had been assigned to her. Once inside she took a deep breath and lay down on her stomach across the bed.

Beth hadn't intended to sleep, but she did. She woke to near darkness and sat up on the side of the bed. Five o'clock. She hadn't given a thought to fixing an evening meal. Then a wave of uncharacteristic resentment rose in her. She hadn't come out here to be a cook! Let them fix their own damn dinner! She'd take a bath.

A couple of hours later she felt as if she couldn't stay in the bedroom another minute. Not for anything did she want Tom to think she was avoiding him. It would put too much emphasis on what had happened between them. She glanced at herself in the mirror and was satisfied with the way she looked. The velour pants and top showed off her willowy figure to its best advantage, and the blue did wonderful things to her dark hair and blue eyes. Not that she was dressing to impress Thomas Clary, she hastily told her image in the mirror. She needed to know that she looked reasonably attractive, needed it to support her sagging self-confidence.

Tom was standing at the kitchen range. He glanced up and the look on his face knocked her heart backward a beat. The look was there for only a few seconds, but there was no mistaking it. He looked like a kid who had got up on Christmas morning and found his stocking empty.

"Need some help?"

"No, thanks." He glanced at the clock above the kitchen sink. "Herb will be in soon."

She hadn't expected this quiet indifference. She glanced at his profile. He was staring down into a skillett, stirring vigorously, ignoring her. The phone rang and for an instant Beth was startled. Her eyes were still on him when he looked up.

"Get that, will you?"

Beth picked up the phone. It was Pat.

"I just wanted to let you know that I made it back to the big metropolis."

"I wasn't worried about you, Pat, but it's nice of you to call and report in."

"I almost wish I hadn't called, if that's the attitude you're going to take. Didn't you worry even a little bit?"

"Well, maybe a little." Through the screening veil of her lashes Beth studied Tom's face. He was still stirring cream gravy in the skillet, although he had turned off the burner.

"Are you coming into town tomorrow?" Pat asked.

"I plan to come in and consult with Sarah's doctor. She's coming home tomorrow."

"Will you have time to have lunch with me?"

"I'll ask Thomas." Beth put her hand over the phone. "Will we have time to have lunch in town tomorrow?"

He shrugged. "It's up to you," he said indifferently. "But Jean and Sarah will be anxious to get home."

Piqued by his nonchalance, Beth was tempted to accept Pat's invitation, but out of consideration for Sarah, she said, "We won't have time, Pat. But thanks just the same."

"Okay, sweet thing. Another time."

"Bye, Pat." Beth hung up the phone.

"Sorry to throw a monkey wrench in your little tête-à-tête." The words were half muffled.

Beth was tempted to tell him to speak up if he had anything to say, but the phone rang again. She lifted the receiver without being told to.

"Hello?"

"Elizabeth!" Sarah's excited voice broke into her thoughts. "I can hardly believe I'll be there with you this time tomorrow night. I swear the last few days have been the longest of my life."

"Mine too. Have you made an appointment for me to talk to your doctor?"

"In the morning at nine. Can you make it here by then?"

"I'm sure we can, but wait. I'll ask Thomas."

Sarah laughed. "He'll be here, or Herb will. What's he doing, anyway?"

"Here he is, you can find out for yourself." Beth held out the phone. His eyes held hers for a long moment before he reached for it.

"Hi, Sarah."

Tom's eyes made a continuous, searching study of Beth's face while he talked. In the oppressive tension between them, she suddenly had trouble breathing; her lungs hurt with the effort. Jarred into action, she went past him to the table and rearranged the silver he had placed beside the dinnerware.

"We've missed you, too, honey." The tender tone of Tom's voice spoke a thousand silent words and caused excruciating pain to Beth's already wounded heart. "No, Herb hasn't heard if Susan will come for Christmas. He'll probably pick you up tomorrow. You can ask him then." Beth took a deep breath during the silence that followed. "Do you want to talk to your sister again? Wait, I think Herb's coming in. You can ask him about Susan."

In a few moments Herb stood in his stocking feet, his face and hands red from the cold, and talked to Sarah in a low, patient voice. For just the tiniest second Beth felt a stab of envy. Her beautiful sister had all the love and respect a woman could want from two very special men.

Tom seemed preoccupied during the meal. He spoke

only when Herb asked him a question, ate sparingly, and left the table to watch the evening news while Beth and Herb lingered over coffee. While Beth was arranging the dishes in the dishwasher, it occurred to her that the quiet foreman was aware of the undercurrent of tension between her and Thomas and had made an effort to ease things for her.

The bedroom was her sanctuary.

Beth glanced at the clock. It was only eight o'clock. Thank God she had brought a supply of paperbacks with her. She admitted, now that she was in the safety of the bedroom, that it was rude of her to come upstairs without a word to Thomas or Herb. But, dammit, she wasn't ready for a confrontation with Thomas, and it was bound to happen if she was left alone with him. With a painfully aching heart she prepared for bed.

It was ten o'clock. For the last couple of hours Beth had been trying to get interested in first one novel and then another. She lay propped on the pillows, her feet tucked in the bottom of her granny gown. In exasperation she tossed the novel to the bedside table. The story had all the right ingredients: handsome, virile hero; feminine, but strong-willed heroine; an exotic setting. Yet nothing was happening in the story that could compare with what was going on in her own life. She pulled the covers up under her chin and sank down into the bed.

The door to the hall was just beyond the end of the bed. Beth was looking at it, her mind on how she was going to approach Thomas about moving into the tenant house, when it opened slowly, and Thomas was standing there. It happened so smoothly that she blinked, unsure whether the figure lounging against the door frame was real or imaginary.

"Is something . . . wrong?" she stammered.

"You know damn good and well there is."

"What is it? What's happened?"

"You know *what's happened*. Cut the dumb Dora act." He came to the side of the bed.

"We can discuss whatever is on your mind in the morning," she said coolly. She didn't like the disadvantage of lying in bed and having to look up at him.

"We'll talk about it now." His glance moved from the bedclothes to her face.

"Say what you've got to say. I've a few things to say myself." Better to attack than be attacked, she thought bitterly.

"I'm listening."

"I'd like to move into your tenant house and live there while I'm here with Sarah."

"You think you'll need more privacy to entertain O'Day? Is that it?"

"Sarah won't need a live-in nurse," she said, ignoring the barb. "She and I can still spend a lot of time together, and I can give her the moral support and the medication from there as easily as from here."

"Pat just separated from his wife. Did he tell you that?"

Again she ignored his words. "I have savings. I can pay rent and utilities. It isn't as if it would cost you anything to allow me to live there."

"Shut up!" he roared. "Shut up about the damned house! You've got your tail over the line and I want to know why."

"I don't know what you're talking about."

"The hell you don't!"

"If you're referring to— If you think that because we

had a romantic interlude it's going to be a permanent affair, then you're painfully mistaken."

Tom's hands reached for her. She was sure he was going to shake her. Volatile anger simmered beneath every move he made and every breath he drew. It took all her willpower not to cringe from his wrath.

"How could I have been so wrong about you?" Soft words came through his face of stone.

"How could I have been so wrong about you?" She threw the words back at him. "You lay down the rules!" She was shouting now. "You said pretend! Do you think that every woman you take to bed is in love with you?" Tears spurted. Angry tears. Dammit to hell! Why did she have to cry every time she got angry? Ashamed of her tears, she lashed out at him to hide her shame. "So we had a one-night frolic. It didn't mean any more to me than it did to you. We're living in the twentieth century, for God's sake! It happens all the time, even between people who don't know each other. Haven't you heard of the swingers who swap wives? Just because you love one person doesn't necessarily mean you can't enjoy sex with another. Right?" Only later did Beth ask herself how such utter nonsense could have spewed from her mouth.

"Wrong!" Tom gripped her shoulders and lifted her upright in bed. "I could slap you!" he gritted.

The violence of his gaze locked with the anger of hers. She sensed the power struggle within him as he fought to bring his rage under control.

"Damn you!" she shouted. She lifted her hand to hit him. He flung her down on the pillows. "You're a bastard," she hissed. She was too angry to care what he did to her.

"What are you?" He rammed his hand into his pocket,

brought out a fistful of bills, and flung them on the nightstand. "Your pay for the other night, and tonight!"

"No!"

"Yes!" He fell across her, pinning her to the bed. His strong fingers curled into the tender flesh of her upper arms.

"No!" She struggled wildly, hating him as much as she loved him, twisting and kicking, her movements hampered by the weight of the bedcovers. Rolling her head from side to side, she tried to evade his lips, but his mouth came down to ravage hers, plundering its softness and smothering her frantic cries of protest.

There was no escape. She was held so tightly that she could feel every bone in his body even through the bedclothes. The brutal kiss seemed to go on and on, and Beth wondered vaguely if this helplessness was what a woman felt when she was being attacked by a stranger. Blackness swam on the fringes of her consciousness as the strength was drained from her.

When she stopped struggling, Tom lifted his lips from her mouth and moved them to her temple. His hand moved up from her shoulder to slide beneath her head and hold it firmly in his grasp. Beth was trembling, drinking in air while her bruised lips throbbed. She could taste the blood on her tongue where he had ground her lips against her teeth. Tears spilled from her eyes. She was so steeped in misery that at first she didn't realize his lips were caressing away the wet rivulets that streamed down her face.

His lips returned to hers and she flinched from the pressure of his mouth on her cut lips. He raised his head. Beth's eyes were tightly closed, but she knew he was looking at her.

"Oh, God! Oh, sweetheart . . . What have I done?" His

husky voice broke. Beth could feel the uneven motion of his chest against her breasts, and she squeezed her eyes tightly to hold back the tears. "I'm sorry! Sweet . . . sweet . . . I'm sorry. . . ."

Gently his lips stole over her face and gradually moved to hers, pried her lips apart and began sensually to lick away the hurt. His tongue sought to heal the cut, his lips caressed, and his mustache, soft and sweetly familiar, brushed her cheek.

His tenderness offered her a release from her own frustrations, and she returned his kisses eagerly. Just for a while nothing mattered as long as he touched her, held her, and made love to her.

CHAPTER ELEVEN

"I'M SORRY! I'M sorry I hurt you, darlin'." Tom's lips traveled over her face, blotting her tears. He placed the softest of kisses on her bruised, swollen lips. "Are you okay now?"

"Yes." Beth knew she would have fought to the last breath if he had attempted to overpower her physically, but she was vulnerable to his attack of seduction. What he couldn't obtain with sheer force he could easily get with a sensual caress.

"I'm sorry." He kept repeating the words. "I'll never hurt you again. I never want to see that look of terror on your face." A groan came up from deep in his throat and he nuzzled his face into the side of her neck as if writhing in pain.

Sensations buffeted Beth in waves. The vulnerability of this man, the pleasure of his hands tracing the contours of her body, the stimulating caress of his mouth against her neck, all combined to lull her into a sensuous limbo. She was lost.

Tom lifted his head, letting the heat of his breath fan her lips. "Am I forgiven?" he murmured thickly.

"Yes," she whispered in the frustration of guilt over loving him.

Seconds later she was swept away by his deep, passionate kisses, until she didn't care anymore. Drugged with erotic sensations, Beth was only slightly aware when he moved away from her to throw back the covers so he could stretch out beside her and curl his arms and legs around her. With gentle pressure he fitted her body to his. His hand cupped her rounded bottom, his arm held her breasts crushed to his chest. She could feel his throbbing hardness and his warmth through her nightgown. He seemed content merely to hold her, and Beth fought to block out everything but this moment, this night.

"What are you thinking?" He placed sweet, chaste kisses on her mouth.

"I'm . . . pretending. . . ." The words were wrenched from her. Her hand crept up over his shoulder and her fingers moved in his hair, pulling his lips to her waiting mouth.

He drew in a long, shaky breath and stroked the hair back from her temples, his fingers caressing her cheek.

"What do you really feel for me?" he asked wearily.

She moved her hand to his chest and felt his heart thudding beneath it. The rest of him was still, with a peculiar, silent waiting. She moved restlessly against him.

"Why bring that up now? Don't you want to love me? Can't you pretend one more time?" she whispered.

"I want to love you now, tomorrow, forever. . . ." The hand on her buttocks pulled her against the surge of his groin and held her there. "But I want more than to have sex with you."

"Can't you pretend, if I can?" Her voice rose with her disappointment. She tried to push him away with her hand on his chest. She needed time to think. Something hurt inside her, and she swallowed hard.

"If that's what you want." The muttered words, barely coherent, were thickly whispered in her ear. "I'm no saint! I'll take you this way if it's all I can have." He began to stroke her, whispering words of seduction as he teased the corner of her mouth with his. "Beautiful . . . sweet . . ." His hands slid under her gown and lifted it to whisk it away. "Perfect. Your body is perfect . . . beautiful . . . heaven . . ." He muttered reverently, and kissed the rosy peak of her breast.

He left her to sit on the side of the bed. In the few seconds it took him to take off his clothes, Beth fought a battle with her pride. *No!* it screamed. He's using you to satisfy his sexual lust. What about my sexual lust? her nerves screamed back. I want him to make love to me one more time.

Her arms were open and welcomed him when he turned. The deeply buried heat in her body seemed to flare out of control. She sought his mouth hungrily and moved her hands over his sides and back, digging into the smooth muscles, loving the feel of his flesh. She felt the powerful tug of desire for him and admitted what her subconscious mind had known since the moment he entered the room. She wanted him and was glad he had come to her.

"Thomas, Thomas—" She was hungry for him and returned his caresses with all the instinctive sexuality of her young body.

"Shh . . . darlin'. Be still and let me love you." He kissed her soft rounded breasts, nibbled with his teeth, nuzzled with his lips. He was deliberately slow, giving her pleasure and at the same time pleasing himself. His lips moved to her mouth, exploring its shape and the texture of her lips and tongue until she was gasping for breath. He whispered endearments during the brief intervals when he was not taking the lips she offered so eagerly. "Sweet, sweet, darlin' girl . . ."

His hands moved over her, touching her from breast to thigh. She tangled her fingers in his hair and the strands fell across her breasts in an exquisite caress. He made small biting tracks across her shoulders and down the sides of her breast, then nibbled his way across her stomach, causing her to suck it in as wild desire swept through her. His fingers replaced his lips and traveled lower, as if compelled to know every inch of her.

Beth had never felt anything like the sensual enjoyment his seeking fingers were giving her. She knew the excruciating drive to be satisfied and to satisfy him. Her hand moved between them and enclosed the hard muscle that leaped and thrust in primitive desire.

Tom's muscular body slid over hers. It was hard, warm, and satin smooth. The velvety touch of him, hard and throbbing, nudging, seeking to fill her, started a fire that surged through the seat of her femininity, causing involuntary shudders of delight. He continued to speak to her in snatches of tender, soothing words.

"Is this what you want, my sweet love?" His fingers stroked; the tumult in her body grew. "Be mine and let me be yours," he murmured. "I'll take away that sweet ache. Be still, love. Soft is best—trust me." He entered her slowly. There were no sharp or hard thrusts. He lay still and she could feel his great body tremble with the effort it took to hold back. "Ah . . ." He sighed. He lifted his face to look at her. His green eyes were dark with feeling and burned into hers.

Beth had the strange sensation of not knowing where his body ended and hers began. She could feel the pressure deep inside her as he gradually tilted her hips while his eyes held hers. She knew at that moment she would be forever his.

"Slowly, sweetheart," he murmured as she began to move. His mouth came over her mouth, his breath and hers one. He caressed her lips with his, his tongue making little jabbing forays along the inside of her mouth. Ever so slowly he penetrated her deeper with a slow, sensuous motion.

Beth clutched him tightly and ran her hands over the warm skin of his back. Heat radiated from his body to hers, sending her into a rapture of love so exquisite it made her head spin with desire. A small sound came from her lips, and rippling tremors ran through her inner being. Her arousal intensified to so great a pitch that she thought she would cry out. Fire ran along her nerves and her eyes flew open to look directly into two bottomless green pools.

"Talk to me. Tell me what you feel."

"Oh, darling . . . I feel you everywhere!"

"Look at me. We'll soar together." He said the words slowly, carefully.

"Yes, yes . . ." Beth gazed into eyes luminous with desire, knowing that nothing would ever compare to this moment.

The strokes came with a driving, primitive rhythm; mutual strokes of belonging and possession. *Soar! Soar!* The word ricocheted through her mind as they climbed together to the cloudlike formation that cradled them. Beth's open eyes were unseeing as the world exploded and sent her spinning into warm, misty darkness. The only solid things in the universe were the arms around her, the lips that moved to cover hers, and the pulsing hardness inside her that she held cradled in the loving folds of her body. Beth felt as if her soul were reeling somewhere above her as Tom's passion erupted and filled her to the core.

They settled to earth once again. He lay with his face nestled in her tumbled hair, breathing deeply. When he finally stirred, it was to ease himself up on his elbows. He looked solemnly into wide blue eyes and reverently kissed her eyelids, one after the other, smoothing the damp hair back from her face with gentle fingers.

"Don't say anything," he murmured, and rolled onto his side, taking her with him. He reached for the covers and tucked them around them, groped for the light switch, and the room was plunged into darkness.

Beth lay tightly against his body, her head resting on his shoulder. A sigh trembled through her, and she closed her eyes. She had to sort out her emotions, untangle the confusion that had brought her to this state. She needed this time to think, but she couldn't remember a time when she was so weary in body, weary in soul, confused in mind. She stifled a groan as her mind began summoning back, in feverish detail, the words Thomas had murmured in his fever about Sarah.

The tears that trickled from her eyes rolled down her

cheeks and onto his shoulder. He slowly stroked her back in silent communication. He didn't speak, and she was glad. How could she tell him she was sick with self-disgust, sick with guilt for wanting him, sick because she knew what he felt for her was only lust.

His hand touched her gently, as though she were fragile and infinitely precious. "Are you warm?" He tucked the blanket close behind her.

"Uh-huh."

"Go to sleep." Low, husky whispers came to her ears. "Things will work out. Trust me. Things have happened too fast for you. Time will take care of it." His lips pressed tiny kisses on her forehead, his voice a shivering whisper. "This is only the beginning for us."

"No," she groaned, but the thought of never having this pleasure again was a stab of agony in her heart. "There's more to life than this."

"Give us time and we'll have it, darlin'," the seductive voice whispered in her ear. "Shh . . . sleep."

The completeness of their lovemaking had left Beth exhausted. She fell asleep almost immediately, falling into a deep, satisfying slumber. But all night long she was subconsciously aware of the warm, male body pressed to her own, the heavy weight of the arm across her body, and the hand that cupped her breast.

"Elizabeth." Her name was a soft whisper wooing her from the depths of sleep. "Wake up, Beth." The voice was a little louder, more urgent. "C'mon, sleepyhead. Wake up."

Reluctantly she opened her eyes and pushed her hair back from her face. Thomas was standing beside the bed.

"What time is it?"

"Time for you to get up if you're going to town with Herb. He'll leave in about thirty minutes." He squatted on his heels beside the bed. "You were sleeping so soundly when I got up, I didn't have the heart to wake you, although I wanted to." His eyes glittered, and his mustache tilted when he grinned. Beth rolled her face into the pillow. More than anything in the world she wanted to reach out and put her arms around his neck. "I brought you a cup of coffee. Don't you think that deserves a morning kiss?"

"Sure." She made a kissing sound with her puckered lips and reached for the mug on the table.

"Won't do." Thomas captured her reaching hand with his, leaned over her, his mouth just touching hers. "Good morning," he whispered against her lips, then increased the pressure of his moist kiss. His lips moved with incredible gentleness over her mouth. It was a giving kiss, tender, and if she didn't know better, loving. It was almost more than she could bear without bursting into tears.

He sat back on his heels and looked at her. "I've got work to do this morning, but I'll try to be here when you get back. I thought we'd have a celebration tonight to welcome Sarah home. We'll have everyone in for steaks. How does that sit with you?"

"Fine." She didn't know what else to say. Besides, she thought, why should he be asking her?

"Okay. I've got to get going." He leaned toward her and covered her lips with his. "See you later." His voice was a whisper when they finally broke the kiss. He went to the door, turned with a happy smile on his face, and winked at her.

Beth sat up in bed and reached for the coffee. She didn't understand him at all. What's more, she didn't understand herself. No wonder he was smiling, she thought angrily. The woman he loves and a mistress both under one roof; what more could he ask for?

She was still thinking the same thoughts while sitting in the station wagon beside Herb. She had very carefully gone over every word Thomas had spoken last night, and he hadn't said a word about love or a lasting relationship. All she meant to him was a warm body in bed.

"The highway is completely cleared in spots." Herb's voice cut into her thoughts. "There'll be a lot more snow in town, but they've got good equipment and a good crew. They'll have most of it hauled away by now."

"How long have you worked at the ranch?"

"About ten years, off and on."

"Then you knew Steven, Sarah's husband."

"Yeah."

Beth waited for him to say more. When he didn't, she said, "My parents and I met him when Sarah brought him home to be married. He looked an awful lot like Thomas, though not as big."

"That's where the resemblance ended. They were nothing alike." His voice was suddenly curt, and he changed the subject to remark about the new wing being added to the hospital. "It'll be there on the west side." He parked the car in a snowpacked parking lot. "When we get ready to go, you and Sarah can meet me at the emergency entrance so she won't have to walk on this snow."

The long gleaming corridors, the rattle of carts full of

dishes, and the familiar smell of medication brought a quiver of homesickness to Beth. This had been her world for a long time. She had moved in it with an awareness of all that went on, but now she was here as a visitor, and she accepted the cheerful smile given by the nurse on duty.

"Hello, Herb. Mrs. Clary is waiting for you. Are you Mrs. Clary's sister? I thought so," she said when Beth nodded. "Dr. Morrison will see you. Come this way."

Beth liked the doctor immediately. He was young, balding, and very professional. He was also very interested in Sarah's case. Beth was able to spot that at once. She could tell that he was impressed when she stated her qualifications and was able to converse with him about her sister's condition. When she left his office twenty minutes later, it was with his neatly typed instructions in her purse and his assurance the medication and the equipment she needed to give the shots would be waiting at the reception desk.

The door to Sarah's room was open when Beth reached it. Dressed in warm slacks and a heavy sweater, her blond hair combed in swirls around her carefully made-up face, her eyes bright, Sarah looked young and happy.

"Elizabeth! I'm so excited about going home. Herb said he's going to sit on me if I don't calm down."

"How are you?" Beth embraced her sister.

"Fine. Just fine now that I'm going home." Sarah turned and held out her hand to the woman beside her. "Beth, this is Jean, one of my dearest friends."

Only one word could describe Jean: plain. She was a heavyset woman with flyaway gray hair and small eyeglasses perched on her nose. When she smiled, she showed more gums than teeth, and it was evident she smiled easily. Beth took the hand she offered.

"No matter what, she'll say she's fine," Jean said, still smiling.

"I'm glad you were able to be with her," Beth murmured.

"It wasn't no chore a'tall, let me tell you. Sarah and me can always find something to talk about."

"I'll take the cases down to the car," Herb said, and picked them up.

"Did you bring the things I asked for?" Sarah asked quickly.

"Sure did." He set the bags down, reached into his pocket, and handed her a couple of small packages carefully wrapped in white tissue paper. "I picked out the ones I thought you liked best."

"Little gifts for my nurses," Sarah explained. "Herb and I made these stained-glass leaded ornaments." She unwrapped one and held it up by the string attached to the top. It was a beautiful little owl with brown wings, a blue body, and large amber eyes.

"You *made* this? It's beautiful!" Beth exclaimed.

"Herb and I together." Sarah's eyes flashed to the tall silent man standing beside the door. "Herb's very artistic."

Herb gave a snort of disgust—Beth was sure to hide his embarrassment—and picked up the cases. "I'll bring the car up to the door."

Sarah said her good-byes. It was obvious that she was a favorite patient. Nurses were still waving and smiling when the elevator door closed and they descended to the lower level.

With Sarah tucked into the front seat of the station

wagon, Beth and Jean in the back, they headed back to the ranch. Sarah and Jean exclaimed over the amount of snow that had piled up during the storm and asked questions about what had happened at home since they had been away. Beth mentioned the two stranded motorists they had picked up, and Sarah picked the details out of the usually quiet foreman. Beth thought he talked more on the ride from town than he had during the whole time she had known him, and she wondered if Sarah was aware that the man was in love with her. What were Sarah's feelings? As far as she could tell, she didn't treat him any differently from the way she treated Thomas.

When they reached the ranch yard, Herb drove down to the tenant house and let Jean out, then back to the house and pulled into the garage.

"Oh, look! Shiloh is waiting for me." Sarah opened the car door.

"Watch that hound," Herb growled. "She'll get you all wet."

"Are you glad to see me, girl? I'm glad to see you too." Sarah patted the shaggy head, and the dog wagged her tail so hard it swung her body from side to side. Sarah's happy laughter rang out and Beth caught a glimmer of a smile on Herb's face.

In the house Sarah went from room to room, looking at her plants. "They came through just fine, Beth," she called. "You didn't finish the puzzle, Herb."

"I was waiting for you," he said quietly, and continued on up the stairs with her bag.

Suddenly Beth was almost as sorry for him as she was for herself. "Would you like some lunch?" she asked when he returned. "I could scare up a sandwich and soup."

"Thanks. Then I've got to get crackin'."

"Are you going down to the south pens, Herb?" Sarah asked. "Thomas said he wouldn't be in until the middle of the afternoon."

Beth's hands trembled as she opened the soup. Thomas must have called Sarah before he left this morning.

"He drove the semi down. I'll go in the pickup and bring him back." Herb settled himself on a kitchen stool. "Now don't you two be doin' anything about the bash we're having tonight. Tom laid out steaks to thaw, Jean said she'd throw something together, and we'll microwave potatoes. After that, everyone's on their own."

"How many will be here?" Beth was trying terribly hard not to feel left out of the plans.

"Probably about twelve," Sarah said, then to Herb, "Is everyone coming?"

"As far as I know."

"Twelve?" Beth said in a worried tone.

"Don't worry. We've had as many as twenty here for supper on the spur of the moment, and my two men handled everything perfectly."

My two men. Beth slumped against the counter and kept her face turned away from the two, who continued to chat about the celebration they planned. All her life Beth had been a fighter, fighting for what she wanted, what she considered right. One time in her life she had been forced to retreat, and that was when Thomas made no attempt to get in touch with her when he came back to Wyoming after the wedding, after she had fallen so desperately in love with him and her pride had refused to allow her to get in touch with him. The hurt had not lasted nearly as long as she had expected it to. Would it be the same this time? she wondered.

She'd better begin to set the wheels in motion to get out of this house, she thought, or else she would lose her mind.

CHAPTER TWELVE

IN THE EARLY afternoon Beth thought it might be a good time to speak to Sarah about the tenant house. They had been visiting for more than an hour, getting caught up on little tidbits of family gossip. Sarah lounged in the recliner, Beth curled up on the couch.

"This is a lovely house," Beth told her sister. "You did an excellent job decorating."

"It was the therapy I needed after Steven was killed. Thomas suggested that I do it, and I think it may have saved my sanity. He gave me a free hand, and I stretched the project out for months and months." The tight lines on each side of her mouth softened a little. "Poor man. I'm surprised he didn't go stark-raving mad with the house torn up for so long. Thomas is the homebody of the Clary family," she explained. "He'd like nothing better than to marry and have a large family."

"Then why hasn't he?" Beth couldn't hold back the bite of irritation in her voice. "I doubt he'd have any trouble getting a woman."

"That's true. He's a handsome, virile man, and a beautiful person on the inside."

"Steven was handsome too."

"Yes, Steven had a beautiful exterior." Sarah turned her face away, but not before Beth caught the haunted expression in her eyes.

"I'm sorry I mentioned him. But it's been a couple of years, and I thought—"

"That part of it is all right. I'm not grieving for him. I just have not wanted to talk about that time in my life."

"It's all right. Thomas told me how he was killed."

"Thomas only told you what I asked him to tell you. Now I want you to know it all, and then maybe you'll be more comfortable about Thomas . . . and me."

Beth felt as if the props had been kicked out from under her. "But I'm not . . . I don't . . . you don't have to explain anything to me."

"I want to. I can't help but feel the hostility whenever Thomas's name is mentioned. I want you to stay here, be happy here. The best way to ensure that is to have everything out in the open. The truth is, all the time I was married to Steven, except for the first few weeks, was a living hell. He abused me terribly."

"Sarah!" Beth sat up on the couch, rigid with shocked disbelief. "You don't mean . . . I can't believe . . ." Her voice trailed away as words failed her.

"I'm just now able to talk about it. I know you'll want to know why I stayed with a man who hurt me. Everyone wants to know that. I don't know, now, why I did. At the time I was so humiliated, I couldn't bear the thought of anyone knowing. Deep down inside I felt as if I had failed somehow, or else my husband wouldn't be doing these terrible things to me."

"You could have come home. There was no reason for you to stay here and put up with that!"

"I couldn't! How could I explain to Dad that my handsome, charming husband, who treated me with such loving consideration while in the company of others, had fits of temper and beat me until there were days I couldn't get out of bed?"

"That certainly changes my opinion of the men on this place!" Beth's face was mutinous.

"No one knew about it but Jean, and she didn't find out for a long time. I made her swear not to tell. Jean is a true and loyal friend." Sarah's eyes pleaded with Beth for understanding. "Don't blame anyone but me for what happened here. I could have left him, but I was too big a coward." She paused and swallowed. "Steven was so clever. Usually there were no visible signs of his cruelties. He knew that Thomas would take me away from him if he knew how he was treating me. Thomas was the only person in the world Steven was afraid of."

"I don't know what to say. I never imagined such a thing happening to you. Women have come to the hospital with bruised and swollen faces, broken noses, ribs, arms, legs, and still insisted they loved their husbands and refused to file charges against them." Beth shuddered. "That it could happen to my own sister! How could Thomas *not* have known?" she asked angrily. "Why didn't you tell him?"

"I think Steven would have been furious with me. He always seemed to be competing with Thomas."

"Herb was here. Surely he could see what was going on."

"Herb was having trouble with his wife. She had taken their daughter to Denver and he spent every spare minute down there. Anyway, Steven never allowed me to associate with what he considered the hired help. He disliked Herb immensely and thought him inferior because Herb hasn't had much formal education. He constantly complained that Herb ignored his orders and took orders only from Thomas. The men all liked and respected Thomas, but they didn't like Steven. His explosive temper alienated them. He needed a whipping boy and I was it."

"I've seen the Clary temper in action," Beth said with cold finality.

Sarah smiled. "Thomas's little bursts of temper are nothing compared to Steven's. Thomas is aware he inherited the temper from his father and he never lets it get out of hand."

"I don't know about that." Beth told her about the unnecessary force Thomas had used on the stoned Jerry Lewis, and about the incident that took place in the cafe during the trip out from Minnesota. "He could have given that boy a concussion."

"But, Beth, dear, he was protecting you. He can't bear to see anyone being mistreated. It riles him quicker than anything." She shifted restlessly, as if her memories were painful. "The night before Steven was killed, he was in an extremely bad mood. That night, instead of beating me on the body and taking his frustrations out on me . . . sexually, he hit me in the face. It was one of the most severe beatings he had ever given me. The next morning I was lying in bed, waiting for Jean to come and help me, when Thomas came to tell me that Steven had been killed on his way to town. I could barely open my eyes to look at him. I remember saying 'I don't care, I don't care.'

"When Thomas saw my condition, and realized what his brother had done to me, he knelt down beside the bed, put his arms around me, and cried." Tears were now rolling down Sarah's cheeks. "Herb and Jean took me to the doctor while Thomas made burial arrangements for his brother. I couldn't attend the services, and I pleaded with Thomas not to notify you. I couldn't bear the thought of you seeing me in that condition. Steven's mother was on a cruise and Thomas delayed notifying her until it was too late for her to come. She had lost a son; there was no need to compound the grief. The doctor, Herb, Jean, and now you, are the only people who know about this. Thomas and I cling to each other. He's my friend, my brother, and at times, my father." Sarah's face brightened. "I think the world of him."

Sarah went upstairs to rest, and Beth sat on the couch staring into space. She couldn't bear to think of what her sister had been through, the horrible years married to Steven, the silent suffering. She didn't know how Sarah had found the courage to come through such a terrible ordeal. If only she could have helped.

Some of the questions that had nagged her had now been answered. She understood Sarah's feelings for Thomas, and why she'd seldom mentioned her late husband. And she knew the reason behind Thomas's words the night he was sick and she'd held him in her arms. But one question remained. What were Thomas's feelings for Sarah?

"Hey, girls, shake a leg. We're going to have a party!"

Beth heard Thomas's shout despite the fact that her door was closed. She had escaped to her room, having admitted to herself that she was a coward, as soon as she heard Thomas and Herb in the foyer. Now she stood before the mirror, blow-drying her hair, telling herself that understanding the bond between Thomas and her sister would make acceptance easier.

Oh, that's a crock!

A feeling strange to her nature surfaced: jealousy. Close behind that, guilt all but smothered her. She ground her teeth, despising herself, despising Thomas. There was something special about Sarah. The tragedy of her marriage and her illness would have broken a weaker woman. Sarah deserves all the happiness she can get, Beth told herself sternly.

When Sarah came down the hall to Beth's room looking so beautiful, Beth wished she had worn something else. She tugged the bulky ragknit sweater down over the hips of her jeans and felt gauche and uncomfortable.

"You look lovely. I didn't realize this was a dress-up affair."

"It isn't. But this is a special night for me, and I wanted to dress to fit the occasion." Sarah smoothed her long, maroon velvet skirt, then plucked nervously at the maroon ribbon around the stand-up collar of her frilly white blouse. "Do you think the colors match well enough? Poor Jean hunted all over Cody to find this ribbon."

"It matches your skirt perfectly. But don't you think I should change? I didn't bring a long skirt, but I could wear a dress."

"You're fine just as you are. Oh, Elizabeth, what I wouldn't give to be your age again!" A few seconds later Sarah laughed lightly. "I don't mean that. I wouldn't want to live the last five years over again. This is the happiest time of my life."

And the unhappiest time of mine. Beth kept the thought screened from her face as she kissed her sister's cheek. "Let's go. The Marshall sisters will wow'em tonight."

Beth looked down from the top of the steps and met Thomas's measured look. He stood watching them without a flicker in his eyes to hint at his thoughts. It was the first time she'd seen him since he had left her room early that morning. Butterflies began a boisterous dance in her stomach.

"Careful of the stairs."

"Yes, Father." Sarah's happy laughter rang out.

"Hold onto the railing," he cautioned.

"Thomas and Herb are so afraid I'll fall down these steps that they've forbidden me to come down them unless one of them is here."

"They're right, you know. You shouldn't be using the stairs."

"Hi." The smile on Thomas's face was beautiful. His brilliant green gaze shifted from one sister's face to the other's, then settled on Sarah's. "Welcome home," he said softly, and kissed her cheek. "My, my, don't you look pretty tonight. Did you get all dressed up for me?" His eyes flashed at Beth, and she desperately wished she had worn something more glamorous.

"Sure," Sarah quipped. "I've got to make sure you don't throw me over for my pretty, little sister."

Beth felt the pressure of emotions rising in her throat. Relax, she told herself. Stop being an idiot—Sarah doesn't know.

"I've got a big heart. There's room for both of you." Thomas moved between them and, with an arm around each, led them into the family room.

Informality was the rule. Beth felt much better about her attire when she saw that every person in the room, including Jean, was wearing jeans and flannel shirts. Flushed and smiling, Sarah greeted everyone and introduced Beth. The names failed to register individually, but collectively they were Jim, Shorty, Frosty, Melvin, and so on, until Beth no longer tried to remember them. Everyone seemed genuinely fond of Sarah and greeted her as if she were returning from a trip around the world. Beth left her with her friends and slipped into the kitchen to offer assistance to Jean.

"Land sakes, no! You're company tonight. I've done 'bout all I'm goin' to. Tom's got the grill goin' in the garage and after a while we'll put on the steaks." Jean's small dark eyes circled the room. "Everybody's here but Herb. He ought to be comin' along."

The ranch hands seemed to be perfectly at home in their boss's house. They milled around, laughing, teasing Sarah about her plants. One of them put a fresh log on the fire, kicked at the grate with his booted foot to shake down the ashes, and replaced the screen. Beth kept her back turned to whichever group Thomas was in, not wanting to meet his eyes, wanting more time to build a barrier against the hurt that was bound to come.

For several minutes she had been aware that Thomas was stalking her. Finally, when there was nowhere else to go, she stopped circulating and waited. He came up behind her, slipped an arm around her, and rested his hand on her hipbone. Beth lowered her eyes and carefully studied the plates and silver laid out on the countertop.

"How did your day go?" The query was a whisper in her ear.

"Very well. Yours?"

"Busy." A pause. "Are you avoiding me?"

"Hey, Tom, where're the tongs for the salad bowl?" Jean's intervention was a godsend.

Herb came in carrying a large bucket filled with snow and bottles and set it on the counter. Sarah came to greet him, her face radiant. He smiled happily down at her. Beth moved sideways along the counter until she could stand with her back to the wall, watching, but being out of the way.

"Gather 'round, you hungry crowbait." Thomas's voice boomed across the room. "Step up and get a glass. I've an announcement to make."

"Well, I'll be a humpbacked maverick! The boss has bought us champagne!" Charlie, the bowlegged cowboy, led the way to the bar.

Queasiness knotted in Beth's stomach. She stood straight and still while the iron taste of fear rose in her mouth. Fear of what? She didn't have time to answer herself.

The cork flew from the bottle.

Jean jumped and squealed.

The men laughed.

Everyone started to talk at once.

"Step up and get a glass." Thomas spoke to the group in general, but his eyes were on Beth.

She moved into the circle. Someone handed her a glass and reached for another. Beth smiled, feeling like a comet on a collision course.

Thomas held up his glass and waited until the room was quiet. Beth couldn't see his face because he had turned to her sister. Sarah's face was glowing as she looked at him.

"First, I want to say welcome home, Queeny. This ranch isn't the same place without you, love." He kissed her solemnly on the forehead. "Now for the big news." He paused at just the right time and glanced around to make sure he had everyone's attention. His eyes rested briefly on Beth and a handsome, brilliant smile covered his face. Her heart jerked painfully.

"It is with very great pleasure that I announce the engagement and approaching marriage of my lovely sister-in-law, Sarah Clary, to Mr. Herb Rogers. Drink to their future together."

A full ten seconds of quiet followed the announcement. During that time Beth wasn't conscious of taking a breath. She stared at her sister, whose face was lifted for her fiancé's kiss. Her beautiful blond head was nestled against his shoulder, his arms closed protectively around her. Beth couldn't remember ever seeing anyone more radiantly happy.

With tears blurring her vision, she moved forward and embraced both of them. "I'm so happy for you."

"Thank you, darling."

"Why didn't you tell me?" Beth was trying not to cry. She kissed Sarah's cheek, then Herb's. "Welcome to the family. There are three of us now."

"I've loved Herb for a long time," Sarah said, darting loving looks at the tall dark man. "I wouldn't marry him though, until Dr. Morrison assured me my disease was in remission. Thank God, it is!"

"When is the wedding?"

"Soon. Very soon," Herb said emphatically.

Someone came up to pound Herb on the back and offer his congratulations. It gave Beth the excuse to move away. She desperately needed to be alone to blot her eyes and wipe her nose. She walked quickly into the dimly lit living room and stood at the bay window. The yardlight lit the snow-covered landscape, but all she could see was a teary girl reflected in the window.

Beth's mind was having difficulty grasping and holding onto all that had occurred. *Sarah and Herb!* It could so easily have been Sarah and Thomas. Tears spurted anew. Thomas seemed genuinely pleased that Sarah was going to marry his foreman. Were his feelings being carefully covered, as hers would have been if he'd been the one who was going to marry Sarah? She dabbed at her eyes again, knowing that she should join the celebration going on in the kitchen.

"What's the matter? Why the tears?" Thomas was behind her. He pulled her back against him and pressed his cheek to her wet one. "Aren't you happy for Sarah?" His voice was dear and raspy, and she cried harder.

"Of course I'm happy for her," she said between sniffs. "I wish someone had told me."

"They didn't decide until last night. Herb said they

talked for hours on the phone after the doctor told Sarah there was no reason why she couldn't live a reasonably normal life, and maybe in time they'll have a cure for MS. Herb is the best man I know, honey. I wouldn't want anything but the best for your sister." Beth was so choked with feeling that she couldn't talk. "Herb's walking ten feet off the ground," Thomas told her with a chuckle. "He's going to remodel the house down there, make it larger, and have everything on one floor to make it easier for Sarah. She owns a third of the ranch, you know, but Herb isn't one of those men whose pride would keep him from the woman he loves."

"Don't you love her too?" It had to be said. Beth couldn't bear the uncertainty any longer.

"Of course I do. I love her very much. She's the sister I always wanted." He turned her in his arms and lifted her face to his with a firm finger beneath her chin. "Don't tell me you thought I was in love with Sarah."

"You talked about her in your sleep the night you were sick. Naturally I thought that you—"

"What did I say?"

"You said you'd take care of her. That no one needed to know. . . ."

"What else?"

"That's about all. I know, now, why you said it. Sarah told me, but . . ."

"Say it, Elizabeth. I'm tired of you jumping to conclusions and making my life miserable." He gripped her arms and held her away from him so he could stare down into her face.

"I didn't know . . . I don't know where I stand with you!" she blurted.

"Is that the reason for the on-and-off treatment you've been giving me? You thought I was in love with your sister and yet I'd make love to you? I could shake you! Dammit, what kind of a man do you think I am? You put me through hell!" He gave her a couple of shakes and pulled her into his arms. His angry face loomed above hers. He lifted her arms and placed first one and then the other around his neck. "Tell me that you love me, Elizabeth." His eyes met hers and held them steadily. "You love me, so say so, dammit!"

"You big jerk! Do you think I'd go to bed with you if I didn't?" She watched his face. The frown fell away, and his eyes began to sparkle as smile lines fanned from the corners.

"You ornery little mule! You stubborn, cantankerous, little jackass! Say it!"

"No! Not till you do."

"So help me God, Beth, I'll turn you over my knee. Say it!" He moved his hands down to her hips, his fingers digging into her soft flesh, and jerked her against him so tightly that she could feel the movement of his arousal between them. He turned the full impact of a coaxing smile on her, and she gave in.

"I love you, you . . . peabrain! If you had half the sense you were born with, you'd have seen that I've been eating my heart out for you since the day I drove out of Rochester with you. Stop laughing!"

"Kiss me, Beth."

"And before that, when you came to the wedding—"

"You were just a baby. I was waiting for you to grow up—"

"I was nineteen. You broke my heart!"

"I liked you a lot, but I wasn't ready to settle down. I had to be careful of you because of Sarah. But when I saw you again, it was like I'd been kicked in the stomach by a mule. I tried to tell you, when I sang to you, that day in the truck."

"Will you sing to me again?"

"I don't know. You've put me through the wringer these last few days. Kiss me and stop talking so much—"

"You deserved it—" His kisses swept her words away.

"I love you, darlin'. I thought you knew that. I told you plenty of times," he whispered in her ear, flicking his tongue around the rim. "I'll take care of you always. I'll never hurt you, darlin'." He turned his head to look into her star-bright eyes.

"You don't have to tell me that," she said breathlessly.

"I want to tell you. You never have to worry that I'm like Steven." He held her, eagerly exploring her mouth, before easing her back a few inches so he could see her face.

"I know. I love you."

"I love you." His hands tightened on her hips. "But you're dangerous. How can I go back in there in this condition and tell that bunch there's going to be another wedding?" He cocked one eyebrow in mocking inquiry.

Beth ran nimble fingers over the evidence of his discomfort. "Did I cause *that?*" she wailed.

"Stop that! I'll never be in shape to go back to our guests." It was his turn to wail, but his mouth widened in a slow, satisfied smile.

"Let's not tell them yet," she whispered impishly. "We don't want to steal the spotlight from Sarah and Herb. We'll have our party later."

"Are you propositioning me?" Laughter gleamed in his eyes.

"You bet!"

"Your room or mine?" He kissed her thoroughly and slipped his hand beneath her sweater, searching for her breast with long warm fingers. "I want you to get rid of this thing." His fingers plucked at her bra.

"Now, stop that! Get your sneaky fingers out of there. Someone may come in." Beth's indignant protest turned into a groan of pleasure, then faded into nothingness when she tilted her head to look at his face. It was all there—all the love she had dreamed about. "I wish we didn't have to go back to the party—"

"Beautiful idiot! You're no help at all."

Book Two

Gentle Torment

CHAPTER ONE

LINDY CLOSED THE door behind her and hurried down the hall, her footsteps echoed by the music and laughter from the party going on inside. She let herself out into the welcome silence of the long corridor that led to the office section of the camp. One of several in northern Alaska, the camp was built to accommodate the nearly one thousand workers who had come north to work for the oil companies and their suppliers.

A gas flare illuminated the area outside the ultramodern structure, and reflected in the small windows set along the corridor. The dim light outlined her gliding figure, slender, with short straight hair, almond-shaped eyes and delicate black brows.

When Lindy had first arrived, awed by the look of lunar landscape in the stark sophistication of the camp, she felt as if she was entering a space station of the future. Oblivious to her surroundings now, she unlocked the door and let herself into the office. The temperature outside was in the fifty-below range. The frigid wind swept the snow over the bleak landscape, but the office was warm and quiet. Lindy was relieved to be away from the rooms she shared with three other girls, anticipating three or four hours of blessed quiet to work on her canvases.

When she first came north it had seemed an ideal situation to share the two bedrooms and sitting room. It was cheaper than a private room and, after all, she was here to make and save as much money as she could in the shortest possible time. The arrangement had been a learning experience for her and, although she was usually able to adjust to most situations, she couldn't get used to the new morality the girls seemed to take for granted. The party tonight was almost the last straw. The last thing she wanted to do was spend her evening sitting in the darkened sitting room fending off the advances of the sex-starved steelworker Peggy's friend had brought along for her. He tried to pull her down on his lap as she passed and grinned cheekily when she jerked away from him.

"What's wrong with you?" he asked curiously. "Why do you think I'm here? To look, but not touch?"

"You're not here by my invitation."

He tilted his head to one side, his long hair almost reaching his shoulder, and a smile of cynical amusement came over his rather good-looking face. Confidently unabashed, he lowered one eyelid in what he intended to be a flirtatious wink.

"Okay by me, doll. If you don't want to play there's plenty that do."

"Then I suggest you find them," she snapped.

He was undaunted. "You know, you're something else!" He stood up and tried to grasp her wrist.

"You're right. I am something else." She evaded him easily.

"If you're worried about the little woman, doll . . . don't. She's happy with the big check she gets every month." He grinned cockily.

"You're contemptible." All the scorn she felt for him and his kind was reflected in her voice.

"Yeah?" The smile said he was proud of it. "Maybe I am, but I'm not a frigid iceberg like you."

"It may surprise you to know that I'm not interested in what you are."

In the bedroom she packed her painting supplies in a tote bag and allowed herself one brief thought of Jake. How lucky she was that she discovered his true character before she was tied down with children like the wife of the conceited ass in the other room. Yet . . . at times her heart ached almost unbearably and she wished with all her heart that things could have been different for her and Jake.

Laying out paints, sketches and brushes in the office, she adjusted the light and was soon absorbed in her work. This canvas would be added to the growing inventory she was accumulating for the opening of her needlework shop when she saved enough money to go back home to Houston. Some evenings she painted in the small bedroom she shared with Peggy, but tonight she had received a broad hint the room would be occupied.

Time went so fast when she was doing the thing she loved most that it seemed she had been working only minutes when she heard the click of the doorknob. It would be Amos, her boss. When he guessed she would be here in the evenings he would come to work quietly at his desk, to be near her, to walk her back to her room later. Quiet, reserved and patient—also unmarried—he would be the ideal man for her . . . if she wanted a man. She shouldn't have let him start making love to her. He had kissed her—and it hadn't ended the way he'd so fervently desired! She was slightly ashamed, afterward, that she hadn't halted his ardent attempts sooner. She liked him, but that was all. He was good, sweet and kind to her, and she didn't want to hurt him. It was a problem she didn't exactly know how to handle.

Lindy wanted no attachments. She had had enough of philandering men to last two lifetimes: a father who made her mother's life miserable and a husband who broke her heart with his infidelities just months after the wedding. It had been like the end of the world for her, as if she had walked off a cliff, or been hit by a tornado. She had wanted to scream and tear her hair, but she had done neither of those things. She did the only thing possible for her to do. She left him.

"Hello, Amos." She wished he hadn't come. She wished she didn't know how he felt about her. Life could be so damned complicated at times.

There was no answer. No sound at all. The silence became obvious. Reluctantly she turned, ready to give him a tender smile to mask her feelings. Her gaze clashed head-on with the man standing there. She blinked. Oh, my God! Had she lost her mind? She took a deep breath and held it for an eternity while she stared.

"Disappointed?" The voice! It caused her spine to sag. She hadn't heard it for two years. She sat there stupidly, her emotions like a crazy seesaw, struggling for words.

"Jake?" she choked. He stood there looking at her. Why didn't he say something? "Jake! What are you doing here?"

"Why shouldn't I be?" As if that was sufficient explanation, he moved toward her, glancing around the room. Then he stood still again and stared at her.

She moved uncomfortably and her pulse raced under the intense scrutiny. He must be as shocked to see her as she was to see him. On the other hand he didn't appear to be shocked at all. Two years was a long time and a lot had happened to both of them. But . . . oh, her eyes seemed glued to his face.

"This is a surprise." Her throat was tight and she just barely managed the words. Surprise wasn't the right word, it sounded so trite, but she had to say something.

"Is it?" Mocking words that dripped with sarcasm.

"You haven't changed!" she flared, finding release in anger. "Still as arrogant and impossible as ever." It had been a long struggle to erase his image from her subconscious. Night after night she had dreamed of him, despising herself for her inability to control her mind. Lately she had begun to believe she had escaped him, would never see him again. And now this . . .

"Leave it," he said coolly. "You've made your opinion of me clear. I didn't come here to start the war all over again."

He turned to remove his coat and hung it on the rack beside the door. He was a tall man; leaner and more muscular than in the old days. The mustache gave him a mature, worldly look, also missing in the old days. His light-brown curly hair was sun-streaked and his skin brown from a tropical sun. He was the only man she had ever known with hair like that and with ice-blue eyes that turned green when emotionally aroused. Although her love for him died when she discovered his betrayal, he still remained the most fascinating man she had ever known. She had been twenty- two and helpless with adoration. Now she was twenty-five and far more capable of assessing a man.

"How are you?"

"Fine." She didn't look at him. What the hell did he care? He hadn't been in touch with her in two years.

His eyes assessed her critically, moving over the short, shiny brown hair that fit her head like a cap to the widely spaced blue eyes with their dark fringe of lashes. His eyes narrowed as he gazed at her mouth and her lips trembled at the image that came swiftly to mind: Jake probing hungrily, Jake taking possession of her mouth. Letting his gaze travel to the firm breast rounding out the sweater she wore, he smiled a secret smile and she burned with resentment. Slowly, coolly he let his eyes roam over her from the narrow waist on down over slim hips and long legs to the tips of her boots and back to her eyes now sparkling with indignation.

"You're thinner."

She did her best to return his gaze coolly. What she really wanted was to tell him to get out and not come back. She felt tears close to the surface now. How long could she hold them back? Instead, she repeated flatly, "I asked what you were doing here, Jake."

"To see you. What else?"

"You needn't have come to ask for your freedom. I offered you that when you made it plain you needed more than one woman. Papers are waiting with your attorney. All you have to do is sign them and the proceedings will be started."

"Is that why you think I'm here? You're as far off the track as you ever were."

"You came all this way to tell me that?" Her bitter gaze locked with his while her mouth tightened with anger. "Well, you've said it. Satisfied?"

Jake raised dark eyebrows. "What are you doing in the office at this time of night?"

"It's none of your damned business." Defiance blazed in her eyes. "But if you must know, I'm here because it's quiet and I can work on my paintings."

"What paintings?"

"Needlepoint canvases. I plan to open a shop when I go back to Houston . . . if I go back to Houston."

His brows came together in a frown she recognized as one of displeasure and a little pleased flutter punctuated her already rapid heartbeat.

"I'm sorry about your mother." She didn't look at him. She knew he meant what he said. He had been wonderful to her mother. She would always owe him for that.

"Do you have a man in your life?" Jake could never be accused of being tactful if there was something he wanted to know.

"After my father? After you?" She looked at him as if he had lost his mind. Her face was tight with emotion and her blue eyes, though slightly misty, looked defiantly into his.

"Bull!" He muttered the word, but she heard it. Almost casually he walked over to where her paintings lay on the desk. "Very good." He picked up a canvas and held it at arm's length. "A whooping crane?"

"Yes. I'm doing a series of birds." Her voice was strained.

"Have you turned frigid, Lindy?"

Her back stiffened with surprise and her head came up. Her voice, when it came, quavered with anger.

"What do you mean by that?"

"The party in your room. Why aren't you there?"

He heard her catch her breath and turned to see the color rising up her neck to cover her face.

"I'm still the prudish spoilsport I was, Jake Williamson! I still have a few old-fashioned principles. I don't smoke pot and I don't sleep around!" Her voice was shrill and didn't sound like her own.

"Regular saint, aren't you?" He made it sound as if it was something disgusting. "You've got some pretty tarnished friends, saint."

"They're not my friends. I was assigned to the rooms when I came here to work. They just happened to be here at the same time I am." Damn him . . . she didn't have to defend herself to him.

"Why did you come up here? You had a good job in Houston and the allowance I paid into your account was substantial." He picked up the stack of designs and looked at each one carefully.

"I took my personal account to another bank. The money you paid into the joint account is there waiting for you. I don't want it. I came here to make the big money, the same reason everyone comes here. In a few months I'll have enough to open my shop and I'll go home."

"The main reason you came here was to get away from your father so you wouldn't have to see him and his new wife." He said this casually while still looking at her designs.

She didn't answer and he turned to look at her stricken

face. Her eyes were bright with tears. Push . . . push . . . push! Wasn't he going to leave her anything?

"I thought so. You see I know you very well, Mrs. Williamson."

She wanted to snatch her designs out of his hand and run out of this place. But the party wouldn't be over for several hours yet. And . . . how did he know about the party? Damn, damn him! He'd always been able to figure out everything about her; how to touch on just the right nerve to stir her up to say things better left unsaid. In the three short months before they were married and during the six months they lived together they had shared every thought. With him she had reached her greatest happiness and her greatest despair. After two years she had adjusted to life without him and here he was again, in living color, and with no effort at all, he was stirring up emotions she had long thought dead.

"Don't you have a girl waiting for you, Jake? Waiting in some dingy little apartment?" She wanted to pierce his calm shell.

"Is that what you thought of ours, Lindy? A dingy little apartment?" She ignored him and was shocked at the bitterness in his voice when he added, "Why do you ask? You didn't want me."

"I never ran with the pack, Jake."

"Don't rake over old coals." He was upset now. Had she finally gotten to him? "And to satisfy your curiosity, I've got women stashed all over. I'm a regular Bluebeard! I take four to six women to bed every day and a dozen virgins on Sunday!"

She sucked in her breath and bent her head as if

concentrating on her work, but was intensely aware of him moving about the office.

"Tell me about this company."

"Amos Linstrom is the manager. I'm sure he can explain the company better than I."

"I doubt that. What's your job?"

"Same work I've always done—bookkeeping, payroll, tax, log sheets and anything else that needs to be done."

"What's in the thermos?" His way of changing the subject was so familiar she didn't even stop to think about it.

"Hot cocoa, but I only have one cup." She shook the bottle. The action was unnecessary. The bottle was almost full.

He grinned. "I don't mind."

She poured the steaming liquid, but made no move to hand it to him. He picked up the cup and turned it to the spot where a faint trace of lipstick was visible. Looking directly into her eyes he ran the tip of his tongue lightly over the rim of the cup before he drank. His eyes sparkled at her, his lips twitched in an effort not to laugh. He was flirting with her, but it wasn't going to work! Lindy felt a small impulse to smile indulgently at his efforts.

"You still haven't said what you're doing up here." She tried to make her voice sound casual, uncaring.

He ignored the question and asked one of his own. "Is there anyplace open where a man can get a meal?"

"The bar and restaurant never close."

"How about coming with me?"

"No."

"Afraid to come?" he taunted.

"Why should I be afraid?" She deliberately chose to

misunderstand his meaning. "You may want to cut my throat, but you won't."

"You know what I mean. Are you afraid you may have some feeling for me after all this time?" His tone was teasing.

"You flatter yourself."

"You may as well come along. It's too early to go back to your room." He was laughing at her now and not even trying to hide it.

"No." Picking up her pencil, she bent over the sketch, but her hand was too rigid to move.

"Suit yourself." Her eyes raked her, then rested on her trembling lips. After a full thirty seconds to take in the sight of her he turned and shrugged into his coat and she had to suffer another going over by those piercing blue eyes. Then he was saying in a demanding, grating voice, "Stay here until I get back."

A burst of almost hysterical laughter rose in her throat. It was unbelievable, but there he stood . . . commanding her! She glared at him defiantly. Her feeble attempt to defy him was short-lived. His eyes narrowed and his mouth compressed into a grim line.

"Well?" he demanded through clamped teeth.

She swallowed and nodded her head and hated herself for doing it. He opened the door and went out.

That one grated word almost shattered her control. Tears stung her eyes, but she dashed them away impatiently. She had done enough weeping over Jake Williamson: she wasn't going to let the tears start again, no matter what happened. Although he hadn't said so, there was only one reason why he could be here—he had met someone else and was ready for the divorce. Two years was a long time for a man like Jake. Time for him to meet dozens of women. Then the thought crossed her mind that he wouldn't have come all this way if it was just a divorce he wanted.

The shock was evaporating now, but deep tremors of unease still chased through her body as she was forced to relive those days of agony, when each day seemed to stretch like an eternity.

The only child of an unhappy, mismatched couple, Lindy had known from an early age her parents had problems. She had watched her mother become sullen and withdrawn as the years went by. She didn't remember ever spending a weekend, during her childhood, with both her parents. In later years her mother lived in a small world of her own, a fantasy world where she was happy and content.

Hers had been a story-book romance. Jake owned a small transport company and they met when he came to the office where she was employed by a friend of his. "Lindy and Jake," he had said. "I like the sound of it. We go together." They had been drawn to each other as steel to a magnet and married a few months later. He was everything to her. Jake was Jake. He was kinder, smarter, sexier, more loving and understanding than she had imagined a man could be. She firmly believed he would never hurt her, be unfaithful, disappoint her. Lindy understood things like unfaithfulness and disappointment after watching her father flaunt his "flings," grinding them into her mother's heart until he broke it. They had a private language, she and Jake. They laughed at each other's bad jokes, remembered things that mattered and were inclined to accept each other as they were. He was hers. Her husband, lover, best friend.

There had been nothing unusual about the beginning of that day, nothing to warn Lindy that a change was about to twist her life. In the months to come she would clearly remember everything that happened, every little minor detail, and relive them over and over again.

She sat in the living room long after the girl had left. She was waiting for something. Something that would make things right again. This couldn't be happening. Not really. Jake would come home and it would be as it was yesterday, last week, last month. He knew how she felt about being faithful. The girl claimed he had stayed with her each week when he went through Orange, had done so for months, had made her pregnant. She was in love with him, had gone off the pill deliberately so she would get pregnant, sure he would marry her. Jake! Oh, God, no! He had broken his promise! He had come home to her after sleeping with another woman. He had pretended love for her. Oh, God, she had to find out for sure. But who would tell her? Liz? Liz had worked for Jake for several years. Lindy didn't really like Liz. There wasn't anything she could put her finger on. Liz seemed to be too possessive with Jake, but she was an ambitious woman and that could account for it.

She drove to the office, her desperation making her reckless and oblivious to the horns that blared their irritation as the small Pinto sped through the streets. She ran up the steps of the loading dock, burst into the office and confronted the cool, smiling, attractive blond whom Jake had dubbed his "right arm." When she left a half hour later, her body weary, her mind tortured, Liz's words were ringing in her ears.

"I'm sorry you had to find out this way, Lindy. All the fellows know . . . just go out and ask any of them. They'll tell you it's true because they do the same. It's the nature of the men on the road. Don't take it so hard, honey. You'll get used to it. No one woman is ever going to satisfy Jake. That's why I didn't encourage a permanent relationship with him. Go on back home and make a good dinner. You'll have him most of the time."

A wave of sickness rose in Lindy. Liz didn't care at all that her world had crumbled. Was she imagining that Liz looked pleased? Liz and Jake? No! Jealousy was causing her to lose her mind.

"Most of the time . . . most of the time." All the while she was throwing her things in a case the words went through her mind. Tears almost blinded her as she wrote about the girl from Orange who was having his baby. On her way out of the apartment she dropped the note on the kitchen table.

She had gone to Debra, her friend of many years, the only person in the world she could turn to. Debra had urged her to see Jake, to confront him with his betrayal, but she had refused and locked herself in a room while he banged on the door with his fist. She lay on the bed, rigid, her fist pressed against her mouth.

The doorknob went sailing across the room an instant before the door flew open. Jake set the large sledgehammer beside the door and came toward her. There was nothing warm or soft about the expression on his face. He stared at her for a moment without speaking. The savage flame in his eyes spoke for him.

"You would take the word of some cheap floozie over mine?"

"Do you deny you've slept with her?"

"No," he said heavily. "I can't deny that."

The admission felt like a dagger plunging into her heart. She looked at him with quivering torment, hatred in her eyes.

"You could go to . . . her after me?" Anger dried her tears. "Do you expect me to ignore what you've done? I'll hate you till the day I die for doing this to me." She was shaking uncontrollably with the desire to hit him.

"I was with her one time. Before I met you." His eyes were sharp and narrow, searching her face. He had made a flat statement. She could either believe him or not.

"You forget I've seen her, talked to her. I've . . ." She broke off there. A tiny ray of hope had begun to burn in her heart. His words were so simple, so sincere. He hadn't played on her love for him, or made elaborate denial.

"Do you believe me, Lindy?" She saw the tremor pass over his face. His eyes fastened onto her eyes. "Lindy?" He sounded ill, but he couldn't be. She was the one dying inside.

Her throat hurt. She swallowed. "I want to believe you." There was shock and pain in her eyes.

"Darling," he whispered and sat down on the bed. "Darling," he said again as she abandoned her pride and went into his arms. Her eyes were damp, but no more than his. This was the Jake she loved. He felt so good, smelled so good. He felt and smelled like Jake. She was home. They kissed again and again with a hunger that made them shake.

"I was scared, babe. I was so damned scared I'd lost you." He rocked her gently in his arms. "Life would be damned lousy without you." He took a deep breath and held her tightly to him as he slowly stroked her hair.

"I love you." There were tears in her eyes and in his.

"I know, and I love you." He looked down at her, smiled tiredly and whispered. "Let's get out of here and go home."

Jake opened the door to their apartment, clasped her hand and led her through the darkened rooms to their bedroom. Once inside, they reached blindly for each other, each wanting to love and be loved, possess and be possessed. Wherever he touched her, Lindy felt sweet waves of desire, at first gentle, then growing in urgency as they tasted and savored each other. Finally, with his arms holding her firmly, insistently, against him, together they felt the world fall away as they reached that ultimate moment of ecstasy. Afterward, her face buried in the curve of his shoulder and neck, inhaling the familiar smell of him, they lay side by side, touching, kissing, murmuring to each other.

After a time Jake said gently, "You've got to know, honey, that girl couldn't possibly be carrying my child." Lindy wanted to believe him. She had to believe him or lose her mind. "She was in the office today when I got back from Dallas. I recognized her, but didn't know the mischief she'd been up to. She's just a girl, sweetheart, who travels the highways in a motor home with a citizens'-band radio. One night, in a rest area, she crawled into the cab with me and, feeling in the mood, I took what she offered. When I realized how young she was I gave her some money and a stern lecture on the dangers of highway soliciting. It was before I met you, honey. Long before I met you. I don't know how she found me, but I don't owe her a thing. Not a damn thing!"

Lindy tried to banish the incident from her mind, but the oneness they had shared before was missing. Jake was attentive and his whole attitude indicated that he felt the misunderstanding was behind them. Lindy, on the other hand, had a deep-seated ache in the center of her body, a jealous ache she recognized with reluctant dismay. She wanted to be immune to it, but every glance, every softly spoken word that passed between Jake and an attractive woman, brought it all back.

The days of wine and roses were over. The heady bliss of life with Jake was being destroyed bit by bit. Lindy, tormented by jealousy, realized that Jake had no idea what his flirtatious ways were doing to her. Still, she could not help what she felt. She was hungry for possession of every little corner of her husband's heart and resentful of any other demands on him.

It all came to an abrupt ending on the night the company held a welcoming-back party for one of the drivers who had been injured and spent several months in the hospital. It was Liz's party from beginning to end. She reserved a small darkened room at the Holiday Inn, ordered the food, the drinks, and arranged for dance music. She shone, glittered in a skintight evening pants suit. She played the hostess, seeing to everyone's comfort, especially Jake's. Liz, all smiles and fluttering lashes, was treated by Jake with a teasing indulgence that pricked at Lindy's heart. The men teased, fondled and danced with her while Lindy and the other wives sat quietly by and danced only when their husbands asked them. By one o'clock Lindy wanted to go home. Jake wanted to stay. He and Liz had been giving their version of dances from the thirties and forties. It was evident they had danced together quite a lot.

"Don't be a party pooper, sweetheart." Jake stood swaying, one arm flung across Liz's shoulders. "I can't leave yet." He had drunk far too much. Lindy had never seen him this drunk before.

At two o'clock she left alone. She went to bed tense, filled with anger and jealousy, but sleep overtook her anyway. When she awoke it was five o'clock and she was still alone. Slipping out of bed, she went down the hall to the living room and the image of what she found there haunted her day and night for months; Jake, his face flushed in sleep, his hair tousled, lay entwined with Liz on the couch. His head was pillowed on her bare breast. The girl smiled triumphantly as she looked across the room at Lindy.

Lindy gave a choked gasp of pain as if a knife had been plunged into her stomach. She knew, of course, it was the end. Jake had sworn fidelity and she had tried to believe him. Her own blindness now infuriated her.

When she came out of her bedroom carrying a suitcase Liz was dressed and sitting in a chair beside the couch.

"Bye," she said softly.

Lindy checked into a small hotel, wildly furious at being caught in the same trap as her mother. Jake relayed messages through Debra that she was childishly immature to kick up a fuss over one drunken spree, that she should have enough love for him to forgive and forget. Lindy lost all hope and filed for divorce, sending him word she never wanted to see him as long as she lived.

Shortly after that a card came in the mail. It was unsigned and and simply read, "Never is a long, long time."

Jake left the country almost immediately. Her lawyer sent the necessary papers to his lawyer to be forwarded for his signature and each time she had inquired she received the same answer. He had not been able to locate Jake.

Fighting to regain her composure before Jake returned, Lindy dried her eyes and reapplied her makeup. Determined to stay aloof, she intentionally brought to mind the picture of the young girl standing nervously in the doorway of their apartment. The picture of Liz and Jake on the couch was too painful, too humiliating to remember.

She heard the door open and close, but didn't look up from her desk. Jake took off his coat and came to stand beside her. He set a brown sack on the sketch she was working on and she was forced to look up. He drew up a chair, sat down, and moved the sketch to a nearby table. Ripping the sack down the side, he laid out sandwiches and french-fried potatoes.

"I only have one cup," he said, and uncapped a Styrofoam cup of steaming coffee. "We can share it."

She tried not to look at him. He was deliberately antagonizing her.

"Eat," he commanded. "You're beautiful, but too skinny."

"You're taking a lot on yourself." She had had all his arrogance she could take. "A . . . mistake from my past trying to change my eating habits."

He was silent for so long that she looked up and surprised the shadow of pain in his gaze, then his eyes narrowed.

"You think that's what I am? A mistake?" She had touched a raw spot. Resentment burned in his eyes.

"What else would you be, Jake?" She enjoyed seeing him on the hook for a change.

"Lover?" He was back in control.

"Certainly not!" Angrily she pushed the sandwich across the desk toward him.

He laughed aloud. "You've become bitchy, little pussycat. It doesn't suit that angel face." The sandwich was back in front of her. "Eat and stop hating me. I'm not your father."

"But very much like him!" Sparks of anger glittered in her eyes.

Jake expelled a heavy breath and reached out and grasped her wrist. "Don't ever say that to me again!"

His sharp words whipped her like a lash, and tears sparkled on her long lashes. The blue circles from her previous weeping were already painted under her eyes. She shook her head and started to say something. Her mouth opened and she closed it again. She took a breath and braced her thin shoulders defensively.

"Regardless of what you think about me, never again tell me I'm like your father. I'm me, Jake Williamson, and nobody else."

She turned her face up to meet his accusing stare. She had regained a measure of control, and although her eyes were still swimming with tears, her mouth was taut and there was an air of unconscious dignity about her poised head.

"You're a . . . bastard, Jake." The words came out quietly.

"Don't talk like that. The Lindy I knew would have never said that!" Now he was the one who was ill at ease.

"That Lindy is dead, Jake. You killed her. I'm no longer the stupid, trusting little soul you once knew."

His gaze flicked to the set, defiant face, then to the red marks his fingers had made on her arm.

"You're talking nonsense and you know it." Her slender fingers whitened as they gripped the cup she was holding. Her wide gaze traveled to his face. "Can't you accept my apology?"

She betrayed surprise at the question. "For what?"

"Not for what you're thinking," he said curtly. "I didn't mean to grasp your arm so tightly."

She stared steadily at some point beyond him as she said slowly, "It's all right. I don't break easily."

He rubbed his fingertips slowly back and forth across her arm. She wanted to jerk it away, but darned if she would let him think his touch bothered her. She forced herself to allow it to lie still. Keeping her eyes averted, she was aware of his close scrutiny. Her heart pounded like that of a scared rabbit and she was sure he could feel it beating through the fingertips on her arm.

She sensed, rather than heard, him sigh. He got to his feet.

"Party must be over by now. I'll walk you back to your room."

"That isn't necessary."

She rolled the remainder of the meal on the paper sack and placed it in the waste container and stuffed her art supplies in the tote bag.

Jake was waiting with her coat. She slipped her arms into the sleeves. With his hands on her shoulders he turned her around and deft fingers worked the buttons on her coat. She stood perfectly still. His movements seemed to be very slow and deliberate. Before she realized his intent or could prevent it he bent his head swiftly and kissed her gently on the lips.

This unexpected action took her by surprise and she jerked away from him and picked up her bag to cover her confusion.

"Don't . . . do that!"

"Okay. " He was good-naturedly amused.

He turned out the light and hesitated just a moment before opening the door. That minute seemed an hour to Lindy, not knowing what he was going to do. Whatever it was, he changed his mind, and they went out into the cold corridor.

The rooms were quiet, the sitting room dimly lit, when they reached it.

"The party is over, or they've gone to bed." He would think of that, she thought dryly.

"Good night." It was dismissal.

He took the knob out of her hand and pushed the door open, following her into the room. It showed signs of the party. Glasses on every table, cigarette butts filled the ashtrays and bits and pieces of food on the table and floor. Lindy caught him eyeing an undergarment that had been tossed into a corner. She wanted to laugh. Jake had never been embarrassed in his life!

"Which room is yours?"

She indicated the room. He went to the door and flung it open.

"What the hell ya want, Yank?" A slurry Southern voice called.

Jake slammed the door. The thundercloud look on his face was laughable.

"Where will you sleep?"

"On the couch. I've done it before." Something in the amused tone of her voice made him frown even more. "You can get a room in the bachelor quarters."

"I'm no bachelor. Remember?" He was looking at the two sofas at the end of the room. "Got any extra blankets?"

She stood helplessly in the middle of the room, not knowing exactly what she was going to do.

"Did you reserve a room?" She wanted him out of here.

"Didn't need to. My wife has a room. I'm tired, Mrs. Williamson. Where's the john?"

While he was gone she made a feeble attempt to clean up some of the mess from the party, but realizing it would take hours she abandoned the job and spread the blankets on the sofas.

Jake came back into the room, sat down on one of the makeshift beds, removed his boots and stretched out.

"Just think, this morning I was in Houston. God, but I'm tired." He looked at Lindy and his lips twitched. "Here I am, spending the night with my beautiful wife and I'm too tired to make love to her." He laughed as she stalked to the bathroom.

CHAPTER TWO

LINDY'S HEAD WAS pounding. She was unable to get her thoughts together, she was confused, tired, and wanted desperately to go off somewhere and cry. It was as if her heart had been pounded to a pulp and her mangled emotions heaped on top. She felt limp and drab as a pile of wet laundry. Her only escape was to force her numb mind to concentrate on her work. Even that was difficult. Betty, the junior clerk and the only other woman in the office, was a pert blond just out of business college. She had come north thinking there was a woman shortage, sure she would land a rich, handsome husband. She spent her evenings at the disco looking and her mornings telling Lindy what she had found. This morning was no exception. She had rattled on insistently.

Amos came in, grunted a greeting, and went into his private office. Lindy's brain was so full of turmoil it didn't occur to her to wonder why he didn't pause for his morning chat.

The door opened again and a rush of cool air from the

corridor hit her back. She knew who it was for Betty perked up immediately.

"Hello." She was practically purring. "What can I do for you?"

"It depends on what you have to offer." The familiar voice was mocking.

Betty laughed. "Would you like a dossier?"

"Complete with pictures?"

"Absolutely!"

Lindy refused to acknowledge him. Let him flirt with a featherbrain like Betty. It came as natural to him as breathing.

"Introduce me to your friend, Lindy."

"Jake Williamson meet Betty Haver."

"Williamson?" Betty exclaimed. "Williamson? Same as yours, Lindy? Any relation? Long-lost cousin, maybe?"

Jake's eyes, sparkling with deviltry, went from Lindy to Betty's flushed, excited face.

"Do we have a family resemblence?"

"Hardly none at all." Betty was almost panting.

The heat of anger passed through Lindy. She knew, without looking up, that Jake was watching her reaction to his little flirtation. Her fingers moved swiftly over the calculator while she waited for him to drop the bomb that they were married. He knew what she expected him to do and chuckling at her discomfort he trailed his fingers across the nape of her neck as he passed on his way to Amos's office. "He's a dream, Lindy!" To a girl like Betty he would be.

"Yes, he is," Lindy murmured aloud and then to herself, "a nightmare."

"Tell me about him. Will he stay around for a while?" The petite blond rattled on, not waiting, or expecting an answer. It left Lindy free to settle into her work.

When Amos and Jake came out of the office she turned to the file and pretended to be selecting a folder.

"Lindy, Betty." Amos cleared his throat. "Mr. Williamson is the new owner of the company."

"How exciting!" This from Betty, of course.

"He plans to merge this company with two others he owns and that means there will be a lot of extra work. During the next few weeks we will be changing procedures. You will be paid double for all overtime."

Jake's eyes never left Lindy's face while Amos was talking. She was aware of this and proud she was able to keep from crying. It seemed her stay in the frozen north had come to an end. She would never work for Jake!

Amos stood silently after making his announcement. Betty let go a stream of gushing comments that made Jake laugh. Lindy bent her head over her work.

"I've got some things to do, Amos. I'll be back later and we can go over a few things. Okay?"

"Sure, Mr. Williamson. I'll be here."

"Jake. Call me Jake. No one calls me Mr. Williamson except my wife when she's mad at me."

Amos went into his office and Jake went out. Lindy could see him jogging down the corridor as her desk was in line with the door. He hasn't changed, she thought. Hasn't changed one little bit. Still flirts, still jogs, still has an eye for business.

"You didn't tell me he was married," Betty wailed. "Oh, for goodness sakes! Maybe he's separated or divorced. I hope so!"

"May I see you for a moment, Lindy?" Amos stood in the doorway.

Lindy followed him into his office, glad to get away from Betty, but one look at his glum face told her he was anything but happy. He waved her to a chair, then seated himself behind his desk and fumbled with the papers stacked neatly in front of him.

"Wasn't really a surprise. I knew the company was being sold, but didn't expect the new owner to show up so soon. Seems to be a right kind of guy. Knows what he wants and insists on getting it. I've heard about him. They say he can truck anything, anytime, anywhere, and after meeting him, I believe it. What I can't understand is why you didn't tell me you were married." He looked at her now. His face was tight, almost as if he faced an enemy. Christ! She hadn't thought about Amos.

"Amos, I . . . I didn't think it was important. We're getting a divorce." She hated having to explain even to Amos who had been kindness itself. A resentment welled up inside of her. She had made it plain to him from the start that she was not interested in a personal relationship and if he had hoped for more she was sorry, but it wasn't her fault.

"Not according to him you're not." His voice now held resentment.

"We're not what?"

"Getting divorced. He said you were working out your problems and he . . . warned me off." Amos's face reddened. "He said if I had any notion of having an affair with you to forget it."

"He said that?" Lindy was trembling with anger.

"Damn him! What I do is none of his business and we are getting a divorce!"

Amos stood up. "I'm only telling you what he said, Lindy. I'm sorry you didn't tell me yourself. I have become . . . fond of you. You're the only woman I've met since my wife died that . . . that I've wanted to be with. I'm disappointed." His brown eyes seemed to plead with her, expected her to say . . . what? He ran his hand over his perspiring forehead and thinning hair. When she didn't speak he said with resignation, "If and when you decide what you want and if I fit into your plans you can let me know."

"Amos . . ." She went to stand beside him. "I'm sorry if . . . well, if you're disappointed. I never wanted anything more than your friendship. Please believe that."

His face lost its stern lines and he smiled. "I know that, Lindy." He took her hand. "If you need a friend, I'm available."

"Thank you." Somehow her eyes were misty and she blinked rapidly. She took his hand in both of hers and squeezed it tightly.

The door opened and Jake stood there, his narrowed eyes going from one to the other and then down to their clasped hands.

"Anything pressing to be done this morning, Amos?" His voice was clipped, impersonal. "I'm taking my wife for a couple of hours."

"Nothing I can't handle. I'll send the payroll cards out, Lindy. The plane leaves"—he consulted his watch—"in about half an hour. Go along, I can finish them in plenty of time." Amos released her hand, but not before he held it in both of his. The act was deliberate and Lindy secretly applauded his courage.

Betty sat with her elbows on her desk, a mutinous look on her face. She had heard Jake refer to Lindy as his wife and the high hopes she had nurtured for a new affair were dashed.

Lindy took her coat from the rack, grabbed up her purse and walked rapidly out the door ahead of Jake. When they were several yards down the corridor she turned on him.

"What the hell do you think you're doing coming up here and interfering in my life, telling Amos we're going to work out our problems?" Her chin was lifted and there was rebellion in every line of her body. "Do you really have the . . . gall to think you can come here and I'll drop all my plans and take up with you again? If you think that, you're the most conceited wretch I've ever known."

For a long moment he stood there, his blue-green gaze locked with hers, while her voice lashed him with bitter, unguarded words.

"We are not getting a divorce."

Lindy closed her eyes. Had she really heard that appalling statement? The stark words hung on the cold air. Anguish worked in her face, threatening to break through her control.

"You won't have anything to say about it. After a certain length of time I won't need your signature." She trembled with the force of unspent emotion and backed away from the cold fury in his eyes.

"I'll fight you to the last ditch to keep our marriage intact." He stood on spread legs, his arms folded across his chest.

"Why?" she gasped. She was truly shocked.

He watched the emotions flick across her face. For a long moment he searched her anguished features, the mouth set so tight it was colorless, her eyes bright with anger and unshed tears.

"Because I choose to." The words had more meaning because they were softly spoken.

Her mouth twisted bitterly. "It's a pity you were not born a sultan. You would have been right at home with a harem."

He unfolded his arms and laughed. "You're being childish. I suppose you're still sulking over my . . . indiscretions."

"Don't tell me you're going to deny them?"

"I wouldn't attempt to do so."

"I'm past sulking, Jake. I'm tired of you hanging about my neck like an albatross. I want to be free to plan a future without you in it."

Cynicism curled his mouth. "I never thought you would still be so prudish, my sweet. Seems I got here just in time. Your . . . friend, Amos, almost dropped his jaw when I told him you were my wife. What's wrong for me is okay for you, eh?"

"You're impossible! Amos and I never . . ."

"Given time you would. For God's sake grow up!"

Lindy tried to control her shivering and failed. She stared at his dark, mocking visage. She took a deep breath.

"Why did you come here?" Suddenly Lindy's stomach lurched. She felt like throwing up.

His mood changed abruptly. "To see my wife. Husbands and wives should be together. I know that now. I made a mistake going away. You can bet I'll not make that mistake again. Remember it's Jake and Lindy. Lindy and Jake." He smiled down at her as if they had never exchanged a harsh word. "Come on." He took her arm. "Don't pout. We have work to do."

Lindy allowed him to propel her down the corridor. She was so wrung out from the emotional scene that she went through the line at the cafeteria in a daze. She followed Jake to a table by the double thickness of glass that made up the wall of the building. At one o'clock in the afternoon it was almost dark here at the top of the world. The gas flares which gave off an eerie light burned continually. The biting wind swept across the snow-packed surface with a boldness that would sweep your breath away if not for the protective shield of the heavy glass. A snowmobile roared past the window, the driver buffeted by the wind.

"It must be seventy below out there," Jake said.

Lindy glanced at him accusingly; she couldn't have possibly put all that food on her tray! He ignored her glance and went to get the thermo-pot of coffee from the service bar.

They ate in silence. The food rolled around and around in Lindy's mouth before it would go down. She avoided looking at him and focused her attention on the other diners. Amos and Betty came in and went down the line together, but sat at separate tables. Betty gave her a definite snub as she sailed past and for the first time all day Lindy wanted to smile.

Jake caught the slight lift to her lips and his eyes held hers in conspiratorial amusement. Her heart gave a sudden sickening leap. The ability to read each other's thoughts and to communicate without words was still there. She looked down to hide the knowledge he was sure to read in her eyes. She understood the bond between them, just as she knew that the almost unbearable longing that swept her at times was more than a physical need. But none of it would make any difference to their relationship. It was better to remember her true motive for leaving him, to steel herself against the dangerous knowledge that his lips, his arms, his masculinity, the whole essence of him, could make her long to surrender on any terms. Giving way to moments like this could only lead to more heartbreak. Jake would take all she had to give, and her own need, her own pride, would be swept away like so many grains of sand. A shudder ran through her limbs and with trembling hands she picked up her bag and got to her feet.

"Thank you for the lunch," she said as if thanking a business acquaintance. She forced a composure she was far from feeling. "I must get back to the office."

"Afraid the new boss will fire you?" His blue eyes were darkly amused.

"He won't have to. I'm giving notice." It was the only defense left to her now.

"Well, in that case . . ." He was cheerfully confident. "Come along. We got a chore to do."

With a firm hand beneath her elbow he ushered her out of the cafeteria and toward the living quarters. She clamped her lips tightly together. Not for anything would she ask him where they were going. They walked silently down the long darkened corridor, her legs working furiously to keep up with his long stride. They stopped at the door to her room and he held out his hand for the key.

"What are you trying to pull now, Jake?"

"I'm not going to rape you, if that's what you're thinking. Although I'm not so sure it would be rape." His words shattered her composure.

"Stop this, Jake!"

The amusement on his face infuriated her. Nothing made her so mad as to be laughed at and he knew that very well. She turned to go back down the corridor, but took only a few steps and he was in front of her. The smile gone from his face.

"I've arranged for you to have another room. A private room where you can paint to your heart's content."

"I can't afford a private room. And I'll be here only a few more weeks. Only until you can get a replacement."

He shrugged his shoulders. "Another girl is already packing to move into this room with the girls. So give me your key, we're wasting time."

Angrily she slapped the key into his hand.

He followed her into the bedroom and they both stared at the disorder. Clothes of every description were strewn around the room, the bed was unmade and wet towels lay on the carpet. Lindy went to the closet for her cases. Long arms from behind her reached over and lifted them from her hands and put them on the bed.

"Let me help so we can get out of this mess. We have two choices. We can make several trips carrying this stuff down what would amount to five city blocks of corridor, or we can load it on a snowmobile and cut across to the other wing in one trip. Which shall it be?"

"Whatever takes the shortest time."

"I thought you'd say that." He grinned. "I've a snowmobile waiting."

She gave him a disgusted look and then her eyes fell on the box in the corner.

"I can't let my tubes of paint freeze."

"Leave the paints to me." He picked up the box and began to wrap the tubes carefully in a suit of thermo underwear he picked up from the pile she dumped on the bed. "How will you take your finished pictures?"

"They will lie flat in the suitcase."

"Be sure and leave out enough warm clothes for the trip over."

They worked quickly and silently together. The first embarrassment of his handling of her intimate things passed and it was almost as if time had rolled back to the days of their love. He always knew what she was going to do before she did it. Their understanding of each other was uncanny . . . up to a point. She begrudgingly admitted it was good having someone to help her. She was tired of being a loner, but being married to a cheat was worse!

Jake looked like a man who had walked on the moon when he came in after loading the snowmobile. He raised the ski mask and grinned at her before adjusting the mask over her face and pulling the fur-lined hood up and over her head.

The wind was blowing so hard it would have been impossible for Lindy to stay on her feet if not for Jake's arm around her. The roar of the Arctic blast crowded out the sound of the snowmobile engine. He lifted her in and slid into the seat in front of her. Gratefully she leaned her face against the shelter of his broad back. It didn't take but a few minutes for them to reach the other wing of the giant building, but in the blowing gale it seemed much longer. He pulled the machine into the wind shelter beside the door and hurried her inside before plunging out again to bring in the cases.

The room was big and square. It was furnished more tastefully than the other one. There was thick pile carpet on the floor and colorful slip covers on the couch and chair. Jake proudly showed her around. He pointed out a small refrigerator and electric burner, microwave oven, hidden cupboard with dishes and utensils and a small stock of quick-to-prepare food. There was no doubt that they were in the executive section.

"Jake, I don't belong here."

"Whatever gave you that idea?" He opened a door to allow her to glance into another room. "Here's the bedroom." It was small but beautifully furnished. "Bathroom is over there." He was trying not to grin. "It only has a shower, but you prefer a shower."

Her face burned. Slowly things were becoming clear to her.

"And who is going to occupy the other room?" My God! Why wouldn't he leave her in peace? Her face had gone from red to white and he was startled at the expression of despair in her eyes.

"Your husband, that's who."

"No!" She was painfully aware that his flat statement was a summing up of his intentions in more ways than one. At least she had no illusions about that. She went quickly to the door. His whiplash voice kept her from opening it.

"For God's sake, quit being such a prude!" He advanced a couple of strides and caught her by the shoulders. "Don't tell me that you're so unsure of your feelings for me you can't stand to be near me for a couple of weeks. If that's the case, Lindy, it tells me quite a lot."

His grip slackened and she spun around, dreading that he should see the betraying tears. With a quick movement of his hands he forestalled the move and seized her arms. For a long moment he searched her anguished face, then released her abruptly.

"Lindy . . . Lindy, you're still a worrywart."

He unzipped his snowmobile suit and stepped out of it. His sun-streaked hair was ruffled. It looked glossy and healthy and brushed the collar of the turtleneck sweater that matched the blue of his eyes. He was not the most handsome man she had ever seen, but be was definitely the most masculine; lean, but with a powerfully built body. His eyes had always disturbed her the most. Between the longest lashes she had ever seen on a man, they seemed to look into her and through her.

Realizing she had been staring, she turned away. It was at moments like this she could imagine nothing had changed, that love still lay unspoken and the words he said so easily were to be believed. He knew she had no choice when he engaged these rooms and had blatantly taken advantage of the fact. What was she to do now?

Gently Jake pushed her into a chair and tugged at her heavy boots. She was too worn out to resist. Kneeling there, he took her stockinged foot in both of his hands and squeezed it.

"Warm feet, cold heart!" He laughed, his lips spreading to show even white teeth. The small wrinkles at the corners of his eyes had not been there before and as she openly studied his face the thought came to her that he was older, not the man she had known before, but a man not to be trifled with. He was hard and experienced, and yet at times she had caught a tender look in his eyes. Jake had a sentimental streak, if but a small one, that surfaced frequently during the time they were together. Possibly it included her, for old times' sake, along with his sister and her two boys.

He was still kneeling there holding her foot. "You're trying to decide if I'm a hero for getting you out of that place or a villain that's dragged you into his den of iniquity."

She smiled rather tightly. "Not . . . exactly." Her eyes shifted to the hands holding her foot. They were lean and brown and beautifully shaped. Strong, responsible hands, ruthless hands. She couldn't allow herself to become intimidated. Hands like Jake's held on to what they wanted, they took, they bruised . . .

"I've got to be getting back. The mail will be in and I'll have a lot to do."

His brows raised. "How about unpacking?"

"I'll do it tonight."

"1 had other plans for tonight." And noting the sudden flare of her nostrils he hurried on. "While I was in South America I dreamed about a pot of Texas chili and a pan of golden corn bread. How about cooking it for me if I can scare up the makings at the commissary?" His brows raised in question. "Besides I want to see how you fill each one of those little holes with yarn to make a picture."

"I want you to know that I've forgotten nothing, Jake. Absolutely nothing. Your vanity needs to believe that I'll come back to you, but I won't."

He didn't speak, only looked at her, defying her in silence.

She gave a twisted little smile. "Nothing to say, Jake? That makes a change."

"I'll walk you back. There's a network of corridors in this place. You might get lost."

It was late in the afternoon when Amos came by her desk and asked if she was settled into her new quarters. She told him she was and he went out toward the coffee shop. Lindy waited for a remark from Betty. She wasn't disappointed.

"Why did you keep your marriage such a deep, dark secret? Have you been separated? The girls will get a charge our of our Little Miss Priss being married to that man. How come you never mentioned him?"

Lindy was suddenly ice and daggers. "My marriage is none of your business, dammit, and I don't want it mentioned again. Do you understand? Furthermore, don't ever refer to me by that ridiculous name again."

"You don't have to get so huffy. I tell you about my affairs."

"That's right. You tell me. I don't ask you."

"Hello, girls." Jake stood in the doorway, his eyes compelling her to look at him. He held her eyes and she seemed powerless to look away and wondered for the hundredth time how she could be attracted to a man who took her faith, her heart, her body and her innocence and then threw them away.

"You've worked long enough, sweetheart." His eyes held a roguish twinkle. "Let's go. It's been a long time since we've been alone."

Lindy burned and wished desperately for a way to deflate him. She grabbed her coat and took off down the corridor, anger speeding her steps. She didn't want to feel anything toward him. He had come back into her life when she was feeling particularly lonely and that accounted for the flutter in her heart when she was near him and she angrily resented it.

He walked easily beside her. "I got all the fixin's for the chili." She said nothing and he took her arm and slowed her pace. "You keep that up and you'll be worn to a frazzle by the time we get there."

"We don't have an oven." She stiffened her facial muscles and gritted between her teeth.

"I know that. We can cook it in the microwave or on the grill like hotcakes. Remember when we went on a picnic to Galveston and . . ." She turned her head and looked at the wall. She didn't want to hear what she knew he was going to say. "And I asked you to marry me."

When they reached the apartment she went through the sitting room to her bedroom and closed the door. She looked around for her cases. The room was neat as a pin. She opened the closet doors. Her clothes were hanging in a neat row—coats, slacks, skirts, dresses. Her shoes and boots were on the floor beneath them, empty cases on the shelf above.

With tight lips she went to the bureau and opened the drawers. Her underthings were neatly arranged. A quick glance at the dressing table showed her that her cosmetics were there. Her anger flared, then exploded when she saw her one and only filmy nightgown lying on the end of the bed.

Fighting the feeling of being on a roller coaster, she flung open the door and confronted him.

"How dare you handle my things!" She clenched her hands together so they wouldn't fly out and hit him.

Jake looked up from the small work counter in the kitchen, genuine surprise on his face.

"Now what's bugging you?"

"You know perfectly well what's bugging me, Jake. You know every trick in the book, don't you? It isn't going to work! Whatever your motives you can be sure of one thing, Jake Williamson, and that is I'm not going to allow myself to be taken in again."

He gave a bewildered shake of his head. "You've got yourself in a stew because I unpacked for you. This is the twentieth century, for chrissake! We've lived together. I've seen plenty of panties and bras."

"Of course you have!" She was mad clean through. If only the darn pounding of her head would go away so she could think clearly. "I want a divorce, Jake."

His eyes were disturbingly intent. "Do you?"

"You know I do." She brushed a hand across her forehead. "Why, Jake? Why did you come here?"

"You're a smart girl. You figure it out."

Lindy felt sick and empty. She wasn't prepared for the agony of confronting him again, but she was compelled to ask, "Are you here to tell me again the girl lied when she said you had slept with her and that you did not have an affair with Liz?"

"No. I'm not saying she lied. What I am saying is that I never stopped in Orange, Jake Charles, Dallas or any other town to look up a woman after I met you. You won't let yourself believe that."

"No, I don't believe that. A whore wouldn't have come to Houston to look you up, Jake."

"Of course you don't believe it. You're so full of your own self-righteousness you only believe what you see. Did it never occur to you to trust your husband? I got drunk that night and you went off like a spoiled kid. Liz brought me home. You wouldn't even believe Liz when she said that was all there was to it. She begged you to stay and let me explain and you wouldn't even do that!" As she shook from head to foot, the vision of Liz cuddled in his arms on the couch flashed before her eyes.

"She said that?"

"And more, but we needn't go into that." He brought a brandy bottle from under the counter and poured himself a stiff drink. "I've known wives to trust their husbands when they were accused of heinous crimes and all the evidence pointed to the fact they were guilty."

"Isn't it ridiculous to be so blind that you can't see the truth?"

"Perhaps my example is extreme, but if you love someone you usually give them the benefit of the doubt. In our case there was not enough love and too much doubt."

Lindy had to defend herself. "There was no way I could doubt that poor girl. She was distraught, desperate."

"My God!" He slammed his glass down on the bar. "You couldn't doubt her, but you could doubt me and we had lived together for six months."

"Not all the time."

"I was away maybe one night a week. Do you think I was so starved for sex I couldn't do without it for one night? The subject is closed, Lindy. I didn't come up here to start an argument over something that happened two years ago. Go take off your coat and let's get on with more pleasant things. And try, for once, to see things through your own eyes and not through the eyes of your mother."

Lindy had to admit that the evening was enjoyable.

They prepared the chili together. He told her about the famous paintings he had seen in museums around the world. He was a stimulating companion and his knowledge of paintings, although recently acquired, was extensive. Lindy listened with interest in spite of herself, hungry to hear about places she longed to visit. She told him how she got started painting for needlepoint. Painting first for herself, then for Debra and her friends, and finally deciding to branch out commercially. There was a sense of unreality in having him here, sharing in the preparation of the meal, talking to him as if two days instead of two years had gone by.

They shared the cleanup and afterward sat on the couch. He insisted she show him "how she filled all those little holes to make a picture." He stretched his long legs out in front of him, his head resting on the back of the couch. His eyes watched the rhythmic movement of her hands as she stitched.

"I've missed this." He let out what was a half sigh, half yawn. "It's what I missed the most, I think. The peaceful quietness, the companionship, the . . . just being with you. This is the way it used to be."

She went pale. His blue eyes darkened when she glanced at him. He looked tired, she thought. The hard bones of his jaws were clenched, and there were shadows under his eyes like bruises. The lines on each side of his mouth were lines of fatigue. Her breath caught in the back of her throat, but when she spoke she chose her tone carefully.

"No. This isn't the way it used to be at all."

He surveyed her through half-closed lids. "Maybe not,

but you're still as tranquil as a harbor in a storm. You'll have to admit it's been a nice evening."

He drew her hand from the needlework and down between them on the couch lacing his fingers with hers. She began to tremble, the easy companionship of the evening was gone and in its place an alarm was sounding that the situation could get out of hand. She tried to pull her hand away, but he tightened his grip.

"Were you still seeing Dick Kenfield when you left Houston?" The question was delivered suddenly.

"How did you know about that?" Her heart was beating heavily.

"Were you trying to hide the affair?"

"No, but . . ."

"He isn't your type."

She looked up with wide-eyed disbelief and her gaze focused on his face, her mouth set in a grim line.

"Dick is a nice person, a really nice person, and if I thought you had anything to do with his being transferred to Chicago, dammit, I'd . . . I'd . . . You have absolutely no right to interfere in my life, Jake. You really are impossible. Do you know that?"

"Think about it. He wasn't your type."

Lindy stared at him, dumbfounded, and he stared back as if he was not seeing her at all, but something that suddenly made him go pale and haggard. He was shaking, as if with a chill, breathing roughly, as if he had just completed a long run. Was he ill? She jerked her hand free and got to her feet.

"Don't move!" The words were sharp as a pistol shot and frightened her into pausing. He was beside her in two steps and his hands closed around her upper arms. She winced at the tightness with which he held her.

"Are you never going to listen to me? There's a limit to how far you can push me, Lindy."

"There's a limit to how far you can push me! I won't take much more! You can't dictate what I do any longer."

His face turned a deep red as their eyes did battle. Dragging her against him, he lowered his head and fastened his lips to hers, kissing her bitterly, cruelly, hard, unloving kisses that took her breath from her. She struggled without success and finally surrendered to his superior strength. At last he lifted his head. His arms held her so tightly she thought she would faint and her blood pounded in her temples like the beat of a tom-tom. She turned her hot, aching mouth to his shoulder.

Anger at her helplessness caused her to raise her head. "Do you think I don't know why you want me?" she said accusingly, hatefully. "It was a blow to your ego having your wife walk out on you. You've come here to punish me, to make me pay and pay and pay. You hate me, don't you, Jake?"

"My God, but you are blind . . . and stupid! You're the only person in the world I've ever loved besides my sister and you know that isn't the same."

"No!" She tried to push herself away from him. "You only want to hurt me more."

"You're damn right I want to hurt you." He was shouting now. "I'm human. You hurt me almost more than I could stand when you walked out on me, when you took the word of some cheap tart over mine."

"That wasn't the only reason I left you. She wasn't your only affair."

The words tumbled from his mouth as though she hadn't spoke. "When I left for South America I hated you so much I was sick. You stuck a knife in my guts and twisted all the illusions out of me. I thought I had found perfection and discovered it was as phony as a three-dollar bill."

"How do you think I felt? Still feel?"

"Still feel?" He laughed without humor and pushed her from him. "Go to bed, Lindy. I won't ask you again to believe in me. You don't know what trust means."

She stood with head bowed. She felt sick and empty and her head was going around and around. She had known that sooner or later she and Jake would have a confrontation like this but she hadn't prepared herself for the agony she would feel.

"I did what I had to do. The sooner you accept that what we had is over, the better off we both will be."

"Yes." His lips twisted. "We will, won't we?"

She watched him until the door of his room closed behind him. Her head was throbbing and when she bent to pick up her needlework she was so dizzy she had to hold onto the couch until the room stopped spinning. She turned off the lamp and with leaden feet went to her room.

CHAPTER THREE

IT SEEMED TO Lindy it had been years since she had been alone. It was pure heaven to strip off her clothes and get into the cotton pajamas without stepping over Peggy's discards. She put away her pants suit, then dug into her purse for her sleeping tablets.

Before opening the door to the bathroom she listened for sounds of occupancy, then went in and shot the bolt on the door going into the other bedroom. The click of the metal resounded in the small room. She gave herself a quick sponge bath and filled a glass with water to take back to her room.

The room was unusually warm, or else her distraught nerves made it seem that way. She lay down across the bed and after a few minutes shrugged out of her pajama top. The satin spread felt cool against her breast. She lay with her head hanging over the side of the mattress, staring at the floor, wondering why the knowledge that Jake slept in the other room didn't fill her with alarm. For the first time since she packed her bags and left the apartment in the middle of the night she allowed a figment of doubt to enter her mind. What if Jake had told the truth? What if Jake had been so drunk he didn't realize he slept with Liz on the couch? That was no excuse! Jake was attractive to women. And he liked them! So . . . Her brain was too tired and too confused to think about it. Thank God for the sleeping tablets. She'd take a couple and her mind would find rest.

Blindly she reached for the bottle and the glass of water went crashing to the floor. In her haste to grab for it the bottle of pills rolled off the table.

"Idiot . . . ," she muttered in frustration, and a mist of nervous tears came to her eyes. She was straining to reach the bottle and the blessed rest it contained when the door was flung open. Jake stood there.

"What happened?"

She barely looked at him, but she knew he was coming toward her, was standing beside the bed. "I knocked my water glass off the table. Is that such a crime? Now would you mind leaving me alone?"

He picked up the glass and reached under the table for the bottle of pills. "What's this?" He held up the bottle, then opened it and poured the small, white, lethal-looking tablets out into his hand. "What are you doing with these?" His harsh tone almost petrified her. When she didn't answer he demanded, "What are you taking?"

She tilted her head so she could see him looming over her and reached out her hand. "Headache tablets. Just give them to me and go!"

"I'm not stupid, Lindy." He looked down at what lay in his palm. "They're narcotics. A measured dose of narcotics that some like to refer to as sedatives—sleeping tablets."

"And if they are, what business is it of yours?"

"Everything about you is my business, you little fool, and this especially! How long have you been taking this stuff?"

She buried her face in the bed. "Not long. Only when I have a headache." She heard him set the glass on the table and looked up hopefully. He stood looking down at her and, as she watched, put the bottle into his pocket. She sighed and turned her face away. She sensed rather than heard him move away from the bed, and when she didn't hear the door close, opened her eyes. He was standing at the bureau with her handbag in his hands.

Without stopping to consider her bare breast she sprang from the bed and tried to snatch the bag from him. He turned his back on her and extracted two more bottles of pills and slipped them into his pocket. She could have scratched his eyes out so frustrated did she feel.

"Don't take them all! Please, Jake, don't take them all!" Her plea was almost hysterical. She flung herself at him, flaying him with her fist. "I hate you, Jake Williamson! I wish I had never set eyes on you!"

He grabbed her wrist and held her away from him. He stared at her disbelievingly, his brows drawn together and his eyes narrowed into a green glitter. They stood like that for a long moment; his attention riveted to her anguished face.

"What has happened to you, Lindy? My God, you know better than to get hooked on this stuff!"

With a gulping sob she tried to wrench herself away from him, but his hands pulled her closer until his arms enfolded her and he pressed her wet face into the curve of his neck. Her control snapped and she begged pitifully,

"Please . . . oh, please don't take them all. You can't know what it's like. The night is so long, Jake. It's like forever. I can't endure it . . ."

The anger died out of him. "Lindy . . . sweetheart," he murmured hoarsely. His hand ran up and down her body, slowly touching her, stroking, caressing. "Darling, darling, sshhh . . ."

All of her resolve had crumbled. She abandoned thought of everything but the sensation of being close to him and of the flurry of excitement his hands were arousing in her. Aware now of her bare breast pressed against the silky texture of his shirt, the muscles of his chest hard beneath, surprisingly she didn't care much what he did to her as long as she could be close to him like this. She wound her arms around his neck, inviting possession.

"Jake . . . ," she pleaded. "I . . . the night is so black . . . so lonely." With closed eyes she lifted her mouth and offered herself to his possessing lips.

"For chrissake, Lindy. I don't want to take you like this!"

She gave a high moan, reacting with panic. "Please . . . Jake!" she whispered feverishly. "Please give me the pills."

His mouth covered hers with a hunger that silenced her, forcing her lips to open beneath his own. One hand moved up to hold her neck in a viselike grip, tilting her head so she could not escape from his passionate kisses.

"Oh, my God!" he muttered. "Is this another dream?"

They strained together, hearts beating wildly, and kissed as lovers long separated. His hands roamed restlessly from shoulders to hips and up to the delicate white glimmer of her breasts. He began to shake and his kiss became deep, deeper, until they both were dazed and breathless. His mouth still kissing her hotly, he lifted her into his arms and carried her to the bed. She kept her eyes tightly closed not wanting to come out of the tranced state, reliving the dreams she had of their nights together. Only now she was wildly, burningly awake, and as Jake's hands moved freely over her she felt the tightness of her muscles relax and the strain of the long, lonely months fade into nothingness. Her fingers moved in his hair as his head moved down her body, feeling the familiar thick, warm hair as his cheek brushed one of her breasts. His mouth gently slid over the white skin until it touched her nipple. Repeating the caress, his mouth became more seductive. His hands moved down her body pushing the thin cloth down over her hips.

Abruptly his hands fell away. She opened her eyes to protest. He was leaning over her, his lips a breath away.

"There's no turning back now, Lindy." The words seemed to be wrenched from him. "Don't tell me tomorrow . . ."

She stopped his lips with hers. "Love me, Jake. Don't think about tomorrow."

He clicked off the light and seconds later stretched out beside her on the bed.

"Don't think, my darling . . . go with the tide," he whispered. Lindy allowed her fingers to roam over his taut cheekbones, remembering the chiseled contours, and her desire was sparked anew with each touch.

It was all so sweet, so much better than she remembered. He was an unhurried, gentle lover, the stroking of his hands on her skin sent waves of weakening pleasure up and down her spine. He was invading every inch of her body, making her give herself up to him. She remembered the first time he had entered her. She had been scared and shy. She welcomed him now. Nothing mattered except her own desperate need for love.

The need for him blazed crazily in her brain. It was dangerous to give herself as she was giving to him now . . . she was vulnerable, asking for rejection, humiliation . . . pain. But she wouldn't think of that now . . . not tonight.

Her arms clutched him frantically as his mouth came down to her pulsing throat, kissing the soft skin. She arched against him tugging at his powerful body as his hands slid under her and she opened her thighs to receive him. His breathing came fast and irregular and his heart thudded above her as his movements quickened and he whispered softly, words whose meanings were muffled as he kissed her soft lips and his tongue probed at the corner of her mouth. The driving force of her feeling was taking her beyond reason, beyond fear, beyond herself into a new dimension. Her hands moved to his throat, slid over his shoulders, and her fingers curled in explosive excitement into his thick hair.

He drew his lips away and buried his face in her throat, kissing it hotly. There was a frenzied singing in her blood and it grew with such rapidity that the words beat against her brain. "Let it last . . . let it last." She heard sounds of his smothered groans as if they came from a long way to reach her ears and then the pleasure rose to intolerable heights and she was conscious of nothing but her own sensations. She felt herself floating down weightlessly and she clung to Jake's shoulders, the only solid thing in the unbalanced world.

She fell into a warm, lazy, languid silence, which was like peace on a summer day at the beach. Jake's head dropped onto her shoulder, his breathing slower, his heart quieter. She lay passively, her arms twined around his neck, while his hands stroked her body gently. The feeling of panic and tension was gone. She had meant to give to him the fulfillment of his desires as well as to satisfy her own. And now she hadn't the necessary courage needed to move away from him. She fought to block out everything but this moment . . . this night. She snuggled against him, her arms locked about him, and sleep overtook her like the dark cloak of night.

Artificial sunshine, issuing from a sophisticated indirect lighting system, awakened Lindy in the morning. Her mind slowly became aware of the disturbing glare. It intruded, shining through her closed lids and penetrating into her brain. She stirred sleepily as a hand began to caress the small of her back.

She lay without moving, dazedly aware that this was an unusual awakening. Then she became alert, realizing she was pillowed on Jake's bare shoulder, lying naked next to his strong, warm body and inhaling the very presence of him. She lifted one hand and delicately touched the hair on his upper lip. Under her fingers the hair was soft and prickled pleasantly. The gold-tipped lashes parted and he looked down into her face.

Her body lay still against him while his hand continued to stroke her back. For a long moment they merely looked at each other.

"I'd forgotten how beautiful you are first thing in the morning." His hand moved to push the dark fringe of hair from her face.

A sigh trembled through her and she closed her eyes. His arms strained her closer as her tears wet his chest. He lifted her face and rained kisses on her brow, cheek, throat and her own mouth sought blindly for comfort, tasting her salty tears on his lips, tasting the tang of his skin and feeling the hardness of his jaw.

Suddenly without saying a word or looking into his face she pushed herself away from him and ran into the bathroom. Locking both doors, she turned the shower to full pressure and stood under it, letting the water beat against her facc. She could never remember a time when she was so weary in body, weary in soul, confused in mind. She clung to the heavy handles of the water controls, half awake, half dreaming, then in an angry gesture she turned off the hot water and for uncountable minutes let the icy cold water cover her, unconsciously punishing herself for her wantonness. Finally she turned off the water and began to rub herself vigorously to get rid of the chill. Wrapping the towel around her, she went back into the bedroom, somehow knowing Jake wouldn't be there.

Taking fresh underwear from the drawer, she returned to sit on the bed. It was then she saw the cup of hot coffee on the bedside table. While she was drinking it she heard Jake in the shower, but her mind was numb from the successive hammer blows which had disturbed it since the night he came back into her life. She stifled a groan as her mind began summoning back, in feverish detail, the events of the night. She had wanted him! She was so disgusted with herself she could scream. She was mad! She was a fool! It had meant nothing to him, she thought bitterly. One more willing woman. Her face burned with self-disgust and she clenched her hands. It had meant nothing to her either! Sex was necessary to him and it had been a way for her to get through the night. She didn't love him, had only thought she loved him at one time. She didn't even like him!

They met in the sitting room almost like strangers. Lindy rinsed the coffee cup at the small sink and upended it on the counter. When she turned Jake was holding her coat. They walked down the corridor without exchanging a word and she would have passed the coffee shop if he had not taken her elbow and steered her inside. He seated her at a table and went to the service counter and returned with two plates of food, then eased his long length down in the chair beside her. Lindy looked at the scrambled eggs, the crisp bacon and the buttered toast. Automatically she picked up her fork. She was hungry and finished every last scrap of the food and held out her cup for more coffee.

The coffee shop was crowded and had Lindy been less occupied with her own thoughts she would have been amused at the curious stares and the female interest in Jake. As it was, her ears barely registered his voice when he asked if she was ready to leave.

Arriving in the office, Jake told Amos he would need Lindy to help acquaint him with office procedures. Lindy was grateful that he maintained a friendly but impersonal attitude toward her during the day, treating her as a capable colleague. And she had to admit he had a flair for the business—his energy and intuition were truly amazing. When he was working he concentrated with all his attention on what he was doing and yet his fingers flew over the pad making notes, all the time reading, and she wondered how he contrived to do both at the same time.

A kind of brittle calm possessed Lindy. She checked and rechecked details, sorted invoices and performed the million-and-one duties connected with the operation of a large company. Noon was marked by sandwiches being brought from the coffee shop and the afternoon passed before she was aware of it. Jake worked tirelessly into the evening and she worked beside him, reluctant to break her concentration for fear other thoughts would intrude.

It was past eight when Jake leaned back in his chair.

"We've put in a good day's work. Let's go eat."

This time as they walked the corridor they passed the coffee shop and walked on to the restaurant where the lights were dim and soft music played. Lindy had never been here. The decor, the service and the prices were geared to the executive incomes. Jake helped her remove her coat and handed it to the attendant. They followed the waiter to a small candlelit table.

"Shall I order for you?" he asked, then proceeded to do so.

Scarcely ten words had passed between them when they left the restaurant. Her mind slightly dazed by the excellent wine, she stood patiently while he opened the door to their rooms.

"Do you want to use the shower first?"

She didn't answer. She walked into her room and closed the door.

Later when she'd turned out the bedside lamp and slid into bed she pulled the covers up over her naked body and burrowed her head into the pillow. She could hear the sound of Jake's shower over the thunderous beat of her heart. She felt panic and dismay creeping into her mind as she realized what was happening to her. Jake was taking over her life. Her need for him was giving him the power to manipulate her as if she was no more than a wooden doll. It angered her and alarmed her and yet when she remembered the darkness of other nights she began to tremble with fear that he wouldn't come. She stared into the darkness, taut with rage. I hate him, she thought savagely. I hate him for degrading me like this.

The bathroom door opened and he came toward her in the total darkness. He turned back the covers and came confidently into bed beside her. Even as his arms reached for her, she cried out wildly, "I still want a divorce!"

For an answer he caught her close, his mouth searching for hers with fierce, possessive demand, silencing all resistance, forcing hers to open beneath his own. She moaned and fought against the rape of her mouth and tried to push him away. His arms held her in a viselike grip and his naked legs held hers imprisoned between his own. Gasping, she struggled as much against the desire he had awakened in her as she did against the arms that held her. Suddenly her mouth was free.

"Jake! Don't do this to me!" Her voice trembled with the agony she was feeling. He didn't love her, she was a diversion for now and she knew that later she wouldn't have the strength to deny him.

"Hush . . . this is our one line of communication," he muttered unsteadily. "You like for me to touch you here . . . and kiss you here." He stroked the flat stretch of her stomach with his fingertips and trailed his lips down over her breast. "I know you better than you know yourself, sweetheart. You wouldn't let me touch you like this if you didn't love me. If we can share this we can share . . . other things." His tongue made a little circle of her lips. "Don't fight me, darling . . . ," he whispered. "I need you. You disturb my nights, haunt my days."

She rolled her head from side to side. "No! It's over! This is all . . ."

"It isn't over!" he grated between clenched teeth and thrust his body deeply into hers.

She raised tear-drenched lashes that scraped against his cheek. "I don't want to love you." She was sobbing helplessly. "I don't have any trust in you, so how can I love you?" She evaded his lips. "Even . . . this has no value. It's been offered to so many others!"

Her words made him go rigid for a few seconds.

"Dammit! You're my wife," he almost snarled. "And you'll remain my wife!"

She continued to roll her head in denial. Her eyes were tightly closed, though tears still crept between the lids. As if in torment she tightened her arms about his neck and hungrily sought his lips.

"Love me, Jake," she begged as if to shut off the turmoil of thoughts that tormented her.

"I will, sweetheart, and I . . . do," he whispered tenderly in her ear and kissed her so gently that her whole body cried out for him.

Morning came quickly. When she awakened it was to full awareness. She was still cuddled in Jake's arms, her bare legs entwined with his. Suddenly she stiffened and wrenching herself away from him sat up in the bed.

"Oh . . ."

"What is it? What's wrong?"

She was frightened and furious, more at herself than at him, but it was toward him her anger was directed. "What if . . . you've made me pregnant?"

He laughed in relief. "What if I have? Would it be such a crime?" He tried to pull her back down into his arms, but she pushed his hands away.

"I don't want a baby! I've no plans for a baby, ever!" she wailed. "It would be different for you," she accused. "You would continue going from one affair to another and I'd be left to be both mother and father to a child. My child will never live the way I lived, Jake!"

She failed to see the hurt look that came over his face.

"Would you hate having a baby that much?"

"Not a baby. Your baby, Jake." She was cruel and she didn't care.

His hands shot out and grabbed her arms and he shook her. His eyes were cold steel and completely ruthless. He continued to shake her angrily, his eyes moving over her face without compassion. She was almost sobbing with frustration as well as fear of him in this strange, cold mood.

"That's it, isn't it, Lindy?" His eyes glittered strangely. "I'm to suffer because of your unhappy childhood? Because of your father? Grow up! Not all men are cast in the same mold, nor all women. You want to believe the worst of me, don't you?"

"What else can I believe?" She was choking on her rage. "I don't want to talk about it. It's over!"

He was shaking her savagely again, unaware of his anger, of his cruel grip on her arms. "It's not over. Admit it!"

"No! I won't!" She bent her head unable to meet those piercing eyes and his anger suddenly left him. He put his hands on her shoulders and pulled her hard against him.

She quivered in his arms, and he put a hand to her throat and tilted her face up to his. His eyes searched her face as his hand cupped her chin. In spite of herself, she opened her eyes and looked at him. A wave of helplessness came over her, and a little whimper escaped from her lips.

"If you feel so strongly about not wanting to get pregnant, sweetheart, we'll do something about it. But . . . for now . . . let's just take our chances, hmm?"

She kissed him as if he was all that mattered in the world and he drew her back down onto the bed and let his hands roam over her warm skin.

CHAPTER FOUR

THERE WAS NO lack of entertainment at the complex. The oil companies had spared no expense to help their workers fight the stress and boredom of isolation. The self-contained camp offered daily movies, videotape television, saunas and surprisingly decent food in the restaurants. Before many evenings had passed, Lindy and Jake had explored them all.

In the weeks since Jake arrived Lindy had lost none of her anxious doubts about the wisdom of what she was doing. But Jake left her no time to sit down and gather her chaotic thoughts and file them in any kind of systematic order. There were so many things to do. Jake completely reconstructed the office procedure; together they made up new weekly, monthly and quarterly report sheets to be sent to the printer. Jake was determined to have a company emblem and they worked long hours on a logo that would be simple, yet instantly recognizable. He left the final design and color up to Lindy and the painting of the logo for the printer to photograph and reproduce took hours of her time.

Lindy allowed one of her rare smiles to surface when she showed her final design to Jake and Amos. The word "Williamson" in block letters was slanted forward as if bucking the wind and the wind lines above and below the letters gave the impression of a company on the move. The letters were emerald green and set into a red frame that was the outline of the state of Texas.

Jake pinned it to the bulletin board and backed away to look at it. He moved close to Lindy and put an arm around her.

"By God! That's great! You're really good, sweetheart." His hand squeezed her waist.

"It can be made up in various sizes. You can use it on the large equipment as well as the small pieces."

"Will it work on letterheads?" He walked away from her so he could view the design from another angle.

"If it's placed on the side of the sheet with the address and phone numbers across the top for balance."

"Good idea. What do you think, Amos?"

"I like it very much. Lindy would make an excellent commercial artist."

Jake laughed. "Don't be putting ideas in my wife's head, Amos. I need her to look after me and that's a full-time job." He intended to make a joke of it, but a quick glance at Lindy's set face told him he didn't succeed.

Lindy was seldom alone. After work hours Jake never left her side and during the day he conducted much of his business by telephone. In the evenings just before dinner they strolled around the complex. They checked what movies were showing, but seldom sat through one. They visited the disco where the girls went in groups of two or three in hopes of meeting someone interesting. Occasionally they entered a gift shop where the imported items were very expensive. Always they stopped in the solarium to watch the northern lights. It was an awe-inspiring sight. The huge cranes used to unload cargo stood outlined like sentinels in the glow of the flickering lights.

They dined quite late and somehow managed to converse easily. Jake told her about various places he'd visited in South America and she told him about her hope of selling at least one of her needlepoint designs to a national stitchery magazine. Much of their dinner conversation was about the business because Lindy was as knowledgeable about some aspects of it as Jake was. They were both careful not to mention the time they lived together or their reason for parting. Usually by the time they reached their rooms she was rather floating from the effects of the wine she had consumed with dinner and went straight to the shower.

When Jake came to her the room was dark. He would slide into bed and reach for her. She would go into his arms willingly. A few times she thought about the sleeping pills. She missed their tranquilizing effect, but after making love with Jake she could relax and sleep. He was a gentle and patient lover, putting her pleasure foremost before satisfying his own desires. His husky voice whispered love words to her and they echoed on inside her brain.

Only one time did she speak of what was happening between them.

"I don't understand myself! I keep thinking . . . I won't do this!"

"Stop worrying about it." He let the palm of his hand

run over her breast until the nipple stood firm. "You like this, don't you?" He moaned silently.

"Yes, but . . ."

"Shh . . . hh . . ." He pressed his mouth to hers each time she started to speak until their hunger grew and there was no time for words.

An air of expectancy hung over the office for several days before the convoy of trucks carrying drilling equipment and replacement parts was due. Jake was impatient for the convoy to get within radio range and called out periodically. Several days after their due date he made contact with the lead truck, via citizens'-band radio, but the transmission was not the best and it was hard to understand the soft Texas drawl coming from the huge eighteen-wheel truck.

"How about it, Buck? You got a copy on this base station?"

"Ten-four, good buddy. I've got you wall to wall and treetop tall."

"How's things going?"

"Well now, we're a keepin' the rubber side down, but it's been the drizzlin's, good buddy. These eighteen-wheel toboggans has been a slidin' since we left the Yukon." The voice coming in was getting clearer as the convoy got closer to the camp.

"What's your ten-twenty, Buck? Do you know how far out you are?"

"No way of knowin' out here on this white desert, Jake. We'll just keep a comin' till we get there."

"You'll see where to go when you get inside the camp. There's a building about the size of Yankee Stadium where you can drive in and leave the trailers. Whatever you do, Buck, keep the rigs running or the fuel will freeze in this temperature. I'll be down to meet you."

"Ten-four, Jake. I've got a man with a bad back who needs to see a doc. He'll never be able to make the return trip. We'll be a man short."

"We'll figure out something, Buck. Keep 'um rolling. I'll clear with you and head on down to the loading docks. My wife will stand by the radio in case you need to contact us again before you get here. See you in a few. I'm gone." Jake set the microphone down and looked at Lindy. He stared at her for a moment, as if in deep thought.

As he left the office he paused by her desk, took her chin in his hand and gazed at her in a penetrating way. She raised questioning eyes to his and he mouthed the words "You're beautiful." She shook her head, trying to free her chin from his hand. He laughed softly as color creeped up her neck to flood her face. She watched him leave and was disgusted with herself for allowing his words to make her blush like a stupid little schoolgirl.

The day passed swiftly. Lindy locked her mind to the work piled on her desk. She wanted to finish so she could leave the office before Jake returned. Betty was excited over the arrival of the convoy and wanted to linger in the office in case the new arrivals came in. She freshened her makeup, ran the comb through her hair and sprayed herself generously with cologne, the fragrance drifting in through the connecting door.

When the outer door opened something deep inside Lindy trembled for a moment.

"Whee . . . ee . . . ee! It sure does smell pretty in here,

Jake. Smells like the Rio Grande valley at orange-blossom time."

The man's soft Texas drawl touched off a pang of homesickness in Lindy. She heard Jake introduce him to Betty, heard Betty's breathless attempts to prolong the conversation, as Jake came through the doorway followed by the giant of a man from which the gentle voice had come. Soft, smiling brown eyes looked down at her out of a rugged face creased with smiles. He held a thick wool cap in his hands and the telltale white streak across his upper forehead told her this Texan was more at home in a wide-brimmed Stetson than the wool cap he was twisting around in his large hands.

"This is my wife." Was that pride she heard in Jake's voice? He waited to see Buck's expression, then grinned.

"Well . . . I'll be swan to goodness, ma'am. You sure are pretty! There's no girls prettier than Texas girls no matter where you find 'em and you're one of the prettiest. But tell me, honey, how'd you happened to get caught up by this here old ugly boy?"

Lindy stood up and although she was quite tall she felt dwarfed beside this big Texan. He was so big, so friendly and his manner so much like the truck drivers she had worked with back home that it was impossible not to respond to him.

"Hello, Buck." She extended her hand and it was immediately lost in his.

"Remind me not to ever call you an ignorant, stupid old boy again, Jake."

Jake laughed and slipped an arm about her shoulders. "Believe me, Buck, I know what I've got." He smiled down at Lindy and before she realized what she was doing she smiled back. "We'd like you to join us for dinner," he was saying to Buck. "Wouldn't we, sweetheart?" His hand caressed her shoulder and arm.

"Of course. It will be nice to talk to someone fresh from home."

"I'll be fresh soon as I thaw out. I'll swear it's colder than blue-blazes out there and I been wonderin' what in tarnation this warm-blooded old boy is doin' up here. I'm for giving this country back to the Eskimos!" His eyes twinkled at her. "I'd better go get all slicked up if I'm going to have supper with the boss man and his lady. 'Bye, for now, Lindy." He went to the door. "And 'bye to you, too, little gal," he said to the disappointed Betty.

Jake closed the door between the connecting offices. "You liked him, didn't you?" He said it very carefully. It was the quality of his tone that caused her to look up. He was watching her when she found his eyes.

"Yes. It would be impossible not to."

"Buck affects people like that. He was with me in South America."

The statement required no answer and she went back to her work. When next she looked up, Jake sat scowling as though he wanted to kick something. When he caught her glance he leaned back in the chair and tried to grin, but it was not an overwhelming success.

Lindy wore a blue dress that night and Buck gave her the usual chaff about being pretty as a Texas bluebell. She had decided she was going to enjoy this dinner and for her own satisfaction she had done her best to look her best. She looked exquisite—tall and elegant and sexy. She didn't know it but she had a kind of naive glamour about her that caused men to watch her. She had an aura of distant reserve coupled with vulnerability and shyness that made them want to protect her. When they entered the restaurant Jake knew what Lindy didn't, that every man in the room would have given his eyeteeth to go home with her.

Buck was an easy companion and Lindy found herself listening eagerly to him and Jake talk of their experiences in South America. Jake included her in the conversation in a light teasing way that didn't require much of her and allowed her to observe the two men who were so alike and yet so different. When the meal was over and they sat with their coffee Jake took her free hand and held it in his lap, his fingers interlaced with hers.

Three evenings later, after they had dinner with Buck, Jake announced, rather casually, "Get your things packed. We're leaving in the morning."

The calm and mildly spoken words stunned her. Time was meaningless while she stood and stared at him, his words echoing through her sluggish mind.

"What did you say?" Her face was a mask of confusion.

"We're leaving in the morning. We're a driver short so you and I are going south with the convoy."

"You and Buck knew you were leaving and didn't say a word during dinner! Why?" A pause while she gave him a scornful look. "I'm not going with you, Jake. Who do you think you are to make plans concerning me behind my back?"

"I didn't tell you because I knew how you would react.

I was right. Now pack your things if you want to take them with you."

Her eyes were blazing with fury. "I'm not going."

"You're going. I've made sure about that." His eyes, turned green like a stormy sea, seemed to pin her back to the wall.

Dear God, she thought, he means it! Rage struggled with the inner terror that he could make her do whatever he wished. Why did he want her? Why didn't he get out of her life and leave her in peace?

"I . . . you're not . . ." She was sputtering and couldn't help it. Her eyes blazed into his. "I'm not buying this time, Jake. Whatever you're up to . . . I'm not buying." In spite of herself her voice dropped to a hoarse whisper. "I don't . . ."

He cut her off as though she hadn't spoken. "We leave in seven hours," he said, looking at his watch.

"Can't you get it through your head? I'm . . . not . . . going!"

He went on as if he hadn't heard her. "The weather is due to take a bad turn and we want to leave ahead of the storm. Otherwise we wouldn't be in such a hurry. So be a good girl and get packed. I've got a few things to attend to first—I can pack my things in about ten minutes."

Lindy sucked in a breath and tried to keep from shaking. She couldn't take her eyes off his face, feeling the blood drain from hers.

"I don't give a damn about the weather!" The words seemed to explode from tense lips. "I have a job here. I have a room here. I have my life planned, Jake. It doesn't include you."

His laugh was dry and short and not really a laugh at

all. "You don't have a job here. You won't have a room here after tonight. Another girl is on the way to take over both your job and your room."

Hating him and herself both, Lindy felt the uncontrollable tears erupt. They gushed into her eyes and swamped her throat. He came to her, caught her shoulders, and she hated him all the more.

"Damn you, Jake!" She was mouthing words, any words. She lifted her head with reluctance, her eyes like two stars between wet lashes and glazed with emotion.

"We're good together, Lindy." He said it very carefully as though he meant it.

She composed herself sufficiently enough to murmur, "Only in bed."

"Thank God for that!" he whispered fervently, and took possession of her mouth, tenderly and eloquent with emotion. When he raised his head he gave a wry smile. "We have our bad moments, but we also have some pretty wonderful ones."

She stood away from him and brushed the thick swath of dark hair back from her forehead. She felt suddenly calm and oddly empty inside. She heard her voice persist. "You're determined to grind me down, aren't you, Jake?"

"Not at all. I'm determined to keep you with me, as my wife, my life's partner, mother of my children. I've had two years to think about it, Lindy. I want a home, family, some permanence to my life." Then he made one of his quick moves and caught her shoulders to spin her toward him. His eyes lost that look of warmth and admiration. He looked down at her with cold, interested eyes that narrowed to mere slits and his voice underwent a rapid change, sharp and cruel. "You're not going to flounder around feeling sorry for yourself any longer." His eyes studied her. The determined tone of his voice convinced her she would never be able to hold out against him. There was a moment of fierce glaring between them. Lindy was first to give in.

"Damn you . . . you . . ." Her own tone lacked conviction and was muffled with a kind of pain.

When Jake finally left the apartment and the echoes of his footsteps died away Lindy's first reaction was that of relief. He'd gone and she was alone. With her accustomed self-reliance she tackled the job of packing her belongings. Carefully she packed her completed canvases and then the rest of her things, much the same as she did a few weeks ago when she moved to the apartment, only this time she left out warm clothing.

Her cases were ready and waiting beside the door before she allowed herself time to think and then her thoughts raced in chaotic confusion. She could not help shivering. The look in Jake's eyes as he had walked away from her made her afraid. Hating him, hating her own weakness for him, her head started whirling dizzily. She lowered it to her knees and hoped the faintness would go away. With defeat in the slump of her shoulders she tried to stand, but she was so dizzy that she held on to the back of the chair while the room stopped swaying. She stood there, her breath quickening, and then a longing almost like a pain washed over her. A longing for the pills that lulled her into unconsciousness and peace.

She walked slowly into the bathroom, catching a glimpse of herself in the full-length mirror as she passed it. It was like seeing someone else. The body was no longer hers. The face, vacant. "You're asking for it . . .

you're really asking for it!" It was weird to look at yourself this way and to feel as if you didn't belong to yourself. She wanted to laugh, but laughter would not come. Tiredness welled up in her, enveloping her like a shroud. She passed on into Jake's room and began opening drawers. She felt so lonely, lost and then . . . frantic.

It was only after she searched every drawer, every pocket in the clothes hanging in the closet that she noticed the pigskin bag. Praying it wouldn't be locked, she tugged it down from the shelf and dragged it out. With trembling fingers she sprung open the catch. Her hands searched under the neatly folded jogging suit, the knit shirts, the jockey shorts for the round bottle. Disappointment making her want to weep, she pulled back the elasticized pocket on the side of the case. Nothing there except two thick white envelopes. Her name, her real name, LuLynn Williamson, jumped up at her. Jake's name was on the other envelope.

Automatically, without will or volition, she opened the envelope with nerveless fingers. The words, the unbelievable words, swam before her eyes.

IN THE DISTRICT COURT OF THE STATE OF TEXAS
IN RE: THE MARRIAGE OF LULYNN WILLIAMSON
AND JAKE WILLIAMSON
UPON THE PETITION OF—LULYNN WILLIAMSON
DISSOLUTION DECREE FILED WITH
CLERK OF COURT
JANUARY . . .

January? January! Her divorce from Jake had become final over a month ago! He had signed the papers without her knowing, the divorce bad become final without her knowing. She bent her head. She was free! No longer married to Jake. She crushed the parchment between her fingers. Why hadn't she been told? Why had he pretended they were still married? What a fool she had been to go to bed with him.

She got up suddenly and waited for her head to stop throbbing before she moved toward the bathroom, taking the envelope with her. After bolting both doors she stripped off her clothes and got under the shower. The water pounded on her head. She had been crazy, stupid, not to take the first plane out of here after he arrived. Why didn't I do it? No one would have stopped me. Don't think . . . relax . . . She held her face to the stinging water, keeping her eyes closed, but her mind kept clicking like a computer. The carefully made plans for her future were not shattered after all. She was once again in charge of her destiny. Oh, God, just one more mountain to climb. She would make it. She had to.

She was hardly aware of the sound of the apartment door closing or Jake's voice calling her name. She was acutely aware, however, of the pounding on the bathroom door.

"So you know." Jake's voice, loud, angry. "It makes not one particle of difference, Lindy. I signed those papers during a weak moment. In fact, after I discovered you were sleeping with Dick Kenfield. It took me a while to realize it was partly my own fault, for going away and that you were lonely. By the time I decided I wanted you anyway it was too late. My lawyer thought he was doing me a favor by rushing it through the courts. We'll be remarried as soon as we get to Fairbanks. Make no mistake about that."

Coming out of her daze she heard his angry words. She hadn't heard right, of course. Either that or she was losing her mind. Dick her lover? Dick could have been her lover. Wanted to be. But, no. She hadn't wanted to have an affair. For the tiniest moment she wished it had been true. Oh, God . . . oh, please . . . please don't let me get sucked in again.

CHAPTER FIVE

LINDY WAS ALONE in the apartment when Buck came for her.

"Will we have time for coffee?"

"Coffee will be waiting for you in the cab." His eyes took in the shadows beneath her eyes put there by hours of sleeplessness. "Jake spent most of the night whipping everyone into shape. We're all lined up and ready to go."

Five minutes later they walked down the long corridor and out into the eerie darkness. It was almost fifty-five degrees below zero and the light from the gas flare made ghosts of the few figures walking on the bleak landscape. The roar of the six huge diesel engines was deafening. A cloud of ice fog floated around each as the drivers revved up the engines. Her appearance was evidently the signal they had been waiting for.

With her overnight case tucked under one arm, Buck firmly clasped his mittened hand around her arm and guided her to the last truck in the convoy. He opened the door and tossed her bag inside. She looked at him with questioning eyes. The step to the huge cab was about waist high. He placed his hands at her waist and as effortlessly as if she were a child lifted her up and onto the seat of the cab. He saluted her with his mittened hand and closed the door.

Lindy had been in truck cabs before and was able to appreciate the luxury of this one. The interior was of soft cream leather and the seats were as comfortable as an easy chair. Between the driver and passenger seats was a compartment for food, complete with a small coffeemaker plugged into the dashboard, and the smell of freshly perked coffee was delicious. It was quiet and warm and had it not been for the turmoil of confusion within her she would have enjoyed the adventure.

The citizens'-band radio came to life. "Break . . . break . . . break, you Texans. We're headin' home to God's country. The boss man and that little ol' turtledove a ridin' with him will have the back door. We'd better check out these CBs. How about it, turtledove, you got a copy on ol' Buck?"

Lindy's fingers trembled as she grasped the mike and pressed the button. "Ten-four, Buck."

"Did you hear that? Ain't that pretty? We're goin' to be hearing that sweet Southern voice all the way to Texas. Come on, now, you truckin' cowboys, check in so we can get out on the avenue."

As the last man answered, the door opened and Jake hoisted himself up into the cab. He tore the ski mask from his face and glanced at her. "Morning."

His calm manner irritated her and she grunted an answer.

He swung his parka and her case into the compartment

behind the cab and picked up the microphone. Holding the mike in his hand, he turned to look at her.

"You'd better get out of that coat or you'll get too warm." He set the mike down to assist her.

Lindy accepted his help grudgingly without looking at him.

He spoke into the mike. "We're ready, Buck. Head 'um up and move 'um out."

"Ten-four, good buddy. Take care of that little turtle-dove. She's mighty pretty."

"Ten-four." Jake turned to her with a half-amused grin on his face. "Turtledove."

"It wasn't my idea," she said tartly.

"Fits, though. You can depend on Buck to come up with something fitting."

He leaned over the wheel and pushed various levers. The big engine rumbled and the truck moved slowly ahead. The headlights sprang on and forged a path into the darkness and Jake coolly maneuvered the big rig out onto the frozen highway.

Lindy stole a glance at his sharply etched profile. Not only was he handsome, but he was strong, capable and . . . ruthless. What a stinking thing it was of him not to tell her about the divorce.

"Wake up and pour some coffee."

She poured a small amount in two cups. Digging deeper into the hamper, she found sandwiches, cartons of salad, deviled eggs and a variety of snack foods.

"Anything else?" she asked grudgingly.

"Doughnut." He held out his hand. "Good," he said with his mouth full. "But not as good as the ones we used to get in south Houston. Remember?"

She didn't answer, but she did remember the all-night bakery and the warm chocolate-covered doughnuts. She saw a flicker of humor in his blue eyes as he swung them away from her and concentrated on his driving. The truck picked up speed and she found she didn't want to turn her gaze out the window just yet. Pretending to rest her head back, she watched the powerful hands deftly swinging the wheel. There was something terribly attractive about him in a rugged, masculine way, of course, and especially when he was doing the thing he liked best to do. Love or hate . . . it had to be one or the other she felt for him. There was no doubt he stirred and aroused her physically, but then, she considered, how do I know another attractive man, Buck for instance, couldn't do the same?

She gave an involuntary shiver at the thought of making love with any other man. No, dammit! I'm just trying to fool myself. Demoralizing as it is, I love him! It was insane that she could love him after the agony he had put her through. He had no need for the love, enduring love, of a woman. With that arrogant face, the imperious set head and flashing eyes, he could have any woman he wanted. Now that she had admitted to herself she still loved him her lips curled with self-disgust.

"What's the matter?" The strangeness of his voice made her look down at her hands clasped tightly together in her lap.

"Nothing," she said much too reasonably. "I was only thinking."

"About . . . us?"

Suddenly she wanted to cry for all those nights so long ago when she was young and blindly in love. Not being able to define in thoughts or words what she was feeling she turned strickened eyes toward him. "Oh, please, Jake!" Her voice was soft in protest. "This is all so . . . useless."

"Useless?" He echoed the word.

"You know what I mean!" Why couldn't he understand, for chrissake? "We're different people now. I have made a life for myself, just as you have."

He gave a muffled curse and looked across the intervening space between them, his eyes glittering under the lids. "Good God! We're right for each other. Haven't I convinced you yet?" There was a hard, mocking quality to his voice.

"The only thing I'm convinced of, dammit, is that I'm no longer married to you and you didn't even have the decency to tell me!" She stared at him helplessly, also convinced she would never, never be rid of him. Everything about him, his physical attraction, his personality, was making that impossible.

Jake set his mouth in a straight line and concentrated on his driving. The loose snow stirred up by the trucks ahead made for poor visibility at times. It was easy to be bored with the scene. It seemed to go on and on with nothing to break the monotony.

Lindy picked up the road map lying over on the dashboard. Vaguely she wondered about the need for a map. There was only one highway south. But looking at it she couldn't suppress a small thrill at the sight of their journey plotted out across Alaska.

"How long before we reach Happy Valley Camp?"

"It's hard to say." His eyes were on the road. "Buck says it's slow going ahead."

"I didn't get to see any of the country when I came up. We flew from Houston to Anchorage, then on north."

He brought his gaze in from the road. "Actually, I haven't seen much of the country either. Alaska is a very poor and stark region; there are large numbers of animals only because this environment is spread over such a large space. I doubt if we will see many of them."

They were moving slowly now so she sat back and sipped her coffee. Jake, with his eyes on the road, was blindly reaching for his cup. She picked it up and placed it in his hand.

"Tell me about Buck. Have you known him long?"

"Why do you want to know?"

"No reason. He seems nice."

"He is. He was given a rough time by a woman." His voice was hard with cynicism.

She didn't say anything thinking he didn't want to talk about it.

"Buck had it rough," he said again, his voice softer. "He's over it now, but it took a while. His trucking company was about to be taken over by his creditors and I bought it. He had spent every last dime he could get his hands on trying to keep his wife happy. I could have told him it was impossible, but at the time he wouldn't listen to a word against her. She was just plain no good. After a time he came to realize it more than anyone else. Now he can't stand the sight of her."

Lindy settled back in the seat and closed her eyes, trying to relax, but they flew open again as Buck's voice came in from the radio speaker. "Breaker, boss. You and turtledove still back there?"

"Ten-four, Buck. We're about a mile back. How's the road ahead?"

"That's what I want to tell you. I'm stopping here. Some joker got himself crossways on the road and is being pulled out. We better keep the rigs spaced in case the traffic on this boulevard gets heavy. If he don't treat you right, turtledove, you just come on up here and ride with ol' Buck."

Amusement, curiosity and surprise all mingled in Jake's eyes as he looked at her. "Forget it, Buck." He hung up the mike.

He pulled the heavy truck over to the side of the road. After pulling several levers and adjusting gears he leaned back and flexed his arms over his head. Turning sideways in his seat, he reached for the coffee.

"Tired . . . turtledove?" His tone was a mixture of ridicule and teasing.

"Don't call me that ridiculous name!" Her face suddenly showed the agony of last night and he watched her, puzzled by the torment he saw mixed with fatigue. He took her hand and stroked it lovingly, holding it tightly when she would have jerked it away.

"Give in, Lindy. Don't torment yourself. Our marriage can be a good one if you'll give it a chance."

Lindy was sitting up very straight, looking at him defiantly from beneath half-closed lids, her hand cold and taut in his. She forced her lids open, although they felt as if a lead weight was attached to each one. His face was grave and his eyes held a tenderness she didn't expect.

"We are worlds apart, Jake. Oh, I admit the marriage would be good from your standpoint. A little woman waiting at home, one that is good in bed, a loving, trusting, dumb little wife who would take care of the babies and go to PTA. That scene is not for me. I'm simply not interested. I prefer a man who doesn't lie and cheat. When I'm with you, Jake, I'm treading on quicksand. There's no feeling of stability. I prefer a straightforward life with a straightforward man to match."

He tilted his head and took a deep breath of air into his lungs. His face was a dark mask and there was harshness in his voice.

"Someday . . . someday you'll push me too far and I'll take a strap to your butt!" His eyes flickered over her face, the firm classical lines, the perfect contours, the flawless skin. A movement in his throat betrayed the fact that he was swallowing his anger. He looked dangerous, his steely eyes sweeping across her face, lingering on the pulse that beat so frantically at the base of her throat. "Life can't be played out like a romantic novel with all the characters neatly conforming to what's expected of them. How dull to have each event of the day marked out all prim and proper! You can't deny the pleasure you feel when I hold you against me. Don't try and tell me our lovemaking isn't as pleasurable for you as it is for me."

"That's all you think about." She flung him a tormented look. "That's all I am to you, a body! You don't want a wife—you want a live-in mistress."

"Shut up!"

Jake's eyes were suddenly so furious that she felt as if the strength drained out of her, leaving her limp in the grip of the hands that clutched her forearms.

"You look like a woman, but you're really a child, Lindy." His dark face was adamant as he looked at her, the lean jaw set and firm. "You're welcome to hate me, if you really do. Frankly I know you love me and you'll marry me again when the time comes." He slid a panel aside and folded down a section at the back of the seat which made a step up to the door behind. "Get on back there and rest. You look like you've been run on a rim for five miles."

Lindy gazed back into his eyes, so astonishingly green and luminous in the dim light. "I'll never live with you," she said distinctly. "It would make me ill to have to see you day and night for the rest of my life. Haven't you got it into your arrogant head, Jake, that I despise everything about you, the look of you, the sound of you and especially the touch of you? I'm free and nothing . . . I mean nothing, would cause me to marry you again."

He flinched when she said that and, if it were possible, went a little pale under the suntanned skin. His facial bones seemed to stand out with additional clarity and the pupils of his eyes expanded and darkened. He looked as if she had kicked him in the throat.

Lindy felt a thrust of pleasure that she had actually bruised his pride and climbed into the back compartment and slid the panel shut with force.

She lay down on the bunk, pulled the blanket up over her and gave herself up to the flood of misery that engulfed her. Her torment was all the more difficult to bear because there was no one with whom she could share it. She longed to be home where she could talk with her friend, Debra. Calm, practical, reliable Debra whose own marriage ran like the romantic novel Jake scoffed at.

Lindy's troubled mind was unable to separate fact from fantasy, now. Built-up emotions of the last few weeks found release in the silent sobs that shook her thin body. All at once tiredness attacked her with an odd sense of detachment and she slept, her tears making a damp pillow under her cheek. She awoke once, conscious of the moving motion of the truck, but was lulled again into the sweet oblivion of sleep, where her mind need not strain to work out the problems that confronted her.

Sometime later the unfamiliar stillness of the truck awakened her. The only sound she heard was the soft purr of the motor which she knew would not be turned off until they reached warmer climate.

She was wide awake immediately, tense and alert. Raising her head from the pillow, she saw the covered figure on the narrow pull-down bunk opposite her. His back was toward her and the blanket was drawn up to his ears. She sank back down into the warm nest of blankets trying hard to resent his being there. Her face touched soft fur and she recognized Jake's fur-lined parka. He must have placed it over her while she slept. By the feeble light she checked her watch. She had slept hours and it had seemed only minutes. She settled herself down to wait out the remaining hours until morning. Unconsciously she drew the fur collar under her face and snuggled her nose into it. Strangely the masculine smell was comforting. She felt safe, contented, and fell into a tranquilizing inertness, then into deep peaceful slumber.

CHAPTER SIX

LINDY AWAKENED TO the sound of buzzing and her sleep-drugged mind thought it was made by hundreds of bees. Full consciousness came to her and she opened her eyes to see Jake sitting on the other bunk, using a battery-powered shaver. He was rubbing the instrument over his face and his eyes were on her. She looked into the blue depth and saw the twinkle of amusement there. His mood had changed, but hers hadn't. She glared back at him.

"Good morning."

"Good for what?" she replied shrewishly.

"I can think of a number of things and so could you if you weren't feeling so sorry for yourself!"

She clamped her mouth shut and tried to look away from him, but in the closeness of the compartment there was no other place to look. He seemed to fill the tiny space. She wished desperately that she wasn't lying down.

He read her thoughts and lifted his brows in a way that made her want to strike out at him. "When I finish shaving I'm going to kiss you," he said, trying to keep his mouth from spreading in a wide grin as her eyes opened wide and her mouth set stubbornly. He was shaving under his chin and tilted his head back, but his twinkling eyes never left her face.

"You're hopeless, Jake. A real imbecile!"

"Yeah?" He turned off the shaver. "But you love me."

"You're not only an imbecile, you're conceited!" In her agitation she sat straight up on the bunk.

He laughed aloud, produced a comb from somewhere and ran it through his hair. "You're even more attractive when you're mad. I don't remember you getting mad in the old days."

"The old days are over!" she almost shouted at him. "This is now!" That reminder of the past tore at her heart.

"Yeah." He said it softly and took her chin tightly in his hand. She tried to twist away from him, but he held her firmly and ran the comb through the tangles of her hair.

She strived to close her heart against the thrill of his warm fingers on her face and the gentle look in his half-closed eyes. His magnetism seemed to draw the anger out of her.

He tucked the comb into his shirt pocket, then brought his hand up to smooth down the hair that fit her head like a cap. His fingers lingered on her ear, then slid to the nape of her neck. The thumb of the hand holding her chin rubbed gently back and forth across her tightly compressed lips. Suddenly he laughed.

"The first time I kissed you you're lips were just like this . . . shut tight!" His laughing eyes searched hers. "But you soon opened them . . . you liked my kisses, remember?"

Her eyes glittered. "I didn't know what kind of an idiot you were then."

"But you know now," he said softly, laughingly, "and you still like them."

She shook her head in denial, knowing that he knew she was lying.

"Shall I prove it?" With her head in the powerful grip of his two hands she was helpless as he slowly lowered his lips onto hers. He kissed her with slow deliberation, his lips playing, coaxing. He had kissed her many times before with passion and urgency, but never did she have to fight so hard not to surrender completely. He caressed her gently, almost delicately, encouraging her by his very control to lose hers utterly. Oh, sweet Jesus! She had to hold out against him. She had lost so much already!

His hands left her head and slipped down her back, pulling her tight against him. She felt herself sliding down on the bunk until she could slide no further and the pressure of his body on hers made every nerve and sense in her body suddenly vibrantly alive.

"You . . . beautiful, tantalizing little witch!" His shaking voice said into her ear. "Tell me you don't love me, if you can."

Her eyes were haunted and dark with despair when she looked at him. "I never said I didn't love you. I said I didn't like you and that I won't . . ."

"Hush," he said quickly. "I don't want to hear what you won't do!"

"No . . . no!" She tried to push him away. "I must be out of my mind! Get away from me, Jake! Get away from me!" Resentment burned like wildfire. With blinding clarity the truth hit her like a tangible blow. He realized his power over her!

He got up and sat on the opposite bunk and ran his hand through his hair. "You're warped."

"I may be warped, Jake, but I'm not stupid. Marriage to me didn't keep you from taking another woman and you've had other women since you left me . . . deny it, if you can."

"You know I can't! What did you expect me to do?" The tender look was gone from his eyes and his voice was fringed with sarcasm. "Dick Kenfield and then Amos and you dare to criticize me!"

"I wish I had slept with every man that asked me!" Her sarcasm matched his.

He got to his feet and stood towering above her, glaring down at her as if he hated her.

"I would have killed you!" he snarled. Snatching his sweater from the bunk, he went through the door of the compartment. Once again they had parted in anger

Lindy lay on the bunk staring at the closed door. Peaks and valleys, heaven and hell. It would always be like this with Jake.

The last twenty-four hours seemed to set the pattern for the days ahead. The convoy furrowed its way south across snow-packed plateaus, one-way bridges, detoured past overturned rigs and slid down icy mountain sides. The atmosphere inside the truck cab was comparable to the conditions outside. One moment smooth going of an easy comradeship, the next stormy battles of will against will.

They passed through Atigun Pass and on south to Old Man Camp settlement, crossed over the first permanent bridge over the mighty Yukon River, stood by on the siding while dozens of dependable rigs passed heading north with their loads of long pipe—the most sophisticated ever designed to meet the requirements of the rugged terrain. After Five Mile Camp the road was considerably better, and knowing the next stop would be Fairbanks and hot showers, good beds and a few days of rest, the men settled down to the job of getting there in the shortest time possible.

"Won't be long now." Jake grinned at her.

"I'm going to sit in a hot tub and soak away all my aches and pains."

Looking straight down the road, his next words were spoken matter-of-factly, belying their importance.

"We'll be married again in Fairbanks."

He hadn't mentioned the marriage since the first stormy quarrel they had shortly after they left the camp and Lindy was about to think he had given up on the idea of a quick ceremony.

She tightened her lips and looked straight ahead, resentment in every line of her face.

"Now don't start balking again," he said sternly, and then trying to joke her out of her sulky mood, he added, "I think I'll start calling you Muley."

"Call me anything you like, but you're a fool if you think I'm going to jump back into the frying pan!"

"Dammit! I don't know why I bother with you!"

Lindy's chin lifted, her own pride fighting to control the pain inside her. She turned her face away and looked out the side window at nothing in particular.

"Break! Break!" Buck's voice came in on the radio.

"Number two's jackknifed. It's still upright, but a-sittin' on the side of the ditch."

Jake slowed the truck and at the same time picked up the microphone.

"Ten-four. John, you and Charlie go on ahead of Buck. Don, you stay on this side of the wreck and I'll pull up behind you."

Jake turned on the flashing emergency lights and steered the heavy truck as far as he dared to the side of the road. Pulling on his parka, he glanced at Lindy's set profile, muttered a muffled curse and got out of the cab, slamming the door behind him.

Lindy watched Jake lope down the highway and out of sight beyond the truck ahead. Her tense body relaxed and she slumped againsl the seat. This was the first time in two days she had been alone and no longer needed to keep up the pretense of the self-assurance she had assumed since the start of the trip. Not wanting to think about the problems she would face in Fairbanks she looked out the window trying to find something that would catch her interest. There was just a lot of ice and snow, occasionally a small hill, or a drift.

She could see nothing of what was going on up ahead and was tempted to get out and walk just for the exercise and to break the boredom of waiting. A northbound truck stopped ahead and suddenly, she had a powerful urge to see for herself what was happening. Something was wrong, she could feel it. Her heart started to pound swiftly and she reached into the compartment for her parka and boots.

When she was ready to face the biting cold she crawled over into the driver's seat and let herself out of the cab, holding onto the door until her feet could feel the firmly packed snow. Up ahead she could see the men running back and forth in a frenzy of activity. Spotlights were being focused on the truck which had slid down the incline and was lying precariously on its side.

Lindy stood hesitantly in the shelter of one of the truck cabs, the roar of the big engine drowning out the voices of the men. Try as she might she couldn't spot Jake. It was Buck's bulky figure at the top of the bank shouting instructions to the men. Where was Jake? She ran across the snow and grabbed Buck by the arm.

"What's happened?"

"What are you doing here? Didn't Jake tell you to stay in the cab?" They were the sharpest words she ever heard him speak and for a moment she was taken aback. Then it came to her . . . something had happened to Jake!

"Where's Jake? What's happened?"

Buck looked down into eyes wide with anxiety. "Jake went around the trailer to attach a cable and it slipped over on him."

Lindy's face went white, she caught her breath and felt the sandwich she had eaten an hour before rise up in her throat.

"Can't . . . you get him out?"

"We're trying, honey. We've got an emergency call out for help. That's all we can do for now."

"Is he . . . hurt . . . bad?"

"We don't know. That's the God's truth!" Anguish was in every line of Buck's face as he stared down at the bedlam in hers.

"Do something! We can't wait!" Her voice was rising to an almost hysterical pitch and she started toward the overturned truck.

Buck grabbed her arm. "Stay back!" he said sternly. "We can't risk it slipping more."

She stopped in her tracks, sure that she was going to fall apart. Jake couldn't be . . . gone. He would come climbing up over the bank and be mad because she was out in the cold. He wouldn't leave her now! He had sworn . . . had promised he was never going away again! Oh, God! She couldn't face all those nights alone again! Why didn't he come up from behind that truck, dammit? He was just doing this to teach her a lesson! Jake, damn you!

One of the men was talking to Buck. "If we had a way to get a chain through that small hole and get it hooked onto the undercarriage we could use the winch to lift it enough for one of us to drag him out. If he is alive he won't last long as cold as it is."

"It's a good idea, Don, but there's no way in the world we can get a chain under that truck. The hole is just too damn small."

Don looked at Lindy. She looked back and suddenly read his thoughts.

"How big is the hole?"

Don made a circle with his hands, but still said nothing.

"I can get through a hole that size, Buck. I can do it!"

Buck looked at her as if she had lost her mind. He shook his head and glared at Don before bringing his eyes back to Lindy's anguished face.

"If Jake's alive it's because the truck hasn't settled and

it could do that any minute. If that happens he won't have a chance and neither would you if you were under it."

"I can do it, Buck! You've got to give him a chance! Let me do it! Please!" The determined ring in her voice and set to her shoulders caused Don to grin.

Buck looked down at her for a long moment before sudden hope flared in his eyes, then died slowly.

"If anything happened to you, Jake would kill me."

"He won't be here to do anything, for chrissake, if you don't make up your mind!" There was something agonizing in her eyes that tore him.

"You understand if that truck slips it will crush you like a melon?"

"Just tell me what to do." She felt as though someone else was speaking the words for her. She heard them, but couldn't feel them in her mouth. There was an incredible numbness that settled on her like a giant cloak.

They walked to the truck and knelt down in the snow to peer into the hole. Suddenly everything was functioning; her mind, her body. Her manner was of total control; it was only her eyes that shouted her anguish. She shrugged out of her coat. Someone handed her a toboggan cap and she pulled it down over her head.

Buck put a chain with a giant hook in her mittened hand and explained what she was to do.

"Straight through the hole and to the right you'll see a big round steel loop on the underside of the frame. Put the hoop in the eye from underneath so when we pull up the strain will be on the outside of the hook, understand?" She nodded. "Now, honey, I don't know what you'll find when you get under there. Get the hook fastened as fast as you can and we'll pull you out." She nodded again and lay flat on the snow. Buck tied a rope to one of her ankles. "Yank on the rope and we'll pull you out," he said but she barely heard him.

Lindy inched her way carefully into the small hole. There wasn't much room for maneuvering the big chain, so she dragged it along with the big hook looped into the belt of her jeans. She didn't dare use her elbows to push herself forward, so she clawed with her fingers and the toes of her boots. The blood was racing through her veins now and her heart pumped madly, but her mind was clear and her nerves steady. It took several minutes of crawling before she could see Jake lying at the end of the small tunnel. She kept her eyes fixed on his face trying to see some sign of life. Oh, God! Please let him be all right . . . she wanted to tell him she was sorry for her bitchiness . . . that she loved him . . . that at this moment she would forgive him anything.

The eyebeam where she was to attach the hook was ahead. Her eyes once again sought Jake's face. His head was lying in blood-soaked snow and his leg was twisted and out of sight beneath the frame. She had to force herself to move away from him.

Lifting the hook from her belt, she slipped it securely into the hole and pulled on the rope to let Buck know she was ready to come out. As she was pulled backward she kept her eyes on Jake for as long as she could see him. Fear tightened her throat at the sight of him lying there so pale and defenseless.

Don untied the rope from her ankle, helped her into her parka and enveloped her in a blanket. She had started to shake uncontrollably. Buck shouted orders and the men hurried about preparing to lift the machine.

"We'll have only seconds," Buck was saying. "I'll shout when I get to the other side. Start the winch slowly. When it's clear enough I'll drag him out. The frame will buckle. Let's pray to God it don't buckle before I get him."

Don and one of the other drivers stood beside Lindy. "Good girl," one of them said. "At least he's got a chance. I hope Lady Luck's ridin' with Buck. He's gonna have to move fast."

Lindy stood as if in a trance while the winch tightened the chain. She knew only one thing. Jake was under those thousands of pounds of steel, and she might not ever see him alive again, might not feel him, touch him, argue with him. He had broken his promise to her, had slept with other women, had been unfaithful to their marriage vows . . . but what did that matter now? Tears ran down her face like summer rain. Dammit, Jake! Don't you dare die on me! Cold to the heart she watched the heavy chain tighten, heard the groan of the straining winch. Her glance shifted to Buck poised beside the end of the trailer.

Suddenly he darted out of sight and the group on the road held their breath. Seconds later he was dragging Jake's limp body out and down the ditch. He had only just cleared the wreck when the metal began to twist and the trailer buckled, settling heavily on down the steep grade. It was all so quiet. Like a silent movie. Even the men who ran to help Buck bring Jake up the bank didn't speak.

Gently they placed him on folded blankets and covered him with several more. Lindy knelt down beside him.

"He's alive! Thanks to Lindy, he's alive!"

"We've got to stop the blood!" Lindy was losing control.

"The ambulance is almost here. I can see the flashing lights. We called for it on the emergency channel as soon as the truck turned over on him." Buck put his arm around her. "You were great, honey, just great. If he lives he'll owe his life to you."

"Don't say that!" Her anxious eyes watched the still face on the ground. Oh, God! She felt so helpless.

Buck pressed a cloth to the wound on Jake's head, trying to stem the flow of blood that ran down his face which had taken on a gray tinge. Time hung like a black cloud while they waited for the attendants to come with the stretcher. Fast and experienced, they made every move count and within seconds of ther arrival Jake was in the ambulance.

Lindy and Buck stood outside the door of the emergency vehicle while the skilled rescue team worked over Jake. Lindy could never remember any of this with clarity; she was conscious only of the heavy dread around her heart and the weakness of her limbs. The tension mounted as the team continued to work. Just when she thought she couldn't stand the suspense a minute longer the door opened and one of the attendants called out.

"Does anyone know this man's blood type?"

Buck shook his head, but Lindy came to life.

"Yes, yes! It's the same as mine!"

"You're sure?" The attendant looked at her closely. "It may save his life if we can give him a transfusion."

"We gave blood to the Red Cross two years ago. Our blood type is the same." She was shaking violently and Buck held her arm.

"Are you his wife?"

"Yes," she said without hesitation.

"Come on then!" He pulled her into the ambulance and almost before she got inside the door he was taking off her coat. "Lay down." He briskly pressed her to the cot beside the one where Jake lay.

While preparing the instruments for the transfusion the doctor questioned her about any recent illnesses. She told him she had not been ill.

"Good." He injected the needle into her arm.

In seconds she could see the tube between her arm and Jake's filling with her blood. The strain and the tension were taking its toll on her and she felt giddy. Closing her eyes, she willed herself to stay conscious. She wanted desperately to question the doctor and stared up into his face trying to read his reactions.

"We're going now." The doctor's voice was quiet, unhurried. "Any message for the men?"

"Ask Buck to come to the hospital." For the first time since the accident she was conscious of the large tears in her eyes.

The siren started, the ambulance moved, the doctor sat between her and Jake, his watchful eyes on the needles in their arms.

A little color had come back into Jake's face by the time they reached the hospital; weak tears streamed down Lindy's when they were separated. Jake was taken to the emergency room and Lindy to a small office where she was given orange juice and a few crackers which she forced herself to eat. The weakness in her legs made her realize she needed the food. While she was resting she gave the registrar as much information as she could about Jake. Married? She had to say no. Age? Thirty-three. Service record? Vietnam. Next of kin? Her heart almost stopped at that question. It seemed hours before she was allowed to leave the room to wait in the small anteroom reserved for relatives of patients in emergency. She rested her head against the wall and closed her eyes wearily.

CHAPTER SEVEN

LINDY REACHED FOR a magazine and let her eyes wander over the pages hardly reading what she saw. She was filled with apprehension, her heart fluttering, her fingers trembling as she turned the pages. Was no one ever coming to the little room? Her ear was tuned . . . listening for footsteps. Waiting was agonizing. She threw the magazine down onto the table and went to the door. The long hall was empty except for a white-coated orderly pushing a cart at the far end. She was surprised at the lack of activity, then remembered it must be terribly late at night. The long day had turned into a nightmare. On almost uncontrollable legs she went back into the room and sank down on the sofa, covering her eyes with her hands.

Footsteps were coming along the corridor. Her heart lurched. Dear Lord, let it be good news!

Buck's big frame filled the doorway. His face looked tired and drawn, his eyes searched her eyes, asking the question. "Any news?"

She shook her head despairingly. "No. No one has come at all."

Buck looked down at the tired pale face. Her dark-circled eyes were dulled with fatigue. She still wore the clothes she had worn when she crawled under the truck. She had gone through quite a lot today, both mentally and emotionally. She had also suffered physically, but she was holding up pretty well.

"Had anything to eat?"

"A little," she said wearily. "I could use coffee, but I was afraid to leave in case someone came with news."

"There's a dispenser around the corner. I'll be right back."

Lindy sank down in the chair, refusing to give way before the tears that wanted to spill over again. How desperately she had wanted someone to come! It would be easier now, sharing the waiting with Buck.

He brought coffee for the two of them. Lindy accepted hers with a bleak smile of thanks.

"It seems like I've been waiting forever, Buck." Her voice was tired, old. She swallowed something in her throat, something that felt like a large lump of cotton that wanted to rise up and choke her.

"I came as soon as I could, honey. I stayed only long enough to hire a couple guys to take my rig and Jake's on south. The men are at the terminal now loading the cargo. Don will handle things and I'll stay here with you."

"Thank you," she said, took a deep breath and felt as though things would never be right again.

"Why don't you lie down on the couch and rest?" Buck suggested.

"I couldn't. Oh, Buck, I've done so many stupid, childish things! I don't know what I want anymore!"

By way of answer, Buck held her hand tightly. They

didn't talk, but they were mentally in tune with another. Buck cared for Jake too.

Lindy tensed at the sound of voices in the hallway. She rose like one compelled by a force many times stronger than herself and faced the door. It was as if her whole inner being was about to dissolve as she waited for someone to appear.

A tall gray-haired man entered the room. "I'm Doctor Casey."

"Yes?" She was breathless.

"Mrs. Williamson?"

"Yes."

Buck was on his feet, extending his hand. "Buck Collson."

"The blood given to Mr. Williamson at the scene of the accident saved his life," the doctor said after he shook hands with Buck. "He has several injuries, but what concerns us the most is the head injury. We don't know the extent of the damage. We had to remove a small piece of his skull to relieve the pressure from an optic nerve. He must be kept absolutely quiet for the next twenty-four to thirty-six hours." He quietly studied Lindy for a moment. "You told the emergency doctor he was your husband and the registrar he wasn't married."

"We're divorced," Lindy said quietly.

"I see. Well, he's fretting about something and calling for you. It may calm him to hear your voice, but I wanted to see you first. You must not allow any of your anxiety to be transmitted to him. He must not be upset. I cannot stress that too strongly."

The doctor was regarding her keenly, assessing her. Lindy looked straight into his eyes. "I can do whatever has to be done. Doctor." Her voice was calm, steady, even to her own ears. But, oh, God! If he only knew how she wanted to cry.

"Good. Come with me."

Lindy hesitated and reached for Buck's hand. The doctor nodded his permission for Buck to come and they followed him out of the room and down the hallway. The long white corridors seemed endless and Lindy was glad of Buck's reassuring fingers beneath her elbow.

When they reached the door of Jake's room the doctor paused and looked at Lindy's calm, composed face once again, then opened the door for her to pass through.

The room was of generous proportions with wide windows and light green walls. The dark-clad figure of the sister nurse stood on one side of the bed, a white-coated orderly on the other, his hands holding the shoulders of the man thrashing about.

Lindy's eyes were drawn immediately to Jake's tanned face. His head was swathed in bandages that came down over his eyes and was held firmly in position by supports placed on either side. The part of his face that remained visible was unrecognizable to her. His mustache had been shaved, the cuts around his nose and mouth stitched, long scratches extended from his jaw to his neck. Restless hands moved back and forth over the white sheet and periodically he tried to lift his shoulders only to be gently pressed down by the strong hands of the orderly. Protruding out from under the sheet that covered him was a leg, encased in a cast, resting in a sling suspended on the foot of the bed.

She stood there for a long moment, afraid to go in, but knowing she had to. Then slowly, one foot after the other, she walked into the room and stopped again. Her brain started to resume its normal function. The murmured words of the man on the bed reached her ears.

"Lindy . . . Lindy . . ." The words came from puffed lips in a hoarse whisper.

The sister stepped aside and made room for her beside the bed. She came close and took his long, slim hand in both of hers. The swollen lips parted and he breathed out words that only she understood.

"Lindy . . . believe me . . ."

Tears coursed down her cheeks and fell onto her hands that clasped his. The hand that had always been so strong and capable was weak and clung to hers. She leaned her head so her lips were close to his ear.

"I believe you, Jake darling. I believe you and I love you. Please lie still. You must lie still and rest . . . sleep, darling." She whispered into his ear and touched her lips gently to his cheek.

The hand in hers trembled slightly and then clutched hers with a strength that surprised her. She brought it to her cheek and spoke to him softly and soothingly.

"Go to sleep. I'll be here. Everything's going to be all right."

He murmured something once again. She bent over him talking softly, reassuringly, scarcely aware the orderly and the nurse had gone to the end of the room to speak in low tones to Buck and the doctor.

Someone placed a chair behind her and she sat down close to the bed. The hand in hers was still holding hers tightly but the restless movement of the other hand had stopped as had the movement of the shoulders. Lindy looked askance at the doctor, who nodded to her, and motioned Buck and the orderly toward the door. He followed them out after giving instructions to the nurse who seated herself at the end of the room.

Jake's breathing was more even now, as if he were sleeping. The fingers holding hers gradually loosened their hold and lay passive in her hand. All at once she felt herself trembling uncontrollably. The shock and surprise of seeing him so helpless, vulnerable, was just now catching up with her. She held the limp hand tightly. He had called for her. Could it mean that he loved her? Really loved her after all? She sat gazing at his face and gradually her nerves calmed. An inner strength exerted itself and she put all thoughts of the future from her mind. All that was important, now, was Jake's complete recovery.

The minutes and the hours ticked away. She was silent and motionless, her eyes never leaving the bruised face. She didn't let herself wonder why his eyes were bandaged. For now it was enough that he was alive. The fact that he wanted her, needed her, and she was able to comfort him was soothing to her troubled mind. The traumatic experiences of the long day were taking their toll on her strength. She leaned over and rested her cheek on Jake's hand where it lay on the bed. Her eyes drifted shut and she slept.

She awakened gradually, her drugged senses resisting consciousness. When full awareness came to her she was lying on a bed, a light cover over her. Buck was sitting in a nearby chair, his head resting on his arm. He appeared to be sleeping. Lindy sat up and threw off the covers, her thoughts flying to Jake.

"Buck!" Her wildly frightened heart pounded.

Buck got quickly to his feet. "He's sleeping, honeychild. Rest while you can." He came to her. "The nurse will let us know if there's any change."

She sank wearily back onto the bed. "Oh, Lord, Buck. What would I do without you?"

"You'd manage, honey. You got starch in that backbone."

She smiled weakly. "It only appears to be so, Buck. I'm really scared spitless."

"Yeah, I know. Me too." He was tired. It showed in the lines in his face and the bleak expression in his eyes. "I've checked us into a hotel. After a while we can go shower and change clothes. That'll make us feel a hundred percent better."

"What time is it?"

He smiled wearily. "It's morning. Can't you smell the breakfast being carted down the hall?"

"As late as that?"

"Rest a while longer. I'll go see what I can find out."

Later, while luxuriating in a warm, scented bath, Lindy let her mind mull over the information Buck brought back from the doctor. Jake's condition had stabilized and he was sleeping, which was what the doctor wanted him to do. Buck had broken the rest of the news to her gently. The doctor feared Jake's eyesight was going to be affected by the blow he had received on the head. He said he wouldn't know for several days the extent of the damage. He also suggested the possibility that the nerve would repair itself and Jake's eyesight would return to normal. It would require long and patient care and he would need to be kept quiet and relaxed. The joy Lindy felt that he would live was replaced by a cold dread of him being unable to see. How would he handle it . . . how could a vigorous, active man like Jake accept blindness, even for a while?

The hotel was a new modern structure that fairly screamed the word "expensive" when they walked in the door. Lindy had been hesitant but Buck propelled her toward the desk and demanded their keys with all the confidence of a Texas millionaire. On the way to their rooms he had assured her the company could afford the expense.

"Old Jake would have my hide if I put you up in anything less than the best." Buck's drawl and humor was coming back.

The room had been far more luxurious than anything Lindy had stayed in before and under different circumstances it would have been a delight to sink into the big tub and sprawl out onto the giant bed. She wanted to linger in the warm tub, soaking her tired body, but she hurried through her bath and was ready and waiting when Buck rapped on her door.

Buck was a good-looking man. Several feminine heads turned to look at him as they passed through the lobby. He was wearing a Western suit that had been tailored for his large frame. His raven hair was shiny as if he had just come from the shower. The ever-present cowboy boots and sheepskin coat flung over his arm fairly shouted this man was from Texas. Why couldn't I have fallen in love with a man like Buck, Lindy thought. He's gentle, thoughtful, comfortable to be with. He's so different from Jake who constantly sets my blood to racing and my heart to pounding.

She was too tired to notice what Buck ordered for her to eat, but when the waiter set the bowl of steaming soup in front of her, she realized she was hungry.

"You know about Jake and me two years ago?"

He was watching her and she found his eyes. "Jake told me."

"Tell me about him. About what he's been doing the last two years." She hesitated. Damn! She wanted to know and she didn't want to know. Her eyes picked out a spot past Buck and she gazed at it intently. "I've wondered . . ."

Buck drained his cup and set it aside carefully. "I've known Jake for a long time. Even before you came into his life. It wasn't until after you two split that I got to know him well and to find out what a really fine person he is."

The waiter refilled the coffee cups.

"I ran into him one day in Houston. He had just got back from South America and was going back again. The fact that I was about to lose my company was common knowledge and Jake asked me, right out, if I needed help. He offered either a loan or to purchase the company, leaving me in charge." Buck's fingers twisted around his cup. "You know the answer to that. He bought the company. But more than that, he stood by me through a messy divorce and helped me get my personal life straightened out. He went off to South America and left me on my own, saving my pride before my men. I had to produce; I couldn't let him down."

Lindy wasn't surprised by the story. It was something Jake would do. She was surprised that he would have the money for such an investment.

"He made several trips back to the States," Buck said, taking up the threads of his story. "He'd stay a few days and be off again. I went back with him about a year ago.

We came back to Houston a few months back and Jake set out to buy the Prudhoe Bay company." He grinned. "I couldn't understand at first why he had to have that particular company." Looking away from her, he continued. "Jake's a very shrewd businessman. Dead wells he leased years ago are now pumping close to eight hundred barrels a day. Financially he's pretty well set. Once he starts the ball rolling he usually gets what he wants. But you should know that. Before he left Texas he bought a house on Galveston Island and left exacting instructions on how it was to be furnished. He set a time limit of one month for the work to be finished." Buck looked at her searchingly. "He came north to get you, girl, and take you back to that house on the island."

Lindy felt as if her heart had turned over inside her. She wondered if, in fact, the loud thump of her heart could be heard all over the room and she had an almost uncontrollable urge to cry. Biting her lip hard, she looked at Buck with agony behind her eyes, making them look large and bleak.

"We planned to have a house on the island one day." The words were whispered and her lips trembled. "And we window-shopped for furnishings." Now . . . why did she have to remember that?

"Didn't he tell you about the house?"

"No. He never even told me about the divorce being final. I happened to find the papers in his suitcase."

Buck smiled at that. "He was mad as hell at himself for signing those papers and fit to be tied when we came back and the divorce was final."

"I'd made up my mind not to marry him again and I

was going to leave him when we got to Fairbanks, but now . . ."

"And now?"

"And now I don't know. I couldn't leave him like this in spite of . . ."

"In spite of what?" he urged.

"In spite of the fact I'd be standing in hot water if I marry him again!" she blurted. "I'd never know from one day to the next if he . . ."

"If he what?" Buck persisted.

"If he was out with another woman! I'm old-fashioned, Buck. I want to be the only woman in my husband's life."

Buck sat back in the chair, lit a cigarette and regarded her with thoughtful eyes. He marveled at her self-control. Her voice was steady and direct when she spoke again.

"Women gather around him like flies wherever he goes. I was told by someone who knew him very well that no one woman would ever satisfy him and I believe it. I know what it means, Buck, to live in a home where there's love only on one side, where the laws of religion keep a couple together until death do they part. I'll never raise a child in that atmosphere. If I marry Jake again it will mean I will never have children!" Tears came to her eyes. "And more than anything I would love to have a child of my own."

Buck's dark brows drew together. "Honey, I don't know what to say. Guess I never gave no thought to that side of it. One thing I do know, Jake's a proud man. It would be a bitter pill for him to swallow to be accused and have his wife refuse to believe in him."

So he did know the reason for the separation. She wanted to cry. It seemed to be all she did anymore. So much had happened. It was all so crazy sitting here talking to practically a stranger, but she had to get it out.

"But what about me, Buck? What about me?" The question seemed to be wrung from her tortured heart.

He shook his head. He longed to reassure her, but the words he chose seemed so terribly inadequate.

"You'll have to decide if you love him enough to take him as he is. One of you will always give more than the other. Accept it or you'll end up hating each other like my former wife and myself."

CHAPTER EIGHT

LINDY SPENT EVERY possible moment with Jake, moving from his bed to the corridor to his bed and back to the corridor. Buck joined her on this treadmill for there was no getting her away from the hospital except for short periods of sleep. Although Jake was kept heavily sedated and fed intravenously, he seemed less restless when she was there.

One time she thought him awake. He gripped her hand tightly and said in a clear audible voice, "My love . . . my life . . ."

Poignant tears sprang quickly to her eyes. He had whispered the familiar words many times while making passionate love to her, holding his ardor in check, infinitely patient, waiting to take her with him in the final floating away.

She gazed at the bruised face. He was sleeping. She leaned over and placed a feather of a kiss on the swollen lips. She felt afraid suddenly, as if by his very helplessness he was binding her closer to him.

Forty-eight hours after the accident the doctor intercepted Lindy and Buck on their way to Jake's room and invited them into his office.

"Mr. Williamson is conscious and alert this morning. I don't think it wise for you to see him for a few hours. I prefer we give him time to adjust to what we have told him. Oh, yes, we told him the absolute truth—the fact that we are not sure he will be able to see when we remove the bandages and also that we have every hope his eyesight will return." The doctor paused and looked at Lindy. "He was concerned about your reaction to his temporary blindness, Mrs. Williamson."

"What do you mean?"

"I got the impression he wasn't sure that you'd stay with him," the doctor said bluntly, and looked away as if not liking to say these things to her.

"I won't leave, now. That is if he wants me to stay."

"I suggest you tell him that." Doctor Casey's voice was kind. "It's important to his peace of mind. He will recover much faster without mental stress of any kind."

Buck spoke up. "How long will this temporary blindness last?"

"We have no way of knowing how long it will take for the nerve ends to heal, but I will say this . . . if his sight hasn't returned within six months, his condition will have to be reassessed and the decision made at that time on further treatment. He'll be able to get around in a few days. We'll put a walker on the bottom of the cast on his leg and he can move about. Well, that is about all I can tell you for now. Come back this afternoon. We're going to remove the bandages now and Mr. Williamson will rest for a few hours. I'll assure him you will be back." The doctor smiled. "Mr. Williamson is a very lucky man."

"Lucky?" Lindy echoed.

"Why, yes. I understand you and his friend risked your lives to get him out from under the overturned machine. Another few minutes and he would have bled to death. You also gave him blood and will stand by him during what is going to be, for him, the most traumatic few months of his life. I would say he's very lucky."

Lindy looked from the doctor to Buck, feeling that the doors were being firmly shut behind her and there was no way out.

Later that afternoon Lindy paused at the door to Jake's room and clutched Buck's hand.

"I'm scared!" Her voice was barely audible.

"Relax, honey, and play it by ear. That's all you can do." Was there ever a man so calm and reassuring? "I'll wait and see him later."

Bracing herself, as if to do battle, she opened the door, slipped inside and closed it softly. Hesitant steps took her toward the bed, her eyes going immediately to Jake's face.

The large bulky bandage she had become used to seeing had been removed and in its place was a smaller one that covered the upper part of his forehead and extended into the hairline. A pair of dark glasses, more like blinders than glasses, covered his eyes. His face had lost its puffiness and except for the pallor under his tan he looked much better than when she saw him last. Her eyes never left his face as she went toward him, her heels making small tapping sounds on the tile floor. He was covered with a sheet that reached only to his bare chest and his arms were lying at his sides, his fingers spread out and pressing against the bed. She could tell by the tilt of his head that he was alert and listening.

"Lindy?" He raised his hand toward her.

She put her hand in his and he gripped it so tightly she winced, but kept the pain out of her voice as she spoke to him. "How did you know it was me?"

"Your perfume. Have you always worn the scent I gave you?" His voice was surprisingly strong.

"Always." Her eyes misted over.

He brought her hand up to his face and rubbed the back of it against his cheek. She had to strive hard to keep from sniffing back the tears.

He seemed to relax a little and a slight smile hovered around his lips. "Do I rate a kiss?"

"Several." She bent over him and placed light kisses on his face and laid a gentle one on his mouth.

"That's not the kind of kisses I want," he complained.

"That's the kind you're going to get until the cuts around your nose and mouth are healed and the stitches out."

"Do you plan to be around when they're healed?" The question was asked tensely, abruptly. She was startled by the question and the tone of voice.

"What do you mean by that? Do you want me to leave?"

His answer came promptly. "You know damn well I don't! Well . . . are you?"

"Of course I'm not going to leave if you want me to stay." Her voice was low and vibrated almost angrily.

He lay very still. Finally he released her hand and his fingers moved up her arm. "You're still standing. Is there a chair nearby?"

"Yes. I'll get it."

She sat down close to the bed and let her fingertips touch his arm so be would know she was near. He made no attempt to reach for her hand so she moved it away.

"I want us to marry again," he said bluntly. "I've been thinking about it all day."

She watched him for a moment and said nothing. He was like a caged hawk. "All right."

He didn't move, but lay with his head turned toward her.

"All right? But it isn't what you want, is it?" He spit the words out bitterly.

She was shaken because suddenly it was what she wanted. "Yes, darling. It's what I want."

"Darling?" He echoed her words for the second time. "Quite a . . . switch." An unyielding look settled on his face. "Well, never mind that now. The doctor said Buck was with you. He'll help you to make the arrangements. Where is he?"

Lindy swallowed hard before she answered. "He's waiting outside. Shall I call him?"

"Not just yet. Tell me about the accident."

Not knowing how to deal with his sudden change of mood she tried desperately to keep the tremor from her voice.

"I don't know much about it, Jake. Buck will be able to tell you all the details. The convoy left two days ago. Buck stayed here to be with you."

"With me or you?"

Lindy drew her breath in sharply. The cynical question hurt her and she tried to keep it from her face, then remembered he couldn't see. "To be with you, of course." Now what was he thinking?

There was a short silence.

"I'll need help, there's no doubt about that!" His fingers formed a fist and pounded on the bed.

"Yes, you'll need help." She said it more sharply than she intended. "We'll see if you're man enough to accept it graciously."

To her surprise, he laughed. It wasn't a real laugh, more like a grunt. "I'm man enough to accept help, little cat, but not pity. Not from you or anyone. Understand?"

"Perfectly, Jake." She felt cool, calm.

Uneasy silence hung heavy between them. Jake clasped his hands together across his chest and turned his head as if looking away from her. She was confused. She had said she would marry him. She had been going to say she loved him, but his aloofness had hit her like a dash of cold water. What thoughts could be going through that handsome head? What had caused him to turn so cold and remote all of a sudden?

"Jake? Why can't we wait until we get back to Houston to remarry?" She reached over and placed her hand on his clasped ones and was encouraged when his fingers captured hers. He turned toward her, his voice hard.

"What's the matter? You getting cold feet about marrying a man that can't see?"

"Don't say that!" She got to her feet. "Your blindness is temporary. Doctor Casey is sure of it."

"And if it isn't?"

"It is! Won't you ever change, Jake? You're being a stubborn fool!"

His face was so pale. Oh, Jesus! Why did she have to

argue with him? The doctor said no stress and here she was lousing up everything.

"Trying to figure out a way to back out, my love?" He said it with a sneer that cut into her like a knife.

"I won't back out, Jake." He made a contemptuous, dismissive sound. "I'll leave you and send Buck in. I don't know if I'll be back tonight . . ."

He interrupted her with a sharp, "Why not? Got another date?"

"No," she answered equally as sharp and thought, oh, darling, don't be such a grouch! "A good-sized blizzard is going on outside. The taxi that brought us here may not be able to bring us again."

His body was still except for the faint rise and fall of his chest. He was quiet for a moment, then held out his hand. She placed hers in it and he pulled her closer.

"Bend down."

She leaned over and his hand found its way to the nape of her neck and he drew her lips down to his. He kissed her soundly. She knew the effort hurt him for when she raised her head she could see beads of perspiration on the part of his forehead not under bandages and he let his arm fall weakly to the bed.

"Get Buck," he said hoarsely.

Through a mist of tears she made her way to the door and paused to look back before she opened it. His face had gone so white she took an instinctive step toward him and drew in a great gulping breath to steady herself.

"Is there anything I can do for you before I go?" She made no attempt to disguise the concern in her voice.

"No. Nothing." The coldness of his tone was unbearable and somewhere deep in her heart a small hope died a quiet death.

She walked slowly down the hall. Somehow she felt humiliated and dreadful doubts assailed her. She paused at the drinking fountain, and as she drew a cup of water a quote came to mind, "Humiliation must be borne with head held high." Oh, darn! Let some other jerk hold his head high. She wanted to tuck hers under her arm and cry.

"How did it go?" Buck asked when she reached the waiting room.

"He wants us to be married again right away." Her voice was not ringing with joy.

He smiled warmly and kissed her cheek. How dare he be happy when she was so miserable?

"I'm glad, honey. You'll make it go this time."

"He's not in a good mood so . . . be patient with him."

"Sure, honey. You can count on it. I know Jake pretty well. He's an independent, ornery cuss, and this will be hard on him, but he'll hack it with our help."

"That's just it, Buck. We must not help too much."

"Smart girl. You're right, of course."

"I'll wait for you here," she called to him as he retraced her steps up the hall.

Sinking down on the couch, she leaned her head back and closed her eyes and tried to imagine what it would be like to be blind. Total darkness . . . for weeks, months, a lifetime!

Her eyes sprang open. "No!" she said aloud, and began pacing back and forth across the small room. She tried to drive the cold dread from her heart by remembering Doctor Casey's reassuring words, "No permanent damage, however . . ." Danm that "however"!

Buck's visit with Jake lasted much longer than Lindy's. When he finally came from the room he suggested they have a light dinner in the hospital coffee shop. He looked more sober than he had an hour ago. She saw him watching her as she watched him. He held her long in the grasp of his eyes.

"Well . . . how is he?"

"His physical condition is far better than I expected considering what he's been through, but . . ." He paused. "He's bitter, inconsiderate. It isn't like him to be so cynical, so hard-nosed about what he wants."

"He's facing all those months of darkness, Buck. He can't help but feel frightened and bitter. We'll have to overlook a lot."

They sat silently while the waiter served their food and when they were alone again Buck pulled an envelope from his pocket. He studied it for a moment and returned it to his pocket.

He chuckled. "His mind runs like a computer. I had to make notes. He wants to see you before you leave the hospital."

"He needs to rest. Do you think I should?"

"Yes, honey. Humor him. He told me exactly what he wanted me to do. Number one, take you to dinner and see that you ate well because your voice was weak and he thought you were tired. Number two, bring you back to his room while I check the weather. Number three, I was to give him the weather report and he would decide if you were to go back to the hotel or spend the night here."

"You've got to be kidding me!"

"He was dead serious. His mind is sharp as a tack and he's taking nothing for granted."

Lindy's eyes grew large as bewilderment spread across her face. "You mean he is that concerned about me?"

"Concerned isn't the word I'd use."

Quick tears sprang to her eyes. "I can take care of myself and him, too, if he would let me."

"Go along with him. Keep him happy and free from worry as best you can. And love him. A man needs love." His wistful tone caused her to glance at him. It wouldn't be hard to love him. Not hard at all.

"A woman needs love even more, Buck."

He left her at the door of Jake's room. She tapped lightly. After a brief hesitation she reached for the knob only to have the door open suddenly and a sister, in black habit, blocked the doorway.

"Tell her to wait, nurse." Jake's voice reached into the hall.

When the door had closed she leaned her forehead against the cool wall of the hallway. The harshness in his voice cut into her like a whiplash. Buck was right when he said Jake was inconsiderate.

She was so busy with her thoughts the time flew. The door opened and the nurse came out carrying a tray. She indicated with a nod of her head that she could go in.

Jake was lying much the same as when she left him, but he had removed the dark glasses. For a moment her heart leaped with the hope he could see. His head was turned toward her. She looked into his eyes and caught her breath. How odd that they could appear just the same, only expressionless. Her gaze shifted to his hands and the spread-out fingers pressing down on the bed.

An almost overpowering feeling of love for him came over her, a feeling of protectiveness, such as a mother would feel for a helpless child. A chair had been placed close to the bed and she went to it. Taking the hand he lifted in both of hers, she held it to her cheek before her lips moved across the knuckles, made white by the tight grip he had on her hand. Neither had made a sound, but a great sigh left his lips and she could feel him relax as she continued to hold his hand to her face.

Presently his fingertips loosened themselves from hers and sought her cheek. His dark lashes shuttered his blue eyes and a half smile came to his lips.

"Talk to me, sweetheart." His fingers traveled over her face, caressing her cheek and chin.

"About what?"

"Just talk. Tell me what you're wearing." The blue eyes were open and he had turned toward her. His hand reached out to caress her hair and his eyes closed wearily.

Trying hard to keep the lump from her throat, she deliberately made her voice light. "I'm wearing the tan sweater I wore the night we made the Texas chili."

His hand left her hair and traveled down over her shoulder and across her breast and came to rest at the slender curve of her waist. His forefinger forged its way into the tight waistband of her skirt.

"And . . . ?"

"A heavy wool skirt and knee-high boots. The skirt is flared and has huge square pockets."

"A skirt? I haven't seen you in a skirt since . . ." His voice trailed away. "But if it's blizzarding, why didn't you wear snow pants? Or did you want to look nice for Buck? It couldn't have been for me! You knew I couldn't see you!" His voice was unmistakably harsh and his nostrils flared angrily.

Lindy couldn't believe that he was angry. In seconds his mood had completely reversed. "Why would you say a thing like that? I . . ."

"Don't bother to explain!"

He removed his hand from her waist and laced his fingers together across his chest. He turned his head straight ahead as if looking at the picture hanging on the wall. It was then she saw the soiled spots on the bedclothes. A tiny line appeared between her eyes and she chided herself for not understanding. He had not wanted her to see him dribbling his food!

She leaned over him and gently kissed his tightly compressed lips. He remained impassive and her eyes grew dark with hurt, but being determined to make things right again she laid her head on his chest. She could hear the rhythmic beating of his heart and after a while his hand came up to smooth back her hair and fondle her ear. Again she could feel the tenseness go out of him. They remained thus until they heard a soft knocking on the door.

Buck came in and stood at the foot of the bed.

"The storm is over," he announced. "They got a snowplow out there as big as a Texas bulldozer, Jake. You just never saw the like. They plow that snow up into a row in the middle of the street and another machine comes along and scoops it up into trucks that haul it away. It's the darndest sight you ever saw."

"Maybe I'll see it sometime," Jake said, his face rigid. "Did you find out anything?"

"Yup, I sure did." Buck took the envelope from his pocket and scanned the scribbled side. "The chaplain here at the hospital will call on you. There's a chapel here where the ceremony can be performed. As for the blood test required for the license, yours has already been taken and Lindy can stop at the emergency room on her way out. The technician on duty will take her blood sample. We'll apply for the license in the morning and the wedding can take place day after tomorrow if Doctor Casey approves."

"He'll approve." Jake had a cold sardonic smile on his face. He lifted his hand to Lindy. Dazed by the rapidity of the arrangements, she put her hand in his and he held it tightly.

"Tomorrow buy a white wedding dress. Buck will give you the money."

"Why should I buy a white dress? I'm a married woman! Remember?"

He chuckled dryly and turned his head toward Buck. "She didn't used to be so difficult, Buck. It takes some getting used to." To Lindy he said, "Buy something pretty."

She didn't answer at once.

"Lindy?" His voice reached her again.

"Yes, Jake. I'll buy a pretty dress." She stood numbly looking down at him, all her assertiveness gone. "I think we should leave now. You've had a tiring day."

"Yes, I have. See that she gets safely back to the hotel, Buck."

"You can depend on it, old man. I'll wait outside, honey."

"Honey?" Jake said as soon as the door closed behind Buck. "What else does he call you? Sweetheart? Darling?"

"Stop it!" She had thought he couldn't shock her anymore, that she was attuned to his moods. She was wrong. "What's the matter with you? Good Lord, Buck is your best friend. For him it's just a matter of speech. He doesn't even realize it."

"Doesn't he?" he said dryly. "Well, never mind. Were you going to kiss me good night without me having to ask you?"

"Yeah. Hello, good-bye and all that stuff in between and you don't have to ask me, you . . . turkey!"

She kissed him tenderly, sweetly, trying to avoid the stitched places on his face that might give him pain. She tried to be gentle, but he resisted her attempt with his hand behind her head and held her to him.

"I don't want you to go," he whispered. "Stay with me. Stretch out here on the bed beside me." He breathed the words into her ear.

"You're insane. Do you know that?" She bit him gently on the neck and raised her head. "I'll be back in the morning."

"Buy your dress first so you can tell me about it." His voice was polite, almost casual.

Hurt again she nodded, then remembering he couldn't see, said, "All right, if that's what you want."

He held onto her hand until she started to move away from him, then let his fall to the bed. She went quickly from the room.

Buck was waiting outside the door and they walked silently down the hall.

CHAPTER NINE

LINDY SAT ALONE in her hotel room. She and Jake had been married that afternoon in the hospital chapel. It was beyond her understanding why he had insisted on making a production out of this ceremony. Their first nuptials were spoken before a justice at City Hall and were just as binding as this one.

Jake had been standing and waiting for her when she came down the short aisle on Buck's arm. When she took his hand it was cold and trembling and she knew he was making a supreme effort to stand erect. The red scar lines around his mouth and nose showed vividly on his cleanly shaven face. It was one of the few times Lindy had seen him in a dark suit. She had chosen a light blue wool dress and matching pumps. The ensemble was simple in design, but well suited to her slender figure. She had resisted the saleswoman's attempt to sell her a matching hat.

During the ceremony Jake slipped the ring she had worn once before back on her finger and seemed to be surprised when she slipped one on his. She had bought the ring, on impulse, the day before. At the proper time he kissed her deeply. She was careful not to cling to him. Still in a state of shock, still stunned by the enormity of what she was doing, she stood firmly beside him, being as supportive as he would allow.

Doctor Casey, who with Buck was witness to their marriage, gently urged Jake back into the chair that had wheeled him to the chapel. He sank into it wearily as he had used up much of his strength getting ready for the wedding and standing during the ceremony. Lindy followed him back to his room, where, at his insistence, a reception, of sorts, would be held.

Standing beside his chair, she could tell by the lines around his mouth that he was very tired, but when she spoke to him he smiled and held out his hand to her. They were served champagne along with the tall wedding cake complete with miniature bride and groom on the top. It was beautifully decorated and Lindy described it to Jake in detail. Adhering to tradition, she cut the cake and placed the first bite in his mouth. The cake as well as the champagne would be served to the hospital staff and those patients whose conditions would allow it.

It all seemed so unreal to Lindy. She hadn't got used to not being married to Jake and here they were going through a ceremony that seemed to be totally unnecessary. She left the room when the orderly came to undress Jake and get him back into bed. He was exhausted and almost asleep when she returned.

"God . . . I'm tired. This is a hell of a wedding night for you, babe."

"It isn't as if I'm a blushing bride." For once he didn't argue; he was too tired to do anything but just lie there.

For a moment she felt a wave of pity rush over her. Why did she feel so protective of him? Why did she have the feeling he couldn't cope with his blindness without her? Was it because for the first time since she had known him he was in the position of needing someone? For this short while she had all his attention, could hold him, take care of him. It wouldn't last. There would be awful times ahead; terrible times full of hurt and humiliation. He would disappoint her again and again and a little of her would die each time.

Looking down at him, as he slept there like a very tired little boy, she knew she was going to lose in the end. It was insane to look at one's own ultimate heartbreak so calmly. There was a brief flash of bitterness as she thought of her mother and wondered if there ever was a time when she looked down on her father with this inner feeling of resignation.

In her hotel room, Lindy fingered the one rose she saved from her bouquet. Three dozen white roses here in the frozen north must have cost the earth. It had been a very emotional day. Less than two weeks after discovering she was free of Jake she had married him again. Her mind was a little numb, but she had set her course for better or worse and with that thought in mind, she went to bed.

When she left the hotel room the next morning she intended to take a taxi to the hospital, but decided to walk instead. After a huge breakfast she needed the exercise.

The air was crisp and she breathed deeply. The sidewalks had been cleared. In places the snow was piled so high she couldn't see over the top. This was a new experience for her and she walked briskly, being careful not to slip on the icy spots. Several small birds hopped ahead of her on the walk and she wondered how they managed to survive the blizzard. Cars passed her with a foot of snow on their tops, snow tires allowing them to move in the soft snow. Children, bundled in snowsuits, played in the snow. It all seemed very normal.

She was greeted by staff members as she walked down the hospital corridor. Her friendly but quiet, unassuming ways had made her popular with the nurses as well as the aides and orderlies. Before reaching Jake's room her hand went automatically to smooth her hair, forgetting, once again, that he couldn't see her. She stood hesitantly in the doorway. Jake was talking on the telephone.

"The oil stock, Mark. Yes, all of it. I want her to have some security if anything happens to me. Hold on, Mark." He covered the mouthpiece with his hand. "Sit down, sweetheart. I know that's you hovering in the doorway. I heard you coming down the hall. I'm talking to Houston."

"Let me wait outside, Jake."

"No. Come here to me. I'll be just a minute more." He held out his hand and waited until she put hers in it. "Here again, Mark. Take care of that for me right away. Buck will be getting in touch with you. I was thinking of sending him on back down there, but Liz is such a wonder. She'll keep things running slicker than clockwork until I get there. God, I don't know what I'd do without her right now." He squeezed Lindy's hand. "Lindy and I will be coming back soon." Another pause. "Thank you, Mark. Yes. Yes, she's very beautiful. That's the hardest part of this . . . not being able to see her. Yes, all right. 'Bye." He handed the telephone to Lindy and she returned it to the table beside the bed.

"Come kiss me, Mrs. Williamson." He was sitting almost upright in the tilted bed. "Sit here." He patted the bed beside him.

His arms reached for her when he felt her weight on the bed, then clasped her to him, his lips hungrily seeking hers. A terrifying sweetness swept through her veins, sending her pulses and her blood racing. Jake, too, was trembling. When he finally took his lips from hers, his voice shook as he said, "I dreamed of this last night. This . . . and other things."

"What other things?" She would have pulled back from him, but his arms refused to let her go.

"Like you being here so I could do this . . . and this . . ." His voice was a soft whisper and his hands moved beneath her sweater and roamed over her bare skin and into the lacy cup that held her breast. "You smell so good and your skin is smooth and soft and you don't seem to have any bones," he said softly. "Have you always gone limp and trembly when I've kissed you like this, and touched you, like this?"

"Always."

"Then I think you should know that I'm about to drag you into bed with me," he murmured, and his mouth kissed every part of her face.

This was the Jake she had fallen in love with, the gentle coaxing lover. She knew there was much more to him than this and that loving him meant accepting the whole man. Her love for him seemed to well up and overflow.

"Jake . . . someone might come in." Her protest was weak, her words fading as his mouth moved to cover hers. His kisses were sweet, giving, tender in their urgency, and then as if beyond his control, hard, possessive and demanding. He was breathing heavily and broke the kiss to allow his lips to move to her cheek where he murmured so softly she almost lost the words.

"You love me. I know you love me."

He held her quietly for a moment and stroked her hair. When he released her she sat up and looked at him. His face was different this morning. No longer tense, scowling. His lips twitched because he knew she was looking at him. She couldn't resist placing one last kiss there.

"You'd better get away from me, woman, before I have you between the sheets."

"And risk having the sister catch us?" She laughed. "Oh, no!"

"It might be worth it! But . . . I suppose I'll just have to wait till we get to the hotel. Now sit still. I want to tell you about our new house on Galveston Island."

Watching the expressions flit across his face, Lindy thought about his almost unconscious arrogance, but his enthusiasm disarmed her and she found herself softening as she watched him.

"It's down the coast a couple of miles . . . a nice area. You'll like it. The house faces the gulf and has a covered deck going around three sides of it. Not much grass yet, but quite a few palm trees. The beach is fine white sand, not too many people go out there. It's nice and private. Just the kind of house we talked about having." He reached with uncanny aim for her chin and squeezed it gently. "I ordered furniture before I left, but if there's anything you don't like you can send it back."

"How many rooms?" A woman's curiosity coming forward.

"I don't know, sweetheart. I didn't count them. I do know that there are several bedrooms. I'm going to board them up . . . all but one. I don't want any company for years and years!"

"Stop teasing, turkey. I was thinking about the kitchen." Her tone was heavy with indignation.

"I was thinking about the bedroom in general and the bed in particular." His tone mocked hers.

"Sexy man!"

"You better believe it! What else?"

"And an egotistical, insolent libertine!"

As she ended the words he pulled her firmly back into his arms. He held her tightly for a while, then swatted her behind.

"I forgot to tell you, there's an apartment above the garage, which by the way is large enough for three cars and a boat."

"Three cars and a boat?" she echoed. "My . . . my . . . You've come up in the world, Mr. Williamson."

"I didn't say we had them, dumb-dumb. But . . . we could if we wanted to. The oil leases I bought up the year before we were married have paid off. You could say we're loaded, Mrs. Williamson."

"You mean to tell me that I've got to start putting on the dog? Have teas? Crook my little finger and all that stuff?" She tried to sound pained, but her tone lacked conviction.

"Be as uppity as you want, Mrs. Astor. But not with me. I'll spank your royal butt!" His hand slid around and under her hip and he pinched her.

"Masher!" She could hardly keep her eyes from his face.

"Hush and listen. A Mexican couple live in the apartment. I've known Carlos for years. He hasn't been married very long, but his wife, Maria, is a fabulous cook. They'll be a big help."

Lindy was silent for a long while before she said, "I don't want help in the house, Jake. I like to cook. What will I do all day?"

He laughed a clear boyish laugh. "Guess!" His lips hovered over hers. "You'll be taking care of me! Anyhow, Mrs. Williamson, I have to leave the country every once in a while. Carlos and Maria will take care of the place while we're gone." He paused, the kiss he intended for her lips landed on her nose. "You'll go with me until our baby comes. You may have to stay at home then . . . for a while."

Lindy lay still in his arms as a tinge of fear swept through her. No baby! No baby . . . ever! He can make all the decisions but that one. I relied on this man once before and it almost killed me when he let me down. I grew up . . . fast. Nothing lasts forever. As wonderful as this is right now I can't count on it lasting. And I know better than anyone the price a child pays living in an insecure home.

Jake touched her cheek. "What's the matter?" His hand moved down over her shoulder and over her breast. "Why is your heart beating so fast? Does it excite you to think about us making a baby together?"

She was trembling. "We won't start a family right away."

"Not right this minute, but I'd like to." He whispered the words between kisses.

"But . . . Jake." He was so intoxicating, so seductive.

Not allowing her to talk he kissed her again, his mouth burning hers. She responded to his kiss, and yet a terrible ache tugged at her heart.

Disengaging herself from his arms, she moved away from the bed and sat in the chair. Her eyes were clouded with worry, but she didn't allow her apprehension to show in her voice.

"I love my ring. I didn't realize how much I'd missed it."

"Would you rather have a larger diamond?" he asked quietly.

"No!" she stated definitely. "I'm not the type for large, flashy diamonds."

He stretched out a hand to her. She met it with hers. His fingers touched the ring. "You won't take it off?"

The question was strange and she looked at him sharply. It seemed his eyes were looking down at the hand he was holding.

"No. I won't take it off," she promised.

His head on the pillow rolled wearily away from her. She hadn't realized he had been so tense waiting for her answer. Then he said another strange thing that was to linger in her mind. It was simply, "Thank you."

She was touched by the humble remark. New hope began an elusive dance through her thoughts. Deliberately she stilled those thoughts, closed her eyes and emptied her mind. When she looked at him again he lay still, his eyes shuttered.

"Would you like me to go so you can rest?"

"No. Of course I don't want you to go." His voice was curt, his eyes springing open. "I'm getting up this afternoon. I've got to get my strength back so we can go home."

The telephone rang and she asked, "Shall I answer it?"

"Please."

"Is this Jake Williamson's room?" a soft Southern voice asked.

"Yes." Lindy's heart began to pound frighteningly.

"May I speak to him?"

She placed the phone in Jake's hand. "I'll wait outside."

"No. Stay here!" The words were spoken softly, but the tone was a gentle command.

He waited until the tapping of her heels on the tile floor told him she had returned to the chair beside the bed before he put the phone to his ear.

"Hello." After a moment, he smiled. "I'm getting along fine." Another pause followed with a short laugh. "Don't worry, Liz. I'm fine. Hey, don't worry. I'll have Buck call and give you a full report. Will that make you feel better?" Pause . . . "That's my girl. Now, tell me about the Allied contract." He listened while Lindy stared at his bruised face. "Yeah? Of course I knew you would. Thanks, honey. I'll make it up to you. Yeah? Losing my sight is damned inconvenient, but with your help, love, I'll get by."

Blood drained from Lindy's face and the fear she had felt since the phone rang materialized into a sickening knot in her stomach. She thought she would surely be sick. It couldn't be starting again so soon! Liz! She was evidently more to him than an employee, Lindy thought miserably.

"Liz . . ." Jake's voice reached her through the ringing in her ears. "Lindy and I will be coming home soon." His hand reached out to Lindy and for the first time since his blindness she ignored it. "Yes." He let his hand fall to the bed. "Yes, she's changed during the last two years. We both have. Her change is for the better. I know how to pick my women. Didn't I pick you? Thanks, love. I'll tell her. 'Bye for now. I'll call you tomorrow. And, Liz, remember what I said about not worrying. Yes, well . . . 'bye."

Jake held out the phone. Lindy took it and hung it in the stand. A thought went winging wildly through her mind: Liz and Jake! She was consumed with jealousy, Jake appeared to look straight at her. The silence which stretched between them was taut, like a wire stretched to breaking point. Tensely she waited for him to speak while her own muscles ached with the effort to keep still. She wanted to speak, to ask him why he had come back into her life, but the words would not form themselves. She realized with a quiver of guilt that she was glad he couldn't see her, glad he couldn't see the misery she was feeling.

Jake leaned back, a faint smile curving his mouth, yet she had the impression of a wariness about him as if he were waiting for some reaction from her.

"You like Liz, don't you?" he asked softly.

Had he been able to guess her thoughts while she stood there? Guilt made her quiver again and she said quickly, trying to stifle it, "She's not important enough for me to either like or dislike her."

"She is to me." Under slanting brows his eyes did not seem blind between narrowed lids. She stepped back a pace.

"Your business," she said with a nervous laugh. "I want to give the flowers some fresh water." Her heels against the floor made rapid clatter as she left the room.

Holding her breath for fear Jake would call her back, she hurried down the hall, the water in the vase spilling onto her sweater in her haste. She reached the door of the public restrooms in time to avoid meeting Buck who was coming toward her down the hall. She darted into the sanctuary and leaned against the wall with her eyes tightly closed. A wave of self-pity engulfed her. What had she let herself in for? How could she have been so stupid? A man like Jake never changes. He had even used his temporary blindness to get what he wanted.

She pushed herself away from the wall and emptied the water from the jar. She refilled it and jammed the roses into the vase. They were hateful to her, as if they represented something tarnished and false. The stricken eyes that looked back at her from the mirror on the wall were large and bright with unshed tears. She couldn't weep. Her misery struck deeper than tears could wash away. She gazed at herself and as she did so a cold hard shell of indifference settled over her. Did she love Jake or only need him as a buffer against loneliness? For a few minutes she thought she was crazy . . . then things began to clarify in her mind.

Debra had insisted once that she attend an assertiveness training session. What was it that the instructor had said? "Lack of action and indecision increase your feeling of helplessness." She came to a decision and breathed a sigh of relief at having made up her mind. Hell . . . she was a person with her own fundamental worth. If Jake was such a shallow person he constantly had to build up his ego with extramarital affairs that was his hang-up, not hers. Her obligation to Jake would be over when his sight returned. She would stay with him until that time. She owed him that.

She went back down the hall, carrying the vase carefully now.

"Hello, Buck." She set the vase in the same spot from which she had so hastily removed it only a short while ago.

"Hello, honey. Been watering the garden?"

"Expensive flowers take a lot of water." She picked up her purse. "I'm going to lunch."

"To lunch? After all those flapjacks this morning?" Buck's voice was laughing, but his eyes were not.

"Suddenly I'm hungry. I'll see you later, Jake."

Going down the hall, she was quite proud of herself. None of the pain, sorrow, loneliness, disillusionment she was feeling, showed in her face.

She killed several hours in the downtown area. She bought a novel for herself and several magazines and newspapers. In a new and up-to-date needlework shop she examined commercially painted needlepoint canvases with a critical eye and compared them to her hand-painted originals. She was pleased with the comparison. Her one-of-a-kind canvases would find a market in Houston where needlework-conscious women would appreciate their quality.

Reluctantly she hailed a taxi to take her back to the

hospital for her afternoon visit with Jake. She wanted to hurry and get it over with so she could go back to the hotel, have a hot bath and perhaps work for a while on her own needlework. Her visit to Jake had become a duty, an obligation, and nothing more.

CHAPTER TEN

THE DOOR TO Jake's room was open when she reached it. She was surprised to find him sitting in a chair by the window, a blue robe over his pajamas and his broken leg propped up on a footstool.

"Lindy?"

"Yes. It's me."

"I thought those were your footsteps coming down the hall."

"Yes," she said again. "My heels are quite noisy. I should have rubber put on."

"I like to hear them."

"I brought the *Dallas Herald*, the *Des Moines Register* and the *Chicago Tribune*. I couldn't find a Houston paper. I think they must sell out fast with so many Texans in Alaska. I also brought a hunting magazine. Shall I read to you?"

"Not just yet." He said it tensely. "Why did you leave so suddenly this morning?"

"Suddenly?" She laughed. "I was here for several hours."

"You know what I mean, dammit. You know damn well what I mean." His face was turning red and his hands gripped the arms of the chair.

"I'm afraid I don't, Jake. Now, do you want me to read to you or not?" She ignored his angry tone and deliberately made her voice conversational. He could take his damned arrogance and shove it! Did he expect her to be all sunshine and light after listening to him seducing Liz over the phone?

"I sure as hell don't want you to read to me until you tell me where you've been for the last four hours." There was a low vibrancy to his voice, an indication he was keeping a tight rein on his anger.

"You mean I'm to keep a log and report back to you, in detail, all my actions?" Her voice was soft, controlled.

"Where are you?" he demanded, turning as if his sightless eyes would find her.

"Beside the bed." She looked at him and was truly sorry he couldn't see, but that was as far as it went. He had hurt her deeply, dammit. Let him squirm. "What do you think I was doing, Jake? Out soliciting?" Her words sounded childish and the look on his face confirmed it.

"I still want to know why you left so abruptly."

"You and Buck had things to talk about," she said patiently. "Things that didn't concern me." For a fraction of a second she closed her eyes and hated him for making her lie.

"Everything about me concerns you. Everything about you concerns me."

"Not everything." Let him figure that out, damn him.

"I know what's the matter with you. You're ticked off about Liz." His voice rasped queerly.

Surprise held her silent for a moment. Dread lay heavy within her until pride cast it aside.

"I could care less about Liz, Jake. She's your affair, not mine." She said this in a matter-of-fact way that infuriated him.

"Yes, she is my affair." He smiled viciously to hide his anger. "She's been loyal and faithful to me for quite a few years. I can depend on Liz."

"How nice for you," she murmured softly.

He compressed his lips, too angry to answer. The silence hung heavy between them. Lindy placed the sack from the bookstore on the bed. Jake heard the rustle of the paper.

"So you're leaving," he muttered coolly, turning away from her so she couldn't see his face.

"Not if you want me to stay," she answered equally cool.

"I'm not the type to beg," he snapped.

"I don't expect you to. I came prepared to read to you and it's up to you if I go or stay."

"Stay then, damn you, and read!"

He kept his sightless eyes turned toward the window. He was tired and tense and the bitter lines around his mouth reflected his inner turmoil. This exchange had done nothing to speed his recovery and Lindy promised herself she would try to avoid quarreling with him in the future, for more than anything else in the world she wanted him well again . . . so she could pick up the threads of her own life.

She read to him for over an hour. She read the political news, the report on the progress of the pipeline, the problems the Alaskan conservationists were having with the migrating animals. She read the entire contents of two editorial pages. Jake didn't make a sound, just sat back with his eyes closed. Lindy doubted if he was listening, but she continued to read; her soft Southern voice breaking the silence of the quiet room. When she started the story about the great gray whale in the hunting magazine he interrupted.

"You can stop. You must be thirsty."

"I would like something to drink. Can I get something for you?"

"Yes, please. There's money in the drawer by the bed."

Ignoring what he said about money, she picked up her purse and went out.

"I brought you a Coke," she said when she returned and guided a cup into his hand. "They give more ice than Coke in that dispenser."

"Thank you."

She noticed how carefully he lifted the cup to his mouth and felt a flicker of sympathy for him.

"Would you like a radio?"

"No, thank you," he said almost formally. "I'll be getting up every day now. The orderly will be here soon to walk me down the hall. I walked about the room by myself, but I need eyes to guide me when I leave it."

"I can do that."

"No. I won't impose. Not even on my . . . wife."

"If you feel this way, why did you insist on marrying me again? It isn't imposing to ask your wife for help."

"A real wife, yes. But not an accusing, untrusting, suspicious, immature little . . ." He bit the words off and threw the cup containing the soft drink across the room. It hit the wall and splattered the windowpane.

Lindy was stunned momentarily by this display of temper.

"Then you admit our marriage was a mistake?"

"A mistake? Perhaps, but we're married and we're going to stay married. You try leaving me and I'll make you sorry you ever lived!" His lips curled and the puckered scar on his forehead stood out as his face whitened with anger.

She brought a towel from the bathroom. "I'll clean up this mess."

"Leave it."

She continued to clean and when she finished she tried to keep the nervous tremor from her voice when she said, "I'll go, now."

"Go, then! I sure as hell can't stop you."

"I don't want to leave you like this." She didn't know what made her say that. It just came out.

"Why not? You've left me before. You can't help being the way you are any more than I can help being the way I am. I was wrong. I thought my . . . But forget it. Tuck your tail and run."

"I'll be back in the morning."

"Come here." His voice commanded and she moved toward his outstretched hand. "You're such a paragon of virtue. Come kiss your sightless husband good-bye."

He grabbed her hand roughly and pulled. Trying to avoid his leg on the footstool, she lost her balance and allowed him to pull her down on his lap. He crushed her to him so hard the air exploded from her lungs. His mouth found hers and mastered it cruelly, his teeth cutting into her soft lips. He kissed her long, hard, and when he finally lifted his mouth she could taste the salty blood from the cuts. His hands handled her ruthlessly, bruising, gripping, as though he wanted to hurt her. But she heard the heavy thud of his heart above her own and her body slackened as she listened to it.

Gradually his hands gentled and moved over her, roaming, searching; but she forced herself to lie still, straining to reveal none of the wild and tremulous sensations that quivered into being beneath the adventuring hand that slid into her shirt and over her breast until her nipple was hard in his fingers. She lay passive in his embrace as he kissed her face, going again to her lips which he kissed gently this time. She offered no response and no resistance and presently he loosened his arms and pushed her from his lap.

"Go," he said tiredly.

She left the room without a backward look at the man who sat in the chair by the window.

Lindy walked slowly back to the hotel and tried to convince herself she had made a mistake marrying Jake. She weighed the pros and cons. She heard again Doctor Casey's words that Jake would recover much faster if he was relaxed and free from tension. Her own previous thoughts about grabbing bits and pieces of happiness came to her mind. The lonely nights she had spent with only the sleeping tablets for relief hung in the back of her mind like a black cloud and the time she spent in Jake's arms was the silver lining. She had known what to expect . . . but it had come so soon . . . too soon. Her mother's life flashed before her eyes. She would be walking the same path her mother walked, but unlike her mother, she would never be walked upon. Did she love Jake or hate him?

She drew a warm bath and tried to soak away the nagging feeling of uneasiness inside her. She was nervous and jumpy and on leaving the tub put on her pajamas, crawled into bed and buried her face in the pillow. She didn't want to remember her childhood. She must think of now, the present. A deep, shuddering sigh convulsed her body as the questions throbbed in her brain. Did she love him so much she wouldn't be able to leave him, even knowing what he was? Was she crazy? This morning she hated him.

She pulled the coverlet up over her ears and drifted into a sort of trance. Arousing once, she looked at her watch; it was past midnight. Sleep had eluded her during these long miserable hours. Finally a deadly lassitude crept over her and she slept.

She awakened suddenly. The telephone was ringing. Frightened, her trembling hands searched for the light switch. The light sprang on, harsh against her sleep-drugged eyes. With fumbling fingers and pounding heart, she reached for the phone. "Hello."

Silence on the other end while her heart throbbed painfully, then a familiar voice whispered her name. "Lindy."

Her heart rose up in her throat. "Jake? Are you all right?"

Silence, and then, "I'm all right. I just wanted to talk to you. Just wanted to talk to you," he repeated. "But I had to threaten to pull this phone from the wall before they would ring you."

"Oh, Jake. You didn't?" She was so relieved she dropped back on the bed. "What must they think of you?"

"I wanted to hear your voice, sweetheart." The humble tone of his voice and the endearment tore at her heart.

"It's three in the morning. Haven't you slept?"

"Yes . . . no . . . I don't know. It's all the same."

"The same?"

"The darkness. Sweetheart, sometimes I don't think I can bear this darkness." His voice had a catch in it.

She had to swallow the sobs in her throat before she could speak. "It won't be for long, Jake. Doctor Casey is sure . . ."

"He can't be sure!" He said it with rocklike certainty.

"Nothing in life is sure. You said yourself that nothing lasts forever. Remember? There's every reason to believe your sight will return."

There was silence on the other end of the line. Presently he said, "Are you leaving?" There was a darting note of pain in his voice, but she didn't notice, her mind too bewildered by his call.

"Of course not. Whatever gave you that idea?" It suddenly occurred to her that she was about to do that very thing. Run. Get back into her safe cocoon before it was too late.

"You've never asked me what I've been doing the last two years." The words seemed to embarrass him. She wanted to say it was none of her business, but she wanted to know. So she asked the question.

"What have you been doing, Jake?"

"I've been running my butt off!" His voice was bitter. Lindy waited. "I threw caution to the wind and gambled every last dime I had on a played-out oil field. Worked till I dropped in my tracks, chased every woman who turned me on and some that didn't. Denied myself nothing. I found out that there aren't very many women out there that are worth a damn. They'll sleep with you, get a free meal, a few clothes, a couple nights in a swanky hotel, all the time looking for a bigger fish with more clout, more money, more prestige. Do you know what I got out of all that? A sick, empty feeling in my guts! That life out there isn't worth a hoot in hell. I finally realized there was nothing to run after. It's a phony world, sweetheart. A lot crazier and lonelier than anyone can imagine. And one time around is all you get."

He hesitated, then said tiredly, "Then once in a lifetime, during one small speck of time, you get a chance to have everything you ever dreamed of having. The prize goes flashing by and you grab for it. You grab for the whole chunk. If you miss it, you've lost your chance. I don't want that to happen to me. I don't want to lose you, sweetheart. I don't want to wander for a lifetime. That's why I came back. I grabbed and I got you, but I'm selfish. I want it all."

For a moment Lindy couldn't speak, and then, uncomprehending, tears poured down her face. Her voice was a pathetic croak when she spoke at last. "What are you trying to say, Jake?"

"I'm saying, dammit, I don't want you to leave me. I want it to be the way it was. What do you want from me? Do you want me to beg? Plead? Crawl? Ask your forgiveness?"

"No. I don't want any of those things." She was tense, tired, and she was doing what she said she would do. She was trying to keep him quiet, relaxed, free from worry. "I've no intention of leaving until we can go together." Would he believe that? She stammered for words to say.

"I was a grouch today. I've developed all kinds of moods these last two years." She laughed a small nervous laugh. "I know I'm not going through the change. Maybe I'm pregnant." She laughed again, hoping it didn't sound too forced, artificial.

"You'd hate that, wouldn't you?" He said it quietly. Then tensely, "You'd beat a path to the nearest clinic and get my baby scraped out of you, wouldn't you, Lindy?"

"Jake!"

He was quiet for a long while. She struggled for something to say. When he spoke his voice was almost a whisper.

"Do you love me at all?"

"There're many kinds of love." Her words were scarcely audible.

"I know that!" He was angry again. "Do you love me in spite of the fact you've got to keep your eye on me every second or I'll go chasing off after another woman? Do you love me like a brother? A friend? Or do you love me because I hold you in the night and chase away the nightmares so you can sleep? It's certainly not like a husband, a lover, a life's companion!"

"If I didn't love you nothing would have made me marry you again. I was free. Remember? Our divorce was final. You had no strings on me at all. Can't you be satisfied with that?"

"Guess I'll have to be. Good night."

"Don't hang up. We've got a whole lifetime to work things out. Let's take one day at a time, shall we? The love, attraction, or whatever it is we have for each other isn't perfect, but it's all we have. It's something to build on. Won't you try?"

"I wish I was out of this damn place. I wish I was there with you. Do you know that I can see you? I can see your mouth. Can taste it. My hands know the shape of your breast, the feel of your hips. Why is the feel of you different from the feel of anyone else?" He didn't expect an answer to his questions. "I know, now, what you mean about the nights being so long."

"Ask the nurse for a sleeping tablet."

"You're not taking them again?" he asked quickly.

"No. But you need to rest." There was a long pause and her heartbeats quickened uncomfortably.

"I think I want to stay awake." He said it slowly.

"I'll be over the first thing in the morning."

"I wish it was now."

"Good night. I'll be over early."

"Early?"

"Yes. Early."

She waited until she heard the receiver go dead on the other end before she hung up the phone. She turned out the light and buried her head in the pillow. There were many sides to Jake's character, but the one he presented tonight was the most baffling one of all. He had only to say he loved her, that he wanted only her. He had only to say he was not having an affair with Liz and that elusive carrot of happiness would have been dangling before her eyes again.

CHAPTER ELEVEN

JAKE WAS RELEASED from the hospital the day before they were to leave for Houston. No husband had ever been more tender and attentive than he had been during the past week. It was a reprieve. Jake was good at reprieves.

Coming into the hospital room to escort him to the hotel, Lindy paused to look at her husband standing beside the window, his proud head erect, his shoulders set in an arrogant line, his neatly trimmed hair already rebelling against the stiff brush that had tried to discipline it.

"Jake?"

No answer, but a smile of gladness spread across his face and he held out his arms to her. She went into them and was locked in a gentle, tender embrace. All was peace, she was home. Releasing a deep and trembling sigh, she raised her lips to receive his kiss.

"I'm only half alive until you get here," he murmured in her ear. Her arms crept around him beneath his coat, and her hands caressed his back. His lips hovered fractionally above hers. "When we get to the hotel I'm going to attack you!"

Just as their lips met, Buck's familiar drawl broke in. "Hey, now! A serpent has just creeped into the garden of Eden."

Jake kissed her one more time and reluctantly let her go. "Hello, serpent," he said dryly.

Lindy moved out of his arms, but not away from him. "Hello, Buck," she said.

"Howdy." He came into the room. "Sorry to be a buttin' in on you-all, but I need to tell the man a few things before I go."

Lindy led Jake to a chair and waited until he was seated. She stood beside him, her hand on his shoulder. "Are you leaving us?"

"I haven't had a chance to tell her." Jake's hand came up to find hers and his fingers interlaced with her fingers. "Buck's leaving me in your care, Mama. Think you can get me on the plane and keep me from spilling soup on my tie?"

"Your tie? More than likely I'll be keeping the soup off your Astro T-shirt!" He was holding her hand so tight it hurt.

"I'm a Dallas Cowboy fan, you dumb-dumb!"

"Well, you're breaking this dummy's hand, cowboy."

"Sorry." He loosened his hold and they both laughed.

"Can I have my say?" Buck was impatient. "That little old cabdriver has got to get me to the airport in twenty minutes."

"Say it, Buck. Did you talk to Mary Ellen?"

"Sure did. I'm going to Mexico City and help her get things lined up so she can come back home."

"Did you tell her that I'll rent a beach house for her and the boys? I want my wife and my sister to get to know each other. Running a tourist business in a foreign country is no job for a widow with a couple of kids. She's been alone since she married that good-for-nothing. Do what you can, Buck, and send the bills to Liz."

Buck handed Lindy an envelope. "Here's your tickets, and some cash to see you through. Your flight leaves in the morning. The time is there on the envelope. Take plenty of time to get to the airport, honey. The roads get bad sometimes. The hotel and hospital bills have been paid. I'm taking your big cases with me and I'll have Carlos take them on down to the beach house. All you've got to mess with is the things in your hotel room and the man here."

"We'll be fine, Buck. Thanks for everything."

"Have Carlos meet us." Jake let go of Lindy's hand to shake Buck's when he felt his touch.

"'Bye, Buck." Lindy watched him leave the room, then looked down at Jake. A broad smile began to take over his face.

"Call the taxi, woman. We got things to do. I plan to spend the whole day in bed."

They almost did.

The long flight back to Houston was smooth and comfortable. Their first-class accommodations were roomy and Jake could stretch his injured leg. He had reluctantly submitted to the chairlift that hoisted him into the plane and the flight steward guided him to his seat. When Lindy joined them the man was just moving away and the forced smile left Jake's face, and as she watched, his features, so dark and strong, sobered. There was something strangely vulnerable about him. It was as though he had shed the hard facade he had cloaked himself with just after the accident. A rush of emotion engulfed her; how she both loved and hated this man!

"You're awfully quiet," Jake said after she had been sitting beside him for a while. "Are you tired?"

"A little. I didn't get much sleep last night."

He sought her hand and held it to his cheek, before bringing it to his mouth and nipping her fingers lightly with his teeth.

"Did you mind?"

"Not a darn bit!" she whispered wickedly.

"Is anyone looking?"

"And if there is?" she teased.

"Then they're in for a treat. I'm going to kiss you anyway."

She reached up and removed the dark glasses from his face. His arms encircled her and he kissed her with infinite tenderness, yet with a hint of fervor that excited her. His hand caressed her intimately and his kiss changed, deepening to a searching delight. Her lips parted, accepting the sweetness, curving with gentle passion.

He lifted his head to speak. "I'm the world's biggest fool."

"Fool?" Fear welled blackly in her mind. Dear God! What now?

"A fool to be so happy," he said softly in her ear. "I've got a beautiful wife in my arms that I can't see, in a place where I can't make proper love to her, and a broken leg to restrain me. And I'm still happy!"

* * *

It was in the middle of the morning when the big plane landed at the Houston airport. Lindy and Jake waited until the other passengers had left the plane before attempting to exit. The stewardess reminded them of the warm weather outside and they turned their coats over to the porter who came aboard to carry off their hand luggage. Jake laughingly refused the offer of a wheelchair to help speed them through the airport.

"My wife leads me around by the nose," he teasingly told the pilot and copilot who had come back to shake hands with him and wish him a speedy recovery.

The pilot stared at Lindy with open invitation in his eyes, admiring her slender figure. Her shirt was tucked smoothly into the waist of her flared skirt, her hair carefully brushed and turned into just the right curve, her eyes bright blue against the whiteness of her skin, untouched for many months by the sun's hot rays.

"Not a bad way to go," he murmured to Jake while still looking at Lindy.

At last they were stepping down upon Texas soil, to familiar scents and sounds, to a sense of excitement that banished the tiredness of travel. The sun was warm on their faces and Lindy's eyes squinted against the unaccustomed brightness. She searched the waiting crowd for someone who might be meeting them until the immediate problem of getting through the airport security demanded her attention.

"I don't see anyone that could be Carlos," she said to Jake when they had passed the inspection point and entered the lobby.

"Don't worry. He'll be here. Take me to some out-of-the-way spot and I'll wait for you to find the porter and our luggage. He'll be here by then."

She led him to a less crowded area and found a place where he could sit without the danger of someone falling over his outstretched leg. Reluctant to leave him, she went toward the baggage room in search of the porter. He found her before she found him and loaded with their hand luggage and heavy coats he followed her back down the lobby. The seat where she had left Jake was empty when she reached it. Her heart missed a beat, then palpitated rapidly as her frantic eyes searched for him.

She saw him almost immediately standing not far away, but her relief was short-lived and in its place she felt dark, smoldering anger. Standing close to him, gazing adoringly into his sightless eyes, was Liz, her two hands clutching his arm possessively.

The petite figure in the flimsy sundress that left her brown shoulders bare was the recipient of every male eye that passed her. The silvery blond hair that had been long two years ago was now cut in a modish style and swung gently about her neck. She teetered provocatively on the slender heels of her sandals as she leaned toward Jake talking earnestly.

Lindy stopped dead in her tracks. The porter coming around from behind to look questioningly at her stared at her stricken face, the smile leaving his lips. For one moment she wished fervently a crack would appear and swallow her up. Instinctively she turned away and her eyes met those of the porter. She wanted to leave, to get away, but . . . she couldn't! She looked back at Jake and knew she didn't have the strength to go to him voluntarily. She stood there too numb to speak or move.

Through the ringing of bells in her ears and the normal sounds of the airport lobby, she heard a trilling voice calling her name. "Lindy. Lindy, we're over here."

She moved toward the voice.

"Lindy?" Jake turned his head from one side to the other.

Making an effort to control her shattered nerves, she stood beside him. "I'm here and the porter is with me." She was dazed at the way the calm words fell from her mouth without difficulty.

"It's nice to see you again, Lindy."

Lindy' s eyes swung toward the voice. The soft, sweet Southern voice came from a girl whose face was cold and still, whose eyes shot undisguised hatred at her. Her mouth was set in a defiant line and her fingers still clutched Jake's arm.

"Where's Buck?" Lindy asked through stiff lips.

"Buck left for Mexico this morning, Jake." Liz's voic played false to the look of her face. "He asked me to meet you when something came up to prevent Carlos from coming."

"What came up?"

"Oh, something about Maria. You know how Mexican men are about their pregnant wives."

"Did Mary Ellen call?"

"She called and they talked for a long while. I think he decided to go suddenly." Liz shook Jake's arm gently. "We just may have a romance on our hands."

"That would be great!" His hand came up to squeeze the hand on his arm. Liz laughed lightly as if she and Jake were sharing a secret and Lindy burned with resentment.

"I'd like nothing better for Mary Ellen," Jake said. "Buck would be just right for her and the boys."

A cold knot settled in Lindy's stomach. This intimate conversation was designed to exclude her and the triumphant look Liz threw at her told her she knew of her annoyance.

Feeling hot and gauche beside the cool-looking Liz, Lindy's temper flared. "The porter has been waiting long enough, Jake, unless you want to make it worth his while to stand and listen to you two."

Jake turned toward her, a frown creasing his forehead.

"I'm sorry, Lindy," Liz said, her voice dripping sweetness." You're hot in that heavy skirt and it's mean of me to make you wait. It's just that Jake and I have so much to talk about, I completely forgot how uncomfortable you are." She looked Lindy up and down. "Let's be off, Jake. I pulled all sorts of strings to get us a parking spot nearby so you wouldn't have so far to walk."

Jake turned, obediently, and let Liz lead him toward the door. Lindy and the porter followed.

Keeping up a constant chatter to Jake and solicitous of his safety to a sickening degree, Liz led the procession out of the building and toward a white Lincoln Continental parked close to the curb.

"I brought the Lincoln, Jake. The right seat will slide back far enough to make room for your leg."

"Good thinking. But I knew you'd have things under control."

With a look of victory on her face, Liz helped Jake into the car. Why am I allowing this? Lindy thought crazily. But then again why should I assert myself? As long as he has her, what does he need with me? Why don't I turn tail and run? There's no one to stop me.

The porter asked for the keys and unlocked the trunk to stow away the luggage and coats. There were two cases already in the compartment and glancing at them Lindy felt once again a choking sensation in her throat. Numbly she paid the porter and moved around to get into the backseat of the car. Liz started the motor and they moved away from the curb and into the stream of traffic.

"All set, sweetheart?" Jake broke into Liz's prattle and extended his hand back for Lindy to take.

"All set." She touched his hand briefly, then recoiled from it as if it burned her.

"You're hot and tired." He said it as if offering an excuse for her silence.

She didn't answer and looked out of the window at the line of moving cars and wished she was anywhere, except where she was.

"Check the air vent, sweetheart. You must open the vent to get cool air back there." Jake persisted in talking to her.

Thc sun was beaming into the window and Lindy could feel the trickles of moisture running down her neck and between her breasts. The wool skirt, which had been so necessary in Fairbanks, was now a weight against her thighs. She was hot and uncomfortable, she was weak, she was angry, she was scared.

They moved out of the city traffic and onto the interstate highway toward Galveston. Lindy grudgingly admitted Liz handled the big car well. But why shouldn't she, she thought angrily. She probably has the use of it anytime she wants.

Liz kept a continual conversation going with Jake about subjects Lindy couldn't have talked about if she wanted to, which she didn't. Liz held a responsible position in Jake's company and they talked at length about company business.

"Now, Jake," Liz was saying in a cool, confident business voice, "Buck need not stay in the office. I'll be able to manage. You'll need him on the road or over at the branch office. I'll be your eyes until you are able to see again. I'll read the contracts to you and we can decide the best way to handle them. As a matter of fact, I brought some things with me that need your immediate attention. And oh, I forgot to tell you that Carlos and I fixed up the small bedroom as an office for you to use until you can come back to the city." Without waiting for Jake to comment, she continued, "I've had a wonderful time arranging the house. I've spent every weekend down there and I think you'll like what I've done. Only one package came that I really didn't like and that was the sheets for the big bed. Can you imagine white sheets with small blue flowers? I took them back and told that silly girl what I thought of them and exchanged them for solid blue ones."

"I ordered white sheets with small blue flowers for that bed," Jake said quietly. "I liked them."

"Oh, I'm sorry. Truly I am." Liz's voice was choked as if she was going to cry.

"It's all right. Don't worry about it. We appreciate you giving up your weekends to straighten up the house."

"I was glad to do it. I've loved that house from the day we first came down to look at it." Liz glanced into the driver's mirror to see if Lindy had caught the implication of her words.

Lindy sat stiffly, numbly, expressionlessly. There is a plateau of suffering which, once reached, results in a blessed state of numbness. The comments about the furnishing of the house had forced Lindy to accept the fact the relationship between Liz and her husband was as strong as she suspected and that she meant so little to him that he made no attempt to hide it.

Questions swirled in her mind. What was his reason for coming to Alaska to get her'? The divorce was final. Why couldn't he have let it go at that? Why did he say he had bought the house for her, when Liz had been consulted about the purchase and had been in charge of the furnishings?

"Lindy . . ." Jake's voice jarred into her consciousness. He had turned in the seat and the hand that reached her skirt was tugging at it to get her attention. "Are you asleep? We'll be there soon. Liz says we're about a mile away. I'm anxious for you to see the house."

The house! The damn house! Any interest she had in the house had been drained away from her. Liz's subtle insinuations had taken care of that. He could do as he damn well wanted with his house.

"You must be hot." Jake's voice droned on, falling on Lindy's ears like a recording. "As soon as we get home you can take a shower and get into something cool. Buck sent your trunk down before he left for Mexico."

Lindy looked down at the hand on her skirt, the hand that had handled so efficiently the monstrous truck and the hand that had gripped hers when he had called for her in his delirium, the hand that wore the wedding ring she bought for him just minutes before she bought her wedding dress.

"I'll do that," she said, because she had to say something.

"Where are we now, Liz?"

"The house is just ahead on the left. I'm turning into the drive now. I'll park here on the side and Carlos can get our cases out before he takes the car to the garage. It's all right, isn't it, if I stay a day or two? Buck suggested . . . we thought . . ." Her voice trailed off waveringly.

Jake was silent, then said, "Buck suggested you stay?"

"He'll pick me up as soon as he gets back. We have so much work to do and you will have decisions to make regarding the contracts I'll read to you. I promise I'll stay out of the way."

Lindy sat there trembling for a minute that seemed an hour. She wanted to scream out that she could stay forever as far as she was concerned. She wouldn't last with Jake any longer than any other woman. Nothing lasts forever. Not you, Liz. Not me. Not even a lie. Damn you, Jake. You used me. You took my heart, my faith, my vulnerability, and you used me. But I'm in my home territory now, damn you, and you'll not grind me down.

CHAPTER TWELVE

JAKE OPENED THE door and got out of the car. He felt for the handle of the back door so he might assist Lindy. He couldn't seem to locate the lever so she pushed the door open and got out. Standing by the car, she turned her face toward the gulf and the gentle breeze cooled her face and lifted her hair. The sound of the surf and the ever-present seagulls were dear and familiar as were the wide expanse of water and the fishing boats headed for port.

"*Señor, señor!*" A short Mexican man came out of the house. His words ran together in his excitement.

"Carlos!" There was a warm ring to Jake's voice and a smile on his face as he held out his hand.

"*Señor*, I glad you come home." Carlos gripped Jake's hand.

Jake reached a groping hand out for Lindy and although she made no effort to meet it he caught her arm and drew her forward.

"My wife, Carlos. Her name is Lindy."

The plump, pleasant face of the man looked up at

Lindy for he was rather short. He smiled, showing white teeth beneath a bushy black mustache.

"Pleaz to meet cha, *señora*."

"Thank you."

"Where's Maria, Carlos?"

"Oh, she come, *señor*. She kinda fat, can't run fast like Carlos."

Jake laughed. "She hasn't had the baby yet?"

"Not yet, *señor*," Carlos said disgustedly. "I think maybe she have it yesterday, but it was false alarm."

His wife appeared suddenly from around the car. They were perfectly matched. She was a little shorter than he was and very pregnant.

"Oh, *señor!*" Tears were actually streaming down over her plump cheeks. "You poor eyes!"

"Maria." Jake reached for her. "Do I dare hug you?" He held her shoulders and bent to place a kiss on her wet cheek.

Liz, standing quietly on the other side of the car, had instant disapproval on her face at this display of affection.

"This is Lindy, my wife," Jake said, his hand searching for her.

Maria turned questioning eyes to Jake before turning big solemn ones to Lindy.

"*Señora* Williamson," she said shyly.

"Call me Lindy for I'm not going to call you *Señora* Santos."

A smile appeared on the smooth brown face. Brown eyes sparkled and went quickly to her husband and then back to Lindy and around the car apprehensively. Following her gaze, Lindy saw that Liz had disappeared.

"Let's get inside out of the sun." Jake reached again to Lindy, but she avoided his hand and turned away.

"I'll go ahead with Maria. Carlos will guide you." She deftly sidestepped around Jake and headed for the house.

Maria led her through a screened veranda porch that ran the full width of the front of the house facing the gulf. The house was set high off the ground to catch the cool breeze and several steps were climbed to reach the veranda. Large double doors led into the main room which was extremely large. All the furniture in the room was white wicker with seats and backs covered with a yellow-and-blue-flowered material. The blue on the furniture matched perfectly the all-over blue carpet on the floor. The room was bright and casual-looking and she wanted to hate it, but she couldn't. It was the picture she had cut from *Better Homes and Gardens* come to life.

The kitchen was perfect. All stark white except for the copper utensils hanging above an island countertop stove. A small glassed-in eating area connected with the kitchen.

Maria glanced anxiously at the silent girl who looked as though she had neither like nor dislike for her new home. "You like?"

"It's very nice," Lindy assured her.

Maria looked relieved and led her down the hall, opening doors as she went along. "This big room." Her eyes twinkled up at Lindy. It was a large square room done in gold and brown and was dominated by a king-size bed. "Nice?"

"Nice." Lindy's voice was flat, but it seemed to satisfy Maria who opened the door next to the master bedroom.

Liz stood beside the bed unpacking her cases. She looked up frowning.

"'Scuse, *señorita*." Maria quickly closed the door and proceeded down the hall. "Next room is little one and now office."

The fourth and last bedroom, the one at the back of the house, was large and also square. The windows were covered with frilly yellow curtains. The furnishings were French provincial, the bedspread layers of ruffles. The only thing missing was a doll with a voluptuous skirt in the middle of the bed. A ten-year-old girl would have loved the room.

"The *señorita* say put your things here," Maria said with a note of apology in her voice. "Say *señor* must have rest in big bed."

Lindy felt a surge of anger, then relief that she need not share a room with Jake. "It's all right. Is there a bath?"

"*Si.* Baths with all rooms, but little one."

"I think I'll shed these clothes and have a cool bath."

Smiling shyly, Maria went to the door. Lindy followed her and turned the small knob that locked it. Her head throbbed, her body ached. Voices, faces, moments, crowded into her head, panic tore at her heart in a way she couldn't bear. She sat in solitary silence on the edge of the bed for half an hour, thinking, trying not to let her mind drift back to the tender moments she had shared with Jake.

Leaving her clothes in a heap on the floor, she stepped into the shower. Standing under the cooling stream, she allowed the full pressure of the water to beat at her body. She was utterly weary. Weary to the bone. She clung to the heavy handles of the water controls, half awake, half dreaming for uncountable minutes until the water turned icy cold.

Slowly she turned it off and reached for the fluffy towel and began to rub herself vigorously to get rid of the chill of the icy water. Wrapping the towel around her, she went back into the bedroom.

Taking fresh underwear from the drawer in the bureau, she glanced into the mirror. Jake was standing quietly, his back against the closed door. He had removed the dark glasses and his sightless eyes were looking straight at her. It was unbelievable he couldn't see, uncanny that he could pinpoint her exact location.

"Well!" she blurted. Did he want a showdown now?

"What are you doing in here?" The tone of his voice was a weapon in itself. It savaged her, sending a shiver of dread down her spine, leaving her shaking.

"Taking a shower." From deep within her nature she scooped up enough courage to say it with exaggerated patience.

"I may be blind, but I'm not deaf. I knew you were taking a shower. I want to know why you are in this room." She saw the tremor pass over his hard face.

She was like ice now. "I'm in this room because your *friend* had my things brought to this room. 'She thought you too sick' . . . and 'need rest in big bed,' to use Maria's words. For once I agree with her. Liz won't take up near the space I would." She had thrown pride to the wind because now this conflict was too bitter for her to bear.

"You'll allow my *friend* to come into your home and take over?"

My home? I had nothing to do with this house, for God's sake! She wanted to scream—instead she merely shrugged her shoulders, forgetting for the moment he could not see.

"Answer me, damn you!" he jerked out. His face was white and his hands clenched. Despite her anger she saw him, like a caged tiger, immobilized, without a hand to guide him, and she felt a small prickle of pity.

"Lindy!" Her name was a hiss as it came from his lips.

She was incapable of replying anything except a stream of accusations so she stood silently as if glued to the floor. In the silence her anger left her and she wanted to cry. It was like two years ago all over again, only a million times worse.

"Very well. Stay here! But don't lock this door. I'll not ask Carlos again for a key to my wife's room. I'll kick it down!"

After a moment, when she didn't answer, he opened the door and limped out, closing it softly behind him.

She seemed to stand there for an eternity after he left, watching a sliver of sunlight on the floor. She didn't move, she didn't think, didn't feel. Her mind dozed like the sunlight. She was numb. She lay down across the bed and relaxed her body, willed her mind to stay in limbo and went to sleep.

She awakened refreshed and resigned to the direction her life had taken during the last twelve hours. She slipped into a cool sundress and pushed her bare feet into brief sandals. Standing before the mirror, she looked at herself critically. True, her brown hair needed a trim, but it was shiny and smooth and lay snug against her cheeks. Her skin was clear and pale from months spent without sunshine and she resolved to spend time on the beach to add a golden tone to her skin as well as absent herself from the house. She added a touch of color to her lips and as was her habit a dab of perfume to her throat and left the sanctuary of the bedroom.

Liz's voice was coming from the small room that had been converted into an office. As she passed the open door she could see her sitting in a chair, her legs crossed provocatively, reading from a legal document. All she could see of Jake was the back of his head and one brown hand holding a cigarette. It struck her odd for Jake to be smoking, for as far as she could recall he had never smoked.

She went on down the hall, her footsteps silent on the thick carpet, and into the large main room of the house. Pausing inside the door, she looked around. When she had first looked at the room her mind had been so confused she hadn't grasped the full meaning that came to her now. The room was the exact replica of a room they had looked at in the window of a furniture store years ago. They had talked about the room and the furniture for days. It was unbelievable to her that he would remember and use this devious method to exact his punishment.

The room was lovely. Lindy reluctantly admitted it was the loveliest room she had ever seen. A white wicker stand, topped with a large green Boston fern, caught her eye. It was placed too near the large windows. The green fern would soon die in the direct rays of the merciless sun. She almost gasped with pleasure when she saw the miniature orange tree, with small yellow oranges hanging from its small limbs. It was growing in a large wooden tub beside the fireplace. She had always had a fondness for growing things. Her apartment in the city had been filled with flourishing house plants. With all these beautiful plants to care for she could come to love this house and hate to leave it.

She went through the swinging doors and into the kitchen. Maria was sitting on a high stool by the sink and Carlos was cleaning vegetables. Maria was scolding. He was laughing and teasing her. The Mexican girl looked up and the smile left her face when she saw Lindy. She climbed off the stool and Carlos turned to find the reason for her silence.

"I help Maria. Her back hurt from big *niño*." A sparkle of adoration lit his dark eyes when he looked at his wife.

The arrangement of the work space was ideal. Lindy cautioned herself not to get to liking it too much. She had learned during the last two years not to let herself get attached to anything. Leaving was too painful.

The couple's eyes caught and held. They were so obviously in love. How lucky they were. A merciless pain stabbed Lindy's heart.

"Will you help me move the fern stand back from the window, Carlos? The fern will die if left there in the sun."

Carlos and his wife exchanged glances. "I will help, *señora*, but . . . I move it one time and the *señorita*, she make me move it back." He shook his head and an anxious look came over his face. "She be mad."

Lindy's head came up. A wave of anger hit her. "Well, now, that will be just too bad, won't it?"

"Sure!" Carlos beamed and headed for the door.

It was almost evening. Lindy stood by the big window watching a small shrimp boat, riding low in the water, heading for home port. Jake and Liz came into the room.

She tensed and forced herself to turn around. She was dying inside, but they would never know.

"Careful, honey. Carlos has moved the fern again." Liz guided Jake around it. "I'll mix you a drink."

Jake stopped and stood perfectly still. "Lindy?" He waited. "Lindy, I know you're in here. I smell your perfume."

"I moved the fern," she said firmly. She was controlled, her feelings in limbo. She had expected to be nervous, angry.

"Do you like the view?" Jake asked quietly.

"Very much."

"Would you like a drink?"

"No, thank you." How could they be so damned civilized? She wanted to laugh, till she saw the smirk on Liz's face.

"Shall we have our drink, Jake?"

"By all means have your drink and Carlos will serve your dinner."

"And you, Lindy?" Jake was holding a tight rein on himself. She knew he wanted to explode.

"I've had dinner with Carlos and Maria. I'll take a walk down the beach while you and your . . . *friend* have dinner." Let him chew on that for a while.

She could see the effort he was making to control his anger. His face turned white, then red, and he ground his teeth together rather than make an angry retort.

"If that's what you want." He shrugged his shoulders. "I'll have that drink now, Liz. You know what I want."

Liz laughed. "I should know by now."

Lindy saw the satisfied look on Liz's face as she moved past them and went out onto the veranda. She hoped and prayed Jake's sight would return soon so she could leave, for those two truly deserved each other.

She walked a mile down the beach. The wind blowing from the gulf sent the waves scampering onto the sandy shore and if her mind had not been busy she would have enjoyed the feel of it against her hot face. Far down the beach a bonfire blazed. Laughter and music drifted on the breeze and when the sound reached her it seemed unreal. It was almost sacrilegious, somehow, that people could be happy, laugh, have fun.

She walked slowly back as if to postpone for as long as possible another meeting with Jake and Liz. What could he possibly say in defense of the position he had put her in? God! Why don't I have the courage to walk out into that water and never come back? She whispered the words into the wind and her sad eyes looked out to where the blue water met the darkening sky.

It was dark when she walked up the steps to the veranda. She could see the glow of a cigarette at the far end and wondered if Jake was alone. She doubted it. Liz wouldn't leave him to sit alone. It was too good an opportunity to miss. She would be sitting there beside him, chatting lightly, showering him with attention, making it obvious to him that she and not his wife was looking out for him. Silently Lindy went through the door and down the hall to her room, grateful once again to escape them.

She sat on the edge of the bed and dialed Debra's number. When the familiar voice answered, it was as if the years had never been and they were once again back in high school.

"It's me, Debbie. How are you?"

"Lindy! For God's sake! I just got your letter. Where are you?"

"Galveston. We got in this morning. I didn't have time to call you from Houston."

"What's wrong? You don't sound happy."

"Happy? I've never been so miserable in my whole life, for chrissake! I'm coming in tomorrow. Will you be home?"

"After ten. I've got to take my youngest in for a shot. I'll be home after that. What's wrong, Lindy? Are you sorry you married Jake again? How could things have gone sour so soon?"

"I'll tell you about it tomorrow, Debbie. How're the kids? How's Jean?"

"The kids are fine, Mom's fine. Is Jake still unable to see?"

"His sight hasn't returned, but it will. The doctor in Alaska is almost sure it will return. Have you seen anything of my . . . dad?" She hurried on as if she needed to give an excuse for asking about her father. "I want to get some things out of the house. My trunk, some pictures, things like that."

"Your dad and Marilyn are living at the house, Lindy. They've redone it. It looks real nice. Of course I've only seen the outside. Mom says your dad seems happy. Looks years younger."

"Good for him!" The words came sharply, bitterly. Debra didn't say anything and presently Lindy asked, "Did you find anyplace suitable for my needlework shop?"

"You're going ahead with that?"

"Of course I am. I've got to do something, Debbie. I'll

see you tomorrow and tell you about it. I don't know yet how I'm going to get there, but if necessary I'll take a taxi to the bus station."

"Are things so bad?"

"Worse than you can imagine."

"I'll see you tomorrow, then. 'Bye."

After Lindy hung up the phone she lay back on the bed and wished the night away. Debbie had been the one permanent thing in her life. From grade school through high school and into the working years before either of them married, Debbie had always been there; solid, dependable, never inclined to go off the deep end about anything. She had married first, falling in love with Brian who was just exactly as tall as she was. They had a house in the suburbs, a station wagon, two boys. Debbie belonged to the PTA, the Women's Club and a sorority. She was as sublimely content with her life as Lindy was dissatisfied with hers.

She was startled when the door opened. Jake came in, closed it behind him and leaned back languidly, but his face was hard. His eyes were concealed behind his glasses, but the set of his mouth told her that if she could see them they would be murderous.

"Do you want me to kill you?" he asked almost wearily.

"There are times when I would almost welcome it." It was the first truly honest thing she had said all day and he ignored it.

"Who were you calling? Kenfield? Crying on his shoulder because you're stuck with a blind husband? I thought the house, the money, would make up for being married to me."

Lindy felt humiliation burning her face, but knowing he was in a dangerous mood kept her voice calm.

"I called Debbie. I'm going in to see her tomorrow. I haven't seen her in almost a year. I also want to get some of my things from . . . home." She hesitated before saying the last word. Home was gone, for heaven's sake! She had no home, no roots, no anything, but Debbie.

His ears, sharpened by his inability to see, heard her move off the bed. "Stay here!" he said tensely.

"I wasn't leaving."

"Is the light on?"

"Yes."

"Good. Then you know my intentions." He began to unbutton his shirt.

"I don't want you here, Jake," she burst out with burning panic in her voice. "I won't sleep with you again . . . ever!"

"You think not?" His lips twisted into a sneer. "My dear wife, you say the most amusing things."

"I mean it. I don't want you in here." What was he trying to do to her? Anger, fear, made her reckless. "What do you want with me, Jake? You've got a willing woman just down the hall."

"I like a variety," he said insolently.

"I won't stay here!"

"You make an attempt to leave this room and I'll . . . I'll break every bone in your body!" The lamplight seemed to drain the color from his skin.

"Jake!" She gazed at him with the dilated eyes of surprise that he would make such a threat. "Jake!" she said again, and for the first time since she had known him she felt a stab of fear; he was so big and dark standing there by the door and the unbuttoned shirt and clenched fist added to his power.

"I'm sorry. I'm sorry, Lindy. I didn't mean that." Very deliberately he pulled a package of cigarettes from his pocket and put one in his mouth. He brought a lighter and with a flick of his thumb the flame appeared. Lindy watched in fascination his attempt to find the end of the cigarette. He missed his mark and the flame came dangerously close to his face.

"Wait." She caught his wrist and took the lighter from him and held it to the end of the cigarette dangling from his lips. He took a deep pull on it and drew down the smoke before releasing it from his taut nostrils. The lamplight gleamed on his thick hair, played over his stoical features.

"I didn't know you smoked."

"There's a lot of things about me you don't know and never cared enough to find out. I learned to enjoy smoking in South America. I've been trying to quit."

There didn't seem to be anything she could say to that. She put the lighter in his hand. Before she could move away his fingers grasped her wrist.

"Where's the bed?"

"Go back to your room, Jake. You're not going to stay here."

"I'm staying here whether you like it or not." His fingers tortured her wrist. "I'll not suffer the humiliation of having my wife, my loving bride," he said sneeringly, "kick me out of her bed on our first night home because she's peeved that my secretary had things that needed my immediate attention."

"Jake! Do you think I'm . . . stupid?"

"Where's the bed?" he asked quietly, and followed when she led him across the room. When he felt the mattress against his legs he dropped her wrist and his hand moved on her breast.

"Don't!" she hissed. His hand continued to move up and down her body, stroking away the thin material of her nightdress. "Please, Jake, don't!" She put out urgent hands to hold him off, but as soon as they touched his chest she withdrew them and tried to find his wrist. He leaned over her, pushing her deeper into the soft bed, and his mouth sought hers and took possession, moving gently yet expertly, coaxing a response. She refused to part her lips and he bit her, the involuntary cry opening her mouth and she was forced to allow him entrance.

Lindy felt sick. Sick with guilt for wanting him. Sick because she knew what he felt for her was lust. Sick because the smell of his skin, his hair, and the sweet wine of his kisses made her mind spin senselessly. Her heart was racing. thundering in her ears, and her body tautened until she felt she would explode with the agony of desire.

"Let yourself go, sweetheart. Jump into the darkness with me." Low, husky whispers came to her ears. "Believe in me . . . trust me . . . love me."

"Love you?" Her voice came out in a shaken whisper because his lips were tormenting hers, moving on to her ear, to the pulse beating so frantically in her throat. "You don't love me. You just . . . want me."

"Wanting is loving," he said softly, his lips nibbling hers, his voice a shivering whisper. "That's how it is with us. Don't throw it away."

"No," she groaned, and the thought of never having

this pleasure again made her wince. "There's more to it than this."

"There could be." His hard cheek was pressed into the softness of hers. "Give us time and we'll have it." She parted her lips to the flicker of his because that was what she wanted to do. "I want you now and you want me," the seductive voice droned on in her ear. "I know you want me. I can tell by the way you're touching me. I'm drunk with the way you feel beneath me and I don't think I can wait much longer . . ."

The tides of their passion for each other met and swirled together and once again she seemed to drown in a flood of sensuous feelings, only to surface to lie close to him, tears of frustration wetting his chest.

CHAPTER THIRTEEN

"LINDY." MANY TIMES she had dreamed she heard Jake calling to her, calling gently, teasingly, as if they were children playing in a dark wood.

"Lindy." Her name was a soft whisper wooing her from the depths of sleep, cajoling her to wakefulness. She wasn't going to open her eyes. She didn't want to awaken, because in sleep there was no regret, no guilt, no pain. She pressed her naked body closer to the warm length against her and snuggled her cheek against the muscled chest.

"Lindy." The voice was a little louder, more urgent. "Wake up and tell me what time it is."

Reluctantly she opened her eyes and pushed tangled hair back from her sleep-flushed face. She freed an arm from the soft confines of the sheet that covered them and pushed herself up and away from Jake. It was morning. The sun streamed in through the yellow curtains.

"I'm sorry I had to wake you, but much as I would like to, I can't lie here another minute. My leg is killing me."

He sat up and swung his leg off the bed. "What time is it?"

"Seven o'clock."

His naked back and buttocks were toward her and she was flooded suddenly with a sense of shame as the memory of the ecstasy she had experienced with him came rushing back. Jake felt around on the floor for his clothes. She turned over, not wanting to see his naked male body.

"I think I'd better go see if I can get another cast put on this leg. Dammit . . . it's a damn nuisance! I can't see, can't walk . . . I'm in a hell of a mess." She felt his weight on the bed as he sat down again. His hand moved up to her body to her head and he knew her face was turned away from him. He fingered her hair and laughed suddenly. "Guess I shouldn't complain. I'm not impotent." She didn't say anything and finally he said, "Is the door straight ahead?"

"Ahead and a little to the right. There's nothing in the way."

"Thank you," he said coolly. She turned her head and watched him grope his way to the door.

Lindy didn't get to Debra's until noon. Jake had insisted she take the small car and go, because his appointment with the doctor wasn't until two o'clock and Carlos would drive him in the Lincoln. Liz would stay with Maria because Carlos was reluctant to leave her alone. The baby was due any day now. Liz was not happy with the arrangement, not that it mattered to Lindy. She was relieved to be away from her, from Jake and the house.

She and Debra hugged each other, stood away and looked each other over and hugged again.

"You're thinner and I'm fatter," Debra wailed.

"You look great."

"Liar. If I looked like a tub you'd say I looked great."

"No, I'd say, 'Hey there, tub, it's good to see you.'"

"We've got hours to talk. I sent one monster to the 'Y' and the other to playschool."

"I'm anxious to see the boys. Have they grown?"

"Like weeds. I've got drinks ready. You'll have to take a diet cola and you don't even need it, dammit."

An hour later Lindy hadn't finished her first glass of cola and Debra had finished her third plus a plate of cookies.

"No one in the whole world makes cookies like you do, Debbie."

"No one eats them like I do either, but you know how I am when I get all steamed up about something. I eat. You've really had it, Lindy. How can a guy be as good to look at as Jake is and be so bad?"

"It isn't that he's so bad, Debbie. We just don't go together. Sometimes I think I'll fly into a million pieces."

"How about using some of that assertiveness training you took? Have you ever thought about going back down there and telling Liz to get her butt out of your house and telling Jake that you don't have to put up with all that monkey business?"

"I've thought about it, but assertiveness in the classroom is one thing, putting it to use is another."

"What do you have to lose? Lay it on the line. Either she goes or you do. It's as simple as that. To tell you the truth, I think Jake is crazy about you, has always been. I was surprised when he let you go without putting up more of a fight. I've always liked Jake. So has Brian. We couldn't believe he went to bed with Liz right on your living-room couch. By the way, what did Jake have to say about that?"

"He said he was drunk and she brought him home. I couldn't bring myself to tell him that I knew the rest of what happened that night. It was too humiliating."

"That's the pit of the whole thing!" Debra untangled her short legs and got up off the sofa to pace the floor. "You and Jake don't communicate. Brian and I tell each other everything. You've got to have it out with Jake. Clear the air. Tell him you love him, but you'll not put up with any more fooling around. He must love you a powerful lot to come all the way to Alaska to get you. Don't shake your head at me, Lindy Williamson. I know you're insane about him and have been since the day you met him. But, love, don't let him use your love as a weapon against you. Just say to him, 'This is the way it's going to be, buster, like it or lump it.' You'll have to decide for yourself if you can forgive him. No one can help you."

"Oh, Debbie. You make things sound so simple."

"I'm a good talker when it's someone else's life. Frankly if it was my life and Jake was my husband I'd kill him."

Lindy left with a sack of cookies and the promise that Debbie would bring the boys down the next weekend.

"But I'll call before I come," she called as Lindy backed out of the driveway.

She drove the few blocks to her old home. It was crazy, but when she eased the car to the curb in front of the house where she grew up she felt as if she had never been there before. The house had been painted and shutters added. To the side of the house was a new screened patio. The lawn was landscaped beautifully. Many of the old shrubs had been removed from the front of the house and in their places beds of bright flowers bloomed in profusion. The big window that her mother had always covered with heavy draperies to keep the house cool and dark was now shiny clean. Crisp cottage curtains framed the window and a row of green plants lined the sill.

Resentment, like bile, came up into her throat. Her father had never taken the slightest interest in the house while her mother was alive. It was true that her mother had definite likes and dislikes regarding the house and Lindy didn't always agree with them. For one thing her mother would have never allowed the thin curtains and the plants.

Lindy got out of the car and walked briskly to the door determined to get in and out in the shortest time possible. Her father and his bride—the word was bitter in her thoughts—had probably put her things in the attic, that is if they kept them at all.

It was insane to be ringing the doorbell of this house after so many years of bouncing in through the screened door, racing to the kitchen or up the stairs to her room, but there she stood, her finger prodding the button. When the door opened she was momentarily startled. She didn't know what she had expected. The woman had short gray hair cut in a wedge, a pleasant smiling face, and was wearing shorts and a T-shirt that said "SUPER MOM."

The smile left the woman's face, then returned quickly. "You're Lindy!" She opened the screened door. "I recognized you from your picture."

"Yes, I am," Lindy said flatly. "I've been away and . . . I left some of my things here. I'd like to get them."

"Of course. come in. I'm Marilyn. Your father and I have been married for a year, now. I'm sorry we haven't met before."

"Well . . . If you'll tell me where my things are I'll try and get them out of your way."

"They're not in the way, dear. Come have a glass of tea. Charles will be here soon. He'll help you carry down anything you want to take with you. You're not in a hurry, are you? Wouldn't you like to look around the house? We have done a lot of work on it this past year. My land, I didn't know Charles could do so many things until we got started. He got so he could refinish woodwork and hang paper right along with the best of them." The woman was nervous. Somehow it made Lindy feel better to know this woman, who could inspire her father to do so much work on this house, was nervous of her.

The house didn't even remotely resemble the house she and her mother lived in, virtually alone, for so many years. The rooms were the same; it was the walls, the windows and the furniture that made it so different. The house was brighter, a cosy warm . . . home.

"Would you care for lemon with your tea?"

She looked at the woman standing hesitantly beside the big combination refrigerator-freezer and shook her head.

"Please don't bother. I want to get back to Galveston before the heavy traffic begins."

"If you're sure you don't have time . . ."

"I'm sure. If you'll tell me . . ."

"They're in your room," the woman said quickly. She

walked past Lindy to the stairs. Lindy noticed she was quite short and a little plump. Not at all like her tall, very slender mother.

At the door of her old room the woman stood back and allowed Lindy to go in. She went through the door and stopped. It was like walking back into the years. Nothing had been changed. The shades were drawn, the room was shadowed, just as her mother insisted she keep it. Everything was in its place from the picture on the bedside table of her and her mother, taken when she was about ten years old, to the bulletin board with the high-school snapshots of her and Debbie. Shocked tears came to her eyes. She looked around, but the woman had backed out the door and closed it behind her.

Lindy stood for a long while. She realized, suddenly, she had been relieved to find the house changed, she hadn't wanted to see it as it was, remember all the lonely hours she had spent here not wanting to go out and leave her mother alone to sit with only the television to keep her company. For as long as she could remember, her mother had been weak, sickly. It had been Jean, Debbie's mom, who took them to the beach, was the Brownie Scout leader, came to watch her in the school plays.

It had all been her father's fault. She had grown up knowing it was her and her mother against him. He was a "lusty" man, her mother had told her. It was more important to him to seek his own pleasure than to spend time at home with them. Lindy didn't want to remember these things. She had enough problems. Let her unhappy childhood stay dead.

She went out of the room and closed the door. She would get her things later. Much later, when she had a place of her own. It seemed her father and his wife had no immediate need for the room, and a few more weeks wouldn't matter.

The hall was empty when she reached it and she went quickly down the stairs. At the bottom she looked around for her father's wife. She came out of the kitchen, looking expectant, the friendly smile gone from her face.

"I'm out of time," Lindy said. "Will it inconvenience you if I leave my things for a while longer?" Lindy looked at the clock on the wall beside the woman's head as she spoke. It began to strike . . . a foreign sound in this house. Her mother couldn't stand the sound of a clock ticking, much less the sound of one striking. She remembered when her father had brought her a clock from Mexico . . . Her mother wouldn't allow her to keep it. Well . . . never mind that now. He knew she hated clocks.

"Inconvenience us? It's your room. Charles and I . . . we were hoping you would come visit us. I have two boys." She was talking fast again. Nervous. Some women were like that. She hesitated and when Lindy didn't comment about her boys she said again, "I have two boys and two grandsons."

"How nice. I really must go." The door behind her opened.

"Charles! Charles, look who came to see us!"

Lindy didn't want to turn around. Why had she come here? Why hadn't she grabbed up a few things and got out of here? She felt her feet moving and suddenly she was looking at him.

"Lindy? Lindy, girl . . ."

"Hello, Daddy."

She didn't think he had changed a great deal. His hair

was a little grayer and he was thinner, but he did look younger . . . happier. She was surprised to see his eyes anxious. He didn't offer to touch her. They just stood there, separated by a lifetime of not even knowing one another.

"I hadn't heard that you were back from Alaska."

She nodded in silent answer.

"Where are you staying? You're welcome to . . ."

"I'm back with Jake." She almost choked on the words. "We have a house in Galveston." For a moment she wanted to blurt out that she had married the wrong person, just as he had so many years ago. It was unbearable to be standing there, being polite. *Won't he quit looking at me, for heaven's sake?*

"You've met Marilyn? We've . . ."

"She told me. I hope you're very happy. I must go. Jake . . ."

"Can't you stay awhile?" He waved helplessly at the glasses Marilyn was holding on a tray. Were there tears in his eyes? No! Her father glad to see her? It was funny, but she didn't feel like laughing.

"No. No, thank you. " She went to the door. "I'll call before I come back for my things. I'll try and get them soon. You may need the room for . . . your grandsons."

"There's no hurry." This came from Marilyn who put the tray on the table and was standing beside her father. Her head barely came above his shoulder. Why should she remember that her mother and father were about the same height? She nodded to the woman and glanced at her father. They were strangers. They had always been strangers.

"'Bye, Daddy."

She went out and closed the door. She heard it open behind her and knew they were watching her go down the walk to her car, but she didn't turn around. It was a relief to get out into the cool air. The wind whipped her hair and dried the tears on her cheeks.

She drove the few blocks to Debbie's old home. To Jean's house. It had been here that she had known her happiest moments when she was a child. Twenty minutes later she sat on Jean's worn sofa and slowly, painfully, she started to sob. She hadn't mentioned her visit to her old home, or her father, but she had to get it out.

"He never cared about me." She said it like a heart-broken child.

"That isn't true," Jean said sternly. "Charlie never tried to come between you and your mother. He realized it would be like a tug of war with you in the middle and you would only be hurt more." She handed Lindy a wad of fresh tissue.

"Poor Mom. She led a dog's life with him."

"Your mother led the kind of life that made her happiest. It's time you realized she was happiest when she was miserable. I would never have said that to you while she was alive, but now . . . more than anything Marsha loved her martyrdom. I knew years before she went to the sanitarium that she was sick in mind."

"It was his fault! He drove her to it with his . . . playing around. He didn't love us. He never loved us. Mama loved him so much she couldn't stand to live with him year after year when he begrudged every minute he spent with us." Anger dried her eyes.

"Marsha never loved a living soul except herself." The bitter words shocked Lindy. She looked with astonishment at this woman who had been like a mother to her, who never said a bitter, unkind word about anyone. Jean saw the shocked look on her face and added, softly, "Lindy, I knew your mother before she married Charlie. She was a sheltered child, pretty, but sickly, and encouraged by her parents to be a clinging, whining woman."

Jean sat with her arms folded over her ample breast while Lindy searched her stern face. "She couldn't help it if she wasn't strong."

"That's true, but you must not blame Charlie for everything. He shouldn't have married her, but give him credit for staying married to her and taking care of her."

Why was Jean defending him? She knew how it was . . . how it had always been between her father and her mother.

"Oh, we had a roof over our heads and food to eat, but that's all we got from him. We would have been better off if he'd left us alone. It was his constant coming and going, his . . . women that drove Mama into a breakdown."

"Did you ever see your father with another woman? Did anyone else ever see Charlie out carousing with another woman? He didn't have time, for land's sake! He held down two jobs for years and years. He was a bartender at night. Marsha's medical bills were so big he had to have two jobs!"

"I can't believe that!" The shock and disbelief made her eyes huge as she stared at Jean. Why hadn't she been told this before? Jean read the question on her face.

"It was Charlie's idea. He thought it best to leave you to your mother. You were all she had and he didn't want to drive a wedge between you, but that didn't mean he didn't love you. He just didn't know how to go about showing it. Who do you think paid for the vacation trip to the Big Bend and to Carlsbad Caverns the year you and Debbie graduated? Charlie did. I didn't have the money for the trip. He didn't want you to know he arranged for me to take you and he certainly didn't want Marsha to know. She would have forbidden you to go."

"Why didn't you tell me? Why didn't Debbie tell me?"

"Debbie didn't know and I didn't think it was my place to interfere. Charlie had enough to contend with without me butting in." Jean was blunt as usual. "I thought after Marsha died you and Charlie would get to know each other, but you took off, right away, for Alaska. You should have told him you were going."

"He already had that other woman on the string," Lindy said stubbornly. "He was seeing her before Mama died. I know he was."

"Yes, he was. I admit it. He had known Marilyn for a long time. He was friends with her husband before he died. It was only a few months before Marsha died that he started seeing Marilyn in her home. He knew it was hopeless with Marsha and it had been a long time since he had had female companionship. Why didn't you go to see him after the funeral and tell him you were taking the job in Alaska?"

"I had to leave right away. There were other reasons why I wanted to get out of Houston." Her voice was tight and Jean watched the expressions of confusion flit across her face.

"I know Charlie wasn't perfect, but he wasn't as bad as you were led to believe. I'm glad he's happy. He deserves it. Don't shut him and Marilyn out of your life, Lindy.

They'll more than meet you halfway if you give them a chance." It stunned Lindy a little to think about it. The idea was too new, the story Jean told too incredible.

"I've got to go." She had to get away, to think, to try and absorb this new information about her parent. You can't change a lifetime of impressions about someone in an hour. "Thanks for letting me cry on your shoulder. I love you." She took Jean's hand and squeezed it hard. "You and Debbie have always been my real family."

Jean hugged her. "Don't let what happened between your mother and Charlie cloud your life with Jake. I know you love him . . . try and work things out."

The traffic took all her attention and she didn't have time to think until she was out on the freeway and then it was only fleeting snatches of thought. Daddy moonlighting the nights he spent away from home . . . her mother knew that, yet let her believe he was out with other women . . . why? Why destroy the love a little girl had for her father? Had Daddy loved her after all? Mama was gone and Daddy was happy. She had to get her own life straightened out. Communicate, Debbie had said. Communicate? What could she say to Jake? Could she say I saw you on the couch with another woman? . . . it makes me sick to see you with Liz? . . . I don't believe you when you say you've not been sleeping around since you met me?

She had accused him of being like her father. Had she placed him in her father's role and she automatically assumed her mother's role? The thought caused her to press hard on the accelerator and the small car leaped ahead.

CHAPTER FOURTEEN

IT WAS POURING down rain when Lindy reached the beach house; a warm, spring squall from the gulf spilled the rain in blinding sheets. She sat in the car and waited for the dark, water-laden cloud to pass before she dashed for the veranda. She slipped off her wet shoes and left them on a mat beside the door and went silently down the hall to her room. What she needed was a brandy, but she would have to settle for a cool shower.

Later Carlos knocked on the door to tell her that Jake would spend the night in the hospital. They had removed the cast and X-rayed his leg. A new cast would be applied in the morning and Carlos would drive in to bring him home. Lindy greeted the news with relief. She would not have to confront Jake tonight.

When Carlos left the next morning he was alone in the big Lincoln. Lindy had expected Liz to have her bags packed and ready to go back to Houston with him, but she didn't come out of her room until after he had left. She came to the kitchen, gave Lindy an insolent glance and asked Maria to fix her toast and coffee.

Lindy spoke up. "Fix it yourself. Maria's going back to her apartment to rest."

It must have been the tone of her voice that stopped Liz when she opened her mouth to reply, because she closed it again and went back into the office.

Lindy went to the blue-and-yellow living room and sat on the couch with her cup of coffee and tucked her long legs under her. The room was even prettier in the morning sun than it had been last night but it looked sad and empty. Just as Lindy felt sad and empty, unloved and frightened. Suddenly she desperately wanted to go home. But this was home! This beautiful house, on the sandy beach, surrounded by the swaying palms was home. But . . . it was a lonely, empty building and no one seemed to live here. It was ridiculous, but she longed to be back in Jean's house in Houston. Why didn't she go? She was a grown woman and could go if she wanted to go. She could get in the car and drive, lose herself in the millions of people out there, never see Jake again. It was absurd to sit in this house and wait for him. She could go and leave him to Liz or . . . she could stay . . . she had the right to stay. The perfect right.

The sun coming in through the window made a bright path on the blue carpet and she remembered the grueling cold of only a few weeks before. On sudden impulse she went to her room and put on her swimsuit. It was Saturday. There were a few sailboats on the water and a few swimmers far down the beach. Armed with beach towels, lotion, sunglasses and a paperback novel, she slipped her feet into scuffs, because of the remembered cockleburs, and went down the path to the water.

Her mind wandered to Jake as she walked, and she was

annoyed at herself. Why should she feel almost guilty because she could see the water, the white sand, could go anyplace she wanted to go without being led? His blindness was only temporary!

She tried to empty her mind of thought as she lay in the warm sunshine, but words kept echoing in her head. Communicate . . . talk it out . . . you've got to decide if you can forgive him. She dozed,woke and applied more lotion, dozed again, then decided to try the novel. She knew it would be foolhardy to fall asleep in the sun. After a time she threw the book down in exasperation—it was no good, she just couldn't concentrate. Giving up, she packed her things and trudged back to the house.

Lindy peeled off her swimsuit and after a quick shower stretched out on the bed. Jake would surely be back from the hospital by now. She looked at her watch and promised herself she would go to his room in a couple of hours for the showdown Debbie suggested. She didn't want to take any more time to think about what she wanted to say to him. She was tired of thinking. She wanted to get it over. Find out exactly where she stood. If he refused to send Liz packing, she would leave. But . . . she would do what she had to do. It was stupid to worry about being alone, about her future, without Jake. She would survive. She was convinced that she was a survivor . . . like Jake. She would swallow her pride one more time and if it didn't work out . . . well . . . Tears, that she shed so easily, wet the pillow beneath her cheek.

She woke up shortly before seven, was dressed and out on the veranda by seven-thirty. Liz and Jake were there, Jake sitting with his leg propped up on an ottoman. A partly filled ashtray with a cigarette still burning was on the table beside him. Lindy hesitated, tempted to go back into the house and return later to talk to Jake. Liz spoke to her before she could make up her mind.

"Did you have a good sleep? Jake asked me to look in on you when dinner was ready, but you were sleeping so soundly I didn't want to disturb you."

Jake held out his hand to her. Somehow she couldn't bear to make contact with him in front of Liz.

"You had better have something to eat." He let his hand drop back down to the arm of the chair and she could see his fingers gripping it as if it were a weapon. "I'll ask Carlos to fix a plate of food for you. Just slip it into the microwave for a minute to warm it up."

"How is your leg?"

"It's all right as long as I don't move it around too much."

"After I eat I want to talk with you. Alone." She shot a glance at Liz who smiled a private, tight smile and raised her brows. The gesture angered her and she snapped, "If you can spare the time, that is."

"Of course I have the time. Liz has work to do anyway. I'll wait for you here."

She hated to hear that name on his lips and she hated herself for allowing Liz to see that she hated it. She took her time eating, trying not to plan on what she would say to Jake. It had to be open, spontaneous, to be honest. That's what Debbie said. Keep an open mind, then decide if you can forgive him.

It was dusk, that time between daylight and dark that the poets write about. One soft lamp was burning as she passed through the living room. Liz was ahead of her, having come from the hall as she came from the kitchen.

She hesitated, tempted to wait until Liz went back to the office, but the desire to get the talk over with was greater than her wish to avoid Liz and so she walked swiftly to the open door.

Liz was standing behind Jake, her palm against his cheek. He reached for her hand and pulled her toward him.

"Sweetheart," he said huskily. "Sweetheart, she won't be back for a while. Come here. God, I can't wait to see you!" He drew the unresisting Liz down on his lap.

Lindy gaped, unable to utter a sound; incapable of accepting what she was seeing. The pain was fresh, sharp and hurt like hell! Shaken to the core she turned and fled down the hall to her room and went straight to the bed. She didn't cry. She didn't think about what she had seen. Strangely she felt relief. Now, at last, she knew for sure! It was like sitting on the edge of a cold pool waiting to plunge in and yet not wanting to. Someone comes along and pushes you and you're glad. She lay there for a long time, staring at the ceiling, wondering if she should call Debbie. She didn't want to talk to anyone right now, but it was a comfort to know she could call if she wanted to. Debbie would come if she called. Debbie would come and get her tomorrow.

She got up and turned the lock on the door, undressed and got into bed. Almost at once a strange sensation began seeping rapidly through her mind, a fuzziness, a distant humming noise sounded in her ears, soothing her, relaxing her. She seemed to float upward, her arms and legs losing their solidity, the tense cords that held her back so rigid releasing, and she lay in limbo.

The knob on the door turned. She didn't care.

"Lindy." Jake's voice was soft. "Are you all right? Open the door. I thought you wanted to talk."

"I've changed my mind," she said tiredly. An endless sigh shook her entire body. It had been an unbearable day. The most unbearable day of her life. The pain and the pressure seemed endless.

"Why did you lock the door?" He was angry. So what? His anger didn't matter to her anymore.

"Go away, Jake. I want to sleep."

"What the hell is the matter with you? Are you sick? Did you get too much sun?"

"Nothing's the matter. I just want to sleep."

Silence and then his voice loud and angry.

"Sleep then, damn you!"

She did. It was strange, but even without the sleeping pills her anguished mind sought refuge in sleep. Curled up in a ball, her hand beneath her cheek, she slept soundly. Later she was to wonder if at that time her mind was slipping away from her.

Suddenly she was awakened. Her eyes sprang open and soon adjusted to the moonlit room. She heard again the soft thump on the carpet that had awakened her. She wasn't frightened. She lay perfectly still, listening, waiting. Before she saw the figure of the man limp around the end of the bed she knew that Jake was in her room and that it was the hard cast on his leg that had made the thumping sound.

She lay motionless and watched his every move. He still had on his clothes as if he had not been to bed. He came to stand beside her, so close she could have touched him had she stretched out her fingers. Breathlessly she watched as his hand came out and slowly, as if not to wake her, touch her hair; then fingertips, light as air, trailed across her forehead. The back of his hand rested for an instant against her cheek. She heard a sound come from him. It was a sigh, a groan or a sharp expulsion of air. She couldn't tell which. With wide and curious eyes she watched him limp back around the bed and out of sight. The soft click of the door told her she was alone.

She drifted off to sleep again and when morning came the scene that had occurred in the middle of the night was as vague in her memory as a dream.

It was dawn when she opened her dry and burning eyes. The emotional upheaval of the night before had left her with an aching head and a listless body. She showered and slipped into a pair of white slacks and a red-and-white-striped sleeveless top. After giving her hair a quick brush she padded barefoot out to the kitchen, sure it was far too early for anyone to be about.

Someone had been there before her and the aroma of freshly perked coffee filled the room. Taking a mug from the shelf, she helped herself to the coffee and went back through the main room to the veranda where she could sit and look out over the water and wait until it was time to call Debbie.

She was about to sit down in a lounge chair when Jake's voice startled her.

"Morning." It was a low, calm voice, but it broke the tranquil silence. Her nerves were jumpy and her hand shook, spilling some of the hot coffee on her bare feet.

"Oh, oh . . ." The sound was out before she could suppress it.

"What's the matter?"

"Nothing. I just spilled a little coffee." She set the cup on the table, not knowing if she should go or stay.

"Sit down and drink your coffee."

She glanced at him. His face was turned away from her as if he was looking out over the water. His hearing had sharpened since his blindness and he was waiting for the creak of the wicker chair.

She sat down and let her curious eyes wander over him. This man, her husband, was hard to understand. There were times when she felt she didn't know him at all. He knew she had loved him before. Did he expect her to love him again? To sweep all his indiscretions into a corner like so much dust? She could never love him as she once loved him—blindly, wholeheartedly, consumingly. What woman with pride and self-esteem and memory could?

Jake had just come from the shower. His hair as well as the cast on his leg was wet. He was wearing walking shorts and his muscled chest and shoulders were bare. The sunglasses helped to hide the expression on his face, but she did see a grimace when he reached a finger down to work it around the top of the cast that came almost to his knee. The leg was propped on a stool and the part of his foot not covered with the cast was almost as white as the plaster. Lindy guessed that he had been careless and allowed water to splash around the top of the cast and an itch had developed.

Slowly she shifted her gaze away from him and the world looked steady again. She drew air into her lungs in great gulps in order to stop her trembling so she could hold her coffee cup. Her heart thumped in her throat when he spoke.

"You didn't come back last night."

"I came," she said aloud, and to herself . . . I came . . . I saw . . .

"I waited and you didn't come."

"I came," she repeated. "You were busy." Her lips trembled at the memory. It was too soon to be completely indifferent although she managed to say indifferently, "You were very busy.""

"Why didn't you ask me how long I would be . . . busy?"

She was momentarily startled at the question. "I didn't even consider asking you that!"

He turned toward her, his hand spread in a gesture of futility.

"What now? Are you leaving me again?"

Quite simply she answered, "Yes."

His face was turned in her direction. He looked tired, haggard: there were deep creases on each side of his mouth. She looked searchingly at him for a long moment. The shock was over. She was able to speak calmly.

"You don't need me, Jake. With all you've got, you don't need me."

He took a quavering breath. "Wedding vows don't mean much to you, do they?"

Anger brought her to her feet. "You . . . can say that to me?"

"You loved me once."

"Yes, I did," she admitted. "But that was . . . before . . ."

"Before what?"

"You know the 'before what' I'm talking about. I don't have to spell it out for you." She crossed over to the door.

"Just a minute. We haven't finished this conversation." She could hear Jake getting clumsily to his feet.

"It's finished. The conversation is finished. We're finished." Feeling the trembling weakness of reaction in her knees and the overwhelming desire to get away from him, she headed, unsteadily, for her bedroom.

On reaching the hall her unsteady legs picked up speed and she was almost running. A door opened and she stood stock-still, staring transfixed, her mouth open in shocking surprise, acute humiliation causing her face to flood with color.

Liz was coming out of Jake's room and through the open door she could see the rumpled bed and the filmy black robe lying on it. The bit of black sheer that covered Liz probably served as an excuse for a nightgown and it revealed most all of her as she stretched and yawned.

Lindy wanted to pass on, but her legs refused to move. Goddamn them! Goddamn them both to hell! The voice inside her shouted her desire to kill them . . . to run . . . to not believe what she was seeing.

Jake came into the hall and Liz called to him.

"Shall we have our coffee now, Jake?" She stifled a yawn.

Jake didn't answer for a moment and Lindy found life in her legs and moved fast toward her bedroom feeling physically sick.

"Get dressed, Liz, and come to the office." There was a strange quality in his voice. "Lindy, go get Carlos." It was a command. With his hand on the wall he walked as rapidly as his injured leg would allow to the small office.

Liz looked as smug as a cat who had just swallowed a canary and her soft quavering laughter sent Lindy's temper climbing. She hurried by her and came face to face with Jake. Her lips curled in disgust and her face was a mask of contempt.

Jake's hand shot out and grabbed her by the forearm. The action surprised her so much she took several backward steps to regain her balance.

"Don't leave this house!" Jake was gripped with a consuming rage. Lindy almost recoiled from the cold fury on his face.

"Get your hands off me!" Her voice was so hard she scarcely recognized it as her own. "Don't touch me . . . ever!" She jerked away from him and went quickly toward the kitchen.

She leaned on the counter. Her head felt light and her vision blurred. She turned the cold water into the sink and held both wrists under the stream. The last few minutes had upset her more than she thought possible. How long would it go on? How much more would she be able to take? Each incident hurt more than the one before it. She turned off the water, dried her hands and dialed Debbie's number. She let the phone ring ten times before she hung up the receiver and went to find Carlos.

Refusing to go back into the house after she had given Carlos the message, Lindy found a shady spot under a palm tree and sat down on the grass and rested her back against the sturdy trunk. She had never felt so alone in all her life and wished desperately she had been able to reach Debbie. She looked at her watch. She would wait a half hour and call again.

A worried-looking Carlos came to tell her *Señor* Jake wanted her to come into the house.

"What does he want?" she asked bluntly.

"He going to Houston, *señora*, and want to say something before he go."

Lindy got to her feet and followed him across the yard. Jake was standing on the drive. He had changed into sports shirt and light trousers. He was leaning against the car, his face was toward her as she approached.

She looked directly at him for if her plans worked, this could be the last time she would see him. He was handsome, no use to deny that. She had thought she could live with the "peaks" and endure the "valleys," but she couldn't. No use to deny that, either.

He spoke immediately. "I'm going to Houston." He waited and she said nothing, so he continued. "Carlos will drive me. We want to be sure you will stay here with Maria. Carlos is worried she may go into labor and not have anyone with her."

The bottom fell out of Lindy's plans. She looked at Carlos's worried face and back to Jake. "Your *friend* will be here."

"Liz is going with me."

"I see."

"I'm sure you do." No mistaking the sarcasm.

"How long will you be gone?"

"Until this afternoon."

"I'll stay while you're gone."

Carlos perked up and smiled his usual toothy smile.

"*Gracias, señora.* I not like to leave her, you know, she will be so scared when the baby come. Maybe it won't be this day, maybe next day and Carlos will be here to take care of her."

"Why can't your . . . friend take you and let Carlos

stay with his wife?" She spoke in the measured tone of a woman who knew her life with this man was over.

Jake answered in the same tone. "Because my . . . friend is leaving and not coming back. Carlos will take me to the clinic and bring me back. After that you can do as you damn well please."

She stared at him. She could see her image reflected in his dark glasses. There seemed nothing else to say.

Liz came out of the house carrying her cases. She hadn't taken her usual time with her appearance. Her hair was pulled back from a makeup-free face, she had pulled on jeans and a knit top. Her feet were thrust into exercise sandals. She dropped her cases at the rear of the car, then got in and sat huddled in the corner of the backseat. Lindy had never seen her other than arrogant and self-assured and she was shocked into confusion. Something very strange was going on, but what it was she couldn't fathom. Jake's voice broke into her perplexing thoughts.

"Find Maria and assure her she won't be left alone. You'll be all right here. Take care of yourself." He started giving his orders in a tense, clipped voice. It softened on the last request and he would have touched her arm, but she sidestepped and went up the steps to the veranda.

Inside the screened porch she turned and looked at the group on the drive, Jake had eased himself into the right front seat. His face was turned toward where she was standing and she could see a sad and serious look on his face that left her puzzled.

Maria came to stand beside her. She waved to Carlos

and he returned her wave. She stood silently and watched the car until it was out of sight.

"I hope baby not come today." Maria's big brown eyes were solemn. "I need Carlos when he come."

Compassion for this young girl flooded her. It had been a million years since she had been this young and this in love.

"Don't worry. They'll be back in a few hours. You feel all right?"

"I don't feel no different, *señora*."

"Come and sit down. I'll make us some fresh coffee."

"I make you coffee, *señora*. You the lady. I the servant."

"Lady? Servant? Who said so?"

Maria blinked her eyes and smilingly shook her head. "You so different from the *señorita*. Carlos and I not stay with the *señor* if she *Señora* Williamson. I glad she go and not come back."

Maria sat in the kitchen chair, a soft pillow nestled in the small of her back. Lindy set the toaster on the table and added butter and jam. It soothed her nerves to be doing something.

"Maria, you can't be sure Liz won't be back. She won't be back today, but she'll be back soon."

"I don't think so. Carlos say the *señor* very, very angry. He call office and say write the *señorita* a check. She don't work for him. The *señorita* cry and say she sorry, but the *señor* say she cost him too much and he not want to put eyes on her again."

Lindy was stunned into silence. Jake had fired Liz? Slept with her the night before and fired her in the morning? Maybe he planned to set her up in an apartment . . .

but no, if that was the case Liz wouldn't have cried and she would have been more arrogant than ever this morning. Jake was a puzzle. Her head ached from all the confused thoughts that floated through it and she wished with all her heart that she had never set eyes on Jake Williamson.

CHAPTER FIFTEEN

AFTER A LIGHT lunch Maria lay down to rest and Lindy fixed herself an iced drink and went out on the veranda. She settled in a lounge chair and tried to sort out the confusing mass of information Maria had given her. After a while she grew tired of trying to figure out the complex person she was married to and allowed her mind to go blank.

A car came into the drive and moved slowly past the garages toward the house. Lindy sat up in the chair, her heart quickening. Could Jake be back so soon? No . . . it was a black car. The man behind the wheel had on a white Stetson hat. The car stopped. A tall familiar figure unfolded itself and got out.

She sprang to her feet and ran down the steps: She was almost blinded by tears by the time she reached him and threw her arms around his waist and buried her face on his broad chest. Sobs shook her slim body and she cried uncontrollably, her tears making wet patches on his shirt.

"Honey! What's the matter?" Buck's voice was anxious.

"Everything!" The word came out between sobs.

"Has something happened to Jake?"

"Jake's all right," Lindy said when she could catch her breath. She stepped away from Buck and saw a pretty dark-haired girl with a small boy clinging to each of her hands. The boys were wide-eyed and silent, the girl's face showed questioning concern. Her resemblance to Jake was unmistakable.

"I'm sorry." They were weak words, but all she could think of in defense of her actions.

"That's okay, honey. It isn't every day I have a pretty girl cry on my shoulder." Buck put his arm out and drew the little group closer to him. "This is Mary Ellen and Mack and Pete. Boys, this is your Uncle Jake's wife."

Mary Ellen embraced her. "Did we come at a bad time?"

"I'm sorry I frightened you. I guess it was seeing Buck again. He was such a pillar of strength in Alaska. Jake has gone to Houston to have the doctor take a look at his leg. I suspect he's developed an itch under the cast." She looked down at the two pair of blue eyes staring up at her. "I'm glad to meet you, boys."

"Are you crying cause you're having a baby?"

Of all the things a child could have said this was the most astonishing and Lindy's lips parted on an involuntary breath. On this unguarded moment her unconscious fear had found voice.

"Pete!" Mary Ellen scolded with her eyes as well as her voice.

"Uncle Jake said he was going to get a baby as soon as he got back. So . . . ," Pete stammered, then halted.

"No, to your question, Pete." Lindy found her voice. "I was crying because it was so good to see Buck again."

Mack turned a serious little face to her. "But . . . Buck is goin' to marry us." His eyes went from Lindy to Buck. "Pete and I are goin' to have a daddy and Buck is it."

Lindy leaned down and hugged him. "You and Pete will have the best daddy in the whole world."

"Then . . . you won't cry no more?"

"I won't. I promise."

Buck had his arm around Mary Ellen and he looked stupidly, gloriously happy.

"They're perfect for you, Buck." Lindy was never more sincere about anything in her life. "And to steal a cliché from you . . . you look like you had the world by the tail going downhill backward!"

Buck laughed. "Well, darned if I don't!" He hugged Mary Ellen tighter. "Who wouldn't be happy as a ring-tailed bobcat with a woman like this and two Texas mule skinners?"

"What's a ring-tailed bobcat?" This from Pete.

"What's a Texas mule skinner?" yelled Mack.

Mary Ellen detached herself from Buck's arms. "Okay, Buck." Her smile was indulgent. "You started it. You explain."

"He can explain in the house while I make a cool drink," Lindy said, and led the way onto the veranda.

In the kitchen she left Mary Ellen to add ice to the lemonade while she made a hurried trip to check on Maria, after explaining Maria's condition.

"That will interest Pete." Mary Ellen laughed. "Right now he has an obsession about babies. He keeps mentioning it to Buck. Honestly, it's embarrassing!"

"Buck is a real gem. I don't know what I'd have done

without him in Fairbanks. He risked his life to save Jake. Did he tell you that?"

"He told me something about it, but said you did more."

Lindy dismissed the remark with a shrug. "Shall we take the drinks to the boys?"

Later, while Mary Ellen and the boys toured the house and the grounds, Buck questioned Lindy about Jake.

"He's doing all right. He's been in to the hospital and had a new cast put on his leg." She decided to change the subject and said the first thing that came to mind. "I was disappointed when you didn't meet us at the airport."

"I'm sorry about that. I phoned Mary Ellen and she seemed to be so glad to hear from me that I hightailed it down there." He grinned sheepishly. "Did Don keep you waiting?"

"Don?" Lindy echoed. "Liz met us." She despised saying the name.

"Don was to meet you so Carlos could stay with Maria."

"Liz. said you made the arrangements for her to meet us and that you would pick her up here in a few days." She looked away from him. The memory was too painful, and she must not let herself cry again.

"Liz came here with you?"

"Yes. She went back to Houston this morning with Jake."

Buck looked out over the gulf, his eyes narrowed in that particular way of his. "You haven't been happy, have you, honey?"

"No." She dropped her eyes and stared at her hands. "I have never been so miserable in my life."

"But . . . you love him."

Her shoulders straightened defiantly. "No . . . yes . . . No! I detest what he is!" she protested incredulously, resentful of Buck's perception when he looked at her.

"Why did you marry him then?" Buck's gaze held hers for a moment longer, grew speculative, then pensive.

She was so damn vulnerable, she realized with a pang. Weak, and vulnerable and pathetically unsure of herself. The complexities of Jake's character forced her to denounce her feelings for him. She thought for a moment before answering, as if she had never thought seriously about it before.

"I don't know." Her lips trembled. "I knew it was the wrong thing to do when I did it. But . . . Jake is so overwhelming, so determined. He's stronger than I, Buck. And not just physically. I mean he has a stronger personality and I thought he needed me. But Jake doesn't need anyone. Jake is a complete unit himself, and . . ." She stopped abruptly, not really knowing how to explain. After a moment she continued. "I'm leaving him. I'd just as soon Mary Ellen didn't know just yet."

Buck waited awhile before he said, "Don't do anything hasty. Jake loves you. That man went through hell when you left him before. You understand it's not for me to be telling you what to do, but I'd swear on my daddy's Bible that he loves you."

"Maybe Jake does love me, in his own way, but it's not the way I want to be loved. I've caught him in situations that I just can't forgive. And to let that woman come to this house . . . I'm just not all that liberated, Buck." Try as she might, she couldn't keep the tears from rolling down her cheeks. They sat silently. Finally, she regained her composure and said, "When is the wedding?"

His dark eyes took on a glow. "In exactly forty-eight hours."

"Great! Where will you live?"

"I've rented a house a mile down the beach. Mary Ellen and the boys will stay there until I move in with them." He grinned happily.

Two bundles of energy burst from the house and threw themselves on Buck. "Ain't we goin' swimmin', Buck?"

Buck got to his feet holding a small wiggling boy under each arm. He took them to the door and set them on their feet. "Out to the car, cowboys. Your mom and I will be out in a minute and we'll go home. Mind, now, or I'll tan your hides!"

The boys bounded down the steps. Mary Ellen looked fondly after them and gazed lovingly at Buck. "You're just what they need."

"And you, little bird?" He put his arms around her.

"Me, too." She wrapped her arms around him.

Lindy watched them leave. They were already a united family, something she had never known. When the car turned the drive and was out of sight, she went back into the house.

By evening Maria was convinced the baby would not arrive that day. Lindy was glad for her company. They sat in companionable silence, Maria knitting and Lindy working on her needlepoint. It was just getting dark when they heard the small blast of the horn.

"That Carlos!" Maria jumped up, clutching her knitting to her full breast, and hurried to the door and down the steps.

Lindy sat as if paralyzed. Damn! It was too late to call Debbie. The dreaded moment had come and she would have to face Jake once again. The lamps were lit in the attractive room and their soft glow fell on her worried face. Would Liz be with him? Had Maria misunderstood Carlos and Jake had not fired her after all? Lindy stood in the middle of the room, waiting. Her eyes looked like sapphires, dark and troubled.

She heard Jake call teasingly to Maria. She heard Carlos laugh. The screen door slammed and Jake was standing in the doorway. The first thing she noticed was that his sunglasses were different. They were light in color and she could see his eyes through the lens. She looked behind him. He was alone. He came slowly into the room holding his hand in front of him.

Lindy trembled violently as she watched him. "Do you need help?" She asked the question to let him know she was in the room.

He came to the back of the couch. "No. I can find my way."

His eyes were on her and she shivered. She wished he wouldn't face her. She felt uncomfortable knowing he couldn't see.

"Did they change your cast again?" She wondered how long she could stand there making polite conversation. Damn you, if only I could bring you the pain and the bitterness you've brought to me. Why didn't she say it? Why did she have to say something as civilized as "Did they change your cast?"

"Yes." He stood there leaning heavily on the back of the couch as if to relieve his leg of the burden of his weight. "What did you do today?"

The question surprised her. He didn't really care what she did today . . . he was the one now who was making the polite conversation. What would he say if she told him she had been out sleeping around? She didn't say any of the things she was thinking.

"Buck was here today with your sister."

"Mary Ellen was here?"

"Buck is going to marry her. He's rented a house about a mile down the beach."

Jake was pleased. His face relaxed and he almost smiled. "They'll be perfect together. What did you think of Mary Ellen?"

She answered truthfully. "I liked her. The boys, too."

Now he did smile. "What did the monsters think about Buck?"

"They liked him. Buck will be a good father." Lindy started to edge toward the door. "She left a number if you want to call her."

"Come here for a minute." He held out his hand.

She stopped, confused. Could he have known she was trying to leave the room?

"What do you want?" Her tone held a shade of desperation.

"Please." His expression was grave, his voice soft.

She looked at the hand he held out to her. The gold wedding band she had given him shone brightly on his brown finger. She seemed to be drawn to that hand, so she went to him. He grasped her hand tightly and pulled her to him. She tried to pull away, but his fingers closed tightly around her wrist and brought it up against his lips. He kissed the soft skin.

"Did you mean what you said this morning about leaving me?"

Her lower lip quivered and she refused to look at him. "Yes!"

"Sweetheart!" His embrace enfolded her, bringing her tight against him. "Sweetheart, don't go! Give it a little more time." He trembled violently and his arms crushed her so close she could scarcely breathe. Her mind whirled giddily and she tried to push herself away from him.

"Don't!" Her words were a whisper coming from her tight throat.

He found her mouth and kissed her hungrily. Her lips already parted in protest, and his unexpected assault found no opposition. The weight of his muscular thighs pushing her back against the back of the couch was in itself a potent intoxicant, but it was his mouth that wrought the most damage, invading and possessing the moistness of hers. She was invaded by that old familiar feeling of weakness in her thighs as his fingers probed beneath her shirt, unrestrained in their caresses.

His withdrawal was as unexpected as his assault. One moment his mouth was on hers, devastating it, moving sensually, causing all the old familiar feelings to surface. The next moment he had lifted his head.

"Don't you love me enough?" The words were wrung from him.

"No! Not *that* much!"

With all her strength she tore herself from his arms and ran from the room. She felt helpless against the storm of emotion he had aroused inside her, dazed by her response to his arrogant assault. It was humiliating to know that he only had to touch her, kiss her, to tear down every defense she built against him. She had to get away from him. He could make her forget all that had happened in the past, and all that would happen in the future.

She leaned on the closed door of her room. Dear Jesus! Would this nightmare never be over? She had to leave this house tonight, or she might never be able to leave it at all. She took her overnight case from the shelf and started filling it with only the absolute necessities. In ten minutes she was ready to leave the room.

It was then her mind paused to grapple with the problem of transportation. What now? She couldn't ask Debbie to drive down here this late at night. The only other person she knew was Buck. She fished in her pocket for the folded paper which she had intended to give to Jake. Glancing at it, she quickly dialed the number.

Mary Ellen answered the phone and she asked to speak to Buck.

"Hi, honey. What's the problem. Jake not home yet?"

"I hate to ask you to leave Mary Ellen and the boys, Buck, but will you come over and give me a ride into town? It's terribly important to me that I go tonight." Her voice shook in spite of her desperate attempt to control it.

"Of course I will, honey. Is there somewhere special you want to go?"

"To a hotel." She was losing her courage and her voice showed it.

For a short moment there was silence at the other end of the line. "If you're sure that's what you want to do I'll be there in ten minutes."

"I'll wait for you out by the garages."

"Okay. See you soon."

Lindy looked at her watch and paced the floor. The

time went slowly, but it went by. She picked up her case and left the room.

Jake was standing in almost the same spot as when she left him. He had a drink in his hand. She walked softly, hoping to slip by without him knowing she was there.

"Lindy." His voice stopped her.

She halted momentarily, then moved on toward the door.

"There's no need for you to sneak out. I won't force myself on you." There was cold sarcasm in his tone.

She looked at him and his blue-green eyes held her frozen gaze with the expertise of the snake with the rabbit, and her heart seemed to choke her with her sudden realization.

"You can . . . see!"

"I'll never ask you to come back." He overrode her statement cruelly and limped to the table and set his glass down. There was a kind of desperation in his jerky movements. "Go! You think you know so God-awful much. Your problem is that you never cared enough to get to the bottom of anything that concerns me." He shouted the last words and she was sure that had he still had the glass in his hand he would have thrown it at her.

She saw the flash of headlights on the drive and turned.

"Good-bye, Jake."

"Lindy, wait. Where are you going?"

She ran down the steps as Buck's car turned into the drive. The headlights, arching in the darkness, found her and pulled to a stop beside her. The interior light came on when she opened the door and she saw Mary Ellen behind the wheel. Indecision . . . she stepped back, confused. Her frightened eyes saw Jake framed in the veranda doorway.

"Get in the car," Mary Ellen urged gently.

She got in and held the small overnight case on her lap. Her nerves were a screaming mass of loose ends that threatened to strangle her at any moment. Mary Ellen eased the big car back down the drive and out onto the highway.

Still unable to relax even the slightest bit, Lindy sat ramrod stiff as the car picked up speed. Mary Ellen hadn't said another word. Presently she pulled the car into the parking area of a closed supermarket, shut down the motor and turned off the lights.

Words fell from Lindy's mouth like rain. They tumbled over each other in their effort to find release. "Take me to a hotel. Please, I know what I'm doing. Tomorrow I'm going to Houston and find an apartment. I couldn't ask Carlos to take me and it's too late for me to ask my friend, Debbie, to come get me. The only other person I could think of was Buck. I'm sorry to get you involved in this."

"I wanted a chance to talk to you. It was Buck's idea for me to come for you. He's worried about you and Jake."

"The last thing I want to do is to worry anyone and especially you and Buck. This is your happiest time. All I can say is that I'm sorry, Mary Ellen." Her voice was hoarse and unnatural and she hugged the case tightly to her breast as if to stop the pounding of her heart.

"It's all right," Mary Ellen said gently. "I'm glad you called us. I don't need to tell you that I love my brother very much. He's all the family I've ever had. Do you love him?" The question was asked earnestly, abruptly, and Mary Ellen leaned toward her to peer into her face.

Lindy waited a while before answering. She swallowed several times to get rid of the aching lump in her throat. "What is love? Is love wanting to go to bed with someone? Or . . . mutual respect, trust, blind faith that the person you love will never let you down, be unfaithful to you?" Looking out the window into the darkness, she stifled a sob.

"Do you?" Mary Ellen insisted. "It's yes or no. You love him or you don't."

"I don't know if I do or not!" The words were blurted out angrily. "I'm human. I like what he does to me, but I hate what he is on the inside!"

Mary Ellen settled back in the seat. "Somehow I think you do love him." She waited for Lindy to find a tissue and blow her nose. "He loves you. You have no idea how much Jake loves you and how badly he wants you to love him in return." She made this statement simply and honestly.

"I think Jake is fond of me in his own way. I said as much to Buck this afternoon. But it isn't the way I want to be loved. I want to be everything to my husband—wife, lover, friend, companion. I won't share him! I lived with a heartbroken mother. My father had many affairs with other women." Oh, Jesus! What was she saying? She didn't even know if that was true anymore.

"Jake told me something about your home life. He came to see me after you left him. He was heartsick! He almost killed himself drinking and messing around in some of the lowest dives in Mexico City. After a while he thought he could build a life without you and he tried. He took on some very dangerous work in revolutionary countries. He wanted the big money, but he seemed to want the risk, too."

She paused to give Lindy time to take in the meaning of her words. "When he came back to Mexico City he seemed to have gotten himself together. He had made up his mind what he was going to do. He said life wasn't worth living without you and that he was coming home and he was going to buy the house you had dreamed of having and he was going to Alaska to get you."

"He broke my heart once!"

"You broke his," Mary Ellen said simply.

"You can't know how it was. A girl came to our apartment and said that Jake had made her pregnant. I tried to believe him when he denied it, but the doubt was always there."

"And you believed a stranger over a man who had never given you reason to doubt him before?"

"Before, no. Afterward, yes. More than doubt. Proof. I saw him on our own couch with Liz. Since we've been here in Galveston . . . they've been together!" The memory was so painful she could hardly speak of it.

"Does Jake know you know about this?" Mary Ellen had a disbelieving expression on her face.

"He knows."

"I can't believe Jake would do that. It goes against everything that I know about him." The dogged look of disbelief was still in her eyes. "Well . . . what does he say?"

"We never talk about it. He thinks I should trust him. He said if I loved him enough I would trust him." The pain of thinking about it was tearing through her again and a small moan escaped her.

Mary Ellen was thoughtful. "He doesn't explain his actions." It was a statement accompanied by a sad shake of her head. "Let me tell you something about Jake's early life. You think you had it rough? You had at least one parent that loved you. Jake had none. Our father died when we were very young and our mother was the type of woman who should never have had children. She was little and pretty and Jake loved her dearly, but there was something about him that made her actually . . . dislike him. He never did anything that pleased her. Any little thing that went wrong, Jake was blamed for it. If a window was broken out in the neighborhood she accused him whether anyone else thought he was guilty or not. If she misplaced money, he took it. She never took his word for anything. Always she believed the worst of him. Even when she was ill, she accused him of not caring if she died. He developed an attitude that he would explain himself to no one. He knew she didn't love him, because she didn't trust him, have any confidence in him. That's a terrible burden for a small boy to carry. I realize it more, now that I have boys of my own." Mary Ellen paused and wiped her eyes. "I understand my brother and I'll never believe in a million years that he was unfaithful to you."

"I saw him with my own eyes!"

"I know you think you saw . . . you did see . . . but talk to him about it. I know he loves you! Ask him to explain. Please, Lindy . . . talk to him."

Talk to him. It was what Debbie urged her to do. She sat silently, thinking.

"Tell him to straighten up or you'll knock his damned

head off!" The unruffled Mary Ellen was now ruffled and Lindy was strangely calm.

How could Jake explain away Liz on his lap . . . Liz furnishing the house . . . Liz in his bedroom? Should she go back and open old wounds? Old wounds? Brand-new wounds! Her hair lay damp and matted around her face, and for what seemed the thousandth time that night she wiped her eyes and her nose.

Mary Ellen took Lindy's silence for an answer and started the car. She didn't speak. She turned in the direction of the beach house.

"I'm scared," Lindy blurted suddenly. "I don't know what to say to him. I don't want to be hurt!"

"Life is full of hurts, Lindy. How do you know when you are happy if you have nothing to compare it with? It's a competitive world. Fight for what you want."

The car turned into the drive and stopped in front of the veranda steps.

"Go on," Mary Ellen said gently. "I'll come back if you call me."

Lindy reached over, kissed her on the cheek and got out of the car.

CHAPTER SIXTEEN

THE SOFT LIGHTS were on in the living room and reached out onto the veranda where she stood. The only sound she heard was the pounding of the surf on the sand beach and the wind stirring the fronds of the palm trees. The sound of Mary Ellen's car had been lost to her for several minutes.

Her life played across the screen of her mind like a movie. Suddenly everything was clear. The guilt she felt for wanting to love her father in spite of his so-called "adulterous" behavior had almost turned that love to hate. The love-hate relationship had carried over into her marriage with Jake. Unconsciously she had cast him in her father's role and herself in the role of the martyred, repressed wife. Lindy felt a surge of rebellion! She would not walk in anyone's footsteps but her own.

She placed one foot in front of the other one until she stood in the middle of the living room. And then, almost before she knew it, she was in the hall. The door to Jake's room was open and the light made a path out onto the carpet. This was the turning point in her life. She was well aware of the importance of the moment. Without hesitation she moved to the door.

Jake lay on the bed with pillows propped behind his head. Only brief shorts covered his near-naked body that looked golden brown against the white sheets.

She struggled against the grayness that engulfed her and through the ringing in her ears she heard him say, "Did you forget something?"

Her lips were dry and she put out her tongue to moisten them. She shook her head to free herself from the daze and suddenly her mind was clear.

She walked into the room and stood looking down at him. Rage such as she never knew existed boiled up inside her. She forced her clenched fists to stay at her sides to keep them from striking him. Words she never thought of saying burst from her lips. "If you ever bring that bitch into my house again I'll knock your damn head off! I've put up with all I'm going to take from you, Jake Williamson!"

Her voice rose shrilly and to her astonishment she found herself shouting. "I've put up with your flirting, your playing around, but when you let that . . . woman come into my house you pushed me too far!" Her finger came out and jabbed his chest. "I've cried my last tear over you and spent my last sleepless night wondering why I didn't kill you!"

Her rage increased with every word. Her face was livid, her eyes wild. "I was becoming reconciled to living alone. I had plans for a business—you had to come and disrupt my life. Well, you've got me, damn you, and you're going to keep me!" She didn't know it, but the tears were streaming down her face. "You had the guts to carry on your affair right here under my nose, in my house! Oh, yes, I'm not so dumb that I don't remember this is the house we planned together right down to the blue carpet and the green house plants. You let *her* furnish it! You let her put me in a back room so she could share yours! I should have horsewhipped her. I should horsewhip you. You're an arrogant bastard, Jake! You're a first-class bastard, as bad as they come."

Although she was screaming and trembling and the sobs were constricting her throat so that her words came out jerkily, her voice dripped hurt and desperation. Now that she had started she couldn't stop.

"I loved you! I loved you with all my heart and soul. I never looked at another man. I couldn't stand for another man to touch me. I'm twenty-six years old and I've been to bed with one man . . . you! I've been kissed by a total of three. How's that for a record?" Her temper was a rapid-rising crescendo now. "I married you again, Jake Williamson, because I thought you needed me. For the first time since I knew you, you needed me for a change."

It was crazy, but she had no control over the words that were coming from her mouth. "I know I'm not streetwise, or even especially intelligent, Jake. I'm just the stupid little sap who was too innocent to know you weren't worth loving!"

She had never felt like this before. It was as if her whole insides had been cut loose. She felt free! She felt strong enough to tackle a tank! She grabbed a magazine from the night table beside the bed and began to strike him with it. He lifted his arm to ward off the blows, but said nothing. She hit him again and again, her eyes blinded with tears.

Jake was stunned into silence. Finally, when she hit him on the side of the head with the magazine he grabbed her wrist.

"Let go of me, you . . . stupid lecher. I ought to kill you! You've put me through hell, but not anymore. Never again! Do you understand? If you as much look at another woman, I swear I'll . . . I'll make you miserable for the rest of your life!" She was lightheaded and almost fell on him. "I hate you, Jake Williamson! I hate you so much I'm sick to my stomach, and . . . I love you so much I . . . I could die from it!"

She was exhausted and did not resist when he pulled her down on the bed and into his arms. She cried. She cried with her mouth open against his naked chest.

"Sweetheart . . . babe, say it all. Get it all out. I love you. Do you hear? I love you so much I thought I'd go crazy. You never seemed to care enough about me. And, sweetheart, why on earth didn't you tell me how you felt a long time ago? Sshh . . . don't cry."

A low moan escaped from her lips and she clung to him as if she could merge with his body. Half laughing, half crying, his arms locked tightly around her, he rolled her over him so she lay on the bed beside him. He smoothed her rumpled hair and traced his mouth along the side of her face and kissed her trembling mouth. His whispered words came against her lips.

"You love me that much?"

"And much, much more, you . . . impossible—"

His laugh was joyous against her face. "Try sweetheart . . . lover . . ."

"You, idiot of a . . . sweetheart . . . lover . . ."

He pinned her to the bed and kissed her hungrily, as if

starving for her. His mouth didn't want to leave hers even to talk, so he whispered against her lips. "I love you, sweetheart. I don't know what made you change your mind and come back to me, but I'm so glad you did!"

Two huge tears slid from the corners of her eyes. "So am I. I decided life with you would be lousy, but without you it would be . . . lousier."

He pulled away from her for a moment and they both laughed happily. "It was this morning that I guessed the reason you didn't come to the veranda last night," Jake explained. "You had caught Liz's little act. She had on your perfume, darling. I would recognize that scent if I were dead. She touched my face and I thought it was you. I was in heaven until I put my arms around her and pulled her down on my lap. I knew instantly it wasn't you. I know every curve, every line of you. The feel of your breast against me is like no other feeling in the world. I told her she was leaving and if she wanted to keep her job she would take a transfer to Dallas."

"Why didn't you tell me last night?"

"You locked me out. Remember? I thought you didn't care enough for me to make a fuss about it or to throw Liz out of the house." He pushed aside the hair from her ears and cupped her head in his hands. He was going to kiss her again, but she began to talk.

"I'd made up my mind to talk to you. To communicate, as Debbie puts it. I wanted to tell you how I felt, that I couldn't live with you knowing . . . thinking that I was sharing you." She put her hands on his face, her lips trembled, her eyes held a world of misery. "And then, this morning I saw Liz come out of your room."

"I saw her, too, sweetheart," he said after he had tried

to kiss the bleakness from her eyes. "She didn't know that my sight had returned in the night. It was while I was sitting alone on the veranda that I suddenly saw the moon. I didn't know what it was at first. Gradually other objects became clear and I got up and went into the house. I couldn't believe it so I moved around. It was true! I could see.

"I went through the house and back out onto the veranda so I could see the moon again. It was wonderful! I got the key from the kitchen and came to your room. I wanted to see you. I had to see you. Your eyes were open and you watched me. I couldn't understand why you were so frightened of me. I could feel the tears on your cheeks and I wanted to kiss them away. I went back to the veranda and sat there most of the night almost afraid to go to sleep. I was afraid that if I did I wouldn't be able to see when I woke up. While sitting there it occurred to me that if you thought I was still blind you wouldn't leave me. Believe me, sweetheart, I was as surprised as you were to see Liz coming out of my room."

He stroked her face and looked into her eyes with a world of longing in his. "I waited, hoping you would fly into a rage, but you walked calmly away as if you didn't care. I never hurt as bad in my life as I did at that moment. I didn't want to go to Houston this morning, but I had to see the doctor and get that damn tight cast cut off and to find out if my returned vision was permanent. Thank God, it is!"

"How could you possibly think I didn't care that you had spent the night with Liz? I cared! I cared so much that I wanted to kill her . . . and you!"

"I've never had an affair with Liz. I took her out a few

times before I met you. After that . . . there was no one else for me. You had my heart in your hands from the beginning."

"Never had an affair?" She looked searchingly into his eyes. "When I left you two years ago it was because I found you and Liz . . . on the couch together." It was not easy to say the words.

"Me and Liz?" His eyes looked down into hers. They were open, honest and puzzled eyes. "You mean the night I got so drunk she brought me home? Why didn't you say something? I was drunk that night, but not that drunk. I admit I was flirting around with her to make you jealous, but I never . . . why . . . that bitch!"

He fell away from her and lay back, his arms folded under his head. "I've been thinking all day about different things that happened. Like Liz telling me that you were living with Dick Kenfield. That was the reason I signed the divorce papers. And somehow I can't imagine the girl from Orange finding me without help."

"You think Liz might have arranged for her to come see me?" She snuggled her face in the curve of his neck so her mouth was against his skin.

"I'm sure of it, sweetheart."

She raised her head and looked at him. She felt as if she hadn't seen him in months, hadn't talked to him in years. At last she was talking to Jake, the man she loved, her husband, lover, the other part of herself. They talked in snatches of whispers between kisses.

After a long, haunting kiss that brought back the gentleness they had lost, Jake said, "By the way, Mrs. Williamson, I never gave Liz permission to decorate your house. I chose the furnishings and had them sent down.

She offered to check the invoices to see if everything arrived okay. As long as I was paying her a salary I told her to go ahead."

"I love my house."

"It was a lousy house without you in it, sweetheart."

"Try and get me out of it and I'll . . . break your arm!" She turned over onto him and held him very tight for a few minutes. They smiled into each other's eyes, reading each other's thoughts.

"I think I've got a tiger by the tail." His hand slipped down inside her jeans and cupped her buttocks. "I'll have to be more cautious." He had a huge smile on his face.

"It's too late to be cautious."

"What do you mean?"

"Ain't cha ever heard about the birds and the bees, fella?"

"Are you serious?"

"I think so."

"Are you sure?" His face was alight and he couldn't quit grinning.

"It's too soon to be sure."

"Want to stack the cards . . . in our favor?"

"Sure. Why not?" She grinned up at him.

He cradled her in his arms and kissed her softly, then hungrily while he pulled her shirt from her jeans.

"The door isn't locked and . . . I love you. Someone may wander in from the beach and . . . I love you."

"We'll just have to take our chances and . . . I love you, too."

"The lights are on."

"I know it, dumb-dumb. They're going to stay on . . . forever."

"Forever is a long, long time."

"You bet!"

He raised his head, and the caressing hand inside her jeans paused. A silly grin spread over his face.

"Would you really do all those awful things to me? Lordy mercy! What've I got myself into? You'd put old Carrie Nation to shame when you get all riled up!"

Her eyes shone like bright stars and her lips twitched with laughter. "Hush up! And get on with what you're doing . . . or I'll . . . kiss you senseless!"

ABOUT THE AUTHOR

DOROTHY GARLOCK is one of America's—and the world's—favorite novelists. Her work has appeared on national bestseller lists, including the *New York Times* extended list, and there are over fifteen million copies of her books in print translated into eighteen languages. She has won more than twenty writing awards, including five Silver Pen Awards from *Affaire de Coeur* and three Silver Certificate Awards, and in 1998 she was selected a finalist for the National Writer's Club Best Long Historical Book Award.

After retiring as a news reporter and bookkeeper in 1978, she began her career as a novelist with the publication of *Love and Cherish*. She lives in Clear Lake, Iowa. You can visit her Web site at www.dorothygarlock.com.

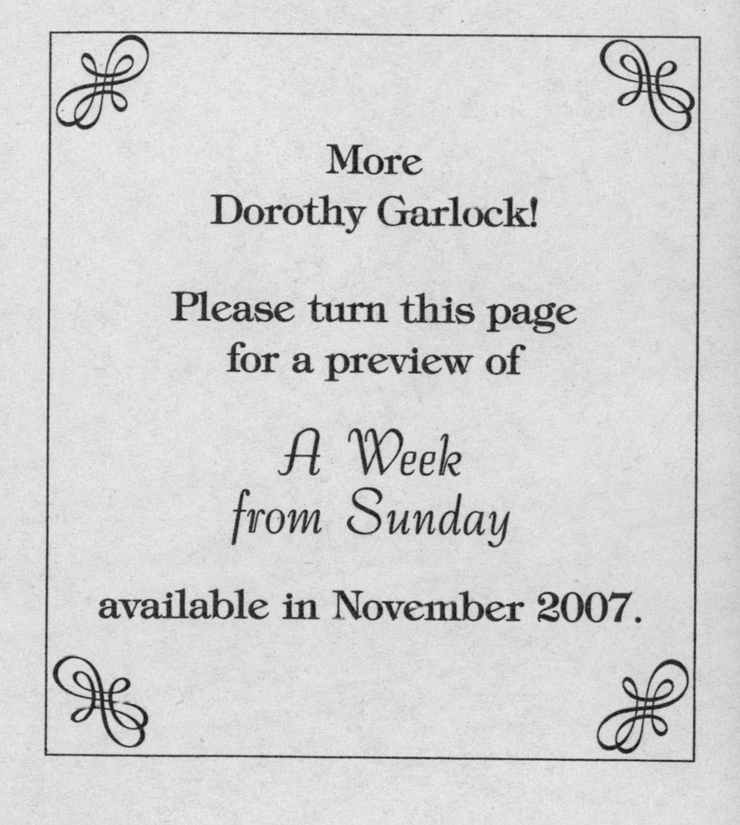
More
Dorothy Garlock!
Please turn this page
for a preview of
A Week
from Sunday
available in November 2007.

CHAPTER ONE

SHREVEPORT, LOUISIANA 1935

"I'M TERRIBLY SORRY, my dear. Your father will be missed."

Adrianna Moore listened to the older woman's condolences with a slight nod of appreciation before moving on. The small parlor was filled with smartly dressed men and women, all wearing black, who had come to pay their respects to the recently deceased. Some of the faces she recognized; most of them belonged to older gentlemen who had done business with her father over the years, but nearly all of the names escaped her. She knew she should say something, at the very least thank them for coming, but she couldn't manage to get the image of her father's coffin out of her head. It all seemed a horrible dream. Her sadness kept her mute amid the soft murmur of voices and the clink of coffee cups against their saucers.

The funeral itself had been a quiet affair. Thankfully, the Louisiana spring had cooperated; although drizzly rain had been falling for days, the morning had dawned with warm sunlight and only a light breeze rustled the treetops. High on the lone hill on the cemetery grounds, they'd laid her father to rest. Now, with that business concluded, she was required to play the role of hostess, a task that normally she'd be well equipped to handle. Today was anything but normal.

She moved from guest to guest, each stopping her for a few measured words of sympathy. She looked into forlorn faces, hands gently holding hers. Adrianna knew that they all meant well, but the things she was hearing only intensified her grief:

"Charles Moore was a lion of a man."

"Regardless of the crippling effects of his polio, he never let it get the best of him."

"I can't begin to tell you how much I learned from him about the banking business. It's a debt that I can never repay."

"He'll be watching down on you, Adrianna." A matron wiped tears from her fat cheeks.

Once, when an older gentleman with enormous jowls was telling her of a hunting trip he'd taken with her father before he had become crippled with polio, she found herself desperately fighting back tears. It wasn't the story that had upset her; she'd heard it a half dozen times before. What made her cry was the realization that her father had *become* a story, a legend in town. It had taken all of the strength she could muster to get through the day, but somehow she'd managed to keep her composure through it all.

Finally, as the last rays of the spring sun shone over the horizon, all of the mourners had gone, leaving Adrianna alone in the large home she'd shared with her father for the last seventeen years. Built from the earnings of Moore Bank and Trust, the stately manor house had been constructed with the finest of materials. The interior was decorated richly but tastefully: a marble fireplace, an antique clock from Germany, as well as a crystal chandelier that hung over the dining room table.

This home was the only one she'd ever known. Her mother had died of a sudden illness when Adrianna had only been fifteen years old. Her father had never remarried. Charles Moore had done everything for his only child. She'd wanted for nothing: piano lessons, private tutors, all the best that his banking fortune could buy. When his own illness had worsened, confining him to his bed or the wheelchair that he despised, she'd done her best to give him the same degree of comfort he'd given her. But still his health slowly and steadily deteriorated.

He was gone and she was alone.

After the mourners left, she went through the downstairs rooms dimming the lights. Glancing up, she caught sight of her reflection in a mirror. At twenty-five years of age, Adrianna Moore had a head of dark brown curly hair that fell to her shoulders. Her soft, oval face was defined by high cheekbones and a warm complexion. Her father had always told her that her deep-set, emerald-green eyes were exactly like her mother's. He called her his "beautiful princess." At the moment, wearing a simple black dress, mourning the loss of her remaining family, she felt anything but beautiful; she was heartsick and exhausted.

"I daresay you get more stunning with each passing year."

Startled by the voice behind her, Adrianna whirled at the sound, her hand reflexively rising to her chest. With slow, measured steps, a man crossed the room toward her. In the scant light, she had to peer intently into the shadows to see her unexpected guest. Finally, there was the spark of recognition, a spark that sent a shiver down her spine.

"Oh! It's you, Mr. Pope. You startled me."

"How many times must I tell you, my dear, to call me Richard?"

He eased out of the gloom to stand before Adrianna. In his late forties, Richard Pope was a man who exuded an air of supreme confidence. Short, with a long face that was marked by a mouth with full red lips, he had colorless eyes that, over a bulbous nose, looked straight into hers. His clothes were immaculate, his shoes polished to a perfect black. The sweet smelling pomade he rubbed into his thinning salt-and-pepper hair made Adrianna's stomach churn.

"I didn't realize you were still here," she said, ignoring his comment.

"I was showing Judge Walters and his wife to the door and walked with them out onto the porch. I don't know if you recognized him . . . the wisp of a gentleman whose wife is as fat as he is thin," he explained. "He has always been very important to Moore Bank and Trust and I wanted to give him my assurances that everything concerned with the company was in good hands. It's all about impressions, you know."

"Thank you for your help today, Mist- . . . Richard," she corrected herself. "What with the funeral arrangements, and all of the guests, I don't know if I could have managed without you." She hated to admit it, but he *had* been very helpful. With his legal guidance, her father's bank had continued to grow ever larger and more prosperous. Adrianna was certain that the only thing that mattered to Richard Pope was acquiring more and more money. As Charles Moore's health had worsened, taking him away from the day-to-day operations of his bank, Richard's influence had grown. For the last several months, he had been essentially overseeing the business.

"It's the least that I could do. How are you managing through all of this?"

"All right, I suppose. I don't think that it has fully sunken in yet, that he's gone, I mean. He was always positive about things. Even after my mother passed away, I could never imagine the same happening to him."

"And yet it did," Richard said matter-of-factly. "He did die." Walking over to a small bureau, he proceeded to pour himself a tall glass of brandy from a beveled decanter. As he contemplated the amber liquid, a thin smile spread across his face. To Adrianna, he looked like a wolf preparing to sink his fangs into its defenseless prey.

"I'm sorry to have to leave you," she said hurriedly, wanting desperately to get away from the man, "but I am going to retire for the night. All of this has left me exhausted. Please let yourself out." Quickly, she turned on her heel and made for the staircase on the far side of the room. But before she could take even a couple of steps, his voice stopped her.

"Actually, my dear, there are things that you and I need to discuss. Business matters that cannot wait even for a night. I'm afraid that you'll just have to bear with me for a while longer."

Turning back, Adrianna felt a slight flare of defiance course through her body. She wanted to tell him that *he* would have to wait for *her*, but something in the way he was looking at her kept her mouth shut. From what her father had told her over the years, recounting his lawyer's smashing victories in court, Richard Pope was not the kind of man one wanted for an enemy.

"What sort of business matters?" she asked. "I'm afraid I don't know much about banking."

"Charles left a good man at the helm. It's not about the bank. Not really," Richard chuckled before taking all of the glass of alcohol in one gulp. "It's actually about you, my dear. You and your future."

"What . . . what are you talking about?" Adrianna asked in confusion.

"I suppose that I shouldn't be shocked by your lack of understanding, sweet Adrianna. After all, you've been cuddled a bit too close to your father's weakened chest all of these years."

"I don't think I like your tone, Mister Pope," she managed, hoping that her voice sounded stronger than she felt.

"There is no offense intended, I assure you," Richard said apologetically and went back to the bureau to pour himself another drink. "But let us call a spade a spade. You've always had household help. You've never worked outside this house a day in your life. You've never wanted for anything! Charles made sure that you were always provided for, and it wasn't until the very last that he saw the error of his ways."

A sickening feeling suddenly washed over Adrianna. Her knees suddenly were weak. *What in the blazes was this pompous ass talking about?* Keeping silent, she waited for him to continue.

"His greatest fear was that you would find yourself all alone, incapable of taking care of yourself," Richard explained. "As I was his closest confidant for all of these long years, it was only natural that he would turn to me to take care of his most precious treasure. And that is why he decided to make me executor of his estate. I am completely in charge of you, your money, the bank, the house and everything in it. It's all under my supervision."

"What?" Like a thunderclap out of a clear sky, Richard's words struck Adrianna with dramatic force. Stumbling on shaky legs, desperately trying to stay upright, she managed to grab hold of a nearby chair and steady herself. Her eyes filled with tears and her voice cracked as she said, "You must be joking!"

"Not in the slightest, my dear. The last legal document that your father ever signed was a change in his will . . . a change that made me executor."

"But not of me!"

"Yes, of you."

"I'm of age."

"Of course you are, but I'm in charge of your money."

As shocked as Adrianna had been by her father's passing, what Richard Pope was telling her shook her even more. *How could what he was saying be true?*

How could her father have done this to her? Richard was lying. He had to be! With anger rising in her breast, she gave voice to her disbelief. "This can't be! My father wouldn't leave my future in the hands of someone else! He wouldn't!"

"And he didn't . . . not entirely."

"But you said that he left you control."

Slowly, Richard crossed the room until he stood before her. She could smell the brandy on his breath. His smile nauseated her. Summoning what strength she had, she straightened her back and boldly returned his gaze.

"He hasn't left you without the means to provide for yourself. This was all part of his plan. All of this," he said, gesturing around the room, "the house, the bank, can still be yours. You can have everything to which you have grown accustomed."

"How?"

"By marrying me."

The words were no sooner out of Richard's mouth when Adrianna's hand shot up toward his face. She'd meant to slap him, the man's boldness on the day of her father's funeral providing the breaking point; but before she could make contact, the lawyer's hand grabbed her own in a tight, painful grip. With a strength she couldn't resist, he yanked her toward him until her body was pressed against his. Try as she might, she couldn't break free.

"Oh, sweet Adrianna," he said, licking his lips. "Haven't you noticed the way that I have looked at you all of these years? I have wanted you from the first moment I saw you. I knew that it would come to this . . . this union between you and me. Your father knew it, too."

"You're . . . you're hurting me," Adrianna pleaded.

"We will be married a week from Sunday. Because of your father's recent death, we'll have a quiet ceremony. I'll have the judge at my house when I come for you. We must keep up appearances, my dear. It wouldn't do to have people gossiping about my wife." His hands tightened on her arms.

"Let . . . let me go."

"I will never let you go!" Forcefully, his grasp tightened even more. "You and I *will* be married!"

"Please . . ." Adrianna sobbed, the tears now flowing freely down her cheeks.

She would never know if it were her words or the sight of her tears that finally broke through Richard Pope's euphoria, but he suddenly released her and stepped away, his hand darting to his pocket where he pulled out a handkerchief and wiped the tears from her cheeks. When he looked down at her, his eyes were flat but still menacing.

"I meant what I said to you, Adrianna," he warned, his voice deep and serious. "By making me the executor of his estate, your father gave his permission for me to provide for you for the rest of your life. To that end, we will be married. The sooner the better."

Stifling a large sob that had filled her throat, Adrianna looked at the man through wet eyes. Never in her life had she been so repulsed by another human being! No matter what were to happen, she would not give him the satisfaction of seeing her fear!

Walking back over to her, Richard once again

grabbed Adrianna by the wrist. While his grip was not as tight as it had been before, it was still tight enough to cause her anxiety.

"Pack up what you'll need. Everything else can be dealt with later. I will come for you a week from Sunday. Dress appropriately for your wedding." Gripping Adrianna's chin, he turned her head until she was looking directly into his face. "This is for the best, my dear. In time, I am certain that you will come to love me every bit as passionately as I love you. As husband and wife, you and I will be the jewels of this town, just as your father intended."

After releasing her, Richard strode across the room and pulled open the door. "Remember . . . a week from Sunday," he said, and then he was gone.

After she had heard the door close, Adrianna finally allowed herself to crumple into a chair, tears streaming down her face. Following so soon upon her father's death and funeral, this was more than she could endure!

Even if her father had worried about her well-being, he would never have given control of his estate to a man like Richard Pope! The lawyer must have manipulated him into signing the papers when he wasn't of sound mind. In those last days, Charles Moore had been robbed of all he had built over his lifetime. Now that bastard Pope was trying to steal her!

But what could she do? She could try to challenge the will, to take the matter to a judge, but how was she supposed to compete with a lawyer like Richard? No, that would not work. But what other choice did she have? Pack up her things and wait for him by the door? He was planning to come for her a week from Sunday. That left her with only eight days!

Suddenly, Adrianna knew what she had to do. She didn't know where she would go, how she would get there, or what she would do to survive, but none of that mattered.

She was leaving Shreveport!

If you or someone you know
wants to improve their reading skills,
call the Literacy Help Line.
Reading...
WORDS ARE YOUR WHEELS
1-800-228-8813